MISSIONARY TO MARS

Lucas Kitchen

FREE GRACE INTERNATIONAL

WHAT READERS ARE SAYING

"Made me cry and rejoice and I couldn't stop reading."

"This Christian Sci-fi book is filled with dangerous threats, dozens of comedic moments, and even a little romance sprinkled in along the way."

"The gospel can change a life and a whole city. That's also what makes it so threatening to hostile powers. Lucas Kitchen brings that spiritual warfare to life and sets it among the stars. I look forward to the next books in the series."

"Missionary to Mars helped remind me that the gospel is important enough to risk your life for. As this captivating sci-fi story shows, the gospel can change a life and a whole city."

"This book could actually be a great long-form gospel tract to an unbeliever who loves science fiction books but would never read a three-page tract or have a three-page conversation on the gospel."

"This book was really good. It was full of action and well developed characters and was clean and had a good message. Can't wait till the next book in the series."

"Believing himself to be the last Christian alive, Eustis is determined to bring the Gospel to the far reaches... The result of his efforts made me cry and rejoice and I couldn't stop reading... Excellent world-building and relatable characters make this story enjoyable and meaningful to read."

"You're bound to enjoy the journey of a missionary to Mars and even be inspired along the way to be bold in how you share Christ."

ALSO BY LUCAS KITCHEN

Fiction

For The Sake Of The King

Isolation

Children's Fiction

Good Enough

Adventures Beyond Mudville

Below The Huber Ice

Non-Fiction

Salvation And Discipleship

Eternal Life

Eternal Rewards

Naked Grace

In Pursuit Of Fruit

All Available At: Lucaskitchen.com

Dedicated to Shawn.
Thanks for exploring the Sol System with me.

CHAPTER ONE

EXECUTE

"Where's Eustis?" asked Fred Gibbs.

"Probably sharing with some street creep," Leena Bickle said with a dismissive wave and a smile. The others laughed. "You know how Eustis is. Planting seeds everywhere he goes. He'll get here when he's ready to be here. I'm sure he wouldn't mind us starting without him."

The others nodded in warm agreement. Martha Grambling laid a gentle hand on the shoulder of her husband, Todd. They sat next to the window. As the motion in the room stilled, Fred brought his voice above the gentle murmur.

"Thanks for coming, everyone," Todd said, smiling as he looked around the room. "Especially thanks to Melone for baking that wonderful apple pie. I can't wait to dig in, but before we do, let's—"

A loud explosion ripped the front door off the hinges. The house rattled as glass sprayed onto the wooden floor. A blast of smoke and splintered shrapnel fired into the living room stinging the skin and eyes of everyone there. Fred Gibbs was on his feet. Everyone's ears were ringing, but they could hear Fred through the din. "They've found us! Scatter!"

The dozen occupants of the living room spread out, moving quickly for the two exits. Leena Bickle and Sue Tuttle were rushing toward the stairs but skidded to a stop across shards of glass. A scream pierced the flurry of footsteps behind them. Leena Bickle collapsed to her knees and interlocked her fingers as Sue Tuttle's eyes locked on a mortifying silhouette. *It couldn't be.* The shape of an enormous man, clad in black battle suit, drifted ominously into view. His head would have hit the wood if the doorframe hadn't already been blown to cinders. "The admiral," she whispered as she tripped backward over an upturned chair.

Black boots crunched the shattered remains of the nearby window, and ozone mixed with the smell of charred wood. The hinges that hung where the door had been glowed orange and set the splintered frame ablaze. Wisps of black smoke swirled around the dark silhouette as he moved deeper into the room. His dark eyes scanned the scrambling contents of the house, logging the IDs of each of his prey.

Leena Bickle did not look up from her prostrate posture and thus did not see the black-clad man charge his power glove and drive his knuckle down on her bowed head. She went limp and splayed across the debris below. Before Sue Tuttle could find her feet, the dark intruder unholstered a sidearm and fired a bolt of plasma through the woman. Her screams were squelched immediately.

"Stop!" Fred Gibbs shouted as he rushed to block the path of the death dealer. "We're not hurting anyone!" Fred's attempt to shield the others was short-lived, as the executioner tapped the back of his power glove and swung his fist in a wide path catching Fred across the temple, sending a hundred thousand volts of electricity into Fred's face. He fell in a heap. Flames spread from the broken door frame to the curtains. Smoke licked hungrily across the ceiling. An overhead sprinkler popped and began spraying water to quell the fire.

"Disable fire suppression," the battle-clad man said. His deep-rumbling voice was calm and detached. A beep followed.

"Yes, Sir," came the response over his cortical communicator. The sprinklers sputtered out, and the hiss of water turning to steam was replaced by the crackle of a roaring blaze.

Two people hiding behind the couch slipped out behind the massive killer and rushed through the growing flames trying for the back door.

"HEXA. Two dissidents at the back exit," the admiral said. A beep confirmed that the command was received, and a spray of gunfire from outside the house cut through the pair fleeing for their lives. "Eliminated. Ceasefire." The explosive cascade of plasma bolts stopped at once.

The man drifted through the house like a shadow. He executed three more people in the laundry room and another hiding under the kitchen table.

"Pulse scan," he said—a beep issued from his cortical implant.

"There's one hiding in the upstairs bathroom, Admiral," HEXA, his A.I. assistant, responded over the comm. "Correction, make that two."

Without a word, the admiral turned and began up the stairs. Before he reached the top, HEXA came across the radio once more. "Sir, one of them is making a call."

"Trace it."

"Can't, Sir. It's an encrypted line," HEXA said. "But I can give you a raw audio feed."

"Put it through." The Admiral paused on the stairs listening to the embedded audio on his cortex implant. A thin voice, a woman's, was speaking.

"Don't come here," she was saying. The Admiral's cortical display blinked with a voice ID notification. The person speaking was someone called *Martha Grambling*. A second notification sounded. Her name appeared on the dissident database. "There's nothing you can do, Sweetie. I know you want to help, but GovCorp found us. They killed—everyone's—they're probably all dead except me and Todd. We're hiding. It won't be long. You have to—" The voice paused for a second. She was listening to the other end of the call. Her ragged breathing set a frantic tempo before it broke into sobbing.

"No," a second voice cut in, a man's. The admiral's visual HUD blinked with a voice ID. *Todd Grambling* also on the dissident registry. "There's nothing for you to do. We knew this might happen." A long pause followed. "Listen, Eustis, you have to get off-world. We can't let this die with us. We might be the last ones anywhere in the Sol System to know about—"

The bathroom door burst from its hinges, and a massive boot stepped in. Martha and Todd Grambling were huddled in the shower. The black-clad man raised his sidearm at them.

"Please," Todd Grambling said. "Let my wife go. You can kill me, but—"

Two bolts of plasma spat from his barrel, shattered the glass of the shower, and ended the conversation. The bodies landed on the tile with a thump as a blanket of glass fell around them.

The admiral glanced through the broken bathroom door frame. The flames had reached the top of the stairs and were spreading down the hall. He turned toward the bathroom window, crouched, and made the hand gesture that brought the mechanized feature of his battle suit online. It pinged, letting him know it was ready for an augmented leap.

He slapped a spot on his chest, which brought a protective visor over his head. He vaulted through the window and allowed his suit to execute a perfect dive toward the ground. At the last moment, his body tucked and rolled before coming up to his feet unharmed. Glass showered down around him as the house fire haloed his dark features with orange.

A superimposed hologram of a man walked through the raining ash toward Admiral Strafe's location on the front lawn. HEXA, Strafe's A.I. assistant, was the best chief logistics general manager he had ever employed. He'd certainly survived longer than his human predecessors who held the post. "You got them all, Sir, and you didn't even need to call in the squad." HEXA thumbed to a row of android soldiers.

"Not all of them," Strafe corrected. HEXA's artificial image displayed a surprised expression.

"None got out, and I'm scanning the house now, Sir. There aren't any more inside. Even if there were, the fire would do them in."

"One was absent. Name is Eustis," Strafe said. HEXA paused and began searching the database.

"There's no Eustis in the dissident registry. The database says they're all—"

"I know what the database says. It's wrong. Make a new entry. File it under Eustis." Strafe slapped his chest to bring down his protective visor. "He's in the city. Get me a location."

CHAPTER TWO

DOCKS

Eustis walked by the endless rows of stalls where vendors sold items from all over Sol System. The market was a multi-kilometer stretch of noise and hustle. In the distance, the reason for the market's location, one of GovCorp's finest achievements, was Earth's only space elevator. It had taken two centuries to build and made space travel accessible to all. All but Eustis, apparently, because he had never been up. He hadn't had a need until today. He had no idea how he would do it, but he had to secure a ride on the next up-shuttle. If only he had a few hundred thousand credits on his account.

"This is useless," a customer said to a pushy vendor nearby, dropping the item and walking away. Eustis came out of his mental fog with a start. He had been on edge since he got the call. He hadn't had time to mourn. That would come soon enough, but for now, he had a job to do. He had to stay focused.

"Ma'am, do you know where I can find—" Eustis tried, but the woman kept on walking. He tried another. "Sir, can you tell me where I can find the enlistment kiosk?"

The man pointed. Eustis glanced in the direction indicated. The scene was chaos and noise. Eustis turned back, hoping to ask for clarification, but the man was gone. "Thanks," he said to no one. He pulled his duffle bag over his shoulder and started walking.

About a quarter of a kilometer down the crowded corridor, and after saying no to about fifty pushy hawkers, Eustis spotted the recruitment bureau sign. A tattered propaganda banner read, *See the Sol System. Be a Part Of Something Big. GovCorp Security Brigade. Join Today!* He glanced down at the little table with a portly recruitment officer snoozing at a one-seat kiosk. It was underwhelming, but he needed off-world, and this was his one idea.

"If this isn't what you want me to do, then stop me." He stood there, waiting, hoping, wishing. "Anytime." Nothing happened. He took a deep breath to calm his nerves. He put a foot out, intending to step toward the recruitment officer, when someone caught his foot.

A young woman tumbled forward, tripping over Eustis' outstretched leg. He reached out to help her, but before he could, someone grabbed his arm with a bone-crushing grip. The woman caught her balance, and Eustis turned to see what had him by the arm. Attached to the grip was an enormous man with a robotic arm bolted to his shoulder. The arm wasn't one of those modern, incognito prosthetics, but instead, it looked as if it had been scavenged from a battle suit dating to the previous century. The man who wielded the arm was in his early sixties but was massively muscular. The mechanical grip was cutting off the circulation to Eustis' forearm and hand. *This is it.* Eustis thought. *This is who GovCorp sent to murder me.*

"You want I should pulverize him, Captain?" The big man said.

"Let go of him," said a kid standing next to the aging giant. The young teen had walked up after the others but clearly had some familiarity with them. His skin was dark, his black hair was a mess, and his speech was too confident for a child his age. "He's just a dirt-licking scobberlotcher. Let him loose, Rudwick."

"You heard him, Rudwick," Eustis repeated. "Let me go." The big man's grip tightened. By now, the young woman had straightened and turned toward the three. Eustis was getting the impression that these were not GovCorp goons.

"Well, Cap," Rudwick said. "What you want I should do with this dirt dweller?"

Eustis turned to the young woman and was about to protest the injustice, but the sight of her face made him forget how to form words. Her soft skin was out of place in this rough environment of grease and titanium. She had the kind of eyes that were sad but strong. Her hair was mostly tied back but hung loose on one side as if her appearance was only an afterthought. Nonetheless, Eustis was spellbound. Her full lips had the slightest hint of a frown. Eustis wondered what a smile might look like on those lips. Her hand lifted a half-filled bottle of unlabeled, amber liquid to those lips. Not a smile, exactly, but not a frown, either. She wiped her other sleeve across her mouth. She was holding a small item with frayed wires jutting out of one end. He recognized the piece of comm gear immediately.

"If you had made me spill this," she lifted the bottle aloft. "Then that would have cost you your teeth." She took another drink. Well, that wasn't what he expected. "Let him loose, Rudwick. He's just a high-G mud sucker who doesn't watch where he's putting his big dumb feet."

Rudwick released his mechanical grip, and Eustis rubbed the spot where he had been squeezed mercilessly. It was sure to leave an indentation.

"I'm Eustis," he said, putting his hand out to shake.

"Earthers," the young woman said, shaking her head, as she turned and walked away.

"They do be a dense breed of bleeders," Rudwick said as he followed his young captain through the crowd and out of Eustis' life. He watched them both go before he looked down at the kid who hadn't.

"People who live most their life in space don't shake strangers' hands." Eustis glanced after the woman and the big man once more and then back at the kid. "Newton's first law. You know, inertia and whatnot." The kid smiled as if he were talking to a baby.

"How old are you?"

"How old are you?" the kid repeated in a mock voice.

"I'm twenty-nine," Eustis said.

"Wow," Enzo said. "When you die of old age next week, can I have your boots?"

"Nice one," Eustis said. He glanced in the direction of the captain's unwelcome disappearance and then back to Enzo. "Are you with them?" Eustis asked.

"Good point. See you later, old dude." The kid was off, chasing after the other two. Eustis glanced at the Security Brigade kiosk with its fat, sleeping recruitment officer and then after his new acquaintances. The choice was clear.

"Hey, wait up," Eustis shouted. He wove his way through the crowd for a few minutes before he got to them. They were entering a shop. The sign read *Earth's Best Shipwright and Parts.* Eustis followed them through the swinging door.

The smell of rocket lube and fission fuel assaulted his nose. The place had the look of a warehouse—Eustis had no idea what most of it was—but he recognized the comms equipment cached twelve shelves high. He had the urge to stop and see what they had, but he resisted. By the time he caught up to the trio, the woman was talking to a clerk at the shipwright's counter. The big guy, Rudwick, was standing near her with his arms crossed, no doubt, intimidating the shipwright. The kid was riffling through some items on the shelves aimlessly.

"Hey, kid," Eustis said. The boy looked up.

"Oh, good grief. What do you want?" the kid said. "Looking to get that beating from Rudwick? I wouldn't. Getting a punch from him is like taking a fission fracker to the jaw bone."

"What's your name?"

"I'm Enzo. Ship's Engineer."

"Eustis," he said, putting his hand out to shake. He pulled it back quickly when Enzo didn't offer his.

"Slow learner, huh?" Enzo said. "Just a word of warning. Captain won't take kindly to you following us. And by the sound of it, she's going to be pretty nuked after talking to that primate of a shipwright."

Eustis looked over at her and Rudwick haggling with the clerk. It was getting heated. "What's her name?"

"Marianna Byrne," Enzo said.

"Marianna," Eustis said to himself as if the name had a favorable taste.

"Ever heard of her?" Enzo said.

"No," Eustis said. "Should I have?"

"So, what do you want, Eustis Shakes-a-lot?" Enzo said.

"I need off-world, like yesterday. I need to get to Musk City, Mars." Eustis said, dropping his voice to a whisper.

"What's in Musk City?" Enzo asked.

"I'm a planter and—" Eustis said.

"There's hydroponics all over the system. It'd be better to go to Enceladus or Ceres."

"Not that kind of planter," Eustis said. "I plant ideas. Ideas that will grow into a movement. The capital is the place where my seeds will have the greatest impact. Where my ideas can spread the farthest."

"Sounds weird," Enzo said. "I'm not sure you really know what a planter is."

"Someday, kid." Eustis looked upward as if there was something to see in the middle distance. "Everything's going to be different. Just takes a seed, and it can grow. You'll see." Eustis straightened up. "So, I was wondering, since you guys have a ship if there might be a spot—"

"Whoah, wait a minute, dust snorter," Enzo said. "Don't even think about it. *We* don't have a ship. Captain Byrne has the ship, and her word is the law. Trust me. She doesn't want a dense-bone gravity hog on her hotrod. We're already—" Before Enzo could finish his thought, the transaction at the shipwright counter spilled into shouting.

"A month?" Marianna shouted. "You told me you'd have it fixed in an hour. We came here from Ceres to see you. What the—"

"It's gotten busy since we talked," the clerk said. "I might be able to get to it in six weeks."

"Cursed be the lips that uttered such rot," Rudwick bellowed. He reached for a holster at his hip and was about to draw on the clerk, but Captain Marianna reached for his trigger hand and touched it with the bottle she was holding. The glass clanked against Rudwick's metal wrist. She nodded him down from his towering rage, lifted her bottle, took a long drink, wiped her mouth with her sleeve, and spoke more calmly.

"Come on, Rudwick," Marianna said. "This place was a bad idea." The captain and Rudwick walked for the exit. When she spotted Eustis, she rolled her eyes.

"Come on, kid," Marianna said. "But leave your pet here." Eustis didn't take the hint. He charged after them with the gusto of a golden retriever.

Chapter Three

BARGAIN

As Eustis stepped out of the shipwright's shop a notification pinged in his cortex display. An unknown caller was trying to contact him. He gulped hard, thinking of the events earlier that day. He gestured to decline the call. It went straight to vid message. He motioned to play the video as it was being recorded. The head of a skinny, sunken-eyed man appeared on Eustis' display. His nasal voice was upbeat and matter-of-fact.

"Eustis Wade Grimes, this is Chief Logistics General Manager HEXA —A.I. Assistant to the Admiral in the office of Dissidence Management. I'm legally required to notify you that you are registered on GovCorp's dangerous dissident database. A formal manhunt has been initiated. You will be terminated on capture. As a convenience, we will turn your remains over to reclamation at no extra cost. If you wish to save GovCorp subscribers the expense of hunting you down, you can turn yourself in at the nearest GovCorp facility. If you attempt to evade capture, your case officer will apprehend you at his earliest available opening. Admiral Kynig Strafe has been assigned to your case and will ensure your capture and termination if you choose not to turn yourself in. Your last known whereabouts are recorded as, let's see." There was a brief pause as HEXA's eyes darted to the data. "Ah, there you are. Earth's Best Shipwright and Parts, Houston City. Your assigned case officer is on his way."

HEXA lowered his voice as a sycophantic pleasure was present in his words. "On a personal note, I've worked for Admiral Strafe for years. He wants you to run. It isn't any fun if you turn yourself in." HEXA's voice returned to upbeat businesslike. "Ok, that does it for us at the Office of Dissidence Management. Have yourself a wonderful day."

The message clicked to black and Eustis remembered to breathe for the first time in three minutes. *Admiral Strafe?* He knew of Strafe by reputation. Who didn't? Eustis gripped the handle of his duffle bag so hard his knuckles went white.

He looked around. Standing a few paces off were Rudwick, Enzo, and Captain Marianna. They were having a heated discussion outside the door of Earth's Best Shipwright and Parts. Under normal circumstances, Eustis would not have interrupted an ongoing conversation, especially one that was proceeding with such vehement urgency, but these were not normal circumstances.

"Let's get off this rock," Captain Marianna was saying to the others. "We'll try that shipwright in Aldrin City, Moon. The sooner we're out from under this heavy G, the better." She lifted the bottle to her lips and eased her nerves with the warm liquid.

Rudwick said, "Could go to Flub's Craft Parts. It only be a short flight over to Europa."

"Flubs?" Enzo said. "The only thing you're going to get at Flubs Parts is a blood disease. Plus, Europa is 657.65 million kilometers away at this point in the orbital." The big man bristled as if each of the kid's words were little daggers driving deep into his skin. "Have you been listening? Without the transponder, we won't be able to land at GovCorp-regulated ports." The kid turned to Captain Marianna. "But, Cap, we can't make an appearance in Aldrin City either. We don't want a repeat of last time we were there, do we? We wouldn't survive a second run in with Mayor Skurg."

"Maybe, maybe no," Rudwick said.

"What are you talking about, you brainless loaf?" Enzo said. "I'm relaying unassailable facts here."

"Maybe it be a truth, brat," Rudwick said. "But you need to learn manners, and I be the one to teach 'em to you." He lifted his metallic fist in the air and looked as if he were going to strike.

"Hey, there," Eustis said, ducking his hand and giving an awkward wave as he stepped forward. "Remember me from like four minutes ago?"

The conversation stopped, and all eyes looked at him. They were not pleased to be interrupted. "So, I'm going to cut to the chase. I need a ride. And from the sound of it, you guys need some help with a busted transponder," he said. "I see a kind of providence here. You see, I believe in—actually, I better save that part for another time. My point is—If you need that, and I need a ride—I was thinking—I mean—after all—"

"Get to the point, mister," Enzo said. "You can do it. One word after the other. Before you know it, you've arrived at some punctuation, and everyone has a clue what you're asking."

"Sorry," Eustis said. "I worked for Comm Interplanetary for five years. I can fix your transponder." Eustis pointed to the device with frayed wires in Captain Marianna's hand. "Looks like a Galaxy Four AIS transcendence unit. If I could just take a look." He reached for it, but she pulled back quickly. Rudwick put a metal hand in his chest and pressed painfully against his sternum.

"Why are you sweating so much?" Enzo asked.

"He do bear a mighty sheen," Rudwick agreed.

"Are you sick or something?" Marianna asked. "Your hands are shaking."

"Oh, no," Enzo said, covering his mouth. "He's got the sickness, and I was talking to him unprotected!"

"I don't have a sickness," Eustis said as Enzo gaged. "The truth is, I have a very important mission. You see, I'm a planter—"

"Looks more like you're a runner," Marianna said. "Anyone in such a hurry to get off earth has trouble screaming up their tailpipe. You in trouble?"

"No," Eustis said but then backpedaled. "Well, yes, but that's not why I'm trying to get off Earth." He paused and ran his fingers through his hair. "I mean, it's not, but it is why I'm in such a hurry. I have a very important mission, and if the trouble catches up with me, it's all for nothing. I really need to get off this rock, like, right away. That's why I'm sweating. My hands are shaking because my only other plan was to enlist with that fat security brigade recruiter back there, but I just learned that won't work. You guys are my only option, and time is running out."

"What kind of trouble be to your taste?" Rudwick asked.

"I'd rather tell you about why my mission is so important," Eustis said. "I need to get to Musk City, Mars. I plan to plant some very important ideas—" Marianna put her hand in the air.

"Look, guy," she said. "I'm sorry, but we have our own kind of trouble. We don't need to pile yours on top. Come on, boys." Rudwick followed her as she left. Eustis closed his eyes, dropped his duffle bag, and put his hands over his face.

"Are you going to cry?" Enzo said. Eustis opened his eyes and looked past the fingers that covered his face. The kid had stayed behind, letting the others go. "Do you want to stay here and cry about it, or do you want some help?"

"You can help me?" Eustis said.

Enzo didn't answer but continued with his own line of thought. "Sorry about the captain," he said. "She's all business, no heart. Or, all heart, no business. I'm not sure which, really, because, in this case, she's making the wrong decision. That's probably a no-business situation. Anyway, we need our transponder fixed, and we can't get a repair manual to do it. Ever since GovCorp blocked the right-to-fix charter, we've been falling apart without knowing how to tape the thing back together. So we're stuck. If you know how to do it, we should take the risk."

"Yes, yes," Eustis leaped. "I can do it. I really appreciate—" Eustis started.

"Do you have a wrist chip?" Enzo interrupted.

"No, we don't really use them on Earth because—" Eustis paused when Enzo put one finger in the air. With his other hand, he gestured to open his comm app.

"Hey, Captain," Enzo said through his internal communicator. "I'm going to hit the toy shop. I'll meet you guys back at the ship." Enzo smiled after a brief pause. "Of course, I play with toys all the time. You didn't know?" He gestured to end the call and returned his attention to Eustis.

"I don't play with toys. I'm 13, by the way," Enzo said.

"Ok," Eustis said.

"And since you're 29, that means you were only 16 when mom had me. You are a single dad, widowed at 20, grandma died, and you just got custody of me, which is why you know nothing about me. Got it?"

"What?" Eustis said.

"Repeat it," Enzo said.

"Uh—" Eustis mumbled. "You're my kid. Grandma died, and what was the other thing?"

"Sheesh," Enzo said. "Normal-person memory freaks me out. How do you people get by with a brain like a drain? Grandma died, and you got custody. You've got it, right?"

"Yeah," Eustis said. "I have it, but I'm not really comfortable lying."

"Come on," Enzo said. "We don't want to miss the transport elevator. It'd be twelve hours before another comes, and judging by the layer of perspiration on your forehead, I'm guessing you won't make it that long."

CHAPTER FOUR

CHIP

"Next elevator transport is in seven minutes," Enzo said.

He followed the kid toward the massive carbonized ribbon that rose overhead and disappeared into the orange haze of the sky. It looked like a black featureless skyscraper whose top was invisible from the ground.

"How does this work?" Eustis asked.

"Man, I'm afraid of how dumb you are," Enzo said. "Top's in geosynchronous orbit. The ribbon is," Enzo stopped and pointed, "anchored to the ground. Ribbon keeps the orbital docking station from flying off into space. Did I use any words you don't know?"

"I know the concept of a space elevator," Eustis said. "I mean, how do we ride it? I've never been on one."

"Wait, what?" Enzo said. "You've never left Earth?"

"Well," Eustis rubbed the back of his neck. "I haven't needed to, but now, well, I need to get to Musk City. I have a very important mission to—"

"Were you lying about being able to fix the transponder?" Enzo asked.

"No, I really can," Eustis said.

"Ok, so what's the transduction eccentricity of an oscillating—" Eustis interrupted, knowing the rest of the question.

"Easy. It's 2.34 unless it has a nine-pin transcoder coupling, then you'd have to retrofit the encapsulator unit to communicate in a digioscilating matrix-style base code. In which case, it'd still be 2.34, but it would be in a truncated form of reverse binary, so technically 2.31."

"Oh," Enzo said. "That actually makes sense. I thought the transponder might need to be transcoded, but I wasn't sure what the—" The kid paused. "Anyway, we'll look at it when we get there. Well, you know your comms stuff, for sure, but you're about to enter the most dangerous environment mankind has ever known. Just do what I say, and it should be fine. Either that, or you might die. Really it's at about twenty-eighty, I'd say. Eighty being your chances of dying." He didn't wait for Eustis to answer. They returned to walking and made their way toward the up-shuttle station.

Eustis let his eyes follow the ribbon toward the sky. A speck, nearly impossible to see, clung to the black thread that hung from the atmosphere. It was descending toward their location. They sat at the terminal with a few hundred people around them.

"When we get on, go straight up to level two of the elevator. Captain and Rudwick will stay on one, so they won't see you up there." Eustis nodded.

With every minute, the elevator's apparent size doubled. When it reached the ground, the speck had become a box as big as a house. It was a rounded multi-deck cylinder covered in windows. On its arrival, the crowd stood and moved toward the transport. Enzo silently pointed and rose, gesturing for Eustis to follow.

When its doors opened, about two hundred people streamed out of the massive elevator. The chaotic murmur surrounded them as they pressed toward the giant lift. When the arrival group had exited the skyward tram, Eustis' mob began to squeeze into the cramped space.

The crowd narrowed near the door. Each passenger was reaching out toward a terminal next to the hatch. Two guards with plasma rifles stood like statues at the opening. The broad-shouldered one had stern eyes that scanned the parade of passengers, while the other appeared utterly indifferent to what was happening around him.

Eustis noticed that the line of people streaming onto the elevator were all waving an empty hand over the terminal. Eustis turned to Enzo.

"What's—"

"Chip," the kid said as he pointed to his wrist.

"But I don't have a chip." Eustis wiped a bead of sweat from his forehead. He felt his face tighten. Enzo nodded calmly.

"Just swipe your hand over the terminal, and I'll handle the rest." Enzo smiled. "It'll be like you're my pet." They were being shoved from all sides. It felt like being pressed into a pasta maker for human flesh. Enzo went first through the glass doors. He scanned his wrist, the terminal blinked green, and he stepped into the transport. Once the kid was in, Eustis was exposed and alone in a crowd of strangers. Enzo had crossed the line, and Eustis was eager to do the same.

He reached out to the scanning terminal. Instead of green light, a loud squawk pierced the chaotic noise of the crowd, and a red light illuminated the terminal. Without intending to, Eustis' eyes sprang to where the fat guard had been standing on duty. He found the barrel of a plasma rifle pointing directly into his left pupil. He followed the length of the gun with his eyes and discovered a uniformed agent attached to the handled end.

"You don't scan green you don't ride." The guard barked.

"I just—" Eustis began to speak. Before he could get three words out, Enzo was at his side once more.

"Dad, come on. We're going to miss Aunt Effy's funeral," Enzo said. Eustis looked down at the kid and lowered his eyebrows. The guard swung his gun and pressed the barrel hard into Enzo's chest.

"Step back, kid. This is between your dad and me."

"It's just a bad scan, Sir. My daddy's chip takes a second scan sometimes." Enzo's voice was childlike. It was an impressive transformation. Eustis was about to speak up, but Enzo moved so quickly that he didn't know what was happening.

With lightning motion, Enzo grabbed Eustis' hand with his left and lifted Eustis' wrist up and over the scanning terminal. Eustis looked down as the terminal flashed green. The guard glanced at it and lowered his gun.

"Ok, Dr. Gatti," the guard said. "You and your son are free to go."

"Dr. What?" Eustis asked, looking down at his wrist. "I don't—" He opened his mouth to say more, but Enzo wrapped his fingers around his arm with an aggressive grip. He tugged Eustis onto the transport.

Eustis stared at his wrist as more people squeezed in behind. Enzo let go of his arm and stood next to him in the crowd.

Eustis pivoted. "How did you do that?" Enzo smiled and pointed to his left wrist, the opposite he had scanned himself in with. "I don't get it."

Enzo leaned close. "They didn't scan you," Enzo said. "Technically, you're not on this transport, Pet."

"So what happened?"

"When I waved your wrist over the terminal, it caught a signal from my chip," Enzo whispered. "Pretty savvy, right?"

"But you can't be scanned twice on the same chip, can you?"

"It's not the same chip." Enzo held up both wrists now. Eustis' eyes darted between them as he made sense of it. "If I scan my right, I'm Enzo Gatti, innocent, unassuming kid. If I scan my left, I'm, well, someone else. Or, in this case, you're someone else."

Eustis brought his voice down to a whisper. "You have two chips? That's illegal, right? How did you get an extra?

"Captain always says, 'use the system to beat the system." Enzo looked at the crowd ushering in. "Ok, dude. Captain and Rudwick are coming. Hit the upper deck. I'll come find you in a while."

"Ok," Eustis said as he clutched his duffle and drifted in among the crowd. "Hey, kid." Enzo looked over his shoulder. "Thanks. I owe you."

"I know. Now, get lost," Enzo said as he turned back toward the thronging crowd streaming onto the transport. Eustis ducked and looked for the stairs to the second level.

He found a spot by a window and watched the hundreds of people entering the transport from a second-level cupola. In a few minutes, all the passengers had entered the ferry. A recorded voice came over the speaker as the doors below closed. Eustis' ears popped as the pressure in the capsule changed. He watched out the window, not realizing, at first, what he was looking for.

"Thank you," Eustis whispered as the up-shuttle lurched and began to rise. Eustis watched the ferry station shrinking below and the marketplace beyond. Although a world's worth of bustle was mingling below, and dozens of aircraft were flying around in the low-level airspace around the exterior of the elevator, one, in particular, caught Eustis' attention. He put his hands on the window's glass and leaned forward as far as he could to see.

A black GovCorp fighter craft with blinking red lights, zoomed up, flying like it was in a hurry. It circled the premises below twice and then began pitching upward. Climbing effortlessly toward the elevator, toward Eustis' position. The elevator pod was a few hundred meters high when the GovCorp cruiser matched altitude. The nose of the craft pointed at the rising pod as it orbited upward around the moving location.

Eustis stared through the window as the fighter craft rose slowly. With its nose pointing directly at his location, the aircraft slowed and held formation. It had spotted its target. The hatch of the cockpit opened and hinged back out of the way. Eustis stepped back from the window as a dark-clad man rose up from the pilot's seat. His hair was tossed violently by the gusting wash of his hovering fighter craft. The man's soulless eyes stared through the glass, the only thing separating Eustis from Admiral Kynig Strafe.

The Admiral made a hand gesture, and Eustis' cortical display pinged a notification. Eustis didn't respond at the first ring, but the notification was persistent. He waved his hand, bringing the comm online reluctantly.

"Hello," Eustis said. *Stupid. Who says hello to their killer?*

"Eustis Wade Grimes," Admiral Strafe said. His voice could have been made by the friction of two metals, and it would still sound more human than what came over the comm. The noise of his fighter's engine roared in the background, and he had to shout to be heard. "So, you've decided to run."

"No," Eustis said. "I mean—It's just that—I," Eustis tried but couldn't put together a clear sentence.

"That's good. It's more fun that way." The admiral made another hand gesture. "I'll see you soon." The cockpit hatch started closing as Admiral Strafe sat back in the pilot seat. The aircraft spun in place and zoomed away. Eustis stared after it. His heart was beating fast, and his stomach was as tight as a pressure vessel. He looked out the window, breathing heavily and trying not to puke.

CHAPTER FIVE

UP

Eustis' tension boiled as the space elevator climbed into the rust-brown sky. Going long stretches without blinking, he watched the world shrink beneath through the glass. He kept thinking the admiral would come soaring through the sky to blow the elevator into bits. That led to visions of what had happened to his friends earlier that afternoon. His stomach turned, and he felt like he might throw up. He cast his eyes out the glass, hoping for a reprieve.

The blues and greens of the scenery below were laid out in a rich array, reminding him of the beauty and comfort he was leaving. The expanse of black was yawning dark and unforgiving above. A new forbidding rested on his heart and squeezed his lungs into a tight knot.

"There you are," Enzo said. The sound of his voice made Eustis jump. "Did you see that fighter craft flanking us? It was weird. Everyone on level one was freaked out. I'm guessing there's someone on board that—"

"So," Eustis interrupted. He was eager to change the subject. "Earlier, when we were talking about scanning your chip, you said I'm like your pet? What did you mean?"

"Well, that was rude," Enzo said. "Generally, we let each other finish sentences before we change the subject. But you know, whatever. You Earthers do it different, I guess. So, yeah. Pets have to be declared. They are basically considered carry-on cargo. Rudwick's cats could enter any port in the system, while the rest of the crew is banned from most."

"Rudwick has cats?" Eustis said. "Wait, did you say the crew is banned from most ports in the system?"

"You're one to talk," Enzo said. "Doesn't sound like you'll be getting a welcome party wherever you're going."

Eustis spun to look out at the vast growing darkness and remained silent for a long time. Enzo chattered about various things, but Eustis couldn't focus on his words.

He felt something changing over the next few minutes, but he wasn't sure what to make of it. His body was tingling. His internal organs were trying to move inexplicably upward. His arms, even his fingers, felt like they would drift away.

"So, why are you in such a hurry to get off-world?" Enzo asked.

"I need to get to Musk City, Mars," Eustis said absently as he rubbed his hands together. The friction felt strange against the tingling in his fingers.

"Yeah, you've said that about a hundred times," Enzo said. "But why?"

Eustis rubbed his hands against his legs. They were tingling as well. He wrapped his arms over his chest. "It's a better place for what I need to do," Eustis said almost without a thought. He put his hand to his stomach. "I feel weird. Do you feel that?"

"Yeah. We're coming up on gravity reversal," Enzo said. "You're feeling weightlessness. You're only about ten percent of your normal Earth weight." Eustis lifted his arm and let it fall. It drifted slowly down. As the weightlessness peaked, he felt his stomach protesting. *Don't puke, don't puke, don't puke.* The sensation of zero-G did not differ from the feeling of falling except that it had come on slowly rather than all at once. He placed his hand over his stomach, willing his guts to understand the peculiar twisting.

All over the elevator cabin, people were floating into the open headspace. It was clear who had been on the transport before because they shoved off the former floor, spun, and landed feet first on what Eustis had been thinking of as the ceiling. He tried to do the same, but his motion was awkward. He fumbled the landing and scrambled for anything to grab. Bumping into a lady, he sent her sprawling in the other direction. He grabbed onto the nearest something but released it when he heard a shrill voice shout, "Hey, creep. Let go of my leg!"

"Sorry," he said. He shouldn't have opened his mouth. His breakfast threatened to come up.

"I got ya," Enzo said, soaring comfortably birdlike and grabbing him by both shoulders. He kept his lips locked around his teeth, but he nodded and let him help.

"Might want to use the foot hook," Enzo said. He glanced up, but no, it wasn't up, it was down now. *This'll take some getting used to.* He glanced overhead at the ceiling-floor and tried to aim for the bench. "I'll give you a boost," Enzo said. Eustis felt the kid's hands press near his center of gravity, a place he wasn't comfortable being touched, but he didn't protest this once.

He reached a shaky hand for the spot he was torpedoing toward. When his grip found purchase, he maneuvered his body, pressed his foot into the loop, and pulled himself into position. He watched Enzo glide like a swan in a pond of weightlessness. Without touching anything, the kid tucked one leg close to his body which gave him a slight rotation. He revolved effortlessly, and then when he was nearly in position, he stuck out his leg, which arrested his rotation.

"Wow," Eustis said. "I need to learn that trick."

"Conservation of rotational momentum," Enzo said as if knowledge of physics was the same as being able to swim in a gravity-free environment like a space fish. "A small mass with high velocity can have the same momentum as a larger mass with lower velocity. Have to be a total throttle-bottom not to know that."

"Are you sure you're just thirteen?" Eustis said. "You talk like you're thirteen and a half."

Within another five minutes, the ceiling became the floor as *gravity*, which was really the earth's centrifugal force, began to grow in the opposite direction. It took his mind only a few minutes to reorient the room. Now the earth was above their capsule, and the gaping chasm of inky void was below. It was strange to have the stars under his feet.

"What's all that?" Eustis pointed through the glass at an expanse of shimmering points of light rising from the horizon.

"That's why rockets can't do low earth orbit anymore?" Enzo said.

"They don't use rockets to get off earth anymore?"

"Where have you been for the last century?" Enzo asked. Eustis didn't respond. "There's too much space junk," Enzo said. "About a billion chunks of junk turn orbital velocity into a death sentence."

In all the history feeds Eustis had seen, space travelers crawled atop giant explosive candles and rode fire into the sky. Strange to think no one left earth in such a blaze of speed. "Dead satellites?"

"Yeah, some. Others are space mines from the war." Enzo gestured toward the window. "A big cloud of swirling explosive shrapnel." He smiled. "It's pretty tough."

"Pretty," Eustis repeated. He peered at the void, dazzling like a molten black pearl. Little sparkling points of light danced across the horizon for as far as he could see. Strange to think that the beautiful twinkle was a nebula of orbiting death waiting to splinter any pilot's attempt to venture through the earth's paper-thin atmosphere. Eustis pulled his jacket tighter at the thought.

"So there's no other way to space from earth?" Eustis asked.

"Nope," Enzo said. "The elevator is the only way. One shuttle every twelve hours."

"Good," Eustis said, but Enzo didn't catch the whisper. It was sad, really. The earth was locked away behind a shield of orbiting death. However, since it was that layer of space debris that made it impossible for Admiral Strafe to make a more speedy pursuit, Eustis saw the fragments of shrapnel as a kind of selfish-providence. "Thank you," Eustis said again in an inaudible whisper.

"There it is," Enzo said. Eustis followed Enzo's gaze through the glass floor. Below, silhouetted by the blackness, the carbonized ribbon pointed to an outgrowth. It was a variety of complex shapes and structures that jutted out in a wide spiral of docking ports and vessels. "Slingshot Station," Enzo said. He pointed to the far end of one of the spiraling arms. "There's our ship. The Scuttle."

"The Scuttle?" Eustis asked. "That doesn't instill much confidence. Why is it called that?"

"Captain doesn't like me to say. But it has to do with how she got it. She rescued it from a scrapyard."

"Again, no confidence instilled," Eustis watched as Slingshot Station swelled to enormous proportions beneath them. "Do you mean it was in a junkyard?"

"My lips are sealed," Enzo said.

"Well, that's a first."

Eustis looked up at the earth, a bold blue ball suspended against the black. He dangled from the glowing orb like a spider on a thin web. Eustis noted the contrast as he shifted, staring between his feet at Slingshot. The artificial glow of manmade lights was a pale comparison to the world above. The station enlarged until it was their entire view. The elevator capsule continued to descend slowing gradually as it neared the geodesic peak of Slingshot.

The elevator shuttered, hissed, and came to a full stop. Enzo spoke fast. "Keep your eyes on the ground, walk fast, and try to look like you're going somewhere."

"What? Why?"

"There are cameras everywhere. You're Dr. Gatti, but you're not looking like yourself today. Also, if you see Captain Marianna or Rudwick, hide." Enzo stepped quickly out of the sprawling hatch that had just opened. Eustis sprinted behind him making the best of the half gravity.

Chapter Six

SCUTTLE

Slingshot Station hummed like a beehive, but instead of honey, it produced grease and a bad odor. A giant billboard that read *Welc me to Slingsh t St tion* hung over the main passageway. It could fall at any moment. It probably clung fast on account of the half-gravity. The people's bustle through the station was erratic and unpredictable. It was filthy, more than Eustis had expected.

The dim lighting left his hungry eyes struggling to capture the glorious vision he had reckoned on for his first foray into space. In all of the interplanetary advertisements, the stations looked clean and inviting, but here the hive didn't fit the hype. The noise and congestion were enough to send Eustis to the exit, except that there was none. Being a hunted man, he could only move forward.

He tried to keep up with Enzo as they weaved through tunnels that periodically opened into glass domes and black nothingness beyond. Despite the ease of movement at his partial weightlessness, he was breathing hard. He paused to catch his breath, something that seemed nearly impossible. Smudge-covered people skittered around him listlessly, with their eyes ever on the ground. The majority of the pedestrians wore air masks over their noses and mouths. Low-hanging lights flickered with spastic rhythms giving him a sickening twist in his stomach.

"Hey, you with the bag!" The voice sounded like it was made of air and dust. Eustis spun and adjusted his duffle bag's shoulder strap. A pedestrian jostled into him and grunted a curse. Eustis scanned for the source of the voice. A man was crumpled against the corridor's bulkhead. Out of his age-puckered mouth came barking jabber. "Yeah, you. Come here."

Eustis glanced along the path Enzo had taken. He was out of sight in the thronging crowd. He looked back at the sagging bag of skin that was wadded up at the edge of the walkway and moved cautiously toward him.

"Hello, my name is Eustis." The broken man looked up at him with surprise.

"You got a breath you could spare?"

"What?" Eustis said as he knelt a few paces away from the man. Foot traffic continued to radiate past in the clogged passageway.

"Come on? You can spare a little wisp for an old man?"

"I—uh—" Eustis set the duffle bag down next to him. "I'm kind of new here. I don't know what you're asking me. I'm happy to help if I can."

"A breath," the man said, closing his eyes and smacking his mouth between the words. "Just a little air."

"Oh," Eustis said, still trying to catch his own breath. "Are you having trouble breathing?"

"They used to keep it at full pressure out here, but now—" the man gulped on the thin air. "Those cheap, mouth-breathing goons cut communal air ration to half. GovCorp's killing us all. Some slow. Some fast."

"What's your name, friend?" Eustis asked. The words apparently surprised the man because his eyebrows rose, making more wrinkles around their edges.

"Ted."

"Ted, I think I have something that could help." Eustis opened the mouth of his duffle and dug through the contents. "Yes, here it is." He pulled out a small emergency air bottle with a face mask attached. The tiny thing wouldn't last long, but the man clearly needed it more than him.

Ted's face became momentarily bright when he spotted the little air tank. His hands went out greedily.

"I'll make a deal with you," Eustis said. Ted glanced at Eustis skeptically. "I'll give you this air, but while you use it, I'd like to tell you about the most important person who ever lived. Would that be ok with you?" The man nodded, not taking his attention off the bottle.

Ted's sad eyes watched Eustis' face as he talked. With the mask pressed against his wrinkled lips, he breathed with vigor as Eustis gave his practiced presentation. He had been talking for three or four minutes when the final gasp of air hissed from the bottle. Ted let the bottle's mask away from his face.

"So, what do you think, Ted?" Eustis said. "Do you believe what I've told you?"

Ted was about to respond, but before he could speak an abrasive voice sliced across the conversation and severed the serene moment.

"Hey!" the echoing noise bounced down the corridor. "No!" Eustis recoiled at the sound. He looked lengthwise down the passageway and spotted a robust figure lumbering toward him.

His black boots had an illuminated GovCorp logo emblazoned on the toe, a toe that looked ready to kick. Attached to the boots was a uniformed officer with his battering stick drawn. He had glowing stripes that ran up the length of his pants and jacket, blinking red and blue. His face was turned down, and his forward-leaning approach promised trouble.

"Don't feed the wildlife!" the officer shouted.

"I'm sorry, he can't breathe. He just needs some air."

The broad man pointed his batterized baton in Eustis' face and pulled the trigger. A warning spark arced like a spurt of angry lightning out of the tip. Eustis jumped back. "Soliciting is against the law, as is supporting vagrancy. Did he solicit you? Did you give him anything?"

"He needs some air. I was just going to give him a—"

"You can't do that." The officer bellowed. "Ted here is a no-script. Isn't that right, Ted?" The officer clicked his lightning stick at the poor man. His face danced with the shocking light as a sickening grin stretched across his face. Ted's lurching wince suggested he was familiar with the feeling of that baton. Eustis looked at the officer's name badge.

"Officer Bragg, I'm new here," Eustis said. "I wasn't trying to break the law. I was just trying to help."

"Let me make this simple. He's got no O2 subscription. Every breath he breathes is on loan from GovCorp, and his payment is way past due. If he begs a breath off you, it's criminal vagrancy. If you give him a breath, it's aiding criminal vagrancy."

"That's ridiculous," Eustis tried. Before he could get another word out, Bragg brandished his baton and let the sparks cut across Eustis' words.

"I don't make the rules," Bragg said. "I just shock the soot out of anyone that breaks them." He sparked his baton once more.

Eustis stared hard for a few seconds before he stepped back and faded into the traffic of the corridor. Bodies passed between him and the man huddled beneath his oppressor. Bragg feigned a lunge at poor Ted, to which the old man leaned over in an attempt to escape the inevitable blow. The officer laughed and spun away from the vagrant, looking like he might leave. Ted sat upright only to find that Bragg wasn't done. The monster took a wide stance so Ted could not escape this time and spat lightning into Ted's tender stomach. He doubled over in a seizing convulsion.

Eustis' heart was thumping against his ribs, and his breaths were flowing in shallow, shattered gasps. People huffed through their air masks at the inconvenience of moving around him. He slid the duffle strap from his shoulder and let it drop to the ground. He balled his hands into fists. His muscles tightened, and his vision narrowed.

"Hey, what are you doing?" A hand caught Eustis on the shoulder. When Eustis spun to look down at Enzo, his eyes were wide, and his nostrils flared. "Whoa, are you ok?" Without saying anything, Eustis looked in the direction of Ted and Officer Bragg. Enzo followed his look and then stepped in front of Eustis, effectively cutting off his plan of attack. Ted let out another scream of pain as Bragg's electric jab found its mark.

"Don't even think about it," Enzo said. "Tangle with a GovCorp goon, and you'll be space dust."

"But he's killing that guy."

"It's just a no-script," Enzo said.

"No one deserves that," Eustis pointed and leaned around the kid. "Don't you see what's wrong with this situation?"

"It's not about right or wrong," Enzo said. "It's just the way it is up here. Don't have to like it. Take one step toward that Govy-goon, and I go to the ship without you. Captain burns hard out of this port. Whatever you're trying to do dies here."

Enzo knelt down and gripped the handle of Eustis' duffle bag. He stood and held it out for Eustis to take. "It's your choice." Behind Enzo, the officer aimed another kick at Ted's stomach.

Eustis closed his eyes and said, "You've been very kind to me, but I have to do something. I just can't."

"Suit yourself," Enzo said, dropping Eustis' bag. Eustis stepped around Enzo and prepared to do, well, something, but he wasn't sure what. Before Eustis could act, Bragg's thick arm was wrapped mercilessly around Ted's neck, but he suddenly shoved him away with a shout and Ted tumbled into the corridor wall.

"The dirty no-script bit me!" Bragg shouted. Eustis stood frozen as he watched Bragg reach for a holstered sidearm.

"No!" Eustis shouted. He was running when the pistol spat a bolt of red plasma and Ted lurched and flopped lifelessly to the ground. Eustis skidded to a stop five paces from the body—the smell of electric ozone and cauterized flesh was sickening.

"We need a reclamation team in corridor three," Bragg radioed. Bragg holstered his firearm, stepped aside, and brushed past Eustis with a satisfied smile. "Two less lungs to fill."

No one stopped to investigate. A man lay dead, and no one cared. He stared down at Ted, hoping, even willing him to breathe, to sit up. Looking down at Ted's body, others came to mind. Leena Bickle. Sue Tuttle. Rod Musker. Martha and Todd Grambling. Murdered by that soulless animal, Admiral Strafe. This wasn't the place to cry, and he wasn't sure he could with how dehydrated he felt. But the tears welled, and he rubbed his face with his sleeve.

A light touch grazed his arm. Slowly, as if his head weighed as much as the earth, he looked down. The kid was blurred by watery lines of sorrow. Enzo had the strap of Eustis' duffle bag. He was handing it up toward Eustis. He didn't say anything but just looked up at the oddly woe-begotten man. Eustis reached for the strap of his bag, silently turned, and followed the kid down the corridor. "Thanks for giving me the chance to talk to him." He hoped beyond reason that it made a difference.

After a long breathless walk in low gravity, Enzo led him through an arched opening that spilled out into a broad landing port. Eustis managed to stow his tears for now, but he sensed he would need to find a place to mourn. He was working hard to push the day's events out of focus, but his mind was having trouble making sense of the world he was now a part of.

Another glass dome rose between them and a ship, if it could be called that. It looked like the loosely erected contents of a scrapyard. It was cable-lashed to the port mooring and remained docked by way of an enclosed gangplank.

"Behold," Enzo said. "The Scuttle."

If the filth and violence of Slingshot station were enough to make Eustis want to return home, the sight of the ship was more than adequate fodder for nightmares. Eustis closed his gaping mouth and blinked his unbelieving eyes.

"Are there pieces missing, or is it supposed to look like that?" Eustis asked. It didn't look like it could make orbit, much less a million-kilometer journey to Musk City, Mars. Maybe the whole endeavor was a mistake. Maybe this wasn't where he was supposed to be. When Enzo didn't answer, he said, "I mean, is it airtight?"

Enzo paid no attention and kept moving toward the gangplank that led to the hatch of the splintered vessel. Eustis took a moment to study the craft.

Compared to many in the Sol System, the *Scuttle* was not large, but to Eustis, it was a hulking giant. It was the size of a city block, and its misshapen form told a hundred stories Eustis couldn't wait to hear. Black scorch marks wrapped the breadth of its bulbous body. Entire panels were curled back, unriveted, and hanging free. Beneath the broken skin, a tangled and corroded electrical skeleton was visible. Its shape resembled that of a lopsided mutant whale whose fins had been severed.

"When we're inside," Enzo said. "Stay quiet. No Questions. You're going to lay low for a little while."

"Aren't they going to be mad when they realize—"

"No," Enzo said. "Not mad. Insanely enraged." Enzo smiled. "It's not too late to back out."

"No," Eustis said, but his tone wasn't convincing. He rubbed the back of his neck and glanced back up the gangplank. There was no other option. "I'm in."

"Ok," Enzo said. "Let's go."

Eustis took a deep breath of rocket exhaust and coughed on the greasy flavor of the thin atmosphere.

"Lord, help me," he said as he followed Enzo through the black tunnel that led into the belly of the titanium beast.

Twenty-seven minutes later, the Scuttle shoved off from Slingshot Station, drifting slowly upward in a lazy orbit. Forty-three minutes later, a smaller, ship drifted from Slingshot port tie-off with a similar heading.

CHAPTER SEVEN

REPUTATION

A thick man propped his illuminated boots on a desk at the back of a crowded set of cubicles. He was eating a rehydrated dish of vacuum-grown beans. It wasn't a meal to be excited about, but it was better than the slop Slingshot mess provided to its station patrol. He heard voices outside his office stall and grumbled something profane. He made the two-finger gesture for music. His cortex implant supplied a mind-numbing deep zone track to drown out the unwanted distraction from his bean stew. A shadow fell across his desk. Someone had entered his office. Whoever it was, wasn't welcome.

"Lunch break," Officer Bragg said. He knew he didn't need to raise his voice over the music since he was the only one that could hear it, but it added the desired severity to his sharp tone. He continued to give his attention to his gruel without looking up. When the intruder's shadow persisted, Bragg said, "I've got another seven minutes. Come back when—"

A sharp whack knocked his feet from his desk and sent them to the deck. The momentum threw his body forward and splattered bean mush across the front of his uniform. He stood, gestured to mute his music, and had his hand on his sidearm in one clunky motion.

"Don't unholster that unless you're ready to use it." The voice was like the deep rumble of metal under a high G burn. Bragg's eyes rose to the face, and he choked on the remainder of the stew that was in his mouth. He swallowed hard.

"Y—you're," Officer Bragg said as he let go of his pistol and put his hands up. "Y—you are," Bragg stuttered. He reached down to wipe the bean broth from his tightly-stretched apparel. He lifted his arm and made the requisite fist to the Temple, the GovCorp salute. Admiral Strafe did not return the gesture.

"I'm looking for a dissident," Strafe said as he glanced down at the name tag pinned to his uniform.

"Looking for a particular one?" Officer Willard Bragg gave a morose laugh. "We have plenty to choose from."

"This person of interest answers to the name Eustis Wade Grimes. He arrived at Slingshot Station twelve hours and forty-nine minutes ago."

"Well," Bragg started. "That's not so easy since the feed drives are on level two, and we're up here in the cheap seats." Bragg stepped back as if he would take his seat. Before his rump reached the chair, Strafe kicked it backward. Bragg tumbled and thumped hard on the floor.

"Men of action remain on their feet until the job is done." Bragg scrambled to get back up. By the time he was standing, Strafe had closed the distance between them and Bragg found himself trapped in the corner of the cubicle. Strafe's stare could have ignited a bar of solid tungsten. Neither of them moved for a second then Bragg broke.

"Yes," Bragg said. "Right. I will just have to... I guess since... I mean, after all... you're the admiral. I'm sure your clearance is in order." Bragg gestured in the air between them as he searched the archive for the file he needed. As he worked, he filled the compartment with empty chatter.

"I'm a big fan of your work, Sir," Bragg chortled. "Maybe after this, we could get a selfie?" He glanced from his task to the big man. The admiral gave no indication that he had heard the request. His eyes were locked on Bragg intently. Bragg went back to the task. "Or not. How silly of me. A selfie. Stupid."

"Finding anything?" Strafe snapped.

"Nope," Bragg said after another moment of searching. "No one by the name Eugene signed into the Slingshot D—"

"Eustis Wade Grimes," the Admiral corrected. Bragg glanced at him once more. He looked taller somehow.

"Right," Bragg said. "Not Eugene. How stupid of me. Eustis, what a weird name." He gestured more vigorously now. "Nope. Closest to it is a Eurie Grey. Is it possible that you might have the name wrong…" Bragg trailed off when he caught another sight of the admiral's icy stare. He was standing closer than before. Why was he so close? The admiral spoke in a gravely severe voice.

"You seem to be aware of my reputation," Strafe said.

"Well, yes, Sir. Who wouldn't be?"

"And what have you heard about me." Strafe was centimeters from Bragg's face. His breath was like the exhaust of an active drive thruster. The security guard was breathing hard and wishing he could look somewhere other than Strafe's face. The deep lines that snaked down from his prominent cheekbones could have been made of concrete.

"You always catch your prey," Bragg choked. "At least that's what they say." He tried to look down, but Strafe took a resolute fist, pressed it against Bragg's chin, and pushed his head back up slowly.

"Is that all they say about me?" Strafe asked. "I'm sure you've heard more."

"They say," Bragg wished he could take a step back, but he felt the cubicle wall against his spine, cold and unforgiving. "They say you do a lot more than just getting your mark. They say you've killed so many people GovCorp doesn't even have you write a report, that you'll kill anyone that gets in the way. That you'd kill the Chief Executive Emperor herself if she happened to be between you and your target."

For a fraction of a second, the sharp lines around Strafe's mouth stretched, arching as close to a smile as Bragg could imagine ever displayed across that grizzled face. "In basic, I learned something about myself," Strafe said as he placed the toe of his huge boot on top of Bragg's and let his weight press down against the subordinate's. "You know what I learned?"

"No," Bragg whispered.

"For most, when they miss the target, they try again and again with the same short muzzle repeater. I take a different approach. The bigger the gun, the harder it is to miss."

"Oh," Bragg said, in a hurry to get the words out. The silence that followed could have been a chokehold.

"I always get my mark. I aim with a big gun. I don't care what else I hit." Strafe paused. "Do we understand one another?" With the words Strafe leaned forward and put his weight on the toe of Bragg's boot. Bragg bit his lip and grimaced.

"Loud and clear, Sir," Bragg said in a breathy tone. "Your mission is my mission, Sir. You can trust me, Sir. If I have to watch every second of security footage from the last twelve hours, I'll do it. I'm on the case, Sir."

"That's more like it," Strafe said, removing his foot from Bragg's.

"Is there any more information you can give me about this Eustis character?"

"Dark shoulder-length hair. Flight suit. Black duffle bag with a Houston City insignia on it."

Bragg stroked his chin, still wishing Admiral Strafe would take even a tiny step backward. "Actually, I think I know the guy," Bragg said. "Or at least I saw him. Brown eyes? Tall chap? Stubborn bloke? Has a problem with authority?"

"Sounds promising," Strafe said as he made a flicking motion in Bragg's direction. An image notification blinked on in Bragg's cortex display.

"Yep, that's the guy. Like you said, he came through here about twelve hours ago. Nearly got the sharp end of my shock stick. Was trying to abed a tramp in criminal vagrancy."

"Where is he now?" Strafe said. "I am going to ground him into nothing."

"Don't know," Bragg offered in a whisky voice. "I'll track him down on the security feeds."

"Bring the vagrant for interrogation," Strafe said.

"Can't," Bragg said. "He expired unexpectedly of natural causes. He's already been sent to reclamation. You know how these transients are. Dying by the droves. Matter of fact, Just the other day I was—"

"The security footage," Strafe said.

"Right. Yes, Sir. I'm on it."

"HEXA," Strafe said.

"Yes, Sir." Bragg continued to pull the footage as Strafe talked into his communicator to his A.I. assistant. "I have an Officer Willard Bragg here. He's going to link access to the security mainframe on Slingshot. Go through it. Look for anomalies."

"I'm not really authorized to give universal access to..." Bragg trailed off at a glance from Strafe. "Yes, Sir." Bragg grabbed the digital credentials and flicked them to Strafe. They stood there in silence for almost five seconds before Bragg broke it. "So, we just wait, or..."

"I think I have something," HEXA's voice returned.

"Give it to me."

"We have nine dissreps that scanned in on that shuttle. One of which is a kid named Enzo Gatti. A few seconds later, another Gatti signed in. Dr. Lorenzo Gatti. Sound familiar?"

"Why do I know that name?" Strafe asked.

"*The* Dr. Gatti. Solologist from Mercury. Known for his work on the flare cycle."

"Oh yeah," Strafe said. "I thought he died in a flare event."

"He did," HEXA said.

"So, how does a dead scientist from Mercury log into a GovCorp terminal on Slingshot?" Strafe asked.

"Security footage from the time of the log shows this," HEXA said. Bragg didn't have access to what Strafe was seeing, but he could tell from his face that they had found their mark.

"I'm going to chop him into little pieces," Strafe mumbled. Watching Strafe talk to himself about how he was going to treat his victim gave Bragg a strange sickly thrill. "I'll end him."

"That's him," Strafe said. "The kid he's with."

"Enzo Gatti," HEXA said. "Engineer on record for a ship called the Scuttle. No transponder signal on ping or private dataset for over a year, but dock manifest shows it was portside up until about eleven hours ago."

"I could get you those manifests," Bragg interrupted. Strafe furrowed his brow, spun, and stepped out of Bragg's cubicle without another word. "Or, we could question the docking authority if you want." Strafe rounded the corner and was gone.

Bragg turned to look at his cubicle. Bean stew was all over the floor and desk. He almost had the urge to clean it up, but he managed to suppress it.

Chapter Eight

STOWAWAY

Eustis had often imagined what his first trip into space might be like. He had envisioned watching the world shrink into a tiny blue marble. He had expected to be awestruck by the vastness of it all and anticipated sharing the moment with someone important, even special. He did not expect to be immediately shoved into a cold lonely spaceship closet to spend his first hours in a real-life spacecraft in the dark. Enzo hid him in a lockup cabinet for spare EVA suits on the engineering deck.

He had felt the engine's vibration and the growing inertia as the Scuttle pulled away from the docking port. Not knowing how long he would be hidden, he unclasped the only EVA suit from its hanger, folded it, and used it as a cushion, doing his best to get comfortable stuffed in the floor of the closet.

He must have fallen asleep because the moments preceding the sound of footsteps were lost to memory, but he was alert now. He held his breath, hoping the footfalls were Enzo's.

A rummaging sound issued from nearby. In the dark of the closet, Eustis imagined the big man, Rudwick, ripping the lockup hatch off its hinges and pulling him out of the closet by the hair. His vision of the scene changed immediately, when he heard the voice.

"Comm app." It was Captain Marianna's voice, a sweet blend of confidence and competence. "Enzo," she said. "Where is that nine-pin coupling unit?" A pause followed, presumably as Enzo responded. "I'm already in engineering. Just tell me where it is." Another pause followed. "That's stupid. Why would I wait for you to come down here? I'm already here. Just tell me where—" She sounded irritated now. "No, just—"

The sound of footsteps falling fast translated through the metal body of the ship. Someone was running. The sound changed as another voice came into audible range.

"It's in that drawer," Enzo said, his voice muffled by the hatch door. Eustis leaned toward the hatch door and pressed his ear against it to hear better.

"What's wrong with you kid?" Marianna said. "You ran all the way down here to point at that drawer. Why didn't you just tell me—"

Under the weight of Eustis' leaning, the hatch door budged ever so slightly. He had forgotten Enzo had left it unlatched to avoid suffocating its contents. The conversation on the other side of the door stopped abruptly. Eustis' breath caught in his throat, and his heart was racing.

"Probably just one of Rudwick's cats," Enzo said. His voice sounded nervous. Marianna didn't respond. Three quick footfalls neared the hatch. Eustis leaned back as the hatch swung wide. A greenish light poured in. It took Eustis's eyes a moment to adjust. When they did, he was both pleased and horrified.

He was pleased to be able to come out of the cramped closet and to receive a gust of relatively fresher air, although it smelled of fusion fuel. Most of all, he was pleased to see the gentle contours of Marianna's face once more, but he was horrified because the look on that perfect face was one of bitter, murderous rage.

"Now, listen," Eustis heard words coming out of his own mouth before he intended to. "I can explain. I'll fix the transponder. Then I just need to get to Musk City. I have an important mission there, and then I'll be on my way. You'll never have to see me again."

"It was my idea," Enzo said.

"PA," Marianna said with a tight hand gesture. "Rudwick, engineering deck. Now!" She paused but then thought to add. "Bring Tiny."

Enzo was chattering at breakneck speed, but Eustis closed his mouth and held eye contact with the Captain. She did not break her icy stare. Over the sound of Enzo's prattle, bigger, louder footsteps echoed through the ship. A softer padding Eustis couldn't quite place accompanied the sound.

Rudwick slid down the ladder and landed with his heavy boots on the decking. He was shirtless and carrying a plasma rifle. Without his shirt, the place where his mechanical arm met flesh was exposed.

"Down here, boy," Rudwick barked as he glanced upward. A blur of fur and teeth leaped down into the engineering compartment. It was a cat, but it must have been a genetically modified breed because it was as tall as Rudwick's hip.

"What be this cad doing aboard the Scuttle?" Rudwick asked. "Be he a castaway?"

"No," Enzo chirped. "I brought him on board. We need someone to fix—"

"Shut it, kid," Marianna said in a grave, controlling voice. She had no need of shouting, for her calm was as frightening as the void outside the ship.

"It wasn't Enzo's fault," Eustis said. His hands were in the air, but he had not yet stepped out of the lockup. "I take full responsibility."

Marianna kicked the hatch, sending it swinging into a closed position.

"We be in good conscious, blasting a bolt through his chest and committing his body to the dark."

"The word is *conscience*, you old goiter bag," Enzo said. "There's no need to kill him."

"I agree with Enzo," Eustis said through the hatch door.

"Shut up," Marianna and Rudwick said in unison.

"He's right, you know," Marianna said. "We are within our rights to space him."

"No," Enzo said. "Not according to GovCorp solitime law, chapter seventeen, section nine, clause four. A stowaway is defined as a human person who acquires passage without the consent of crew."

"Blast your memory voodoo, boy," Rudwick said. "You hardly be crew. You be barely out of diapers."

"I don't care about solitime law. He's on my ship without my permission. That makes him a stowaway."

"He can fix our transponder," Enzo said.

"I can," Eustis added through the door.

"Shut up!"

"But killing a stranger," Marianna said. "Too many unknowns. He could be the chief imperial officer's son for all we know."

"That be bosh," Rudwick said.

"But my point is that we don't know what we're dealing with here."

"Dealing with a man needs a killing." Rudwick was adamant, but Marianna ignored him.

"Isn't he in some kind of trouble?" Marianna asked.

"I'm sure it's no big deal," Enzo said. "We've all had our scrapes."

"Maybe there be a reward for the scurvy cad," Rudwick wondered aloud.

"Enzo. Check." Marianna said, kicking the lockup hatch. It swung open once again. "Slug. Full name. Now!"

"I'd rather not," Eustis said. Rudwick stepped forward and pointed his plasma riffle at Eustis' head. His big cat hissed as he took the ominous stance.

"Give the name or I take off your face," Rudwick said. He touched the barrel to the tip of Eustis' nose.

"Eustis Wade Grimes."

"Residence," Marianna commanded.

"329 Hopper Street, Houston City, Earth," Eustis said. "At least that was my place until this morning."

Enzo was gesturing to a display that he hadn't made available to the others.

"Weird," Enzo said. "No reward posted. But his remains are earmarked for reclamation. But he's obviously not dead yet."

"Check the colonial notary for—" Marianna started, but Enzo cut across her words.

"Already did. Nothing," Enzo said.

"Me thinks Euticus be mighty quiet," Rudwick grumbled. "Spill it, you traitorous nave."

"I uh—well—I got a call," Eustis said. "From the Office of Dissidence Management."

"No!" Marianna said, raising her voice now.

"Say it be a lie," Rudwick growled. "Kid, you invited a shunt aboard. You've doomed us all."

"I didn't know!" Enzo said. "I just thought he was in normal trouble. I didn't know he was a—a—you know."

"We drop his body in the cold of black and burn on as if nothing askew took we on," Rudwick said. "No one be the wiser." Despite Rudwick's words, Marianna did not break her icy stare.

"We could turn him in," Enzo said. Eustis shot a glance at the kid. "Could claim he came aboard without us knowing." Again Marianna didn't look away. Her knowing stare was unflinching.

"Listen," Eustis tried. "I'm really sorry. I should have—"

"Who's assigned to your case, dissident?" Marianna said as if she were asking for the date of his funeral.

"It's all a misunderstanding," Eustis attempted. Once again, he found Rudwick's barrel in his face.

"Who's your hunter?"

"Admiral Strafe," Eustis said, letting his head bow low.

The compartment fell silent. Even Tiny, the giant cat, noticed the change in mood. Enzo leaned against the bulkhead and slid down to the deck.

Rudwick stood his post, ready to eviscerate Eustis. Marianna continued to stare at him. No one said anything for a long time.

"Ok," Marianna said after a long, excruciating pause. "Rudwick, we need him alive for now, but he needs to look unwelcome in case Strafe catches us with him."

"That I can do, me hearty," Rudwick said with a smile. "I never did hear such welcome words."

"So, he's in?" Enzo said excitedly.

"Nope," Marianna said. "We're still headed to Aldrin City. We'll drop him there and burn hard."

"But Mayor Skurg will—" Enzo tried.

"I don't want to hear it, kid," Marianna said. "Now to your quarters. I don't want you to see this." Enzo grumbled as he followed her toward the ladder and started to climb.

Before she disappeared into the upper deck opening, she peered down at him and said, "You realize you've put your black mark on all of us, right? You know they'll kill us all?" Eustis nodded reluctantly. "Ok, Rudwick, do your thing but, don't mangle his face too bad. May need it for facial recognition when that death dealer catches us. Anything else goes, but make it quick. We're going to burn hard out of here in fifteen minutes. Enzo, you're with me."

Enzo followed the captain out of the engineering compartment as Eustis' attention turned toward the giant man standing over him. Rudwick smiled and began.

CHAPTER NINE

GRATITUDE

"Cap," Rudwick grumbled into the communicator app. "This guy be no fun to beat. He don't fight back, but he don't cower either." Eustis took a much-needed breather while Rudwick waited for a response. "Aye, aye Cap'n"

The trickle of blood tickled his burning nose. His cheekbones felt like they had taken a pounding from a jackhammer. His ears were still ringing from the most recent impact. He ran his tongue along the range of his teeth. Only one in the back was missing. He spat a mouthful of pooling crimson on the deck and dragged his sleeve across his cracked lips. Eustis had never taken such a beating, was still on his feet, but he wouldn't be much longer if the enormous man kept it up.

"Captain says, times be up," Rudwick moaned. His giant cat Tiny was sniffing the dubious, crimson stains Eustis had splattered all over the engine room. "Follow me."

"Where are we going?" Eustis question.

"Upper deck, course," Rudwick said as he reached for the ladder leading up to the next deck. The vinegar had gone out of his voice, and he was as friendly as if they had just completed a successful business deal. "You'll be needing to buckle in. We be getting heavy in five minutes."

"Getting heavy?" Eustis asked as he reached for the ladder and prepared to follow Rudwick up. Tiny briskly leaped up the rungs of the ladder before him.

"*We're getting heavy* means we're going to hit the throttle," Enzo said. Eustis glanced up to discover Enzo was peering down through the deck hatch.

"Ah," Rudwick said. "The runt be spying on our fist cuffs."

"You look like you got sucked through a fusion drive and hit every thrust blade on the way out," Enzo said as Eustis climbed onto the second deck. Rudwick laughed proudly at the kid's description.

"I don't know what that means," Eustis said, trying to smile. "But today has turned out much better than I expected." Enzo and Rudwick looked at each other with furrowed brows.

"You're super weird," Enzo said.

"Thanks." Eustis felt rising nausea threaten from within. He reached for the railing to keep from listing too hard one way or another. He felt dizzy, was seeing double, and hurt all over.

"Eutychus here uttered nary a whimper for the duration of the abuse," Rudwick said. "But stood ground and stared me down, smiling as I laid the whoop on his cold bones. It be mighty unsettling to be stared at while I thrashed him about the face and body."

"I'll try to do better next time," Eustis said. He leaned over and was sick all over the deck.

"This stowaway be a mysterious bloke," Rudwick said. "But any man remains standing under Old Rudwick's hammer hand earns me undying respect for sure. It'll be a shame when Cap'n orders me kill him. But orders is orders." Without another word, the big man, vicious assailant as he had been, walked away whistling an upbeat tune. He climbed the next ladder toward another upper deck and disappeared. Tiny followed Rudwick up.

"Well, welcome to the Scuttle," Enzo said now that they were alone.

"Thanks," Eustis said, finding it challenging to stay upright.

"You look like you might pass out or die," Enzo said. "It's hard to tell the difference when you're all covered in blood like that." Enzo stood staring at him as if he wanted to see which one it was. "Well, anyway. Let's find you a place. A couple of minutes until our burn. Better have you in a crash seat before we light the candle."

Enzo trotted down the corridor much quicker than Eustis could follow. Presently his left leg was only responding to about half his commands, so dragging it while gripping the railing was his only option.

Enzo turned and faced a rusted and warped hatch. He pulled at the lever three times before he got it loose. The hatch creaked as if it hadn't been opened in years. Enzo disappeared inside, and Eustis did his best to waddle after him.

"Ship was built for a crew of twenty," Enzo said as he spoke from a dark compartment. Some pile of odds and ins tumbled to the deck. In the dim spill of illumination from the corridor, the room was absolutely stacked with discarded and unwanted items. "It's just been us three since I came aboard." Enzo paused near a stack of crates as tall as he was. Instead of moving them, he just shoved them over. He shouldered the remaining pile out of the way.

"This will be your room, at least until they kill you," Enzo said. He pointed in each direction respectively. "Crash seat. Bed. Lockup for your bag and personal items." He pointed a thumb over his shoulder. "Lavatory's down the corridor." Eustis surveyed the dark room. The compartment was a horror scene strewn with discarded equipment and spools of frayed wire. Jagged metal jutted out at a dozen places. Numerous trip hazards threatened every step. The tiny window that looked out into the heavens beyond was cracked. Eerie shadows cast by the light from the corridor painted the room in a sinister contrast.

"Are there lights?" Eustis asked.

"They would have come on when we entered. So, no, I guess not," Enzo said. "I mean, it's a bit of a fixer-upper. You don't have any room to complain. Seriously, dude, you were about a half inch from gettin' spaced. If you don't like it, you can just—"

"Enzo," Eustis said. "Come here."

"What?" Enzo said. "No. I don't want to be your crutch."

"Please," Eustis said gently. He reached his hand toward the kid. Enzo blinked. Glanced at the open hatch. After a moment of contemplation, he closed the gap, albeit reluctantly. Eustis knelt to one knee, wincing as the pain shot down his leg. At face level with the kid, he put out both arms and wrapped them around Enzo.

"What the?" Enzo said as the strange stowaway hugged him. Eustis let Enzo loose, reached for his shoulders, and looked him in the eyes.

"Enzo Gatti," Eustis said with slow and deliberate intention. "Thank you so much. I'm so deeply grateful for your generosity. You took a risk on me, and I am so thankful. You are more courageous than many grown men I know. I'm tremendously impressed with you. You're helping accomplish things more important than you know. Sometime soon, I'd like to talk some more, but—" Eustis coughed and spat more blood. "But right now, I think I need to lie down."

Enzo stepped back, eyeing him. Eustis rose to his feet with great pain. Enzo moved backward three paces. He looked like he would say something but then closed his mouth and left the compartment without saying anything.

Eustis worked his way into the bed and strapped himself in as well as he could. The growing sensation of weightful pressure gripped him as the sound of the engines ramped. Sleep befriended him before he had endured another minute of the heaviness.

CHAPTER TEN

TRANSMITTING

"Captain," Enzo said. "Take a look at this."

"Did you bring another stowaway aboard?" Marianna said.

Enzo didn't respond to her sarcasm. She stepped over a crate and peered above the back of his chair. The bridge was packed with old gear, broken equipment, and rusted paraphernalia of an inglorious past. Enzo gestured in Marianna's direction, giving her access to his cortex display's readout. He pointed at the hovering data. "It's some kind of intermittent signal. It's in close proximity too."

"How close," Marianna asked.

"Too close to get a parallax reading," Enzo said as he swiped to another screen.

"Admiral Strafe?"

"Nope," Enzo responded. "No GovCorp tag. Plus, it's coming in irregular bursts. A few minutes at a time. It's not lightwave, either. It's an old band spectrum. Radio frequency."

"Who uses radio anymore?" Marianna asked. Enzo didn't respond. "Bring it up. Let's hear it."

"Can't," he said. "It's not broadcasting currently. I can set it to record the next transmission so we can analyze."

"Do it."

"Aye, Cap." He made the requisite hand gestures, nodded, and swiped away the screen. "By the way, we're approaching our insertion burn increase for lunar orbit. Still want to hit Aldrin City, or—" Enzo didn't finish the thought, as the subject of the stowaway was still raw.

The captain stepped across the bridge, maneuvering around various piles of unsorted tech. She slapped the wall lockup, and a small hatch door swung open. She retrieved a liquid pouch. Enzo eyed her as she pierced the seal and took a long drink.

"Starting early?" Enzo asked.

"You have a problem with this?" She glared. He put his hands up defensively. She spun and looked out the large bay window. She drained the liquid pouch in its entirety. "How long can we put a hold on the insertion burn?"

"We're stable," Enzo said. "Long as you want, but with Strafe on our tail—"

"Yeah, I know," Marianna said. She tossed the crumpled liquid pouch at the discard receptacle and missed. She didn't move to pick up the garbage. What was the point? "I get it, you know," Marianna said. "You've got a memory like a computer. You're a smart kid."

"I'm sensing a *but* coming," Enzo said.

"*But*," she emphasized, "no matter how perfect, memory isn't a replacement for experience," Marianna said.

"You made the wrong choice. He can fix the comm. You were three bottles in, and that always makes you cowardly."

"Shut up, kid," Marianna barked. "Just for once in your life, listen to me." She pushed her hair out of her face. "You're just a kid, and you don't understand—"

"Better to be a sober kid than a bitter, blind boozer," Enzo said.

"Get off my bridge!" Marianna growled.

"Oh, there's that nerve I was reaching for," Enzo said.

"Now!"

"Fine!"

Enzo glared as he rose. He moved toward the command deck exit without taking his eyes off her. One hand on the ladder, he paused. He stared at the deck for a second, looking as if he would say something. After a moment's hesitation, he crawled down the ladder silently.

Once he was down deck, Marianna cursed and kicked a stack of crates. They tumbled, but the aggression didn't satisfy.

"Comm app," she grunted. A beep indicated that the line was open. "Stowaway, report to the command deck." She waited for a long few seconds, but there was no response. She tried again, "Fair-dodger, come up to the command deck." She waited again, but there was no response. "What's wrong with this thing?" She slammed her fist down on the control panel, but it didn't seem to fix anything.

A piercing beep sounded from the terminal Enzo had vacated, but the kid wasn't there to receive it. Marianna moved to the kiosk and unlocked it with a swipe. The close proximity signal was transmitting again. She gestured to open the signal readout. It was an audio file. She played it. Her rage metastasized when she heard the sound bite. "That rotten hornswoggler!"

She was in a full run. She slid down the ladder and descended three decks in less than a minute. She heard his voice as she approached Eustis' compartment. She attacked the door with an aggression she usually reserved for emergencies, and this situation fit the need.

She burst into his quarters, and briefly marked that Eustis was sitting in front of a cobbled pile of tech. Wires snaked between varied pieces of active communication gear. A signal indicator blinked as an audio readout bounced. A long antenna was propped up against the bulkhead with a fat strand of braided wire running to his makeshift transmission rack. Eustis was holding a microphone to his mouth and had just stopped speaking when Captain Marianna entered the compartment.

She crossed the room in two quick steps, ripped the microphone out of his hand, threw a well-practiced right hook, caught him across the jaw, and sent him sprawling to the deck. She then turned her rage to Eustis' ad hoc radio transmitter. She gripped the wire to the antenna and cracked it like a whip. The rack of gear went tumbling.

"No!" Eustis shouted. He was on his feet in a second. She unholstered her pistol and released the safety. With it pointed at his face, she used her other hand to rip his equipment apart. The blinking lights went out, and the equipment died with a crash. When each piece of tech was air-gapped, she spun on him. His hands were in the air.

"You intolerable gobermouch!" she shouted. "What were you transmitting?" He didn't answer. She stepped forward and leveled her barrel at his forehead. "Who were you talking to?"

"Anyone who will listen," Eustis said.

"What?" She screeched. "Are you insane? We've got Admiral Strafe on our tail, and you decide to step up to an open mic night?"

"That's exactly why it's so important I do this," he said, gesturing to the broken equipment. "I may not have much time left. Believe me. I wouldn't do this unless it was important."

"Do what?" she shouted. "What are you broadcasting?"

With his hands in the air, he said, "Captain, I can see I've upset you. I will tell you anything you want to know, but I'd like us just to take a moment to de-escalate." He pointed to the gun in her hand.

"De-escalate?" She said, looking at him with her head cocked sideways. Her voice was calm but deadly. "I'm going to ask you once more, and if you don't tell me, I'm going to paint the bulkhead with your brains. What were you transmitting?"

"I'm a believer," Eustis said.

"Believer," Marianna said. "What's that? Is that your dissident faction?"

"No," Eustis said. "I'm part of an ancient belief group. I may be the only one left in the Sol System. I can't let the message die with me. I know I've put you in great danger, but this is so much more important than—" He would have continued, but she lowered her gun and stepped back. She leaned against the hatchway and stared at the floor. Her face went pale white.

"You're a *religionist*," she said. "A religionist on my ship. This is—" Her voice grew quiet, but she continued to talk to herself in rapid terms. Eustis could not quite hear what she was saying as she paced back and forth.

"PA," she blurted suddenly. "All hands muster, stowaway's quarters." It took only a minute for the entire crew, which included Rudwick, Enzo, and four cats, to be huddled around the entrance of Eustis' compartment.

"This insane mud dweller was just transmitting his religionism on broadwave."

"Religionism," Rudwick said with a face that looked as if he might wretch.

"From our ship!" Enzo shouted.

"I know it sounds odd, but I didn't—" Eustis started, but Marianna cut across his words.

"Shut up, stowaway." She turned to the kid. "Enzo, prep for a long-range burn. Get us something in the belt."

"I really need to get to Musk City. I have an important message I need to give to Mars." Eustis interjected. Rudwick stepped over, put his huge hand over Eustis' face, and shoved him backward. He tumbled over a pile of scattered gear.

"We're not going to Aldrin City?" Enzo asked.

"Every GovCorp ship in signal range knows where we are now. They know whatever this dissident criminal has been broadcasting. They know that his contraverbs were being transmitted from this ship. Which means we're tagged. Whatever this rube was being hunted for, now we are too."

"We bear the black mark," Rudwick said.

"Enzo," Marianna shouted.

"Right," Enzo said. "Long-range burn. I'm on it." He rushed away.

"Rudwick, secure the prisoner and make sure he has nothing he can transmit with. If he tries to leave this deck, kill him."

"Aye, Cap," Rudwick said with a smile. "Do you wish me just kill him now, and we be done with it?"

"No," Marianna said. "Without Aldrin City, we still have a broken transponder. Once we're on our way, we'll put him to use."

"Then we will kill him?" Rudwick said.

"We'll see," Marianna said. "But not until after he fixes the transponder."

"Unless he leaves the deck?" Rudwick said.

"Yes," Marianna said. "If he leaves the deck, then you kill him."

"But won't he have to leave the deck to fix the transponder?"

"Rudwick!" Marianna shouted. "Get to work!"

"Aye, Cap."

CHAPTER ELEVEN

WAR SHIP

"What is that sound?" Captain Marianna asked over the ship-wide communicator. She waved her hand to initiate the cued maneuver, which would spin the axis of the ship by a few degrees.

She felt the slight change in inertia, but her mind wasn't on that. She got still for a minute before she repeated her call. "What is that sound?" Again, there was no response. "Why doesn't anyone listen to me?" She climbed down through the hatch from the bridge and listened for the strange echoing moan.

They had been burning engines at 1.2 Gs for days. They were in the deep black pit of space, but no matter how far they flew, she couldn't get comfortable knowing the unstoppable Admiral Strafe was after them. They hadn't spotted any pursuers on the scopes, which had allowed everyone to relax a little.

She banged her flattened hand against the hatch of Enzo's room. The hatch swung wide, and the kid stood shirtless in the opening.

"Why didn't you answer the comm?"

"You look tired," Enzo said. He glanced at the ceiling. "Hey, what's that awful noise? Sounds like a hand towel got stuck in the bathroom filter intake."

"I don't know." Marianna spun and reached for the ladder to the next level down. The sound of footsteps told her that Enzo was following.

She tapped the panel next to the down hatch and crawled through. "Rudwick, is that one of your cats?" She asked as she came around the bulkhead. There were unpleasant and moist smacking sounds coming from his room, but it was not the noise they were searching for. She and Enzo paused at the passage to Rudwick's bunk compartment. Rudwick was feeding his felines. Tiny, the genetically modified giant, Biscuit, Striker, also modified to be indefinitely minutely kittenesque, and Beverly Gertrude Lewis, Rudwick's favorite. The cats gnawed ravenously on as Enzo and Marianna stared into Rudwick's compartment.

"Bleeding stardust, that smells terrible," Enzo said. "What is that? Rotten bilge muck."

"It be synthetic cat meat," Rudwick said. He sliced off a sliver of pink and tossed it to Tiny, the genetically modified tabby that weighed more than Enzo.

"Why are you feeding cat meat to your cats?" Marianna asked.

"If stranded we ever were, I'd wish 'em to eat one another before they turned their teeth on me. So I'm giving each the taste of cat meat. It be a matter of me own life and death."

"Congratulations. You've risen to gross level twelve," Enzo said.

"That's horrifying, Rudwick," Marianna added.

"Thank you, Cap'n. I love me cats, but I love *me* more." Rudwick paused. "What be that tremendous racket? Sounds alike to a variable speed slot socket."

"Don't know," Marianna said and then turned toward the ladder leading to the next level down. This time both Enzo and Rudwick followed her descent. This was the level Eustis had been occupying, and it was also where the sound was the strongest. Crawling down into the narrow passage, she knew at once what the sound was. She gritted her teeth and walked resolutely toward the hatch that led to Eustis' cabin.

"It be the man Eugene," Rudwick said as he climbed through the opening. He followed Marianna.

"Is that—" Enzo slowed to listen when he entered the corridor. Eustis' chamber door was open. Quietly Marianna, Enzo, and Rudwick formed a semicircle around the opening and took in the sound. Eustis had his back to the door and his face pressed against the window that looked out into space. Though his posture was strange, what had their attention was that he was singing.

The melody rose and fell in a haunting lilt that tickled tiny shivers down Marianna's neck and back. She let her clenched teeth loosen as she listened.

The starry sky speaks,
About the glory of God
The expanse explains,
What he's accomplished
Each and every day,
They talk about Him
And every single night,
they reveal knowledge
They have no need,
For spoken language
From celestial heights,
No sound is heard
Yet their words ring,
To the ends of the worlds
Speaking to all the earth

"It don't be a saloon jig, but nice enough in its own way," Rudwick said when the song was done. Eustis leaped at the sound of the crude and unexpected voice. When he saw his audience, he wiped his knuckles across the wet of his red eyes.

"I think he's crying," Enzo said. "Could he really be crying?" Eustis sniffled and once again ran his hand across his face.

"The view is so beautiful," he said. "Everywhere I look, I just see reasons to worship."

"A warship!" Rudwick bellowed. He rushed to the window, shoving Eustis out of the way. "Where be the scalawags?" He called over his shoulder as he craned his neck for every possible angle. "Battle stations!" he yelled. When Rudwick saw that no one obeyed his instruction, he spun and charged out of the room, screaming, "I be doing it me self, you cursed cowards. Battle Stations."

"No," Eustis called after him. "I said *worship*. I couldn't help but worship." Enzo entered Eustis' cabin now that Rudwick had made space. Marianna stood at the door with her arms crossed. "Actually, I did see something out there earlier. It was a bright speck. Caught sight of it as we did that spin move. Thought it might be a ship or something."

"Couldn't be," Enzo said. "A ship would register on lidar if it was close enough to see."

"But," Eustis protested, "it looked like–"

"It wasn't," Marianna barked through the open hatch. She and Eustis stared at each other for a long, tense moment.

"You said it made you want to worship," Enzo said, rescuing them all from the awkward silence that followed. "If it's not a spacecraft full of trigger-happy meatheads, what is it?"

"It's when you show your appreciation to the creator," Eustis explained.

"So, worship is when you put your head in a little window and sing a bunch of meaningless words?" Enzo said.

"Well, if that's where my head happens to be when the mood strikes, sure, but the words aren't meaningless. Plus, worship isn't always singing. Sometimes it's just speaking or even acting in a certain way."

Enzo scrunched his face. "Sounds stupid."

"You could try it if you want," Eustis said. He stood and gestured toward the window. "Come on. I'll show you." The kid cast his eyes toward Marianna, who was holding up the door frame with her hand on her holstered pistol. Her jaw was clenched tight once more. Despite the captain's tension, Enzo walked toward the wall as Eustis stepped aside.

"So I just look out, or what?" Enzo asked.

"Sure, look at that amazing view and say what comes to mind." Enzo leaned into the small hull-mounted window and looked through the glass.

"Uhh—star cluster."

"Express your emotions about the view. Just say what you feel," Eustis said.

"It's the dark between the worlds."

"What else?" Eustis prodded.

"It's a cold, unforgiving void that wants to kill me, and eventually, it will."

"Ok," Eustis said. "That was dark. But it's beautiful, right?"

"In a *die from asphyxiation* kind of way. Yeah, it's kind of pretty," Enzo said.

"Pretty, there we go. Now say something about the source of that beauty. Think about what could have created such a vast, majestic expanse."

"The universe began in a cosmic horizon event which was propagated by a radioactive bed of primordial chaos," Enzo said.

"Kids," Marianna said, letting her arms fall to her side. "They never do what you want them to." Enzo stepped back from the window. Marianna straightened up and took a breath. "Listen, guy. I don't want to hear you singing on my ship anymore. It's weird, and it gives me the creeps. It also reminds me that your stupid religionism got us into this mess. So kill that noise."

"Sometimes I just can't help it," Eustis said.

"Oh, shut up with that '*I can't help it,*' nonsense!" Marianna said. "You will stuff that garbage into the deepest darkest lock box and forget the combination," Marianna said, straightening up from where she stood at the door frame. "Don't do it again. Also, don't fill my engineer's head with your lunacy. He's smart, but he's also an impressionable kid. I need him clear-minded for the trip we're making."

"Captain," Eustis said. "All due respect. I can't promise to follow either of those orders. I plan to sing from time to time, and I plan to talk to anyone who wants to know what I have to say. I'd like to talk to you about the reason for my joy sometime as well."

Marianna stiffened and balled her hands into fists. Enzo stepped back from Eustis as if he expected fire to shoot from the captain's eyes. She closed the distance between them in a few steps and stood nose-to-nose with Eustis. She spoke in a grave unrelenting voice.

"Here are the words that are going to come out of your mouth next," Marianna said. "I promise not to sing while I'm aboard the Scuttle." Eustis took a breath to speak, but before he formed a word, she put one finger in his face. "Those exact words and nothing else."

"I apologize, I just can't—" Before Eustis could get the words out, Marianna rammed her fist into his stomach. The surprising concussion made him double over and grip his belly.

"Enzo," she commanded. "Out!" The kid obeyed as Marianna turned on her heel and moved toward the door. She tapped a string of buttons on the keypad. A beep sounded throughout the ship.

"All hands alert. The criminal stowaway, Eustis Grimes, is to be forcibly confined to his quarters. He is not allowed to come out until he promises not to sing anymore." She slapped her hand against the panel. The ship beeped again as she turned back on Eustis. "No more singing."

She walked out and slammed the door. A metallic thump sounded inside the inner workings of the lock. The small glass window embedded in the closed hatch filled with the face of Enzo. He looked into the chamber where Eustis was still holding his stomach in pain. A muffled voice called him away.

Chapter Twelve

TRIANGULATE

"We have something," HEXA, Strafe's A.I. assistant, said. The Admiral spun his chair, stood, and looked at the hologram in his cortex display. "Old band. Radio signal. Sounds like it could be him."

"Can you link it with any adjacent transponder signal?" Strafe asked.

"Nope," HEXA said. "Doesn't seem to be one."

"Bring it up," Strafe said. It was an analog audio signal. Most ships didn't monitor the radio frequencies anymore, but since black market smugglers occasionally used it as a low-fi comm frequency, Strafe had never allowed their radio gear to go out of repair. The sound of a man's voice filled the command cabin. It crackled over the speakers, and Strafe needed only a second to I.D. "That's him. Triangulate it."

HEXA's hologram stood by with a busy posture as he obeyed. Strafe listened to the audio file, idly. "It's weaponized words. On earth, before the sky rush, it was these words that destabilized everything. It was statements like these that brought down empires. Ruined the peace. Destroyed the world. That's why I'm going to disembowel him. I'll grind his bones."

"Ok," HEXA said. "I've got it on the triangle. Ping network shows his doppler has him moving fast. Really fast. Burning hard away from our position."

"Project the flight plan," Strafe said.

"On it," HEXA said.

"We have to get this one," Strafe said. "It has to be me that watches the life drain from his body." He stood and watched the scene through the viewport. The dark vast of black stretched out before them. They were only twenty hours out from Slingshot Station, and the blue glow of the world below, but the haze of the planet had drifted to sheer black. This was the only place Strafe felt at home. Surrounded by cold nothingness.

"But why?" HEXA asked. "You've bagged every kind of dissrep and dissident there is. Insurrectionists, rebels, revolutionaries. How is this vacuum-sucking novice any more dangerous than all the rest?"

"Because he's the last one of his kind," Strafe said. "We are close. We're one trigger-pull away from inoculating the entire Sol System of these toxic ideas. It's going to be me standing over his lifeless body, knowing I've rid the System of his pernicious brand of dissidence, never to rise again. I'm going to choke him out with my own hands."

"There is a high probability of his death in space," HEXA said. "Why not let him die out on some low G rock, and that will be that."

"Science eradicated ninety-nine point nine percent of diseases five centuries ago. But that last one-hundredth of a percent," Strafe paused. "It's the hardest to kill. Takes ten times as much effort as all the rest. Everything it touches is contaminated. Has to be burned. Ended. Obliterated. I'm fighting the last one-hundredth of a percent. It's the hardest to kill. That's why we need to catch him on that ship. If he touches down on some colony or GovCorp city, who knows how many he will infect before we can extricate him? He's a disease, and I'm the cure."

"We have a problem," HEXA said.

"What?"

"I was tracking his transmission, but we just got bumped."

"What?" Strafe thundered.

"GovCorp contract," HEXA said. "Propaganda Department sold an hour of time on the tracking satellite to IceTech Haulers Incorporated.

We're dark for another fifty-nine minutes." HEXA's hologram threw his hands up in artificial frustration.

Strafe smashed his hand into the console and let off a string of stinging profanity.

"Did you get a projected flight plan?" Strafe asked.

"Not complete," HEXA said. "Though, it looks like he's burning hard toward Ceres. Based on the current drive load, he'd arrive in about three weeks."

"Set a course," Strafe said. Mumbling to himself he whispered, "When I catch him I'll burn him to ash."

CHAPTER THIRTEEN

BEACON

"Where are the distress beacons?" Enzo asked. The comm crackled as Marianna responded.

"Try the mag lock four," Captain Marianna said from somewhere in the upper decks.

"I looked there. Where else?" She continued to offer options. Enzo spun around and tapped the release on a cargo lockup. "Nope, not there either." He turned once more and made his way to the bin next to the EVA storage rack where Eustis had spent the first few hours aboard. The engineering compartment was cramped, so kneeling down was a challenge. He scrounged for a few seconds, but when he didn't find them, he straightened up. As he did, the airlock kiosk swept across his vision, but he didn't pay it any attention.

"Well, I can't find them anywhere," Enzo said. "Can I just mark them as lost on the inventory? I'm tired of doing this stupid data entry." He listened for a few seconds as the captain lectured him about responsibility and initiative. He swiped through a slew of unrelated feeds on his cortex display, waiting for her to finish.

"Are you sure we have any beacons?" Marianna asked.

"Yes, I'm sure. They were there last time."

"Maybe you just forgot—" she stopped as soon as she realized what she had said.

"Trust me. I didn't forget. I wish I could. I think it's Rudwick's turn to do inventory."

"Rudwick can't do inventory. The dumb thug can't count past seven," Marianna said.

"It's not fair. He never has to do—" Enzo paused. The afterimage of the airlock kiosk lingered effortlessly preserved in his mind, like a million other unwanted images he couldn't shake. Although, in this case, there was something amiss.

He took the three steps across the engineering bay and gestured at the airlock terminal. It gave his cortex display access. His brows furrowed at the logged data. "Uh, Cap." She grunted. "Terminal is showing the airlock decompressed a little past zero hundred hours last night. "

"What?" Marianna asked. "That must be wrong."

"Nope."

"I'll be right down." By the time she had descended to the engineering level, Enzo had the closed-circuit video on display. "What is it? Unauthorized EVA?" He gestured for her to see the clip.

"No. No one got in the airlock," Enzo said. The security footage of the airlock rolled as they talked. "It couldn't have been Rudwick."

"How do you know?" Marianna frowned as she looked at the footage.

"Look," Enzo said. "Two hands." In the far corner of the video feed, two human hands set something small on the deck of the airlock. The rest of the person was not visible, but it wasn't hard to imagine who it was. "What's he doing?" The internal hatch closed, and the external opened. With the rush of air that followed the hatch being opened, the device rolled toward the open hatch and fell from view. They looked at each other when the video clip paused. "Did that look like one of our missing distress beacons to you?" Enzo said.

"Sure did."

"I'm going to kill him," Marianna said. "Literally. I'm going to put him out of this airlock. I'll watch him boil in the vacuum."

"But why would he be spacing distress beacons?" Enzo asked. "He'd have to have a good reason." Enzo swiped and gestured through a half dozen data screens to get what he was looking for. He gestured toward an indicator marked *Multiband Scanner.* The scan pinged immediately with the frequency he expected. "There you are." He isolated the signal and brought it up. Enzo laughed out loud.

"Well, I'm impressed," Enzo said as he listened to an audio recording of Eustis' voice. He didn't understand what the recording was talking about, but he attended it with admiration for another few seconds. "I mean, those beacons are encrypted. Hacking one would take some serious talent."

"He hacked a beacon?" Marianna said. Enzo flicked his hand in Marianna's direction, giving her access to the recording. She listened for five seconds before her face was red, and she was climbing the ladder to the next hatch. Enzo stood his ground and listened to the audio file.

"...his only son that whoever believes in him will not die but have everlasting life. You see. Everyone in the Sol System has this amazing opportunity to..."

"Enzo," Marianna shouted down from the upper deck. "Get the brig restraints." Enzo swiped away the recording, but try as he might, he couldn't wipe away the smile from his face. *Crazy? Sure, But how did he do that?* He opened a nearby lockup and found the cuffs he was looking for.

By the time Enzo had climbed the ladder to deck two, Marianna had Rudwick against the corridor wall and was excoriating him profusely. "It was your job to keep that radiation-baked mooncalf on this deck. It was your job to keep him in his room. If you weren't licking those stupid cats all day long, maybe you could do your job!"

"I be mighty tired from the—"

"Stow it, you dumb vac-sucking gnashnab," she said as she ripped the handcuffs from Enzo's grip and thrust them into Rudwick's chest. "Make sure he doesn't go anywhere." She turned and charged freighter-like toward Eustis' room.

"What be her ailment, lad?" Rudwick asked in Enzo's direction.

Enzo laughed with admiration as he said, "That dirt-loving fribble stole our distress beacons, reprogrammed them to broadcast his religionist non-sense, and spaced them last night. Those little probes are floating a few thousand kilometers back, just blabbing on and on about his earther reli-gionism."

"He left the deck?" Rudwick asked.

"Seriously?" Enzo said. Rudwick didn't seem to grasp the obvious. "To get to the airlock. Clearly, he had to leave the deck." Rudwick lit up like a drive plume.

"Cap'n," Rudwick shouted after her. "I'll finish me job. Just you wait." Now Rudwick was running, and he brushed by Marianna in the corridor in a thundering stampede of man and metal. He tapped his mechanical arm as if to prepare it for duty.

In the seconds that followed Rudwick's entrance into Eustis' compart-ment, the tumult of a struggle issued down the corridor. Urgent sounds of grappling were mixed with Rudwick's gruff threats. Marianna entered the room next, followed by Enzo. The big man had Eustis on the deck, his throat in hand, and a pistol in his face.

"Rudwick," Marianna said. "Don't."

"But you said I could off him if he left the deck." Rudwick was genuinely disappointed.

"I know," Marianna said. "But we *need*—" at the word, she paused and then adjusted her stance. "I mean, we can put him to use."

"Torture?" Rudwick asked.

"We're not going to—"

"At least hard labor, lass," Rudwick grumbled.

"Just the cuffs for now," Marianna said. Rudwick groaned with disap-pointment but obeyed. A long rusted piping ran along the compartment interior. Rudwick wrapped the brig restraints around the conduit and cuffed them around one of Eustis' wrists.

"You blasted zounderkite," Marianna said. Her voice was grave and hallow. "What's wrong with you?" Eustis' face was red, and a bruise was forming around his neck. It would soon blend in with the other scars Rudwick had inflicted only days earlier.

"Why'd you do it," Rudwick asked.

"Who cares *why*," Enzo said. "I want to know *how*?" He knelt in front of Eustis, no longer attempting to hide his smile. "I mean, really? Hacking a SAR alert probe. That's got to be at least 64-bit encryption on top of a dual isolated bandwidth modulator."

"128-bit, actually," Eustis corrected.

"So, how'd you crack the encryption?" Enzo asked, his face glowing with the obvious mark of inspiration.

"I didn't," Eustis said. "They are unlocked by voice recognition. They're keyed to Captain's voice. The other day when she came in..." Eustis glanced up at the Captain, who was glaring down at him from a wide power stance. "Sorry, Cap. But the other day, when you came in and tore up my radio gear. Well, I was recording when you entered, so I might have just happened to get a few minutes of your voice recorded."

Enzo started laughing. He understood immediately. The others hadn't caught on yet.

"What be the jest?" Rudwick said.

"He made a voice replica of Cap's voice from his covert recording. Unlocked the beacon with a deepfake of Cap's voice and bypassed the encryption." Enzo turned toward Eustis. "Who are you?" Despite the tense mood, Eustis couldn't help but smile.

"Thanks, kid," Eustis said, looking down at the deck.

"This don't be an award's ceremony, you two-watt twit," Rudwick said. He was about to strike Eustis across the mouth, but Enzo spoke up.

"More like two hundred megawatt genius," Enzo said. He stepped between Eustis and the others. "I don't think you guys understand what we have here. This guy is—well he's—" Enzo searched for words that would communicate adequately. He lit up. "Ok, if we would have had him on that Europa job, remember the one where we were hauling that crate of dropline skimmers?"

"Err," Rudwick bellowed. "Remind me not. The Govvy goons singed me tail feathers on that one. "

"Yeah, well, if we had this walking decoder ring aboard, he could have, I don't know, built a comm jammer from a hand full of Popsicle sticks. We wouldn't have been scoped and marked. Or, or, or the Titan run."

"We get it, kid," Marianna said.

"We were hauling the chipset spoofers, remember? He could have changed our transponder credentials, and we wouldn't have been blasted by that GovCorp gunner. I mean, sure, what he's doing with his talent is super weird, but don't you see? We've had a hole in our team all this time. This guy is the scam-boy we've been missing."

"Enough," Marianna groaned. "Talent doesn't matter if it gets us killed."

"We be just fine without this loose-bolt vent-crack," Rudwick said. The room fell silent for a few seconds.

"You guys haul dropline skimmers and chipset spoofers?" Eustis said. "Those are contrabanded," Eustis said.

"Says the religionist dissident," Marianna said.

"You guys are running dark?" Eustis asked. "Black market trade? Illegal gear?"

"There do be a bit of shadow to what the Scuttle trades in," Rudwick said again with pride. Eustis laughed. He laughed long and hard. He laughed until Rudwick and Enzo joined in.

"Smugglers," Eustis finally said. "Bunch of vacuum-drifting bootleggers. Now, things are starting to make sense. "

"What is that supposed to mean?" Marianna said, leaning forward as if she were ready to explode.

Eustis tugged against his wrist restraints as he shoved a curtain of black hair out of his face. "I expected you would turn me in to the authorities as soon as you discovered I was a stowaway, but then you didn't. Then when you caught me with my radio blaring, I thought that was it, but you just let it slide. I guess God had a plan, all along."

"God," Enzo said. "What's that?"

"Yes, you see God sent his only son to earth so that anyone who believes in him—"

"Nope," Marianna interrupted. "Not happening. Alright, everyone. Show's over. Move out." It took quite an icy stare to pry Enzo from his position, and Rudwick followed him closely behind. Marianna was about to exit, but Eustis' words caught her.

"Captain," Eustis said gently. He did his best to rise, but owing to the cuffs, he could only come up to his knees. He interlocked his fingers and said, "Thank you."

"What?"

"I'm so incredibly grateful that you took me aboard," Eustis said. Marianna cut across his words.

"I didn't." She was going to say more, but he nodded agreement.

"I mean, you allowed me to live once you found I was your stowaway. Thank you. You're an amazing woman. You've become part of something very important." He smiled at her for a few seconds. "Would it be possible to take me to Musk City, Mars? I have a very important goal I need to accomplish there."

She blinked at him twice, spun, and left the chamber. She kicked the hatch and locked it tight behind her. Eustis leaned back against the wall and took a deep long breath.

Chapter Fourteen

INVASION

"He's stubborn," Enzo said.

"Stupid would be a better word for it," Marianna said. She reached for her drink pouch and emptied it into her mouth. After tossing it toward the garbage lockup, she waved her hand at the terminal at the center of the command deck. A video feed appeared on her cortex display. In the security footage, Eustis was swaying in place, still hand-cuffed to the piping in his room, singing at the top of his lungs. "He's been at it for four hours."

"He knows a lot of songs," Enzo said.

"And nary a one suited for a brothel to boot," Rudwick said. Marianna could feel him breathing down her neck. She shoved against him with her elbow. The ignorant lunk didn't move.

"His voice has got to give out eventually," Marianna said. "If not, we could just vent the O2 from his room."

"Why does he get under your skin so much?" Enzo asked.

She harrumphed before waving her hand to dismiss the video. Turning to Enzo's station, she said, "What's our status?" Enzo made a slight hand gesture and scanned the info available.

"Scuttle's living up to her name. She's burning rough," he said.

She grunted. "What else?"

"I looked into what Eustis said about that speck." Enzo glanced at Marianna. Her frown should have been enough to tell him to drop it, but he wasn't getting the hint. He was a persistent little brat. She repressed an urge to go after another drink pouch. "It turns out there is something on our six. Nothing in the vis-base matches its profile, but it's a ship, all right. It's burning at about 1.6 Gs. Looks like it plans to pass us by, but it's going to be a close miss. We probably should–"

"Don't tell me what we should do," She said as she wiped her mouth with her sleeve. "Just tell me what we can't fix on *this* ship."

"Hard to fix anything when the skipper is tipsy," Enzo mumbled.

"Yeah, yeah, yeah. I'm the worst captain ever."

"Not by a long shank," Rudwick said. "Me worst ship's commander were Cap'n Seethe of the Norberg, but the boys called him Cap'n Cadaver. Quietest captain ever sailed the seven heavens. Couldn't get a peep out of him. His icy stare, never blinking, could fill your veins with cold vacuum."

"Do you know what the word *cadaver* means?" Enzo asked in Rudwick's direction.

"Silent strength and slightly greenish tint, I reckon, for he possessed both chilling qualities in mighty abundance. So fierce, were he, at such a point when his sallow skin peeled away from them bones, and be he nothing more than skeletal remains, still he held helm and unswerving command of the ship, albeit silent."

Enzo squinted and cocked his head. "Ok," he said. "I was wrong. You're a slightly better captain than a Commander Corpse. Though, in certain circumstances, I'd prefer the stiff."

"Can we get back to the point?" Marianna said. "We've got a lot of work to do. We need to figure out where we're going. Once we get to the belt, we're going to need a hiding place we can lay low for a—"

An explosion quaked the ship. All three crew listed hard to port and smashed into the metal of the compartment. They struggled to their feet as Rudwick cursed.

"What was that?" Marianna said. Enzo climbed into the nearest flight seat and strapped in. He spun and began gesturing at the closest node.

His hands worked rapidly. In another second, Marianna was strapped in as well.

When Rudwick was on his feet, hand on his head, he shouted, "Me kitties!" He tramped down the corridor screaming, "Daddy be coming, me pretties."

Marianna squinted at the display. "Scuttle's pulling to the side by twelve degrees. Thirteen. Fourteen. She's going into a spin. Cut engines." The computer beeped, and the low rumble of the thrusters died. Immediately the inertial force the engines offered, which gave the ship its manufactured gravity, was lost, and they felt the drift of weightlessness.

"Our center of mass has changed," Enzo said as he gestured for another display. "Almost like we've just gained thirty thousand tons on our port side." Enzo and Marianna looked at one another, both realizing what that meant. Before either could say anything, Rudwick's voice came over the comm.

"There be a scatter of sparks filling the aft compartment," Rudwick said. "Me thinks some privateers be trying to enter by way of cutting torch."

"It's raiders!" Marianna said.

"I told you!" Enzo shouted.

"Not now!" Marianna yelled back.

"We could try the centrifuge maneuver, spin 'em off our back," Enzo offered.

"If Rudwick's seeing sparks, they've already breached the hull. She'll be spinning with a gaping wound in her side. We don't have the O2 to spare."

"So, what do we do?" Enzo said, sounding like a kid.

Marianna waved her hand and made a fist, bringing it down in front of her face. The universal command notified the ship of a hostile intruder and enacted wartime protocol. Enzo's jaw fell open as Marianna said, "Battle stations."

"Zounds! Me thinks I'd never hear such sweet words again." The comm clicked off as a red glow replaced the blue haze of the running lights.

"Enzo," Marianna said. "This is an all-hands muster."

"You mean the religionist too?"

"All hands," she shouted. "Get him a pistol and make sure he knows how to turn the safety off. Muster on deck two in three minutes." The kid worked to unlatch himself from his flight seat. In zero gravity, he shoved off the headrest and rocketed toward the hatch. He flew down the corridor, glided down three decks, and cornered for Eustis' chamber.

Marianna's voice echoed over the loudspeaker as Enzo swam toward his target. "Brace for a quarter-G burn."

"Seriously?" Enzo said. Before he could reach the railing, the engines exploded to life, and the Scuttle lurched forward. Enzo slammed against the wall for the second time in two minutes. He pushed against the quarter gravity to a standing position and rubbed his head where it had met the wall. As he tried to run down the corridor, he had to fight his crooked steps. *I must have hit my head harder than I thought.* He felt for blood. No, it wasn't his head. *It must be the ship.* He paused. It was twisting violently. *Captain must be fighting the torc with manual stick.* After a few seconds of burn, the motion stabilized.

"Got her back on a string. I'll meet you on deck two in three minutes."

Three-quarters down the corridor, Enzo slapped a circular latch on the wall, and a compartment opened. Normally there would be a wall of ammunition and firearms, but there was nothing. Enzo touched the wall next to the compartment. The comm beeped.

"Where are the guns?" Enzo begged.

"You need bunker busters, guided projectiles, or hand rockets?" Rudwick asked over the comm.

"Anything!"

"Compartment 1A," Marianna clicked in.

"Looking at it. Nothing!"

Rudwick's voice interrupted with, "The intruders dropped a cork out of the hull and be set to board. I be prepping me battle kitties for the fray."

"Copy, Rudwick," Marianna said. "Enzo, try the lower drawer."

Enzo's frantic hands shook as he pulled on the lower latch. It should have sprung open, but it snagged. He stuck his fingers in and pried. It popped. There was a pitiful assortment of mostly non-lethal self-defense options, the least of which was a bar of soap in a long tube sock. He shifted the contents around until he spotted what he was looking for. He collected the items and kicked the lockup closed as he said, "Got it!"

"Good," Marianna's voice crackled through the speaker. "Rudwick, I need you on two. Need to make a barricade before these corsairs come through."

Enzo twisted the manual release on the thick metal door that had Eustis entombed for the last four hours. The full-release lever had large letters that read EMERGENCY on it. The hatch swung open, and Enzo stepped in. He saw the last thing he expected. He thought Eustis would be cowering, crying, or otherwise melting into a pile of liquid nerves. Rather than a frantic, panicking space novice, he saw a calm man cuffed but kneeling with his hands folded and his eyes closed.

Enzo transversed the room, unclasped Eustis' wrist restraints, and said, "Get up!" He shouted. "We're under attack."

CHAPTER FIFTEEN

SING

"Safety. Trigger," Enzo said, spinning the sidearm around. "Point. Shoot." He tossed the gun through the quarter gravity in Eustis' direction. Eustis reached for it, and caught it. It felt heavier than he had expected. It was a mean piece of metal, cold in his hand. It made him think of his friends back home. He saw images of Todd and Martha Grambling, Rod Musker, and Leena Bickle. They had stared at one of these in their last seconds alive. Maybe even the same caliber. He frowned at the piece of killer hardware.

"I won't need this. I'm not going to shoot anyone."

"Don't be a rube. Come on." Enzo disappeared through the door and didn't give Eustis any time to respond. He glanced around for a storage compartment. It was another few seconds before he followed the kid through the doorframe.

He stepped down onto deck two, where Rudwick and Marianna were already erecting a cover line with boxes and spare pieces of equipment. The barricade was about waist-high. It didn't look bulletproof.

Eustis stood over them and watched as they shoved junk together. Enzo spotted him, grabbed his shirt, and gave it a violent tug. "Get down, you grunt." He knelt behind the shelter where Enzo was. When he did, he found himself face to face with Tiny, Rudwick's giant genetically modified cat, looking more like a lion than ever. The other cats were lined up, and each wore armor. Eustis had never seen flack jackets on cats, but the trip was full of novelties, so sure, why not?

When the captain and Rudwick had finished pushing the deck's stray paraphernalia into a battle barricade, Marianna sat with her back against it and spoke in a hushed but commanding voice. "Weapons at the ready. When they come through that hole, hit 'em with everything you've got."

Rudwick was already cradling his handheld cannon. Enzo and Marianna pulled out their smaller weapons and prepped them for the fight. After a couple of seconds of chaotic clicking, cocking, and clacking, the crew was ready.

"Hey, guy. Where's your gun? Enzo, I thought you gave this poltroon a pistol."

"He did, ma'am," Eustis said. "I left it in my room."

"You show up to a gunfight without a gun? How could you be so dumb? Go back and get it!"

"No, ma'am."

"Excuse me?"

"I left it because I'm not going to use it."

"This is an all-hands defensive operation. You will retrieve your sidearm and prepare to fight!" Marianna grit her teeth with the words.

"Respectfully, Ma'am. I refuse. I have moral objections to killing, especially without a prior attempt at diplomacy."

"Do you have moral objections to *being* killed?" Marianna leaned forward. Her eyes were a hair's width from Eustis.

"No," Eustis said. "I apologize for not being able to help with the fight, but I don't think it has to come to that. If you just let me talk with them, I'm sure we can come to an agreement."

"I'm going to shoot you myself. That's what I'm going to do. You're a liability. You're not giving me a choice." She lifted her gun and hovered it a centimeter from Eustis' nose. He gulped hard and closed his eyes. She opened her mouth and was about to speak when Enzo interrupted.

"Here they come," the kid said. She lowered her pistol, and all four heads craned to see, eyes just barely above the hastily constructed barricade.

Down the corridor, there was a jagged breach in the wall. Next to it lay a metal cutout that matched the opening's shape. The metal was still glowing orange and smoking from where it had suffered the plasma torch's unrelenting heat. Around the hole, a docking tunnel had been attached, and the umbilical was no doubt connected to the airlock of the enemy ship. Lights danced in the tunnel, and the sound of boots echoed through the metallic passage.

A face, grimy and awful, peeked around the corner of the torch-cut entrance. Rudwick was the first to fire. His shoulder cannon spat bright red balls of angry plasma toward the hole. He had five shots off before the other two found their triggers. Muffled voices sounded in the deep, and return fire exploded from the yawning rift.

Enzo ducked between shots. Marianna leaned down but kept her arm over the top of the junk fortress and lit off blast after angry blast. Rudwick, however, had no reserve in him. He chortled with a giggling pleasure as he blasted blazing bolts from burning barrels. Apparently, the low vantage didn't offer him the angle he wanted. In the fray, he stood and let out thunderous claps of deep-throated laughter as he poured relentless fury on the unwelcome guests. The rupture filled with a cascade of fire. They shouted over the sound of cannon blasts, "This be reminding me of the time Old Rudwick lost his arm in a battle with an Ionian raiding party." His eyes were wild with pleasure.

"Rudwick, get down! You're target practice up there," Marianna ordered. It did no good.

"Prepare for frontal assault, me kitties," Rudwick bellowed. His battle cats rose and stood at attention, armored and ready for war. The old warrior lifted one leg as if he would step over the relative safety of the barricade. A torturous ball of projectile plasma plunged into his right side. His robotic arm took the blast's concussion, and Rudwick went flying one way as the mangled remains of his prosthetic arm went another. The big man bounced off the back wall and scrambled with his one arm for his rifle. In another few seconds, he was shooting again, though more cautiously this time.

Shots whizzed over Eustis' head as he hunkered in the back of the shelter. Bullets screamed and exploded only centimeters from where he sat. He closed his eyes, crossed his hands over his lap, and took a long deep breath through his nose. Instead of simply exhaling, the breath came out in a song. In the chaotic exchange of deadly volleys, Eustis sang, quiet at first, but in the noise, he let his volume grow to match the tumult.

The Lord is my keeper
I do not have a need
He leads to still water,
Lays me in fields of green
The Lord is my keeper
He guides me the right way
He refreshes my soul,
For the sake of his name
While walking death's valley,
Your staff makes me safe
I will fear nothing bad,
Because you're my safe place

Eustis paused, letting the last note linger in the air. When he stopped singing, he realized that the sound of the gunfire had ceased. He opened his eyes to find the crew looking at him. Silence surrounded them for a second.

"Why are you singing?" an unknown voice, muffled by distance, said.

"I want to hear more singing," a much younger voice said. Were there kids behind the breach? Eustis rose to his knees to look over the barricade. Three sets of eyes were peeking around the corner of the hole where they had forced their entry.

Slowly, Eustis put both of his hands in the air above his head, where they remained. When they didn't get blown off his arms by gunfire, he ventured to stand, albeit slowly. On his feet now, he kept his hands aloft and stepped forward. Enzo grabbed his pant leg and said, "What are you doing?"

Eustis stepped over the cobbled barricade, hands in the air, and walked toward the intruders. He heard Marianna ordering him back behind the line, but he ignored her. As he closed the distance between him and the enemies, he continued the song where he had left off.

You pour out your good things,
And set a full table for me
My cup now overflows,
In view of my worst enemy

With the melody, the faces peered out from behind the jagged hole. This was no professional operation. It looked to be a father, a mother, and a young child. Their faces were covered in grime, their hair wild with unkempt negligence. They were gaunt and afraid. Eustis' hands were still in the air, and he continued toward them as he sang the final verse, hoping the enchantment would hold.

Your love will follow me
Your goodness is pure
I will dwell in your house,
The Lord's house forever.

By the time Eustis sang the last note, letting it ring out solid and loud, he was standing in the opening between the two ships. His audience looked up at him from where they hid. When everything fell silent, Eustis knelt down gently.

"Can we talk?" Eustis asked in such a soft voice even his own crew behind him couldn't hear. The skinny child, whose pure blue eyes were brave and relentless, nodded. Eustis glanced at the adults, both scrawny and pale. They nodded as well. When they did, Eustis sat on the deck, cross-legged, and placed his hands in his lap.

"I'm Eustis. What are your names?"

CHAPTER SIXTEEN

BATTLE

After a few minutes of quiet consultation, Eustis followed the pirate family onto their ship. Rudwick, Marianna, and Enzo hunkered behind their battle embankment, trying to decide what to do.

"What be the critter that crawled into that man's brain?" Rudwick asked. "We ought to weld the hole shut and fly on."

"It's not a bad idea. We could be rid of him once and for all," Marianna mused.

"That's dumb. You guys are scoundrels." Enzo said. "He walked straight at them. They didn't fire a shot. I know you hate him, but he just saved your life. We should be thanking him."

"Thus be the thinking of a wee pup."

"Whatever." Enzo leaned his back away from the makeshift fortress. He locked eyes with Marianna. "Why do you hate him so much?" She looked at the deck and then busied her hands by checking her gun.

The sound of footsteps rescued Marianna from the uncomfortable question. They each peeked above the top of the barricade, guns at the ready. Eustis was walking down the corridor, looking calm, even cavalier. A slight smile stretched across his face. Behind him, one of the so-called pirates emerged from the jagged hole. Rudwick, who was still missing his robotic arm, pointed his hand cannon at the pirate, but Eustis put his hand in the air.

"Don't shoot them," Eustis said. "They've agreed to leave." The smudge-covered man scurried around the hole he had made in the hull. They watched him as Eustis stepped over the barricade and sat down against the adjacent wall. Marianna and Rudwick continued to watch the intruders with wary eyes. Enzo spun in place and studied Eustis with a look of awe.

"What be the witchary you be working at?"

"They're fixing the ship." The raider clamped a maglev winch to the jagged piece of the hull that lay in the corridor. He used the winch to lift it. When it was nearly in place, he waved at Marianna and the crew. The winch pulled and fitted the severed piece of metal into its original place. A few seconds later, sparks began to fly.

"They be welding it back in place from outside!" Rudwick stood now that the danger was past. "Shiver me gizzard, I never saw the like." He looked down at Eustis and toed Eustis's foot with his own. "Dirt lover, you needs teach Old Rudwick such scare craft you used upon yon scalawags. You must of treated them to a fear-a-plenty."

Behind him, the sparks dissipated, and the metal glowed orange. The atmospheric system hissed as it equalized the pressure. A mechanical clatter resounded as the pirates disengaged their docking tunnel. Eustis smiled as Rudwick's cat, Biscuit, tussled his hand. Eustis caressed a gentle finger under Biscuit's chin. Not wanting to miss a chance at an itch, the little kitty Striker, giant Tiny, and the plumpest feline of all, Beverly Gertrude Lewis, circled around him, waiting their turn for a scratch.

"I didn't scare them," Eustis said. "They are actually really nice, as long as you don't shoot at them."

"They peeled the lid off my ship like a sardine can," Marianna said. "They fired at us. They tried to kill us. They're criminals!"

"Oh, I don't think so. They're desperate. That's what they are," Eustis said, not bringing his eyes up from Striker, whose turn it was to gain some affection. Tiny put his huge paw on little Striker's back and flattened him to the ground in an attempt to get at Eustis' scratching hand. "Hey, now," Eustis said to Tiny. "There's no need for that. There's enough scratch for everyone."

"You act like you've done some great thing." Marianna's voice was loud now. "Really, you aided our enemy in their escape."

"*Your* enemy. Not mine," Eustis corrected. "Plus, they agreed to fix the ship, and they didn't take anything that belonged to you. I'd say it was an equitable trade."

"No, you air-mouching milksop!" Marianna barked. "Had you let us get on with it, we would have taken care of them and then taken charge of their ship. We would have increased our bounty tenfold. As I see it, you owe me a ship on account of the one you lost."

"You said you would have 'taken care of them,'" Eustis said. "By that, you mean murdered them? That's an odd way of taking care of a person. I not only saved your lives, but I removed the need to kill. I'd still say that makes it a good trade."

"A trade?" Rudwick said. He was gathering the pieces of his dismantled robotic arm, but the word brought him back to full height. "Me thinks, a trade be when two parties exchange trinket."

"Yeah," Eustis said. "It was a trade. I had something they wanted, and they had something I wanted."

"What did they give you?" Enzo chimed in. He leaned forward, eyes wide, eyebrows raised.

"My life," Eustis said. "Yours too. All of you." He reached for Tiny and patted his side. "They gave me a chance to continue the mission."

"Mission," Marianna scoffed.

"I asked for the thing I wanted the most," Eustis said, ignoring her. "And they gave it to me without hesitation."

Enzo opened his mouth to speak, but he was cut short by Marianna's violent rise to her feet. Marianna regarded him for a moment. She walked toward the ladder that led to the upper deck. She reached for the rung but paused. In Eustis' direction, she said, "You're an ignoramus. I can't wait to see the GovCorp goons toss you into a reclamation pod. You're going to die out here. And for what?" She then addressed the others. "Rudwick, get this junk cleaned up. Enzo, check the hull. See if we're sealed. Report in twenty minutes. And you, ignoramus, you're still confined to quarters." She climbed up the ladder and disappeared above.

"Thank you, Captain," Eustis said.

"Shut up!" She shouted over her shoulder.

"She be right, lad. You be mighty touched in the head. And it be your own hand that which signed your death sentence. If you wish me to give you life's end before you meet such a fate, I'd oblige straight away. Out of respect for your iron stubbornness, you understand." Rudwick made a gesture toward his gun, showing his willingness.

"Thanks, Rudwick, but I think I'd like to stay alive a little longer."

"Suit your fancy," Rudwick said as he began shoving the pile of stuff that comprised the barricade back to its respective place. As Rudwick moved on, so did the cats. However, Enzo stayed in his place across from where Eustis sat. He hardly blinked.

CHAPTER SEVENTEEN
RATIONALE

Eustis' heart was still beating fast from the encounter with the family of space pirates. Enzo sat across from him, wide-eyed, questioning him about the endeavor.

"What did you give them?" His mouth hung open, and his head shook from side to side. Enzo scooted closer. "How'd you know that's what they wanted?"

"I asked them."

"That easy, huh?"

"Actually, most people don't tell you what they want right away. They'll usually start with some indirect demand. They started by saying they wanted the ship."

"What'd you say?"

"'I want to help you guys get what you need, but how am I supposed to do that?' Then I got quiet and let them think. See, I didn't really think they wanted the ship. I could tell by the look of them that they were a family. I didn't think they'd want to split up. They could see the Scuttle was well-defended. I figured there had to be something underneath their surface demand."

"So what'd they do?" Enzo asked with wide eyes.

"They asked for valuables."

"Not the ship?"

"That's right. Just like that, they changed their demand, which told me we were getting somewhere. I said I'd like to help you get what you *need*. I asked them if they needed all of our valuables or just a certain amount. Then I let them think and talk among themselves a while."

"Pirates would want it all," Enzo said.

"That's right," Eustis said. "I thought I was getting down to what they *really* wanted. So after talking amongst themselves for a few minutes, the man, who seemed to be the father, said they needed to get commodities worth at least nine hundred and fifty-three GovCorp credits in trade value."

"Weirdly specific," Enzo said.

"Yep. So I said as much, asking what that price would fetch that was worth privateering in such dangerous space. The wife and mother, started crying immediately. It was actually the kid that told me."

Enzo's eyes were wide with anticipation. "What was it?"

"The kid said, 'Grandma is sick.' And pointed to a hatch. I guess grandma was in the other compartment, but I never saw her. The father filled in the gaps. He said they were trying to get his mother-in-law to a hospital on Mercury. They had just enough to make the voyage and pay for medical, but their Comm array was reading the wrong transcendence ID, because the ship was borrowed."

"Stolen, more likely," Enzo said.

"Maybe. But that's between them and the maker." Eustis said. "So the comm array was busted, they didn't know how to fix it, and since Mercury is GovCorp territory, they wouldn't be allowed to dock with a false ID. It was going to cost them nine hundred and some change to get it repaired in Armstrong City. Turns out it was just an Effron 2 single-band transcendence unit. No problem. Fixed it, and saved them big time. When they saw the new readout the woman started crying all over again but with joy this time."

"Unbelievable," Enzo said.

"Yeah, desperate people are always on the defensive. Giving away information makes desperate people feel vulnerable. If you can put them at ease, sometimes they will open up."

Enzo reached out his hand. Eustis reached across the gap and shook. The kid's hand was small but strong. Enzo said, "I know the others don't appreciate what you did, but I do. I, for one, am glad you were willing to take that chance."

"I appreciate you saying so."

"Oh," Enzo said as he let go of Eustis' hand. "You said earlier that you asked them for the thing you *really* wanted. What was that? What did they give you?"

"Yeah, this is the best part," Eustis said. His voice grew louder and more animated. "In exchange for the repair, I told them I wanted to share the gospel with them. They agreed, although, they didn't know what it meant. I explained the good news. The parents listened, but it was the kid that really paid attention. I'm not sure any of them understood what I told them, but it felt good to try. When I was done, I got their comm address and told them that if they had any questions about the gospel, I'd be available."

"You know, if they message you about religionist stuff, they'll be hunted down just like you," Enzo said. His eyebrows were furrowed, and his lips curved downward.

"I know," Eustis said. "But some risks are worth taking." Enzo squinted his eyes and stared at Eustis for a few seconds without saying anything else.

"I'm not sure that's true. At least about the religionism part," Enzo said. "But I'm glad you got them off our back." He glanced toward the place where the intruders had welded the hull back together. It was still smoking, but it no longer glowed orange.

"How did you get into all this stuff?" Enzo asked. "This religionist mumbo jumbo, I mean?"

"My parents died on my eighteenth birthday," Eustis said.

"How'd they die?" Enzo asked.

Eustis glanced at the deck and was momentarily trapped in thought. "I—uh—"

"That bad, huh," Enzo asked.

"I can't talk about it without—" Eustis paused.

"It's ok," Enzo said. "I get it."

Eustis took a sharp breath. He said, "Anyway. I had been raised by a nanny-bot. When I turned eighteen her lease was up. She went back to the dealer the same day my parents..." He gulped hard. "You know. So, after all that, I was wrecked. To add to the mess, I missed the bot more than mom and dad. I loved that A.I. nanny, and basically hated my parents for what they'd done. How messed up is that? I felt so guilty. It was so twisted. Even though I hated my mom and dad, I couldn't stand to go on without them. They had ignored me my whole life, and now that they were gone, it all came to the surface. I had always had it in my mind that I would eventually make a connection with them, somehow, but nope. They were just gone. So, I sat around for a while before I decided to end it. I went down to the euthanasia office and was going to get the procedure, but outside the front doors, there was this man. Long beard, kind of wild looking. I don't know what made me do it, but I stopped and talked to him. Best choice I ever made. His name was Riley Wynters. He was there with his wife, Deb."

"He was a religionist?" Enzo asked.

"Yes," Eustis said, "But I didn't know that at first. They begged me not to get the procedure. Me. A stranger. They cared more about me than any human had, and we'd just met. After talking for over an hour they convinced me to 'try a different approach to life' for thirty days, as they put it. Offered to put me up in their house and help me through things. It sounded weird, but since I was a walking dead man anyway, I agreed."

"They were like the parents I always wished I had." Eustis said. "So, obviously I didn't get the procedure. At the end of thirty days I just went on with life. They asked me to stay with them. I did. It was amazing. They loved me like I'd never been loved. Although, it still took at least a year of endless discussions for me to come to believe like they did, eventually I saw the truth. It changed everything. Not all at once, but in retrospect, I can see it did. This world is so dark and broken, Enzo. You can feel it right? I found the light. Since then all I've ever wanted to do was spread the light. That's what I'm doing out here, you know. You can have that light too. All you have to do is believe in—"

"What happened to the Wynters?" Enzo interrupted. Eustis smiled at his spunk.

"I lived with them until they passed away a few years ago. Riley Wynters left me his Bible when he went to be with the Lord."

"Be with the Lord?" Enzo asked. "That some kind of afterlife thing?"

"Yeah," Eustis said. "You see when a believer passes—"

"Enzo," the ship's speaker exploded with Captain Marianna's voice. "Get back to work!" Enzo looked up to the corner of the compartment deck and made a rude gesture toward the security camera that was mounted there. He rose reluctantly. "Stowaway," Marianna added. "You're confined to quarters. Get back to your place." Eustis looked at the same camera and gave an overly friendly wave and smile.

"You're so weird," Enzo laughed. He stuck out his hand toward Eustis. "To be continued."

"I thought we weren't supposed to shake hands in space," Eustis said.

"And you weren't supposed to survive," Enzo said. "But you did anyway. And I'm glad." They shook hands with a smile before Enzo skipped off to whatever task he had at hand. Eustis took a big breath, smiled, and climbed back toward his quarters.

CHAPTER EIGHTEEN

BREADCRUMB

"This is the spot," HEXA said over the comm. "Signal is strongest, but there is nothing here."

"There must be something," Strafe said. "Sweep the area." Strafe's ship, the Scorpion III, drifted through the black. The admiral manned the command deck as HEXA, his A.I. assistant, piloted the extravehicular drone. "There!" Strafe called out. The tiniest glimmer of light hinted at the location.

"I see it," HEXA agreed. "Reeling it in, now."

Strafe was away. Since they had cut thrust, there was no gravity in the ship. He drifted through the hatch and down the passage through the dark interior of the craft. He passed the barracks compartment, where two dozen robotic soldiers were suspended from hanging racks. He descended another ladder and came into the cargo bay. Shoving off the bulkhead, he glided effortlessly across and arrived at the airlock. The EVD was entering from the other side.

"Entering airlock with the package," HEXA said over the comm.

"Marked," Strafe said.

Strafe impatiently waited for the airlock to equalize. He couldn't identify the nature of what they had picked up from the other side of the hatch glass. When the lock pressure matched the cabin's, he slid the door open and examined what the extravehicular drone had brought in. HEXA's hologram was behind him before he had his hands on it.

Strafe picked up the small metal object despite it being freezing cold on one side and burning hot on the other. He turned it over and examined it.

"Looks like a standard distress beacon," HEXA said.

"It is," Strafe responded.

"Then why didn't we pick it up on the regular frequency?"

"Because it's been hacked," Strafe said. He held up the unit and pointed to the side. There were little scratches in the metal, and scars around one of the screw heads. "Someone broke into this beacon and reprogrammed it to spout that religionist garbage. I'm going to rip him to pieces."

"How is that possible?" HEXA said. Strafe turned and made the gesture to deactivate the hologram. HEXA's voice persisted in his comm. "The hacking, I mean. The encryption is intricate on those. There's no way a mud sucker would know the first thing about hacking a distress SAR beacon."

"I don't know, but it doesn't matter," Strafe said. "When I catch him, I'm going to grind his thick earther bones to powder."

"What did he think he was accomplishing?" HEXA said. "Leaving a squeaking beacon behind to blab about his religionism. It just doesn't make sense. Could it be a decoy to throw us off the trail?"

Strafe lifted the beacon to his nose and sniffed it. "No," he said. "This is why he's dangerous." He held the beacon up. "This shows how desperate he is. He knows he's alone, and he's running out of options. He knows he's trapped. It's going to be me that ends him."

"So, what do we do?" HEXA asked.

"On, to Ceres," Strafe said. "We'll eviscerate him there. I'm going to carve him up into little pieces."

"Aye, Sir."

Chapter Nineteen

DETOUR

Eustis had been locked in his room on the Scuttle in low gravity for an entire day before seeing or hearing from anyone else on the ship. He was still glowing from his earlier encounter with space bandits and his unregrettable opportunity to share the gospel with them. After twenty-seven hours locked in his quarters, he was feeling more than a little claustrophobic. The only thing that he knew to do for comfort was sing and read.

He had not revealed to the crew that he was carrying a priceless artifact, probably the only of its kind that existed in the entire Sol System. He kept the Bible in a protective box at the bottom of his duffle bag. He unpacked it carefully each time he wanted to read. He had gone to great lengths to acquire the relic, and he was not eager for it to be discovered. He ran his finger down the page as he scanned his favorite passage of Scripture.

The mechanism at the door of his compartment clanked, and the latch unsettled itself. Eustis hurried to wrap and box the Bible, replacing it in his bag before the hatch could swing on its hinges. He rose and moved toward the door to peer through the small glass window. Before he was squared with the door, it opened, and Marianna stepped in. She latched the door behind herself as if Eustis might make a run for it.

"Hello, Captain," Eustis said. He did his best to let none of his irritation show. *Lord, help me be patient with her.* "What a treat it is to have a visit from—"

"Ok, cut the slag. I came here to tell you what's going on since it is your fault." She stood between the bulkhead and the bed in a wide stance that exuded authority.

"Yes, ma'am. I'd be delighted to—"

"We're not going to Ceres." She stared at him for a moment. His eyes dropped to the floor. He spent a few moments in his own thoughts before he sat down on the bed.

"Captain, I've been thinking about it, and I believe I owe you an apology. I've been—"

"No," she said. "Don't apologize. It makes you look weak, which I guess is the truth. Anyway, we're rerouting to Bezos City—" she paused and looked at him. "You know, Bezos City, on Phobos. One of Mars' moons. It's a coop colony. It's a dump, but it's where you go if you don't want to be found."

"I'm confused I—"

"Of course, you're confused. You don't know anything about space. The point is, we have to make a stop in Bezos City. It's a dump hole, but it's the only place we can land without having to report it."

"This is good news, actually," Eustis began. "I need to get to Musk City. It's really important that I have the biggest platform to spread my—"

"No," Marianna put her finger in the air. "Don't do that."

"Do, what, Ma'am?"

"Don't try to turn this into a good thing. It isn't. It's the worst place in the Sol System. No one wants to be in Bezos City."

"Listen," Eustis started. When Marianna balled her hands into fists, he relented.

"When you let those pirates get away without repaying us for the damage they caused to the ship," Marianna said. "You put us in a deadly spot. Their docking tunnel was a piece of junk. The whole time they had that leach on our hull, we were venting O2. That meant the scrubbers were working double time. Running on low tanks isn't good for the injectors. We burned up five rotary nozzles, and we've got to dock sooner rather than later. Enzo spotted the problem this morning. Good thing that kid knows what he's doing, or we'd be dead in the ether. We'll be dirt locked until we get it fixed."

Marianna stood silently for a moment, nodded to herself, spun, and reached for the hatch door.

"Captain," Eustis said. She turned on him with violent eyes.

"Listen, guy. I know what you're going to ask, and the answer is, I don't know how long we'll be there." She whirled around once more, making to leave, but Eustis tried again.

"Captain." This time she didn't turn but only paused. "Can we talk?"

"That is what we have just done," she said without looking in his direction.

"It seems like this is a stressful line of work. I think you're doing a good job. I appreciate your leadership," Eustis said. He did his best to mean the words that came from his mouth. "I'd like to someday not be such an ignoramus. If you see ways I can improve, I'd be happy to—"

Marianna's grunt cut his words short. "Listen, you chud-blasted fladge, I'm the owner of this ship. That means every docking manifest, or distress call, or request for emergency port access, GovCorp knows. You know what they see in big red letters every time that happens?"

"No," Eustis said.

"They see the words Marianna Annika Byrne, Captain, and Pilot on record. It's my name you're ruining every time you do something stupid enough to get us noticed. We're done here."

She reached for the hatch handle and twisted. Once she was out the door, she shoved it slightly but then paused, seeming to be caught by a thought. She glanced at Eustis, who was still sitting on his bed. He smiled at her. She frowned at him and walked down the corridor, leaving the hatch open.

He stared at the open hatch. He had expected her to lock it, so its unprecedented level of openness was jarring. Not sure what to make of it, he rose and walked to the opening. Putting one finger out, he pressed against the hatch. It squeaked on its rusty hinges and banged against the metal of the passageway. Poking his head out the opening, he glanced down the corridor. Marianna was climbing the ladder to the command deck. He stuck his toe out the door and was about to touch down on the free ground when an alarm sounded through the ship.

"All hands alert." It was captain Marianna's voice. Eustis' foot hovered over the deck outside his cell. "The stowaway has been granted access to deck one. Being that he's under minimum confinement, if anyone sees him on any deck but one, he is to be shot in the face. Right in the center of his stupid face." The loudspeaker buzzed and clicked off. Eustis let his foot fall on the deck outside.

He turned down the corridor and prepared to take his first walk as a freeish man when the comm buzzed and came back online. "The moratorium on singing is still in effect. That is all."

Eustis sang quietly to himself as he strolled the short length of the Scuttle's first deck. When he arrived at the end, he turned and made his return journey. It felt good to stretch his legs, but it could hardly be called a walk. When he came around the corner and entered his room once more, he started at the sight. The kid was sitting on his bed and looked like he was in a chatting mood.

"Did you hear the news?" Enzo asked.

"That I'm free, sort of?" Eustis said as he sat and leaned his back against the wall.

"No, the other news." Enzo was standing now, looking through Eustis' things.

"Phobos, Bezos City." Eustis rubbed his chin with his palm. There was a patch of whiskers there. He needed to shave soon. "It's the worst. Probably get our arms pulled off by some radiation-baked GovCorp reclamation squad."

"I really need to get to Musk City. We'll be so close. I plan to start something there that will change everything. It's so important."

"Oh really? Sheesh, you nearly let me forget about *Musk City*." Enzo mocked his voice with the last words. "I know where you think you need to go, but forget about it." Enzo unstacked a pile of items Eustis had left at the foot of his bed. "What's this?" Enzo had his hands in Eustis' bag before he could stop him. He pulled out the protective box.

"No, don't," Eustis said.

"What?" Enzo said as he lifted the lid to the box. "You have a book? Where did you get this? Does Captain know? This is worth, well, I don't even know how much."

Eustis shot across the floor in a rush.

"Yeah, I—" Eustis stammered. Enzo thumbed through the pages quickly.

"This should be in a museum," Enzo said.

"It *should* be available to everyone."

"Holy Bible." Enzo read from the cover. "Weird name. I don't know those words. I would remember them if I had ever read them before." Enzo looked at Eustis to see if he understood. Eustis didn't. Enzo tapped his forehead. "It's a brain thing. Anyway." He glanced back down at the thick Bible in his hands. "Is it a tech manual or something?"

"In a way," Eustis said. "Technically, it's illegal." He thought this would make the kid distance himself from it, but it had quite the opposite effect. Enzo's face lifted, and his eyes grew wide.

"You have a book," Enzo said. "And it's banned?" The relish in his voice was clear. Eustis rubbed the back of his neck and looked at the wall.

"Well, yeah."

"Mind if I borrow it?" he said. The words startled Eustis. He had miscalculated the outcome of the conversation. He pondered the opportunity for a long moment.

"I don't know," Eustis said. "It's very special. If I lost it, it would be a disaster."

"Tell you what," Enzo said. "Let me borrow it, or I'll tell Captain you're hiding something in your room that's worth a fortune."

Eustis stared at the floor for a long moment weighing his options. He looked back up at the kid and held eye contact. After an intense staring contest, Enzo's rude exterior cracked, and a smile stretched across his lips. Eustis pointed at his face. "Ahh. You're bluffing?" Eustis said.

"Yeah," Enzo said. "But it was worth a try."

"Listen, I can't overstress this. That book is the most important item in the Sol System right now."

"Well, now I have to borrow it," Enzo said.

"You have to be careful," Eustis said. "Please protect it." He grabbed. "Here, take the box. Keep it safe." He watched the kid. "Don't hold it like that. You'll bend the pages."

"Right," Enzo rose from the bed with the ancient book in his hands. Eustis felt a knot in his stomach at the idea of letting the priceless artifact out of his sight. If it were lost or destroyed, there would be no way to get another one. Enzo headed for the door. "Captain'll notice I'm not at my post if I don't get back."

Chapter Twenty

SPREAD

Eustis had beaten a path back and forth across deck one for three days. Enzo came by often to talk, though Eustis couldn't avoid talking to him about the Bible. As their friendship grew, Enzo asked increasingly intricate questions about the faith. Most were sarcastic attempts to discredit the gospel, but the kid kept coming, so Eustis kept talking. It wasn't long before Eustis considered the kid a friend. His manner was easy and enjoyable, unlike the other two crew who were aloof and downright dangerous. He was skeptical, but there was a kind of unassuming honesty Eustis appreciated.

Rudwick, for his part, was scarce but could often be heard talking to his cats on an upper level of the ship and cussing them out when they didn't please his purposes. Occasionally Tiny, the giant of the pack, came to visit Eustis for a scratch. Gradually the other cats would join the big one for an affection appointment.

Eustis spent hours a day staring out into the black void of space, considering God's greatness and singing quietly to himself. He wished he had his Bible back. His mind often wandered to the awful events, the massacre of his friends, and the devastating way they were murdered. Each day, at least a few tears trickled down his cheek as he observed the lonely stretch of nothingness that yawned away seemingly forever. This led him to prayer. After one of these sessions, he rose and attended to his hygiene.

"Stowaway," Marianna's voice exploded over the loudspeaker. Eustis had been shaving, and his jolt nearly severed his head from his body. Marianna continued. "It's time to fix the transponder. Command deck."

Eustis virtually sprinted down the hall and grasped the ladder so that his knuckles were white. Leaving deck one had been his only hope for days, and he gladly climbed. By the time he was halfway up the ladder, he realized he would need his tools and replacement equipment. He returned to his room for his duffle bag and filled it with various items.

Much slower this time, Eustis went back to the ladder that led to the command deck. To his left was the captain's quarters, and to his right was a row of three unused habitats. In the center of the deck was a ladder that led up the bridge.

He climbed into the cockpit and glanced around at the blinking lights and various display nodes. His personal device hadn't been granted access to any of the data, so all the overlays hovered blankly. It appeared as if the ship had been designed and manufactured before panel nodes were used, but the newer technology had been upgraded without removing the old useless equipment. As a result, the bridge looked cramped and in dangerous disrepair. There were stacks of crates that cluttered the way. There was a persistent smell of liquor that hung in the stale air. As he looked around, a tall pilot's chair at the center of the room spun.

Marianna glanced at Eustis and then spun back around. She made a few gestures at the nearest display. She must have given Eustis authorization because information sprang to life on one of the displays. Without a word, he began to scan the data.

"Well, it looks like you got a lot of life out of that transponder. It was almost a hundred years old when it...." Eustis trailed off when Marianna started talking.

"I would prefer you give your report after you've made a full assessment. I can't stand empty chatter, and I don't need a running commentary."

"Understood, Ma'am," Eustis said. "But, uh—" he glanced around. "Where is the transponder assembly?" Once more, Marianna's chair spun around.

"I thought you knew comm gear," She leaned forward, tapping her harness release. The straps fell to her sides.

"It's just that there's so much stuff in here. I don't know which equipment is still active and which is old. If you want, I could remove some of the old stuff and organize. I really wouldn't mind. It's—"

Marianna stared at him while he spoke for a few seconds. When he didn't stop, she stepped past him, letting her shoulder bump hard into his. She tapped a release latch on a side-wall lock up, and it swung open with a hiss. Without saying anything else, she returned to her chair and spun away from Eustis. He looked at the open cabinet, which was filled with equipment, most of which had blinking red warning lights.

"Thanks." That was the last thing Eustis said for about a half-hour. He had a powerful urge to give a commentary on what he was doing, so to keep himself from chattering, he hummed the melody of an old hymn.

"No singing," Marianna said without turning her chair. He quieted for some time. Within another ten minutes, Marianna spoke up once more. "No whistling." He hadn't even realized he was doing it.

"Sorry," Eustis said. "I fidget too."

He did his best to work quietly, most of the time on all fours, buried up to his waist in the comm closet. On his cortex display, he made a wiring diagram and then an active schematic. Once that was done, he was ready to disassemble the communications gear. The transition point in the project felt too big to keep unspoken.

"Beginning disassembly."

"Understood," Marianna said without turning in his direction. Eustis smiled to himself. It was the first word the captain had uttered to him that was void of spite. He glanced cautiously at Marianna and then back to his own overlay. He brought up his journal. He made a quick remark that noted the date, and he wrote one line. *Mari spoke to me without cruelty for the first time today. More to come soon, I hope.* He made a quick gesture to close his journal. The advancement in human relations was so invigorating he decided he would venture another attempt. As he pulled the rack-mounted transponder unit from the panel lock-up, he spoke once more.

"Comm is disconnected," he said.

"Copy," Marianna said. "Report before you reengage comms. We need to change the transcendence credentials before we reconnect it."

Eustis' hands paused in mid-air. "You mean you want me to change the Ship's ID?"

"Yep," she said.

"As in, rename the ship and falsify its tail number—" Eustis said.

"Yes," she said with a note of acid in her voice. "Is that a problem, Stowaway?"

"Well, it's just that it's a class five violation of interplanetary law."

"So is spreading religionism," She said.

"True, but—"

"Listen," Marianna said. "If the transponder comes back online with the old ID, we're dead. Change the name and ID on the transponder."

"It will take me some extra time," Eustis said.

"Fine."

"I'll have to bring the transponder to my compartment to work on it," Eustis said.

"Whatever."

Eustis smiled, already knowing what he would do. He could envision the modifications he would make. "So, the ship needs a new name. What do you want to call it?"

"Just pick a scramble of letters and numbers, something no one will remember," Marianna said. "It just can't be Scuttle."

Eustis let a wide grin stretch across his face as he turned his back to the captain. He did his best to speak the new language he was learning from her. "Understood," he said.

"Shift change," Enzo's voice came into the room before the boy. Eustis looked up and watched the kid enter with bright eyes. He spotted Eustis elbow deep in wires and smiled. "Hey, the captive has been released." Enzo was effortless and free, but Eustis knew his own leash was not so luxurious.

"Copy," Eustis said, unsure what it meant. Enzo cocked his head and squinted his eyes.

"You're so weird," he said with a laugh. Eustis returned his smile, letting it spill into a goofy shrug. Enzo spun and tapped the back of the chair Marianna was in. "Time for a nap, Cap."

"Roger," she said. Then to the computer, she said, "Transfer command to Enzo Gianpiero Gatti." A beep signaled that the computer understood and complied. Marianna rose, rubbed her eyes, and walked out of the bridge without saying anything.

"You fly the ship?" Eustis asked. "I thought only the captain could do that."

"Course I can fly," Enzo said. "Nothing to it." Enzo made a twisting gesture which flashed a new line of data across the screen.

"What's that motion do?" Eustis asked, mimicking the hand gesture Enzo was using. The kid corrected his technique and pointed to the active display. Having Enzo to talk to and learn from was energizing. Enzo was a wealth of information, and Eustis was a sponge. He felt for the first time that he was part of something, something that was going somewhere, not the somewhere he had intended to go, but it was something going somewhere alright, and he liked it.

Chapter Twenty-One

DINNER

"What's that smell," Eustis said as he entered the galley. The aroma that filled the ship was not pleasant exactly, but it was better than the odor of ozone and sealant lube that permeated every compartment. A few uneventful days had passed since the embarrassing incident, and the legend didn't seem to be nearly forgotten by the others.

Standing at the industrial stovetop at the end of the narrow galley was Rudwick. His massive size dwarfed the cooking utensil in his hand, and the orange glow of the powered cooker illuminated his silhouette as he turned to see who had come in.

"It be a stowaway mouth to feed," Rudwick said, brandishing a dripping spatula like a weapon. "Got a cargo of Jing Leed from Calisto. Fried 'em up for a feast." He scooped a dark object from the stovetop wok and slung it toward him. Eustis caught it and studied the contents of his hand. "They be genetically modified, on account of their hugish size."

"It looks like a—" Eustis said, but Enzo cut across his words as he entered the dining space next to the galley.

"What we having?" Enzo said as he crossed the space and leaned over the frying surface. "Oh, great. More Jing Leed." Enzo grabbed a plate out of the lower lockup and held it out for Rudwick. He scooped a giant pile of the stuff onto the plate before Enzo moved to the table and sat. He shoved a fist full into his gaping mouth.

"Are these—" Eustis said, staring at the dark mass in his hand, but Marianna entered the dining compartment before he could get his words out.

"Smells good," Marianna said. She slapped Rudwick on the back, a stand-in for an actual word of thanks. With plate in hand, she sat, and began eating.

"It looks like a—" Eustis said, but now Rudwick's four cats paraded in, meowing at the sight and smell.

"Ahh, me pretties," Rudwick said. With the spatula, he scooped a heaping portion of the stuff onto the floor, and the cats began gnawing through the pile. Rudwick spun around, eyed Eustis for a second, reached for a plate from the same lockup, filled it with a mountainous pile of fried Jing Leed, and reached over to place it on the table next to Enzo. "Eat," Rudwick said, pointing his mechanical hand in Eustis' direction. Eustis moved toward the table.

Rudwick joined the crew at the table. Instead of a plate, he ate directly out of the giant wok he had been frying dinner in. He used the spatula as a spoon. Eustis stared at his plate as the sound of crunching surrounded him.

"Are these crickets?" Eustis asked. "They look like crickets."

"No," Rudwick said. "They be *fried* crickets." He shoveled a load of the crunchy critters into his mouth. "Big difference."

"They grow well in dark places," Enzo said as he smacked on a mouthful of creepy creatures. "They're easy to ship and packed with protein. Bugs are the staple food of the Sol System, mushrooms too." He swallowed. "Too bad they taste like toasted toenails."

"Food's food, Stowaway," Marianna said. "Eat it or don't." She eyed him for a second before she went back to her meal. Eustis nodded and looked down at his plate. *Right.* He took a deep breath and prepared himself.

"Do you guys mind if I say grace?" Eustis asked.

"What be the meaning of them words?" Rudwick said.

"Sounds like some dumb religionist thing," Marianna said.

"I'd like to hear it," Enzo announced. The other two paused with utensils in mid-air and eyed him incredulously. "Just out of curiosity," he added. Eustis didn't wait for further discussion. They turned their attention to the top of his head as he prayed.

"Dear, Lord," Eustis said with his head bowed, eyes closed, and his fingers interlocked. "Thank you so much for these new friends and their generosity. I pray you would bless them for their kindness to me, and most of all, Lord, please help me eat these weird burnt bugs."

"Well," Marianna said. "That was odd." At the same time, Rudwick burst into an explosion of laughter. Enzo didn't join in the laugh. Instead, he stared at Eustis with a smile, and his brows raised.

"To be true," Rudwick agreed when his laughter died enough for him to talk. "Saying grace, be the kind of weirdness that do put a creeper in me liver."

"You want to know what gives me the creeps?" Eustis said. He lifted one of the black-charred crickets to his mouth and tossed it in. He squinted as he crunched the strange cuisine. The crisp explosion was like an earthquake whose epicenter was his offending mouth. He opened his eyes, smiled, suppressed his gag reflex, and swallowed hard. "Tastes like bacon." Rudwick and Enzo cheered and clapped. Marianna gave a faint smile. He tossed more critters in his mouth and pretended like they were tortilla chips.

"This be reminding me of the time I lost me arm—" Rudwick said.

"Oh great," Enzo grumbled.

"Here we go," Marianna said.

Rudwick banged his robotic arm down on the table. It was still glitchy from recent repairs, but it got the point across. The cats jumped and hissed. Eustis nearly leaped out of his chair. "Curses on you," Rudwick said as his smile dissolved behind a boyish but bearded pout. "You never lets me have me fun." With the giant wok in hand, he stood and started for the exit hatch. He was grumbling something under his breath.

"Rudwick," Eustis said. "I want to hear it. I love stories."

"It won't be true," Marianna said.

"Who cares if a tale be true, as long as it be an entertainment?" Rudwick barked. "A database of telemetry numbers be true, but it ain't no tale. There be no story unless there be a bit of exagerment among the scallied deeds." Rudwick scowled at Enzo, who was laughing harder now. The big man balled his mechanical hand into a fist and looked ready to strike when Eustis interjected once more.

"I mean it," Eustis said. "I'd love to hear what you have to say." At Eustis' words, Rudwick looked as if he had just won the lottery.

"Eutychus, me boy," Rudwick said. "I could kiss the teeth right out your mouth."

"Ok," Eustis said. "Just to be clear. I want to hear the story, but I'd like to keep my teeth, and I'd prefer there not be any kissing involved." Enzo giggled as Rudwick vaulted from rage to revelry in a tenth of a second. He rushed back to the table and performed his tale with such relish Eustis couldn't look away.

"So there I were," Rudwick said out of the corner of his mouth as if it were a secret. "Surrounded by a squad of Musk City's drones, thirsty for me blood. I squared up me blaster and checked the reticle. I knowed I had one shot left. It weren't enough to shoot me way out. The only way were to escape undetected. The microchip in me wrist were me dead giveaway, so I pointed me blaster at me shoulder and pulled the trigger. Me arm blew off in a wild spray of gore as me fleshy tissue disintegrated into a plume of plasma. I walked out free as a bird, on account of the drones having no microchip to scan to ascertain me identity. And that's—"

"How old Rudwick lost me arm," Enzo and Marianna said in unison both mimicking his tone. Eustis clapped and laughed.

"Wow," Eustis said. "I thought you said you lost it fighting Ionian raiders."

"He also lost it on a bombing raid for the colonial first division," Enzo said.

"And by getting it closed in a cargo hatch while trying to tame a barrel-grown tuna," Mari said.

"He's got more amputee stories than cats have lives," Enzo said. "How many lives do cats have?"

"Nine," Eustis offered.

"Eww," Rudwick roared as if the number hurt his side. "Not the dreaded twisty six." They all laughed.

"Your microchip is in your right arm," Enzo said. "You shot off your left. Way to go."

"To be true," Rudwick agreed. "Me plan t'weren't fool's poof." Mari, Enzo, and Eustis laughed again while Rudwick looked on, confused.

"So, I'm not sure if Rudwick's story is true," Eustis said. "But I'd like to share one that is."

"I don't like the sound of that," Marianna said, tossing a cricket into her mouth.

"Tell away," Rudwick demanded. They each quieted.

All eyes were on him. Eustis took on an airy tone as he spoke. "God cared about people so much that he gave his Son so that anyone that believes in him won't die but will have everlasting life." Eustis smiled as if he had achieved some great accomplishment.

All three sets of eyes stared at him below furrowed brows. There was a long pause that was pregnant with negative anticipation. Rudwick met stare with the others. Eustis held his breath, hoping for a positive outcome.

"Awkward," Enzo blurted out. The others laughed louder than before. Eustis wasn't deterred.

"You see," Eustis tried to continue. "The name of God's son was Jesus Christ. He—"

"No more with the Jevus Cripes," Rudwick said. "Me thinks Euticus knows not the guts of telling a tale."

"He paid for your wrongs," Eustis tried again. "You see, Jesus—"

"Your story privileges are revoked, effective immediately," Marianna interrupted, laughing into her plate of crickets.

"But—" Eustis tried.

"Nice try," Enzo said, leaning over and nudging him with his elbow. "I liked it. I mean, it was a total misfire. But hey, marks for bravery. Knowing these two void-bloated thugs might chunk you into space for puking your religionism on them, you went for it anyway. You're as stubborn as a toe wort, I'll give you that."

"Euticus be a rotting story slayer," Rudwick grumbled. "Let Old Rudwick demonstrate tale-craft. Pay attention, all." Rudwick took a grand breath. "Once when me and me mates were taking delivery of a salt load of cargo, I seen yon kid scan into a Govy terminal with that twig-thin ankle of his. Thoughts he, no one saw him cast his feeble leg upon the kiosk. Oh, how the Govies were confused when his ID pegged him a thirty-eight-year-old woman from Titan? Me thinks he has stashed some mighty hoard of microchips beneath that sallow skin." Rudwick roared with laughter at his own tale.

"No comment," Enzo said, still smiling but letting some solemnity touch his expression. Eustis was disappointed that the conversation had moved in a new direction. He fought the urge to take over and force them to listen to his presentation.

"I think that one is true?" Eustis said. "He scanned both wrists to get us onto the space elevator."

"Maybe," Enzo said.

"Come on, kid," Marianna said. "Fess up." Eustis eyed Mari just long enough not to be caught doing so. It was good to see her smile.

"I've just got four," Enzo said. He slapped each wrist in turn and then pointed at both of his ankles. "Never know when you might need to scan in as someone else."

"Or three someone elses," Marianna said with a giggle.

"Where did you get four ID chips?" Eustis said. "Did you steal them from a morgue or something?" Suddenly the laughing and warmth disintegrated as if the oxygen had been sucked out of the compartment. Silence fell. Even the cats glanced up at the sudden lack of sound from their human counterparts. Mari's spoon hovered in the air. Rudwick's eyes were wide, and Enzo stared down into his half-eaten plate of Jing Leed. Marianna and Rudwick glared at Eustis as if he had uttered a curse upon the ship's fate. "I'm sorry. Did I say something wrong?"

"I think that's all for me," Enzo said. He shoved his plate toward Rudwick, who lifted it and dumped it into the wok he was eating from. Rudwick glared at Eustis as he set the plate back down. Enzo stood and moved toward the door with his head hanging low.

"Enzo," Eustis said. "I'm sorry. I didn't mean to hurt your feelings."

"I know," Enzo said. "It's fine. You didn't. I just have a lot on my mind." He drifted out of the compartment without another sound. Eustis stared after him trying to decide if he should follow. His indecision lasted only a second. He stood, but Marianna grabbed his arm and shook her head.

"Well, that zapped the mood," Rudwick said as he stood and dumped the rest of the Jing Leed on the floor for the cats to devour. They happily did their job. Rudwick cleaned the wok and collected the other's plates as they finished. Eustis and Marianna listened to Rudwick chatter about his old war stories as he did the dishes and mopped the floor where the cats had made a huge mess. After about a half dozen amputation stories, Rudwick slapped his full belly. "That be all for old Rudwick," he said. They bid him goodnight and watched him exit with his cats through the hatch that was entirely too small for him. Only Eustis and Marianna were left in the galley.

CHAPTER TWENTY-TWO

LINGER

"I feel terrible," Eustis said.

"Yeah," Marianna said. "The Jing Leed has that effect sometimes."

"No," Eustis said. "I mean, I feel terrible about what I said to Enzo. I don't even know what I said, but I feel bad about it." Eustis had stumbled into a subject, unwittingly, that had sent Enzo out of the room with his head held low. He hadn't been able to get the moment out of his mind.

"Oh," Marianna said. "Don't worry. He'll have to toughen up, eventually. Can't survive in space with a thin skin."

"Or," Eustis said, trying to play the counterpoint gently. "Maybe he needs some compassion, someone to talk to."

"That's not how space works," Marianna said.

"It's how people work," Eustis said. "No matter where they are. Everyone needs that, even you. Do you have someone back home?"

"This ship is my home."

He looked down at his hands. He could feel the conversation moving in that familiar direction. The one that ended in a punch to the stomach or an order to be locked in his room for days. Eustis had the urge to press harder on the point, but something was bidding him to leave it alone. "Sorry," Eustis tried. "Didn't mean to be nosy."

"It's fine."

"So, what set Enzo off?" Eustis asked. "It was something about his microchips."

"The chips are from his parents," Marianna said.

"So, what?" Eustis said. "He stole them? They disowned him for it or something?"

"Not exactly," Marianna explained. "His dad was Dr. Gatti. He was a solologist, studying the sun from the Mercury observatory."

"Wait," Eustis cut in. "Dr. Gatti. Was that the guy that was all over the feeds during the storms?"

"Yep."

"Oh, I thought it sounded familiar," Eustis said. "I haven't seen his broadcast in a long time. Whatever happened to him?"

"Died."

"Oh," Eustis said. A hot rush washed up his neck. His hands tightened into fists.

"Happened a few years ago during a bad flare storm," Marianna said. "He and the whole family died. All except the kid. Enzo was eight at the time, but he remembers."

"Remember's everything as far as I can tell," Eustis said.

"Sure does," Marianna said. "Every vivid, awful detail. The Govies brought the bodies to the family's burrow. Put them there for three days while they waited for transport back to Armstrong City, where Dr. Gatti had requested his remains be buried."

"Buried?" Eustis asked. "I thought in space everyone was—what do you call it?"

"Reclaimated," Marianna said. "Everyone except the wealthy or famous. Anyway, they left the bodies in their apartment, waiting for transport. Govies didn't know Enzo was hiding in the back bedroom when they delivered the stiffs. So the kid was locked in his family's home with the remains of his entire family for three days. Imagine that. Eight years old.

He never talks about it, but he must have pulled the chips off of them at that point."

"Oh my," Eustis said. "That's horrifying. Why did he do that?"

"Don't know, but we try not to mention anything that will trigger him to remember his family. He can't help it sometimes, but we do our best not to add to it." She stood, walked to the refrigerated lockup in the galley wall, and pulled a chilled drink pouch from the bin. "Want one?" she asked.

"No thanks," Eustis said. He wasn't sure if his stomach could handle a second novelty in such a short time span.

"Anyway," Marianna said, spinning the top of the drink container and returning to the table. "He blames himself for their death. There was a flare advisory, and he thinks he should have talked his dad into staying in the tunnelworks that day."

"He shouldn't feel responsible," Eustis said.

"He's a kid," Marianna said, squeezing off a portion of her drink, letting it pool in the low gravity before catching it with her mouth. "Kids don't always think things through."

"*People* don't always think things through," Eustis said as his eyes bounced down to the drink in her hand. She spotted him looking at her beverage, scowled for a split second, and then emptied another pool of the liquid into her mouth.

"What are you trying to say?" Marianna said. "That some kind of jab?"

"I didn't mean anything by it," Eustis said. He tried to stop the words that were shoving their way out of his mouth, but they came anyway. "It must be tiring to be obligated to take offense at everything anyone says. Why are you so defensive all the time?"

She skewered him with a sideways glare. "Defensive?" she spat. "Why are you such a religionist all the time?"

They shared a tense moment that could have broken over into blows, but her hard exterior cracked. She took a drink.

"Listen," Marianna said. "About what happened the other day."

"It's fine," Eustis said. "All is forgiven." A cold silence washed over the room.

"Forgiven?" Marianna said. "Is that what you think I was about to do? Ask for forgiveness?"

"No," Eustis said. "Or, well, yes, but—"

"Forgiveness for what?" Marianna said with fire in her eyes. She downed the rest of her drink pouch, tossed it toward the recycler, rose to her feet, and moved toward the exit hatch.

"Sorry," Eustis said. "I used the wrong word. I just meant—"

"Really," Marianna said. "What am I supposed to ask forgiveness for? Set me straight, you religionist dissident."

"Well," Eustis said, standing to his feet and meeting her fiery stare. He sensed that she had intended the question as rhetorical, but he couldn't resist. He clenched his jaw and spoke softly. "You were drunk, for one." He stepped closer to her. She didn't move. "You tried to force me to—you know. When I wouldn't, you pointed a gun at me and threatened to kill me." He shrugged and put his hands in the air. "It was—" He searched for the right word. "It was unusual."

"Unusual?" She said. "Is that all? You sure it wasn't defensive?"

"Yeah, probably a little of that, too," Eustis said. "There are better ways to let a fellow know you have eyes for him."

"Have eyes for him?" Marianna harrumphed. "That's ridiculous. You're such a rot-gutted bumbler." Nonetheless, Eustis stepped closer, letting his voice grow softer still.

"Maybe under different circumstances, we could get to know one another. We could have—I don't know—maybe a conversation. I mean, I get it. You need some romance in your life, but it's not like cargo. You can't just steal it. It has to be freely given for it to be real. It's kind of like Jesus' free gift of—"

"Need?" Marianna interrupted. "You think I need help? You think I need you?" Her entire body tensed, and her face went rigid. "Listen, you dirt sniffer, I've fought my way through the meanest piece of black sky you could imagine. I was commanding a ship by the time I was twenty-one. I don't need anything you have to offer." Marianna was shouting now. "You don't know the first thing about what I need. I don't need you. I don't need anybody. Just stay out of my way, or I'll vacuum pack you so fast."

"I don't believe you," Eustis said. His voice was calm.

"What?" she said through her teeth.

"You've threatened me since I got on this boat, but you always pull your punches. It's clear you're interested in me. Why are you pretending that you aren't? It's ok that you need some companionship. I do too. Let's just admit how we feel and try to figure out what we're going to do about it."

"That's not how it works in space, you dusk-snorting romanticizer!" Marianna said. "Out here, everything is trying to kill me. That fact that you're trying to get yourself killed at every turn doesn't mean I have to. Just stay out of my way, or I'll shoot you myself."

"No, you won't," Eustis said. "That's not who you are. I see that it's who you're pretending to be, but it isn't you. I know that under all of this, you're kind and caring."

"You're wrong."

"No, Mari," Eustis said. "I'm not."

"Don't call me Mari," tears were streaming down her cheeks now.

"Mari," Eustis said in a gentle whisper. "What happened to you that you have to self-medicate with that?" He pointed at the liquor pouch. "How did you become like this?"

"I wish you were dead," Marianna said before turning and walking out of the mess.

Eustis stood entirely still for a long time. "Well, that's not how I expected that to go."

CHAPTER TWENTY-THREE

CAPTAIN

"Captain," Enzo said as he poked his head through the partially opened hatch. "We're starting our decel toward Bezos City."

"Whatever," Marianna said. There was alcohol on her breath and a slur in her words. "Tell your new best friend."

"Also," Enzo said. "There's something wrong with the reactor. The magnetic containment bottle is giving a red alert."

"Enough, Kid," Marianna said. "I'm getting oblivious,"

"You look terrible," Enzo said. "You should take a shower. We'll touchdown in twenty." He ducked back out of the hatch and scurried down the corridor. His impatience for Marianna's recovery was intensifying. Certainly, the recent changes were difficult, but he wanted a trustworthy and coherent Marianna, not this loose cannon. He slid down the ladder and slapped the hatch on Eustis' room, and he was about to speak but noticed that Eustis wasn't alone.

"Count it out," Eustis said. Rudwick was standing in a wide stance. His human hand was on his chin. His glitchy mechanical fingers were ticking off one by one. "Take away seven, and you would have—"

"It be fourteen," Rudwick erupted with a cheer that was as frightening as it was loud. Eustis rose.

"Nice Job," Eustis said. He put his hand up, offering a congratulatory shake. When Rudwick reached for it with his mechanical hand, Eustis jerked back, "Ah ah ah."

"Me apologies." Rudwick swapped hands and shook with glad abandon. He turned and saw Enzo watching at the door. "Ernest be teaching me math. Turns out, twenty-one plus seven be fourteen."

"Oh, it is?" Enzo asked. His incredulous tone was lost on Rudwick, whose joyous achievement could hardly be damped by matters of accuracy. Enzo glanced to Eustis, who shrugged.

"Either you're a terrible teacher, or he's a terrible student," Enzo said.

"We've still got some work to do," Eustis replied. "But we're making progress."

"I grew up on Zepher," Rudwick said. "Where be the norm to use the base-seven number countage."

"One time, while Rudwick was piloting," Enzo said. "He got confused about the number nine, which he calls the twisted six, and we wound up orbiting Titan instead of Io. Lost money on that job for sure."

"Ahh," Rudwick bellowed. "That cursed twisted six be me unmaking." He laid his hands, both human and mechanical, over his chest and nearly sang the words, "Never had me such a crew mate as which would give attention to Old Rudwick's numerical proclivities."

"I'm happy to," Eustis said.

"Anyway," Enzo said. "We're coming up on decel. Be at Bezos City in twenty." He looked at Rudwick, "Or seven minus seven, for the mathematically challenged."

"Decel? Me gear be loose, and me kitties be free." Rudwick was through the hatch so fast it nearly knocked Enzo into the bulkhead.

"Ok," Eustis said. "And *decel* means?"

"Deceleration," Enzo said as he straightened up. "We'll fire the engines at triple G thrust to bring our momentum near zero. You'll want to stow anything you have and strap into the flight seat." Enzo pointed to the seat embedded in the wall. Without another word, he spun and was nearly through the hatch. "Or you could join us on the bridge if you want. I think Captain's seat is free."

"Hey," Eustis said. "You're really good at this space stuff. And not just for your age, either. I bet you're as good as any pilot out there." Eustis stood up from the bed and laid a hand on Enzo's shoulder. "I'm just saying I'm glad you're here."

Enzo opened his mouth to say something, but wherever his words were normally stored was apparently shut tight. He closed his mouth and blinked at Eustis for a moment. He had the urge to say something cruel to balance the mushy mood. He had the urge to run away. He had the urge to hug the weirdo.

"You'd make a good captain," Eustis said.

"Oh, he would?" Marianna said, shoving her way around the corner and through the hatch. She wobbled into the opening of Eustis' room and reached out a shaking hand toward the wall. Her other hand was gripping a drink pouch. "He's only twelve, you know. I taught him everything he knew."

"Thirteen, actually," Eustis corrected. Marianna turned her head toward Eustis and tried to open her eyes to their full extent. She blinked at him a half dozen times before pointing a crooked finger with the hand holding her liquor bag.

"Religionist," Marianna slurred as she slung a splattering cascade of droplets.

"True," Eustis said.

"You're totally useless," she said. "I'd rrrather have a bay o' dead bees." She turned toward Enzo and patted him on the head, but the pat turned into slaps, nearing an assault. Enzo tried to back up, but the wall prevented him. When it looked as if she was about to strike him with force, Eustis stepped in between and caught her hand. Her woozy stare went from the kid to Eustis once again.

"The stowaway, *Useless Grime*, the religionist scuz ball," she added, tottering forward. She smacked her lips and reached up to pat her cheek. "Can you ffffeel my ffface? Cause I can't." She paused and looked around for a second as if she had forgotten where she was. She pointed her finger in Eustis' face once more and said, "They're gone find your dead body in space. And it's me gone put it there. After I cut—"

"It's time to get strapped in," Enzo said. "We're on approach to—"

"Don't interrupt your captain, you stupid twit," she shouted. The abrupt change in her demeanor made Enzo's body tighten. "I took you in when your dddaddy died. Your momma, too. This is how you replay me. Bringing this good-for-nothing stowaway aboard." She took a long sloppy slurp of her drink. "Mutiny."

"It's not mutiny, it's—" Enzo tried to defend himself, but Marianna wouldn't have it. Eustis tightened his grip as she lashed out at the kid.

"They burned, you know? Your momma and daddy. They fried until they was crisped to a crispy crisp."

"Stop," Enzo shouted, covering his ears and ducking his head.

"Their skin peeled—"

A *whack* cut her words off. Eustis slapped the drink pouch out of her hand. It splattered against the wall and filled the room with the smell of liquor. With frightening speed, Eustis spun Marianna around and shoved her against the wall. Marianna squealed as she tried to get out of his grip. Enzo's eyes went wide as the missionary pressed his hand against her mouth. She fought against his hold, but in her inebriated state, she was no match for his sober, deliberate strength.

"We've had enough of that kind of talk," Eustis said with his nose hovering a centimeter from Marianna's. "Can't you see you're hurting him?" She squealed through her nose and tried to wiggle free, but Eustis wasn't done. "When you sober up, you're going to apologize to Enzo. You can't talk to your crew that way. It isn't right." He turned his head in Enzo's direction. The kid's eyes were wide, and his mouth was hanging open. "How important is it that she be strapped in?" Eustis asked.

"Landing can be rough. If she's not in a flight seat, she could hit her head or worse."

"Right," Eustis said, doing his best to hold her in place. He directed his next words at the wild woman. "You can strap in on your own, or I will make you." He let his hand off her mouth for a split second.

The string of profanity that erupted from her mouth told them all they needed to know. The violent tumult that followed had Enzo entranced. Eustis fought to spin her around and wrap his arms around her torso. She violently protested, landing a few blows about his torso and head, but he had her in his grip. With one foot, he kicked to flip down the flight seat embedded in the wall. He shoved Marianna back toward the seat and fought her into the chair. It took him a minute to get her still enough to strap her in, but her drunken attempt to escape was inadequate. Once he had her harness in place, he pointed to a lockup across the room.

"Enzo, could you grab some tape for me?" Eustis said in a voice that was too calm for the scene it was matched with. The kid slapped the wall and then rummaged through the items before he came to a thick roll of sealant tape.

"Yep, that's it." Enzo brought it over and pulled a piece. Eustis quickly reached for it and wrapped a generous amount around Marianna's wrists and hands. Once they were secure, he sent the roll around her legs to keep her hands in place. He handed the roll back to Enzo and stepped back, breathing hard. Now that Marianna was secure, Eustis spoke gently to the wild-haired woman.

"I'm sorry I had to do that, ma'am, but you didn't really leave me much choice. It's for your own good." When she started screaming again, Eustis turned toward the door. He patted Enzo on the shoulder and said, "Mind if I ride shotgun for landing?"

"Sure," Enzo said. He glanced over his shoulder at Marianna and then to Eustis. "You know she's going to punch your teeth out when she escapes that seat."

"Well, I guess I'll need to find a dentist in Bezos City."

CHAPTER TWENTY-FOUR
TRANSCENDENCE

"Sir, you might want to take a look at this," HEXA said. He had been monitoring the applicable datasets for the last few weeks, trying to spot any information that could lead his human master to his mark. "We have a transponder signature that just came online out of nowhere."

Admiral Strafe stood behind HEXAs' hologram. The bridge glowed with low red illumination. Strafe clinched his fists as HEXA's translucent image stepped aside. "Show me."

"If this is right, we're going the wrong way." He let Strafe study the screen. The transponder signal from a ship called *Resurrection* was broadcasting coordinates.

"We're not looking for a ship called *Resurrection,* you half-wit artificial know-nothing. We're looking for the *Scuttle.*"

"Yes, Sir, I know. I almost passed it up, but take a look at this," HEXA pointed to a second line of data. It was coupled with the first line.

"What is that?"

"It's a rider signal, buried under the carrier wave. It's a quarter-modulated sinusoidal oscillating pattern. This guy is good," HEXA said. His hologram looked up at Strafe as if what he said made any sense at all. Strafe brought his fist down on the place HEXA's forehead would be. Strafe's hand flew right through the hologram. It didn't make contact, but it communicated Strafe's displeasure well enough.

"Sorry, Sir," HEXA said, knowing Strafe had no interest in technical jargon. "There is a second signal hidden inside the transponder transmission."

"What does it say?" Strafe asked. HEXA brought the signal to the display. It had the obvious shape of an audio waveform. "Play it."

Crackling words came through the speakers, thin and static-filled. "God loved the world so much that he gave his only begotten son that whoever—"

"That's him," Strafe growled. "I'm going to torch him. Where is he?"

HEXA changed the display. A brilliant Sol map appeared on the overlay. "He's turned course. Looks like they must have peeled off halfway there. No longer en route to Ceres."

"Projected flight plan?" Strafe said.

"Looks like Mars."

"Set a course," Strafe commanded.

"Aye, Sir."

"I'm going to look him in the eyes as his body goes limp," Strafe muttered to himself. "He's mine."

CHAPTER TWENTY-FIVE

LANDING

For many days Eustis had watched Mars grow through the window of his cabin. Now it loomed like an orange giant before them. To come this far, get so close, and be turned away was heart-wrenching. They would not be landing at Musk City, the main metropolis of Mars and the capital city of the Sol System. Instead, they would land on Phobos, one of the tiny two moons of Mars. Then again, wasn't this as good as any place? It wasn't the shining city on Mars he'd been dreaming about, but it was a start. At least he thought there was a city, but as of yet, he hadn't seen it.

Eustis had expected to see a sprawling cityscape arrayed in lights, but as they descended toward Phobos, there wasn't much to look at other than the rocky crater-marked surface. A massive tower with solar reflectors was the only man-made structure in sight, but the immense size was incredible. The impossibly tall pillar of solar reflectors stretched up like a metal arm from the rim of a huge Crater, able to catch the sun despite the crater's depth. Phobos spun so fast that the shadows were racing across the surface of the tiny Mars moon. *Scuttle*, now renamed the *Resurrection*, worked to match the rapid rotation. The cascade of sunlight that shone into the stony depression was pointed into a cavernous opening in the crater floor.

"Where's the city?" Eustis asked. Enzo was in the pilot seat, Rudwick rode co-pilot, and Eustis was strapped into the spare flight harness at the back of the cockpit.

"You'll see," Enzo said as he waved at the display before him.

"It be hid in the belly of that gray mammoth."

"Are we going in there?" Eustis asked.

"Yep," Enzo said as he pulled the throttle. "And just in time too. Another day in space and we'd be out of O2. Not to mention, the extra strain on the system has cracked our magnetic containment system. It's not going to be cheap to fix. We're going to be grounded until we get it repaired."

Eustis leaned forward to peer into the cave that was depicted on the 3D display. The kid shoved his hands forward and rocked back at the wrists. The *Resurrection* arched sideways, and the metal hull moaned with the upward force of the thrusters.

"Prime the injectors," Enzo said. "Number three is sticking."

"Aye, Kid," Rudwick said.

"Give me twenty degrees of yaw. Let's put our heat shield toward the beam."

"Belly up. Aye, aye."

Eustis' eyes grew wide as the ship descended into the mouth of the massive Phobos cavern. The beam from the solar reflector lit up the thruster exhaust outside, and a blinding light poured in through the viewing port at the head of the capsule. Eustis blinked against the light but couldn't take his eyes away from the vision that came up out of the smoke.

The cave they were dropping into was the biggest enclosed space Eustis had ever seen. A rim of rock formed the mouth of the cavern through which they were arriving. It was off-center and yawned against the black heavens at least a half kilometer above the cave floor. The beam of light that came through the opening via the solar reflector was focused on a giant orb suspended in the open space at the center of the spelunk. The side that received the sunlight was too bright to look at, while the shadowed side glowed orange from the immense heat. It provided light for everything that was above.

About a quarter kilometer off to one side and overhead was a cityscape. Eustis furrowed his brow as he looked. The City was on the apparent ceiling of the cave, not the floor.

"Why's it upside-down?" Eustis asked with an obvious note of amazement in his voice.

"Inverting maneuver," Enzo called out. As he did, the ship rolled once more placing the city below them. Now the City was in the apparent down position, as was the cave opening. Bezos City was surrounded on all sides by towering rock walls. An array of tubes and cables hung down from the glowing sphere like an umbilical to the glowing city beneath. The city didn't have the squarish architecture of an earth establishment. Instead, the buildings were mostly spherical, many of which were transparent. Since buildings in vacuum had to serve as pressure vessels, most were almost entirely buried in Phobo's rock, allowing the smallest portion of the upper domes to be exposed to let in light.

"He be gapping," Rudwick's voice broke Eustis' enchantment with the growing world below. Enzo spun in his flight seat and smiled at Eustis.

"Aww," Enzo said. Eustis reached up with the back of his hand and manually lifted his jaw from its gapping position. Enzo laughed and turned back to his business. Eustis felt the involuntary smile stretch across his own face.

The domes of the city swelled to titans as the *Resurrection* seemed to shrink and descend into an open space between an array of looming structures. The landing pad appeared, and white engine exhaust kicked up dust, which billowed around the window. The last one hundred meters of the decel, they descended into an open dome with a massive hatch in the roof. It slid closed as they passed through. It was comparatively dark outside the cockpit's cupola, and the scene seemed to freeze until a thunk told the crew they had touched down.

"Well done!" Eustis cheered. Rudwick and Enzo laughed at his enthusiasm. "I'm on another planet! I'm on another planet!"

"I'd hardly call Phobos a planet," Enzo said.

"It be nary more than a space pebble," Rudwick chortled. When his harness was off, Eustis stood and bounced, feeling close to his full weight once more. It was still not quite equivalent to Earth's gravity, but it was noticeably more than the inertial stand-in he had been experiencing for the previous weeks.

"Man, I love gravity," Eustis said.

"Not technically gravity," Enzo said. "Centrifugal force. A few centuries ago, they spun Phobos up to .73 Gs. It's tidally locked, so they had to spin it on a second axis. But, yeah, a little rotational gravity does the body good."

"Wow," Eustis said. "I just can't wrap my mind around it. Why are we on the ceiling?"

"There's no up and down in space. It's all relative to acting forces. Phobos' spin pushes everything outward," Enzo said as he swiped away the display and unlatched his harness. "That's why Bezos City has to be subterranean. If it were on the surface, it would fly off into space. Phobos' core is overhead, and a thin couple of kilometers of rock is all that's holding us inside.

"It's amazing!" Eustis said.

"It's a dump," Enzo said as he unstrapped and stowed his flight suit in the bridge lockup. "Let's check on the Captain."

CHAPTER TWENTY-SIX

PRAY

"Are you sure it's ok to leave her on board?" Eustis asked. They were standing in front of where Marianna was strapped to the flight seat in the wall of Eustis' quarters. She was passed out, wrapped in sealing tape, snoring loudly, and covered in the spilt contents of her liquor pouch.

"Sure, Rudwick leaves his cats on board when he goes ashore," Enzo said.

"She's not a cat, though," Eustis said as he stepped toward the cargo lockup on the adjacent wall. He rummaged for a second until he found what he was looking for. With a small knife in hand, he approached Marianna and cut the tape that bound her hands and legs. He was less than gentle, and yet she didn't wake. "Pull down the bed."

Enzo reached for Eustis' bed and unlatched the hasp, letting it swing into place. Eustis undid the harness that held Marianna to the wall-mounted flight seat, and lifted her into his arms. Her weight was heavier than before under Phobos' spin gravity. Eustis stepped across the room and laid her gently on the bed. He knelt and removed her boots, pushed her hair out of her face, and tucked her under the covers. He reached for her hand, bowed his head, and whispered a quick prayer. None of this roused her from a deep slumber. He leaned over and gave her the lightest peck on the forehead.

When Eustis stood and turned toward the door, he found Enzo had been watching him with wide eyes, brows raised, and a big smile.

"What?" Eustis said.

"Nothing." Enzo couldn't keep the smile out of his voice. They moved toward the hatch and stepped into the corridor. They were nearly run over by Rudwick, duffle bag over his shoulder, moving like a meteor for the exit.

"Land hoe, mates," Rudwick said over his shoulder.

"He's in a hurry," Eustis said.

"Oh, hey I need to return your book," Enzo said as Rudwick disappeared down the hatchway.

"My book?" Eustis acted casually as if he'd not been thinking about it every few minutes since he had let Enzo borrow his priceless Bible. He was happy to know it was still intact but simultaneously disappointed. There was no way the kid had read the Bible in the short time he had borrowed it. "Wait," Eustis said, swallowing hard. "Wouldn't you like to keep it a while longer?"

Enzo stopped in the corridor and said, "Are you sure? You seemed kind of uptight about loaning it out."

"It is priceless," Eustis said. "But the worth is in reading it."

"Perfect," Enzo said before pivoting to business. "Once we're off, we need to see the port authority and get our emergency access. Then we visit the manifest officer and get the *Resurrection* signed in. After that, we've got to hit up the shipwright's office and see if they've got the gear we need for the repair. If not, then we'll need to see the shipment manager to get the parts. We're stuck until we have them in hand. It's going to be a long day and a lot of walking. They won't let you off this ship with a gun, so don't—" Enzo paused. "I guess that won't be a problem for you. Anyway, don't bring anything valuable with you, at least nothing you wouldn't want to donate to a pickpocket."

"Got it," Eustis said. The boy watched him for a few seconds as if he were waiting for something.

"Don't you want to–uh–you know–" Enzo pointed to Eustis' head and circled his finger about his eyes.

"What?"

"The thing where you close your eyes and whisper."

"Huh?"

"Like you did for the captain. Could you do that for me?"

"Are you asking me to pray for you?" Eustis said.

"Pray. Yeah, do that."

Eustis stared at the kid for a few seconds before he bowed his head and whispered a prayer just loud enough for Enzo to hear. When he opened his, he found Enzo with wide eyes, brows raised, smiling. Eustis smiled back. They both laughed.

"Perfect," Enzo said. "I'm going to throw a few things in my bag. Let's meet at the down-hatch in five."

Four minutes later, Enzo and Eustis were at the exit hatch, ready to climb down and meet whatever Bezos City had to offer. They were nearly through when Marianna's voice echoed down the corridor from above. It was muddled and impossible to make out.

"Oh, great," Enzo muttered. The sound of stomping clanged from above. She materialized on the upper ladder and tried to climb down. Her hand slipped, and her foot lost its purchase. She tumbled backward and would have crashed to the deck except that Eustis rushed to catch her.

"Take your hhhands offf me you yump," she said. Her brief nap had not improved her inebriated grumpiness. She shoved Eustis away, to which he put his palms to the air, showing he had, in fact, unhanded her.

"Are you sure you're—" Eustis said but paused when Enzo put his hand up.

"Don't try to stop her," the kid said with one eyebrow raised. "It'll get ugly, which will attract attention."

"I'm ffffine. Let's go."

"Won't it attract attention to drag a drunk woman through Main Street?" Eustis asked.

"Not a bit," Enzo said. "It'd be weirder to come to port with the entire crew sober." Eustis shrugged. Enzo nodded. Marianna winked at the wall.

They descended the steps on the other side of the open hatch and followed a long walkway with blinking lights on either side. There was no scanning kiosk, no ID terminal, not even a guard to block the way.

"No security?" Eustis asked.

"Nope," Enzo said. "No need for security when there's nothing of value to guard. You'll see." Enzo put his finger in the air as if he had just thought of something. "We should set up a coordinate coop," Enzo said, as he made a hand gesture Eustis didn't recognize. Eustis was about to ask, but Enzo added, "Location sharing." The kid tapped and swiped a few times before a notification pinged in Eustis cortex display. *Would you like to share your location with Enzo Gatti?* Eustis swiped to agree. "That way we can find each other if we get separated. As long as the data grid is up and running, which is probably rare in Bezos."

"Separated?" Eustis asked, trying not to sound fearful.

"One can hope," Marianna slurred.

The terminal wove between dozens of docking stations where ships of all sizes had airlocks gaping like hungry mouths. Shipmen and crew bustled around the mouths of most of the docked ships. Marianna wobbled, and Eustis reached to steady her. He received a slap on the hand for trying.

Enzo pointed to a turn in the walkway through which light and color were spilling. They had to wait for Marianna, who bent over and left the contents of her stomach on the walkway. When she stood, she smiled and wiped her mouth with her sleeve. She nodded, and the trio continued.

They turned the corner and stepped into a chaotic scene. Vendors hawking everything from rocket fuel to jewelry shouted toward the new arrivals. A multi-tiered dome with spiraling sidewalks rose to a pinnacle that had to be a hundred meters up. The peak of the dome was the only part not buried in Phobosian regolith and was where most of the light cascaded down into every gritty crevice of the sphere. Eustis stopped in the walkway and craned his neck to study the giant structure with people on every level moving around like ants.

Above the upper glass of the dome, the glowing orb which was absorbing and redirecting the twice-reflected sunlight poured amber beams through the skylight. Eustis could see the shapes of grander domes towering above this one and, in the distance, the cave walls that surrounded Bezos City on all sides.

Enzo kept walking through the droning crowd, expecting Eustis to follow. As Marianna shuffled past, she reached out a hand to push Eustis out of the way. It was unclear what part of Eustis' anatomy she was aiming for, but her uncontrolled palm laid across his cheek and right eye. He slapped at her mislaid hand as she moved him aside with a sloppy shove. Apparently undaunted, he continued to gaze up at the domeworks.

Enzo and Marianna walked on for another minute. The kid was looking for the port authority office, and Marianna was using any pedestrian who got within arm's reach as a handrail. The disgruntled complaints and threats let Enzo know she was not far behind. When he spotted what he was looking for, he pointed.

"That's it," Enzo said. "All we have to do is—" Enzo stopped when he realized Eustis wasn't behind him. He made eye contact with Marianna, or rather he looked at Marianna as she looked past him, cross-eyed and slightly to the left.

"Where's Eustis?" Enzo asked.

"I touched his ffface just now," she said as she reached for her own. "Still can't fffeel mine. I have a ffface still, right?" Enzo ignored her slurred question and pushed to his tiptoes to look over her shoulder. Marianna misunderstood the kid's approach as a request for affection because she reached for him and squeezed him in a booze-scented hug. He wriggled free and stepped aside. "Come on. Eustis got lost."

"Good," Marianna said.

CHAPTER TWENTY-SEVEN

HYPER

Enzo wove back through the noisy crowd as Marianna stumbled after. Halfway back to where the dome met the walkway, Enzo spotted Eustis talking to a woman in a white lab coat on the steps of an ornate structure embedded in the dome wall. He furrowed his brow as he read the sign above the opening where Eustis was talking to the stranger. It read *Hyper-Terrestrial Research Commune.* He felt Marianna's unsteady hand grip his shoulder.

"What'sss that wrinkler doing?" Marianna said.

"I don't know. He's talking to a hyper-terrestrial researcher. Come on." Enzo stepped forward. He moved around sideways, trying to catch Eustis's eye line, but not wanting to attract undue attention. When he was at the foot of the steps, he heard what Eustis was saying to the hyper.

"He came to Earth for a very important purpose," Eustis was saying.

"He came?" said the researcher. She squinted at him. "So, he was a hyper-terrestrial? I thought you said he was the son of—" she paused. "What was it you said?"

"Jesus is the Son of God. He came to earth to—"

"Black vvvoid!" Marianna cursed. She began whisper-screaming in Enzo's ear, not nearly as quiet as she likely intended. "That grumble-tongue babbler is talking about his ssstupid religionism to a hhhyper." Enzo tried shoving her mouth away from his ear. Her breath smelled flammable. He put his hands on her face and tried to shove, but she gripped his head and continued to splatter slurred words all over the side of his head. "Run away before that mollycoddle gets us arrested for profitizing." She released him, turned, and tried to run, but stumbled down the steps.

The hyper-terrestrial research scientist heard the commotion that Marianna had made and spun to see her fall down the steps. Her eyes then bounced to Enzo, who was standing only a few paces away, trying to blend in with the stone wall. By now, Enzo was violently gesturing for Eustis to come with him. The researcher buttoned her lab coat tight, pulled down her goggles, and glanced between Eustis, Enzo, and Marianna, the latter of which was trying to sneak-crawl down the steps without detection.

"What is this?" The researcher said, taking a step back up the stairs of the research commune building. She cocked her head to the side as she watched Marianna and then glanced at Eustis, as if she were just taking in what Marianna had said. "Proselytizing," she said. "You were trying to proselytize me. Is this some kind of experiment, or test?"

Eustis took a breath as if he were about to speak, but Enzo stepped in and cut him off.

"I'm so sorry," Enzo said. "It's my fault. My uncle got radiation poisoning on our last flight. He's been saying the strangest things. I'm trying to get him to the infirmary?"

"Her too?" The researcher pointed to Marianna, who was still on all fours and having trouble negotiating the foot traffic that moved relentlessly down the street.

"Oh, no," Enzo said. "She's just drunk." Enzo reached for Eustis and tugged on his shirt. He glanced at the researcher's name badge as he spoke in a calm, even voice. "Listen, Researcher Delphi," he shoved a confused Eustis behind his back. "I'm very sorry that my uncle inconvenienced you. I promise I'll get him to a doctor as soon as possible." Enzo spun and shoved Eustis so hard he nearly toppled over.

"I was telling that girl about Jes—"

"Go!" he said through clenched teeth, trying to communicate the urgency with his flared nostrils and wide eyes. Over his shoulder, Researcher Delphi stared at their backs as they walked away. Delphi made a gesture that they, had they been looking, would have known, opened her communicator app.

As they stepped into the street, Enzo leaned over and tapped Marianna on the back. Apparently, her daring escape had tuckered her so that she needed a nap. The middle of a busy road was as good as any place for a drunk void sailer. She roused with the touch and did her best to dodge pedestrians as she scrambled to follow Enzo and Eustis. When they had walked far enough away to be out of sight of Researcher Delphi, Enzo turned a corner and led Eustis and Marianna down a less-traveled alley. He spun and spoke to Eustis in a grave tone.

"You can't do that," Enzo said. "You can't speak religionism to anyone, but most of all, not to a commune researcher. Sheesh, you might as well go and announce yourself to the Chancellor." Eustis opened his mouth to say something, but Marianna cut in. Her words were slurred, but her point was clear enough.

"You scorn-scorched rattlecap. You can't profffitize— prostitize— proselytize. You're gone get us arrested and get yourselfff killed."

"She's right. No proselytizing," Enzo agreed.

"I'm here to proselytize," Eustis said. His simple words were accompanied by a grin. Marianna reached out, probably aiming for his cheek, and slapped him across the forehead. He rubbed the place where she hit him.

Marianna opened her mouth to say something else, but only gibberish came out. Instead of making a second attempt with more verbal clarity, she tried to slap him once more. This time, Eustis caught her wrist.

"Wherever I am," Eustis said, "I'm here to tell people about Jesus." He let go of Marianna's hand. It fell to her side, and Enzo's mouth hung open.

"But you wanted to spread your nonsense in Musk City," Enzo said. "If you get arrested for proselytizing here, you'll never make it to Musk."

"I wanted to get to Musk City because it's the biggest city," Eustis said. "Musk would have been great, then my message could spread to billions. It's still my long-term goal, but here I am in a city full of people who need to hear the message too. Sure, I'm a little disappointed, but it has to start somewhere. Here is as good a place as any. I'm sorry to disappoint you guys, but I'm a missionary. I had planned on being a missionary to Mars, but I'll settle for being a Missionary to Mars' moon. No disrespect intended, but I've come a long way for this, and I'm not going to be quiet about it. It's a matter of eternal life and death."

They studied his face for a long few seconds. Enzo raised his eyebrows, widened his eyes, and grinned. The expression distracted Eustis just long enough for Marianna to ball her fist and thrust it at full speed into his temple. His knees buckled, and he flopped to the ground with a sickening thump. The punch knocked her off balance as well. She placed a shaking hand against the alley wall.

When he opened his eyes and looked up from where he lay, he found Marianna looming over him with a wobbly stance. She pointed her finger down at him and said, "No prostitizing." She stayed in contact with the wall as she spun and staggered away. Eustis looked at Enzo, who was grinning from ear to ear.

"You're a terrible missionary," Enzo said, offering him a hand up.

"Well," Eustis said, still trying to catch the breath Mari's punch had knocked out of him. "I'll have to do until the professionals arrive."

Chapter Twenty-Eight

FREEBIE

"I'm going in ttthere," Marianna said pointing to a place with a glowing sign which read, Gruff's Fluids.

"Yikes," Eustis said. "Sounds nasty."

"Ok, I'll go see the shipwright," Enzo said.

"Fffine," she spun. "Take the scamp with you." Marianna didn't watch as Enzo hurried away. She staggered through a rusted doorway into a dimly lit establishment that had been burrowed into the cave wall. The smell of liquor escorted her in like a welcoming friend. There were a half dozen other sky sailers spread out among twice as many tables. The little light that filled the space had a sickening green tint.

"What's your poison?" a large man behind the bar said. "Just got in a shipment of zero-G aged whiskey from Ganymede." Her mouth watered as she set her blurry eyes on the shelves behind the man. She had caught the word whiskey, but the rest didn't stick.

"You, Gruffff?" she asked as she reached for a barstool and perched atop it. The room was spinning, but she did her best not to let her eyes cross. She blinked away the haze and let her vision bounce between Gruff and the translucent doppelgänger that shadowed his every move. She rubbed her eyes.

"Yep, I'm Gruff," the man said. His belly grazed the back of the bar, and the shirt threads which covered it were hanging on for dear life. His front teeth had retired from service. He washed a dirty glass as he smiled. "Gruff's Fluids, been in business for over–"

"Can I get a shot offfff–" she said as the sound of his voice caught up with her awareness. "Ooop," she burped. "Were you saying sssomething?"

"Never mind," Gruff said. "Are you going up or coming down?"

"Just came *down* fffrom Earth," Marianna said. "Or we came *up* fffrom Earth, I guess."

"I mean, are you trying to keep your buzz or kill it?" Gruff said. Marianna spun a half-turn on her barstool and looked over her shoulder. There was a dark corner in the room where a large man sat in impenetrable shadow. There was something about him that was calling for her attention, but she couldn't keep her mind on it.

She wanted nothing more than to keep drinking because coming out of this one was going to hurt. She couldn't remember why, but she knew she was running from something. She was curious what it was but knew to trust her avoidance instinct and stay under the influence. That shadowed silhouette looked familiar. She looked down to make sure she was wearing clothes; she didn't remember putting any on. The sound of a crack caught her attention. She straightened up to the vision of two sausage-like fingers snapping a centimeter from her face.

"What?" Marianna asked.

"You staying drunk or getting sober?" Gruff asked.

"Drunk pleassse."

"You got credit?" Gruff asked. Marianna's eyes crossed. She covered her left with a sweaty palm and squinted. She laid her other arm across the bar, offering her wrist. Gruff reached for his device and scanned her embedded chip. A loud, unfriendly beep followed.

"Put it on my ship's tab," she barked. "The Scuttle."

He made a few gestures but then remarked. "There's no ship docked by that name."

"Oh, it's called—uh—the retribution. No, the reverberation. Err—" *What did the stowaway call it?* She gave a blank stare, hoping the name would come to her.

"Ok, then. You got cash?" Gruff said. She patted her jumpsuit pockets, hoping to find a forgotten black bill or two. Her search produced no results.

"I ffforgot where I put my mmmoney," she said. The man spun to the shelf behind him and busied his hands.

A plume of steam rose around him. The aroma of coffee beans mixed with the more appealing smell of lunar-brewed moonshine. He came around holding a mug of something hot. He placed it in front of her, reached below the counter, and produced a small vial. Upending it, he let one drop fall into the mug, shoved the steaming cup across the bar, and stepped away.

"What's this?"

"It's on the house," Gruff said. She took a generous drink.

"Coffffee?" She took another swig. "With a little sssomething extra? I hope." She took another gulp.

"That's right," Gruff said. Although it was scalding, Marianna lifted the cup to her mouth and drained it. She set it down and stared into the empty glass. She furrowed her brows.

"Oww!" she said. "I burned my mouth." She looked up at Gruff. "Hey, I can feel my mouth?" She put her hand to her cheek and patted it. "I can feel my face. Why can I feel my face? What did you put in this?" She lifted the glass and sniffed. Gruff turned around and smiled a toothless smile.

"Buzz killer," Gruff said as he pulled the small vial from below the counter once more. He twirled the stuff between his fingers. "Sobers ya up in seconds. Handy if a pilot gets a sudden duty call. Or a customer drinks their fill but still has dough."

In another few seconds, her head was clear, her eyes were sharp, her buzz was gone, and her temper was raging. She gritted her teeth. "Why'd you do that, you big dumb sause-box? I was going to get another eight hours out of that buzz."

"Buzz killer's got another handy feature," Gruff said.

"What?"

"Helps forgetful customers find their money." Gruff grinned.

"The *Resurrection*," Marianna growled. "The ship is called the *Resurrection*. Give me an old fashioned on the *Resurrection's* tab."

"Now, we're talking," Gruff rubbed his hands together. He checked his cortex display. "Ok, I see the ship is parked at the docks. Good. But..." He paused. "Oops, it's not on the GovCorp registry. Sorry, miss. They won't let us run tabs on unregistered ships anymore. You know how it is. They're cracking down on everything these days. You could register the ship at the port authority office, and then I could get you anything you like."

She reached for the empty glass, lifted it, and was about to let it fly in Gruff's direction but stopped when he put two fingers in the air. "Broken glass costs two bucks." She slammed the glass down, not hard enough to break it. "Chipped glass costs–"

"Oh, shut up." She spun around on her barstool as it all came flooding back. Her failed career, her mutinous crew, her ruined life. That starry-eyed missionary with his broad earth-born muscle tone, those piercing gorgeous eyes, and—her mind lingered on him longer than she wished. *No.* She balled her hands into fists. If she couldn't get drunk, she'd do the next best thing. There had to be some muscle head here who could put up a satisfying fight.

CHAPTER TWENTY-NINE

TROUBLE

Marianna was in a towering rage, and looking for a fistfight. She scanned the room. There was a scrappy bruiser two tables away from the bar. She started toward him but then spotted his leg brace. Too easy. She turned her attention to a short, thick man at the next table and stepped in his direction. When she got close, she saw he was sitting with a woman who had a lab coat draped over her chair. He was a hyper-terra researcher guard. It'd be too much trouble. She paused and looked around. At the table in the corner sat that large man shrouded in shadow. His dark silhouette boasted enough bulk to give her a challenge. She moved in his direction, intending to attack.

She was about to lunge when the big man pushed his chair back and came into the light. She caught sight of his shoulder and saw the familiar shape of a mechanical apparatus attached to tattooed flesh. The light silhouetted the familiar broad shoulders and the unkempt bearded mane. She sighed.

"Oh, Rudwick, it's just you," she said, relaxing her hands from their white-knuckled posture. Rudwick spun in his chair, spilling a cascade of dark ale. When he caught sight of her, he smiled a large goofy grin.

"Ahh, lass, why you be so mighty disappointed to behold an old black sky raider alike myself?"

"I was looking for a good scrap, and you're the only ruffian in here that could knock me out cold."

"Be not fretful, me lady. I be honored to fistfight you here before these sad witnesses," Rudwick said with warm regard.

"That's nice, Rudwick, but fighting you isn't fun anymore. It's just the same old thing." He took a long swig of his ale and no apparent offense. When he put his drink back on the table, she sat across from him and reached for his glass. He frowned and blocked her hand.

"I be willing to fight you as a favor, but mind you, if you lay hold of me mug, I be fighting you for drink and that, me hearty, be a mighty different and messy affair."

"Fine," she said as she retrieved her empty hand and leaned back in her chair. "Why are you here, anyway? I thought you were going to drown your woes at the Research Commune with some young hyper."

"In sooth, Old Rudwick tried, but alas, there be no tab for the *Scuttle*."

"The Ship's called the *Resurrection* now," Marianna said. "I had the stowaway change our transponder signal. Remember?" At her words, Rudwick rose as if he would return to the commune and try again. "It won't work." She said. "I tried it. No tab on unregistered ships." He sat back down. "What about this?" She pointed to his ale.

"Had enough black bills for a brew, so here I be, broke as the day I were born."

"Me too," Marianna said. "Well, actually, I didn't have enough for a drink." She closed her eyes and rested the back of her head against the wall behind her.

"Hey," came Enzos' voice. Marianna's eyes shot open. He was coming through the entrance and bouncing toward their table. He pulled up a chair and sat with breathless urgency.

"Tell me we can get off this rock soon," Marianna said.

"Depends on what you call soon," Enzo said. "Talked to the shipwright. He said he'd need four months to get the part in. It's got to come from Titan."

"Four months!" Marianna shouted. She rose to her feet as her chair slammed against the wall. Eyes all over the room cast her way.

"Broken chair is forty bills," Gruff hollered from the bar. She ignored him.

"We don't have the dough to pay for four months of room and board," she said as she pulled her chair back in place. She ran her fingers through her hair and stared at the artificial grain of the table. After a long, deep breath, she spoke. "Not to mention the cost of parts and repair."

"So what do we do?" Enzo asked.

"We have the emergency cash box," Marianna said.

"But you said we don't touch it," Rudwick interrupted.

"I know, but we're in a tight spot, here. If we park the *Scuttle–*" Marianna caught her error. "I mean, if we park the *Resurrection* in long-term docking and just pay for air and fluids in cash, we could live on the ship while we wait."

"Do we have enough for that?" Enzo asked.

"Not four months," she said. "But, I don't know."

"We'll freeze to death," Enzo said.

"I don't know," Marianna said.

"What about the repair bill?" Enzo asked.

"I don't know, kid," she said, raising her voice.

"There always be space in Maroon Housing," Rudwick offered.

"Sure, we could stay in Maroon Housing if we wanted to get a sampling of the latest trends in deadly orifice-exploding plagues," Enzo said. Rudwick laughed and squinted in thought as if the strain of using his brain was nearly too much.

"Or, if we be in desirous need of a hand shortening by the rusted blade of villainous finger scavengers," Rudwick said. "Then Maroon Housing be our charm."

Enzo chimed in with a smile. "Maroon Housing is perfect for those who want to get their faces peeled off by a powder addict's grit-black fingernails in the middle of the night."

"Or if you want to suffocate," Marianna blurted. They both looked at her silently. "You know because they keep the atmospheric pressure below system standards."

"Yes, well," Rudwick said.

"Yeah," Enzo agreed. "But."

"What?" Marianna barked. "Hypoxia is one of the worst ways to die."

"It be true, but it be lacking in imagination. The joy be in the gruesome detail and grim aspect of thoughty horror."

"Oh, never mind! This is why I don't play your stupid games. As soon as I try, you make up some dumb rule." They all sat silent for a few seconds.

"Or if you want to get a kidney gnawed out by a radiation-mutated Phobos rat looking for a warm moist place to make a nest," Enzo said. Rudwick slapped the table.

"The kid be gifted," Rudwick said. He laughed for longer than was warranted before Marianna cut in.

"Anyway. Maroon Housing is not an option," Marianna said. "We'll put the *Resurrection* in long-term docking with life support hookup and wait it out." They nodded. "Ok, let's make it happen." Marianna and Enzo rose to their feet. "Hey, where's Eustis?" she added. Rudwick finished his ale and stood. They made their way toward the door.

"I thought he was with you?" Enzo said as they passed through the rusted hatch. The kid gestured for his cortex display. After a moment, he said, "Location sharing says he's nearby. Right outside, actually."

They stepped out of the bar and into the passageway. The street in front of Gruff's Liquids was busier than it had been before. There was a crowd of people gathered in a tight group.

"There be Eugene," Rudwick said, pointing his mechanical arm out beyond the crowd. The others looked to find Eustis in the middle of about two dozen people, standing above an audience, speaking. Rudwick, Marianna, and Enzo watched and listened for a few seconds.

"What is he doing?" Enzo asked.

"He be informing the Phobosian folk about his strange beloved alien, Jevus Cripes."

"Oh, no!"

Chapter Thirty

CAPTURED

Enzo was the first to press his way through the surrounding audience. Eustis was standing on a cargo crate, arms outstretched, speaking to a growing crowd of confused faces.

"The Almighty God offered His Son to be the sacrifice for sins, and each of you can receive grace by believing in Him."

"What's grace?" a man called out.

Enzo reached up and tugged on Eustis' arm, hoping to extract him from the very dangerous and illegal activity. He looked around, wishing Marianna and Rudwick would help, but they had not pressed their way through the audience. *Cowards,* he thought. Eustis glanced down at Enzo but didn't stop. "Uh, well–" Eustis tried. "Grace is unmerited favor." Murmuring spread through those standing around. Simultaneous questions about *favor, merit,* and a dozen other things were fired at Eustis all at once.

"Come on, Eustis," Enzo begged from below. "You can't do this." Eustis' eyes met Enzo's.

"This is why I'm here," Eustis said before turning his attention back toward those who were still plying him with questions. "You see, God is infinitely holy, thus any sin required a sacrifice. That's why he–"

"That's him, officer!" A voice rang out over the crowd. Eustis tried to continue, but his audience understood the situation before their neophyte preacher. A bustle shoved through the people. Starting from the outside,

Eustis' listeners spotted the officer and scattered. Still, Eustis preached on, trying to overpower the growing tumult with the volume of his voice.

Enzo saw what was happening, reached up to grip Eustis' arm, and pulled him hard. "Time to go," he said. Eustis tumbled off the crate and stumbled to the pavement beneath. Not knowing what to do next, Enzo froze. When Eustis looked up, he found a GovCorp officer standing over him. His bulletproof jumpsuit was lit with strips of blue light. He had his sidearm drawn as if Eustis was a violent offender. Standing behind him was Delphi, the lab coat-clad young woman from the hyper terrestrial research commune.

The burly officer turned to Enzo. "Good work, son. You brought down a dangerous criminal." Enzo opened his mouth, but no words came out. He wanted to come up with a story that would get Eustis out of this sticky spot, but when he spotted Delphi, he knew there was nothing he could do but watch.

"Is this the man, ma'am?" The officer asked Delphi.

"Yes, sir. That's him. He came to the research commune jabbering about a slew of illegal contraverbs. The kid said he had radiation poisoning, but something didn't add up. When they left, I researched some of the words he was using. Turns out he was talking about one of the ancient religionisms, something called Christianism. Here I have a transcript and my research notes." She made a hand gesture in the officer's direction. He scanned something on his own display and nodded as if the matter was settled.

"I see," the officer said. He looked down at Eustis, puffed out his chest, and said, "I'm taking you into custody for contra action violation three six five, the promotion of religionism with intent to spread dissidence. Don't move." He made a resolute hand gesture and spoke into his communicator. "Evidence bot. Do a 3D scan at my location." A bright flash enveloped the scene for a second. Before Enzo's eyes had readjusted, the officer had Eustis on his feet and was moving him down the street. Enzo and Delphi followed behind. Rudwick and Marianna had slipped away.

"Officer, may I ask why researcher Delphi is allowed to spread her alien nonsense, and I'm not allowed to tell people the truth about the Lord?" Eustis said. Without warning, the butt of the officer's sidearm flew like a rocket into Eustis' stomach. He doubled over and nearly went to his knees. Enzo took a lurching step forward but stopped himself before he did anything rash.

"How dare you make such a nasty insinuation," the officer said. As Eustis tried to catch his breath, Researcher Delphi came around and stood in front of him.

"We do research into hyper-terrestrial contact. Without researchers like me, no one would know what hyper-terrestrials expect us to do. It's not religionism."

"Apologize to the nice lady," the officer said to Eustis. "She's in a prestigious line of work. She's a scientist." The officer turned a smile toward Delphi and said, "Pardon this savage ma'am. I, for one, appreciate your work in pan-alien studies. I make my contributions weekly. Haven't missed in years."

A brief conversation followed between the officer and Delphi. In the fleeting moments, while it lasted, Enzo knelt down next to Eustis' ear. He wished he had Marianna and Rudwick's help, but he'd have to do it alone. He whispered the words, "I'll go for his gun. You hit him in the—"

"No," Eustis said. "Not by might, nor by power, but by My Spirit, says the Lord." Enzo squinted and cocked his head. The conversation was over, and Delphi took up lecturing Eustis once more. Enzo stepped back.

"Like I was saying, pan-alien research is a vital part of a balanced scientific society. We don't proselytize. We study and inform people what acts of service they must perform and what contributions they must make to show allegiance to hyper-terrestrials." Delphi said. "I mean, without that, how would anyone know what they were supposed to do? Appeasing the hyper terrestrials is a vital part of daily life." Eustis was about to respond, but a sharp noise drowned out his words.

Coming up the street was a six-wheeled rover. Its lights were flashing, and its sirens were blaring. The sound rang off the glass of the upper dome and filled the street with an eerie reverberation. People stepped out of its way as it squeezed through the narrow passageway. Its fat tires left tread marks on the dusty gray street.

"Here's your ride," the officer said. The rover came to a stop behind where they were standing. Two more large men got out and made their way toward the crime scene. A crowd, many who had listened to Eustis' confusing sermon, were watching now. "You still haven't apologized to Researcher Delphi."

"Miss," Eustis said. "I'm sorry I misunderstood the nature of your work." The officers, newly arrived, began to usher Eustis toward the rover, but when he continued they paused. "I thought you were part of something new, but I was mistaken." Eustis paused. "Yours is truly an ancient *religion*." At his emphasis on the word *religion,* Delphi gasped and placed her hand over her mouth. The officer bristled and spun Eustis around with violent force.

"It's not religionism," she said in a breathy, thin voice, looking as if tears might spill from her eyes. "It's science."

"Call it whatever you want," Eustis said over his shoulder. "It's a deadly thing when you worship de–"

Before he could get the word out of his mouth, the officer knocked Eustis across the back of the head, and he stumbled into the rover. Everything went black.

CHAPTER THIRTY-ONE

PRISON

Eustis woke in a cave. At least that's what it looked like from the ground. He gasped in a lung of thin air. It wasn't enough to sustain the breath his body wanted. His brain felt like a fried egg, and he wasn't sure if it was because of the low atmospheric pressure or the painful lump that was on the back of his head. He sat up and looked around.

Bars lined one side of the rock-hewn enclosure. On the other side of the bars was a corridor lit in a sickly green. A stainless steel toilet that had already announced its presence to Eustis' nose sat next to the rotten mattress. A small water faucet was placed above the toilet. The cell was so small that he could only lie down in one direction.

"Hello?" Eustis shouted. His voice sounded thin. He gasped for air at the excursion. "Is anyone there?" A long silence followed his words. His ears were pounding, and his hands were tingling. He flexed them as he tried to stand. The cell spun around him. He gripped the bars and waited for the vertigo to abate. He turned, knelt, and puked in the toilet. Once the business was done, he looked for the flush mechanism. There was none. That made sense of the smell. He reached for the faucet, thinking he would clean the bowl with what came out. He spun the handle and only a drip at a time released from the rusted pipe. Since he was on his knees already, he closed his eyes and prayed.

"Father in heaven. Thank you that my friends were not thrown in here with me. Please allow them to discover your love and mercy in this chaotic place. I ask that you would show kindness to them as they grope in the darkness." His eyes didn't open for another hour as he continued to pray for the crew.

The days that followed were the worst he had ever endured. To quench his thirst, he hung his head over the toilet and let the wall-mounted faucet drip into his mouth. The stale water from the corroded tap took a quarter of an hour to fill his mouth each time he wished for a drink. The water never felt enough and was a sad substitute for sustenance.

When the lights dimmed, which he assumed meant it was Phobosian night, he would roll up into a fetal position on the rotting mattress and try to stay warm. There was no sleep, only the still hours filled with headaches and homesickness as he shivered off the jagged sheets of frigid darkness. The cold nights were full of relentless whimpers, offered in stolen gasps as the constant droplets beat their steady tempo.

When the running lights brightened, presumably because it was morning, he wouldn't wake since it was impossible to sleep in that place. He would simply sit up and study the hard surfaces of the cell, the bars, the rugged stone edifices. How many poor souls had sat where he was now sitting? How many had died in these dire conditions? One was too many, but he guessed there were many more.

The wall had become the subject of his daily study. There were eight hundred and forty-nine ridges in the rock of the main wall and six hundred and seventeen on the adjacent. The floor had sixty-four distinct marks, and he had taken to giving each an appropriate name. He christened each with traditional earth names like Verna, Clancy, Taloola, and Buford. He was especially fond of Buford. It was a deep cut running nearly ten centimeters near the corner of his confinement. If he survived long enough, he would also name the ridges on the walls, but he didn't want to set his expectations too high.

When he had the energy, he would pace the confines of his prison, being sure to take no more than centimeter-length steps. His minor movements through the vacuous air were strenuous. Only a few short laps left him light-headed, throbbing, and suffering debilitating nausea.

The loneliness was palpable, and the despair was aggressive. They threatened to take his mind, his wits, his hope. Although his lungs constantly begged for air, and his head ached relentlessly, he filled the endless moments with the only activity, apart from crack naming, that his fragile energies could afford; prayer. He spoke to the Lord constantly. He was a running commentary of supplication.

On the morning of the third day, a loud beep echoed through the corridor, and the green lights turned red.

"Prisoner," came a voice over the loudspeaker. Eustis was on his feet in an instant, already breathing hard from the excursion. "Proceed from lockup to the chamber door and await a custody officer for further instructions."

A metallic click punctuated the announcement. Eustis pressed cautiously on the barred gate. It swung with a protesting squeak. He walked down the corridor and waited by the exit hatch. The excursion made him light-headed, but the hope of escape kept him on his feet. It clicked and swung open. Air rushed in that was so thick he could almost drink it. He closed his eyes and took a deep breath of the richer atmosphere. It didn't smell any better, but it brought a much-needed blast of oxygen.

"Did you learn your lesson?" came a familiar voice. Marianna stepped into view. Eustis stepped through the hatch into the light and put out his arms, a clear request for a hug. He was surprised by the swell of emotion that overflowed from his eyes. The vision of a familiar face was more necessary than the air that gushed in with her arrival. She glanced at his hands but didn't respond in kind. An officer was standing next to the hatch.

"Get out of here," the officer said.

"Really?"

"This person," the officer pointed to Marianna, "paid your fine." Eustis stepped through the door. "Cad-thrashed thing to do. Most who come in here don't leave. It's cheaper that way." The officer slammed the bar door and started walking. Marianna followed close behind as Eustis struggled to keep up atop his tingling feet.

They wove through a maze of tunnels that opened into a bustling bullpen. Large men in illuminated uniforms milled around the room. The officer gestured toward the front door but said nothing more as he plopped down in a chair that was too small for his robust frame. Eustis followed Marianna out through the glass exit and stepped into the illumination of a massive dome. The reflected sunlight that cascaded down in warm, passionate beams generously drenched him. He closed his eyes and faced upward as he said, "Thank you."

"Don't," she said.

"There be the stubbornest man Old Rudwick ever laid gaze upon," Rudwick said. Eustis opened his eyes to find his giant shipmate coming toward him, grinning, and Enzo following close behind. Rudwick slapped Eustis on the back so hard that he could have lost a whole row of teeth. They stood on the steps of the municipal compartment building.

"You survived the slammer," Enzo said. "Sorry it took so long. I had to talk these two thugs into springing you. We had to dip into our cash box. Only for emergencies. How was it in there?"

"Pretty awful," Eustis said. "I could hardly breathe. Guys, thank you so much for—"

"Don't," Marianna repeated. "If you say, 'thank you' one more time, I'm going to break your nose."

"I'm just so grateful to see you all," Eustis said. "It seems like God is watching out for us. It all worked out just the way–"

"You're kidding, right?" Marianna said as she squared off with Eustis. She grabbed his collar and jerked him close.

"I don't get it," Eustis said.

"The little lass be angered on account of your judicial recompense fee."

"The fee?" Eustis asked. "Oh, the fine?"

"Fifty-two thousand," Marianna said through gritted teeth. "All because you couldn't keep your blab trap shut."

"It's ok," Eustis countered with a sunny mood. "I'm sure it will be fine."

"No, it won't," she hissed. "We don't even have enough cash to dock the ship with life support," Marianna said.

"That's why I'm thankful," he said. "I recognize you made an enormous sacrifice on my behalf." Eustis was about to repeat his thanks, but Enzo cut in.

"Well," Enzo said. "We didn't really have a choice." He laughed. "These two crooks would have let you die in there, except that you..." Enzo trailed off.

"You hacked my transponder, you rock-loving skinflint," Marianna was enraged. "Every time I turn it on, it's spewing your religionist garbage. Even if the ship was repaired, we can't go anywhere until it's fixed. It's a religionist megaphone. I can't believe you did that."

"I can," Enzo said.

"Me too," Rudwick said.

"You're going to fix it, and repay me for damages," Marianna said through ground teeth. "But mark this. You will never ride aboard my ship again. Bezos City is the end of the line for you. Welcome to your new home, you useless, lying piece of slag."

As Marianna paced back and forth, Rudwick and Enzo laughed. Clearly, she didn't see the humor. "She be speaking true!" Rudwick said. "You be a savvy black sky farer, playing such a dark and devious con on me and these saps, all to ensure you preserve life and limb. It be a clever ploy. You have me respect, Crewman Eugene."

"It wasn't a con," Eustis said. "I'm just trying to get to Musk City and tell as many people about Jesus on the way."

"You will stay quiet about this religionist stuff until we get our ship fixed and are on our way. Once we're gone, and you're alone on this nasty, tiny rock, you can do whatever you want," Marianna said.

"I left Earth to talk about Jesus. That's what I'm going to do, even if it has undesirable consequences."

"Looked more like you left earth to save your skin," Marianna said. "Remember, Admiral Strafe?"

"No, I left Earth to talk about Jesus. I knew if Strafe killed me, there might be no one else in the Sol System to carry the light. It's a risk, but I have to. It's why I have to get to Musk City. It's the best place to broadcast from. I could reach millions from there."

"That's not your choice to make, you dunderhorse!" Marianna growled. "My life isn't yours to throw away, and neither are theirs." She put her fingers close together and stuck them in his face. "We were *this* close, this time. We dodged death because when that cop showed up, he saw Enzo pull you off that crate. He thought Enzo was attacking you. When they booked you, they didn't know who you were." She slapped his wrist, where there was no chip to scan. "Had they known they were holding a valuable criminal, one with a reward on his head, they would have ground you into hydroponic fertilizer. What's worse, they would have arrested all of us, and done the same."

"She's just mad because we've got to stay in Maroon Housing until the new magnetic restriction coils come in," Enzo said. "Course, I don't know how we'll pay for them when they arrive, but they're coming in from–"

"This kid," she cut him off. With her knuckle, she knocked on the top of Enzo's head. "He's a genius. But he's an fopdoodle too, cause he looks up to you. He doesn't know you're going to get him killed. Him. Me. Even Rudwick. You're going to get us all killed. We don't want to die for your stupid religionism. Stow that nonsense away in the deepest, darkest locker you've got. Otherwise, I'm going to find a back alley and strangle you myself."

"Can't yet," Enzo said. "Need him to fix the transponder."

She spun on her heels and walked away. Before he followed, Rudwick reached out his heavy mechanical hand and laid it on Eustis' shoulder, and said, "Worry not, matey. She be drunk again soon enough, and all will be right as the black sky." Rudwick turned and walked after Marianna. Enzo and Eustis followed behind at a quick pace.

CHAPTER THIRTY-TWO

VICTORY

Marianna marched resolutely through the street of Bezos City, followed by Rudwick. Eustis and Enzo meandered behind with less urgency.

"So, you look up to me," Eustis said as he gave Enzo a playful punch on the shoulder. Enzo reached into the pocket of his flight jacket and pulled out something wrapped in clear plastic. He handed it to Eustis, who unwrapped it. It was a half loaf of bread.

"Thank you!" Eustis said. He bowed his head and closed his eyes for a few seconds and then bit into the bread as his stomach came back online. Enzo talked while Eustis ate.

"At first I thought you were just a know-nothing squawk-box," Enzo said. "I mean, I still think you're a know-nothing squawk-box who's probably going to get us killed, but what you lack in street smarts you make up for in stubbornness. I respect that."

"Thanks," Eustis said after swallowing a big bite. "I think."

"I mean, you've got to be the worst missionary there ever was," Enzo said as they turned the corner and headed toward the conjunction of another dome. "You don't seem to know what you're doing. You're so over-eager to spout the message on anyone who will listen that you sabotage your effectiveness."

"Since I'm the only missionary, I'm the best and worst, I guess," Eustis said before taking another bite.

"I mean, don't you even read your Holy Bible book?" Enzo asked. "Like when Paul was in Athens. He studied their religion. He found a bridge to connect with their culture. He didn't just bust in and spray his eagerness on everyone as you do. That sermon you gave outside Gruff's Fluids. What a dud! They had no idea what you were talking about. You've got to start simple. Build up their knowledge base. Come at the gospel by way of shared understanding."

Eustis stopped, head cocked, eyebrows furrowed. "You read it?" He was gaping at the kid. "You really read the Bible?"

"Yeah, of course," Enzo said before continuing with his line of reasoning. "Or like Peter with Cornelius or Philip with that Ethiopian guy. They found people who were interested. They started from a point their listeners could understand and built up from there. Sheesh, it's like you haven't even read your own book. I mean, I respect your stubbornness, but your strategy is non-existent. We need to come up with a plan of attack. Otherwise, you'll be dead, and this thing won't go anywhere."

"You really, really read it," Eustis said.

"Yeah," Enzo said as if it were nothing. "Above all, though, you need to slow down and pay attention to how people are responding. You need to ask them questions, to make sure they are understanding." When Eustis didn't respond, Enzo glanced over to him to find that he was grinning broadly at the boy.

"Well," Eustis said with an expectant stare.

"What?" Enzo asked. He glanced in the direction that Marianna and Rudwick had gone. They had turned a corner and were descending into a tunnel opening. "Come on, they're leaving us behind." Eustis blinked into the haze of his surprise and caught up with the kid. He took another bite of the bread as he matched Enzo's gait.

"Well," Eustis said. "What did you think about the Bible?"

"It made sense," Enzo said. "Offered a reasonable cosmology. Much more logical than the hyper-terrestrial mumbo jumbo the commune researchers are trying to sell. I really liked the talk about being part of God's family. Since my family is... well... you know. But anyway, my favorite were the parts about Jesus, of course. He's super awesome. He was stubborn, too. Not a squawk-box like you, but at least you've got his stubbornness. That's got to be worth something. I think we can use that."

"Wait," Eustis said. "Are you saying you–" Eustis swallowed. "You believe it?"

"Yeah, I believe it," Enzo said, letting a smile stretch across his face. "I mean, I believe the parts I understood. There are a lot of parts of your Holy Bible book that I felt like I was missing some backstory or something. It says some confusing things. But the parts I got, I believed."

"Did you understand the parts about how Jesus gives eternal life by faith in him?" Eustis said.

"Well yeah," Enzo snickered. "From page 1,525, right column, third paragraph, to page 1,540, fifth paragraph, your Holy Bible book talked a lot about eternal life."

"I don't know page numbers," Eustis said.

"The heading at the top of the page said Gospel of John," Enzo said.

"Right," Eustis agreed. "So you understood what Jesus said about eternal life there? That you receive it by believing in him?"

"Honestly, you kind of primed me for that subject," Enzo said. "Since you never shut up about it for more than thirty seconds at a time all the way from Earth. I had already heard a lot of those sentences so how could I miss it when I came to that part of your Holy Bible book? And anyway, that's the main claim of the whole thing. I wouldn't say I'd believed unless I believed that part."

"Are you serious?" Eustis said. "So you have believed in Jesus for eternal life?"

"Yeah," Enzo said. "I'm in." Once again, Eustis stopped, but this time he reached down, wrapped his arms around the kid, picked him up, and spun him around in a bear hug.

"We're brothers!" Eustis said as he put Enzo down. "When were you going to tell me?"

"I didn't believe until you were in jail."

"Man, I really am a bad missionary," Eustis said. "People only get saved while I'm out of the way. Probably some kind of lesson in that, I guess."

"Actually, it was that thing you said when they were arresting you that made me take it seriously. 'Not by might nor power but by My Spirit says the Lord,'" Enzo said. "I remembered reading it in your Holy Bible book. Page six thirty-nine, right side, three paragraphs from the top. When that cop grabbed you, my instinct was to fight. That's everyone's instinct, except yours. Your instinct was to believe God had a plan and trust Him. My plan would have gotten us killed. Yours worked. So while you were in jail, it just kind of clicked. After that, some of Jesus' words popped into my head about believing and getting eternal life. So, I went back through everything I read and realized I believed it. Although, I do have a question."

"Shoot?" Eustis said.

"I can see that Jesus freely offers eternal life," Enzo said. "I'm happy to have it. But—" Enzo scratched his head. "I mean, why not make people work for it? People are such slobs. They're just the worst. They should have to give something in return, right?"

"Ephesians chapter two says, 'For by grace you have been saved through faith, and that—'"

Enzo cut across his words. "'Not of yourselves; it is the gift of God, not of works, lest anyone should boast,'" Enzo quoted. "Top of page 1,675. I know it says it. I'm just asking why that's the way God set it up. Why not make people work for it?"

"It's right there in the verse," Eustis said. "Lest?"

"'Lest anyone should boast?'" Enzo said.

"Yep," Eustis said. "If you could earn it in any way, it would be something *you* could brag about. God gets the credit for grace. Period. It's his gift, not your effort, that makes it happen. That's how he wants it to be."

"Yeah," Enzo said. "But wouldn't it make sense that we have to do at least a little?"

"I don't think so," Eustis said. "How does it make you feel to give me a gift?"

"Don't know," Enzo said. "Never have."

"You saved my life," Eustis said. "How did that make you feel?

"Totally regretted it," Enzo said.

"No, really."

"Well," Enzo stared up at the ceiling for a moment. "Satisfied, I guess."

"Right," Eustis said. "How would it make you feel if you gave everyone in the Sol system a gift like that?"

"Really satisfied," Enzo said.

"Whenever you have an emotion from doing something good, you can extrapolate. The emotions you have, God has too. That's because you're created in the image of God. So if it makes you feel good to give a gift, it makes God feel good to give a gift as well."

"So he gives grace because it gives him joy?" Enzo asked.

"Yeah," Eustis said. "But now imagine that when you gave me that gift out of the goodness of your heart, I tried to pay you back with the loose bills I have in my pocket. The gift you're giving me is worth a fortune, and I try to pay you back with a hand full of change. How would that make you feel?"

"Robbed," Enzo said. "Actually kind of mad."

"Yeah," Eustis said. "It's the same with God. We don't have anything nearly valuable enough to offer in exchange for what he's giving us. And plus, if we try to earn the gift, it robs him of his joy in giving it. So he doesn't want it to be that way. He wants to give it as a free gift, received by faith alone."

Enzo thought for a few quiet moments, nodded his head, and looked at Eustis. "Makes sense," Enzo said. "Thanks."

Eustis let a broad goofy smile stretch across his face. "Do you know what this means?" Eustis said. "What it means now that you believe?"

"What?"

"It means I'm not useless!" Eustis said. "I'm a missionary. God is really doing something. He hasn't abandoned us, Enzo. We're here for a reason. I just can't tell you how good this is. This is what I've been dreaming about for years!" Eustis was talking at full speed. "I can see it now. This is just the beginning. We'll do what you said. We'll find a way to share the gospel, but we'll make a plan. You and me together. We'll spread the word right here in Bezos City. It'll be great. We can find a way to do it where—" Eustis hardly saw where they were going as he chattered about the next steps of their mission to Bezos City. He barely noticed that Marianna was leading them deeper into the tunnels carved into the rock of Phobos. Downward they spiraled through dark passageways lit by eerie green. When they came out of the mouth of a jagged corridor, the new location with its low cave ceiling and cold, dry air finally got Eustis' attention. The four of them stood together at the breach.

"Wait, where are we?" he asked.

"Maroon Housing," Marianna said.

"Oh, no!" Eustis said with a sinking feeling. He looked around at the frightening scene that lay before him. "I think I'd rather go back to jail."

CHAPTER THIRTY-THREE

CALL

Chancellor Phineas Montobond stared down through the glass alloy at the domed metropolis he had been neglecting for years. Bezos City buzzed with activity—activity that had ground down the resolve and care the old man had shown earlier in his career. What was left was a grizzled caricature with an itchy beard and numb detachment from the affairs of state. The itch in his beard was the only of the two problems he intended to make right. As he dug around in the matted curtain of whiskers, a ding sounded—one he had learned well to ignore.

"Chancellor," Jeera chimed in. Her voice radiated from the desktop console. She was the best assistant he had ever had, but her persistent honesty, the thing he cherished in her, was also what made her the most irritating.

"Not now," Montobond said. "I'm busy."

"Ok, Sir," Jeera said as if she would comply. She didn't. "A few matters for you to consider. You have the water conservation committee meeting at 09:00. Then it's to the port to tour the new hangar facilities. After that, you'll give a speech to the refinery workers. They're considering unionizing." Montobond was about to pitch a fit, but Jeera preempted him. "Don't worry, Sir, it's already written. Prompter notes will appear in your cortex embed." Montobond's stringy muscles relaxed back to their indifferent state as Jeera went on. "You have an urgent call from Admiral

Strafe, dissident management office. His office is waiting for your response. Also, you have a meeting with the attorney for Trenton Sikes, the kid that was taken to reclamation by accident," She continued on as Montobond stroked his beard.

"You ever wonder what it's all for?" Montobond interrupted.

"What's what for?" Jeera asked.

"All this scurrying around," Montobond said. "I mean, the hypers must have some purpose for it all, right?"

"The hypers, Sir?" she questioned.

"There's a quarter of a million people down there scratching around as if any of this matters." Montobond sighed. "They'll all be in reclamation before long." He drove a determined finger deep into his beard, trying to reach the elusive itch. "Did you hear a kid got picked up by reclamation? A live kid. By the time anyone knew, he had been turned into potting soil. Can you believe that?"

"Yes, Sir," Jeera said. "Remember? Trenton Sikes. His parent's attorney. I said that's what your two o'clock is—"

"What scares me is, I don't even care. I mean, shouldn't I care about that? It's a kid for vacuum's sake. But. Wait. Maybe—" A long pause followed. "Nope. I thought I felt something there for a second."

"Are you feeling alright, Chancellor?" Jeera asked. "I can move some things around. If you think you need to take some time to—"

"No," Montobond said. "I'll just keep doing what I normally do."

"Which is?" Jeera said.

"Ignoring the important matters and piddling around with insipid, meaningless tasks while eagerly hoping I'll be dead soon."

"Right," Jeera said. "Are you sure you—"

"Quite certain," Montobond said with resolution in his tone. "What's first?"

"Admiral Strafe's office." She paused.

"Yes, well," Montobond said, bringing his mind back down to Phobos. "I am not going to talk to that ego-bloated no-neck savage. Hang up on him."

"I've got his deputy on line one, patching him through now," Jeera said.

"That zero-G-inflated mercenary isn't getting any of my time," Montobond grumbled louder now.

"It's ringing now, Sir," Jeera said.

"That trigger-happy umpteen toilet stone can grind moon rock for all I care. I'm not talking to that lascivious butcher or his minions."

"Good morning," Jeera said to the other line. "I'm putting you through to Chancellor Montobond right now."

"No," Montobond said. "I'm not going to consort with that hideous troglodyte."

"He's on the line," Jeera said.

"Well, what a flagrant surprise," Montobond said. "What can you do for me?"

"This is Chief Logistics General Manager HEXA with the office of dissidence management. Who am I speaking with?" a voice that wasn't Strafe's began.

"Yourself," Montobond said.

"Your voice print identification matches that of Chancellor Montobond. Thank you for taking my call, Sir."

"Oh, wonderful," Montobond said. "A bot." He moaned. "And as far as taking your call, I was forced."

"I'm calling to let you know about a perp we are hunting in your area. We believe he is on Mars, but it's possible he may find his way to Phobos or Deimos. Just wanted to make you aware. If you detect any suspicious activity, please report it."

"Suspicious activity," Montobond scoffed. "In Bezos? That couldn't be." He glanced down through the glass at the domed city that was falling to ruin almost before his eyes. "Let me check. Nope. Everything's good here. Thanks, though."

"That was supposed to be a joke," HEXA said.

"And that was supposed to be a question," Montobond shot back. "A little inflection at the end lets your interlocutor know you are making an inquiry. Try it sometime. It does wonders for interpersonal communication."

"I tell you what," HEXA said. "Out of an abundance of caution, let's just look at the file together. This will only take a moment. I'm sending the dossier now," HEXA said. A notification pinged on Montobond's visual overlay. "Criminal Eustis Grimes. Religionist. Proselytizing. Illegal broadcasts. Dissidence."

"Sentences. Subject. Verb. Sometimes object," Montobond said as he thumbed through the dossier.

"I didn't get that. Come again?" HEXA said.

"I'm not surprised," Montobond said as he gestured to mute the call. He flipped to Jeera. She was already on it.

"No record of a Eustis Grimes in our system," Jeera said.

Montobond clicked over to HEXA's line. "Nope. Thanks for calling."

"One more thing," HEXA said. "This guy doesn't have an ID chip. He's flying dark."

"He'll fit right in here, then," Montobond muttered where HEXA couldn't hear him.

"Since he doesn't have a chip, we need access to your bioscan datasheets to rule out the possibility that he's hiding on Bezos."

"Not possible," Montobond said. "Bioscan system's been down for years. Couldn't afford to repair it." *Nor did anyone want it repaired.*

"What?" HEXA inquired. "No matter, we'll take another approach. Admiral Strafe will need data shield passcodes so that we can spot if our perp logs on to your data network."

"Also, not going to happen," Montobond said. "We don't use data shield. Never got around to having it installed."

"What?" HEXA questioned as if it were unthinkable. "What about GloboIntercept?"

"Nope," Montobond said.

"Do you use OverLook, BankPeek, or DigiWall?"

"No," Montobond said. *It's why disreps from all over the Sol system come to Bezos,* he didn't say. "We're a bit more analog. But our fire alarms work. Sometimes."

"You *are* a GovCorp municipality, are you not? These are required infrastructure apps for the safety of all—"

"Cut the slag, dumbo-bot. Don't act like you don't know all this already. Your meat-head boss has been to Bezos plenty of times to bag more scum-licking disreps than either of us can count. You know what Bezos is, and you know what it isn't. So don't waste my time with your false virtue. Let's not pretend like your boss is anything but what he is."

"He always gets his man," HEXA agreed.

"I tell you what," Montobond said. "We'll hand paint some wanted posters and paste them up around town hall."

"Another joke," HEXA asked.

"Listen," Montobond said. "I'm very busy. Why don't you have your boss call and we'll see if we can waste some of his time too."

Jeera cut in on the line that HEXA couldn't hear. "We did have a perp that was jailed a few days ago. He was booked for a minor charge. Instant A.I. trial and conviction. Sentenced to a fine for judicial recompense. His fee was paid a few days after lockup. He had no chip. His name wasn't recorded."

"He had a trial, but we didn't get his name. That's Bezos' finest for you," Montobond complained.

"What's that?" HEXA asked.

"Nothing," Montobond said. "We don't have your guy. I need to get back to some more important work. I have this itch in my beard. I might have to contract with an astroid drill ship if I can't reach it by conventional means."

"I—uh—" HEXA said.

"Ok, bye." Montobond swiped the call to the offline position.

"That was handled well," Jeera said.

"Conversation is over, so I'd say it is a total success," Montobond said. "Screen all future calls from Admiral Strafe and his little creepy goons."

"Sir," Jeera said. "I think it's unwise to—"

"Screen the calls. I do not intend to suffer contact with that thug anymore."

"Understood, Sir," Jeera said, but Montobond could feel the anticipation in the air.

"What?" Montobond asked.

"Sir," Jeera said. "I hope you enjoyed yourself because that little performance pretty much ensured that Bezos City will be his next stop. With Madam Electra putting pressure on the custody force already, I don't think we can keep things together if Strafe shows up in Bezos City."

"Good point," Montobond said. "Block his entry permit."

"On what grounds?"

"I don't like him," Montobond said.

"It won't keep him out long," Jeera said.

"Do it."

"Understood."

CHAPTER THIRTY-FOUR

MAROONED

"What's Maroon Housing?" Eustis asked as he looked at the scene before him. A cave chiseled roughly into the rock of Phobos' underground spread out in three directions. The buildings that were erected under the low-hanging stone were cracked and crumbling. Sad, dirty people shuffled around the entrances of various buildings.

"It's the last place you go before you die," Marianna said. She stood and stared at the pitiful accommodations that awaited. "Let's find a bunk." She began to move toward the nearest opening.

"That didn't really answer my question. What is this place?" Eustis asked as they stepped over a man sleeping in the middle of the path. It was impossible to miss the man's smell. "It looks dangerous."

"That's because it is," Enzo said. "Maroon Housing is where people who have nowhere else to go wind up. It's packed with the most rotten sorts." A woman's scream made Eustis spin. A toothless man laughed from the shadow of an overhang.

Enzo waved his hand in front of his face. When it didn't work, he did it again. "Great," he said. "There's no signal down here."

"Not surprised," Eustis said.

"Communication app won't work without it. No calls or messages in or out. No data, downloads, uploads, nothing. It's going to be a long four months in this underground dungeon," Enzo said.

"So, why are we here?" Eustis asked. He pulled the collar of his jacket tighter. "Can't we stay on the ship until the new parts arrive?"

"You can if you want to be dead," Enzo said. Up ahead, a door set in the carved edifice of rock hung ajar. Marianna pushed against the dusty opening, and Rudwick followed her into the darkness that awaited. "After breaking you out of the slammer, we couldn't afford the O2 and fluids cost to keep the ship living and breathing. When you're stranded without cash, this is where you go. Every GovCorp municipality is legally required to have housing for marooned spacefarers, but I've yet to see maroon quarters that didn't look like you might get your eyes carved out by a spoon-toting hypoxic powder addict."

From inside the shadowed building ahead, Rudwick shouted, "good one!"

"You got some powder?" A cracked voice wheezed.

"No," Eustis said, kneeling down to a man who looked more like a cadaver than a living person. "But I have this, and I'd like to give it to you." He handed the remainder of the piece of bread he had been eating to the vagrant. He grabbed for it greedily and devoured it in a mere two bites. "Do you mind if I tell you about My Lord, Jesus Christ?" Before he could continue, the man was on his feet, shuffling away from Eustis. "I guess not," Eustis mumbled.

They climbed the steps and paused at the cracked entrance for a few seconds. Enzo shoved on the door and disappeared inside. The hinges squeaked as the metal panel swung toward Eustis' face. He caught the handle and entered. The interior was lit by one buzzing bulb at the end of a haunted hallway. The horrendous shadows spasmed in the pulsing glow.

Eustis' foot caught something in the relative darkness. Something on the floor said, "Watch it, ya gollumpus!" A tall dark figure shoved past Eustis and Enzo. Dark silhouettes lined the wall of the filthy hall. Eustis followed Enzo into a large bunk room. Again a single light bulb at the corner of the room gave inadequate light. The dry cold air burned his chest and left him hungry for oxygen. His tongue felt like sandpaper in his mouth. The place smelled of blood and body odor.

Enzo slapped a mattress, and a cloud of dust erupted into the air. They both coughed as Enzo put his bag down and said, "Just like I like it–packed with lung-severing astroid particles." Across the path, Marianna and Rudwick had found two adjacent bunks. Eustis sat on the bed next to Enzo's. The sound of a fight replete with prolific profanity came from the hallway. Everyone pretended they didn't hear it.

"So," Eustis said.

"Don't!" Marianna said.

"Don't what?"

"Don't speak." She said. "Don't do that stupid thing where you try to say something positive even though the universe is telling you it would be better if you were dead." She slammed her hand against the bed. "Don't pretend that this is ok."

"I spent the last three days in a jail cell all alone," Eustis said. He was on his feet now. "I know this isn't ideal, but at least we're together."

"You just can't turn it off, can you?" Marianna stepped forward, put her palm on Eustis' face, and shoved him backward. He fell on his mattress as a plume of dust swirled around him.

"Mate," Rudwick said. It took Eustis a few seconds to realize he was addressing him. When he looked up, Rudwick said, "When Mari and Old Rudwick be crossways, the best thing for it is a punch in her teeth or a swift kick in her gut. Relieves pressure faster than a cracked airlock."

"Rudwick," Eustis said. "Thanks for the advice, but I'm not going to fistfight Marianna. I don't think that would be productive."

"Curses, Eutychus," he said as he adjusted his mechanical arm. "I don't mean fair fisticuffs. I say you sneak up while she be sleeping and give her a boot to the jaw. It be a memory she dare not let loose of."

"All the same," Eustis said. "I don't think a fight is what Marianna needs."

"What does she need, then?" Enzo asked.

"Oh, the same things everyone needs, I guess," Eustis rubbed his nose where the dust was still tickling. "She needs the Lord."

"Does you mean Jevus Cripes?" Rudwick bellowed. "You think Mari be yearning for the Cripes?"

"Yeah," Eustis said. "We all are. Even you are."

"Who be Hugh R.?"

"I believe in Jesus," Enzo said. The big man's head turned slowly on a swivel. His eyes were wide, and his mouth hung open.

"Could it be!" Rudwick exclaimed. "You won over the kid to the Cripes?" He bellowed a laugh loud enough to shake the walls.

"Keep it down," a grumbling voice shouted from the other end of the bunk room.

"I do as I please," Rudwick shouted with such violent retribution that the entire place quieted for a few seconds. Rudwick turned to Enzo and smiled as he said, "Watch out for that one. He be lying in wait to flay the flesh of your tender inner thighs for a late-night crafting project."

"Good one," Enzo said.

"Well, boys. I be off to bring me cats to this desolate place before the air on the ship runs out. They be missing me something outrageous, me thinks. Maybe they be in need of Jevus Cripes too." Rudwick disappeared into the shadows laughing to himself. Eustis felt inherently less safe without Rudwick or Marianna anywhere nearby. He eyed the grumbling man in the corner.

Eustis laid back on the mattress as Enzo unpacked his belongings. The kid tossed a small bag onto Eustis' bed. "What's this?"

"I knew you didn't have any of your stuff with you when you got locked up, so I gathered some of your things. I thought you might need them."

Eustis looked into the bag, filled with a thoughtful array of useful items. "Oh, man! A toothbrush. Thanks. My mouth tastes like something crawled in there and died." He was about to upend the bag on his bed when Enzo reached out and stopped him.

"I put your Bible in there," Enzo whispered as he held the opening of the bag closed. "I wouldn't let anyone see it, especially not in Maroon Town. They'd kill you for a silver filling. What do you think they'd do if they saw a priceless antique artifact? Of course, the joke would be on them because when they tried to pawn it, they'd discover they were in possession of a highly illegal relic. Anyway, best not to let anyone know you have it."

Eustis took the bag and fastened the buttons at the top. When it was secure under his bed, he watched Enzo organizing his things in the eerie light.

"You're useful to have around, you know?" Eustis said after a few quiet moments. Enzo laughed but didn't say anything. "I mean it. You're street smart or space smart. Or whatever you'd call it." Eustis rubbed his chin. "Not to mention, you're a believer now, which I am still trying to wrap my mind around. It just couldn't be a coincidence."

"What?"

"Well, you were right." Eustis stood and paced around the bunk. "What you said earlier. I don't know what I'm doing. I'm really lost out here, but you're not. I need someone like you. A strategist; a cross-cultural advisor; a missionary partner. It's like Paul and Barnabas."

At that Enzo put down his personal items and turned around to watch Eustis pace. Eustis said, "You've proved that this whole thing is worth it."

"How's that?" Enzo asked.

"This was all worth it if I reach even one person with the message." Eustis ran his fingers through his hair.

"Well, you've reached one," Enzo said. "Now that you've hit your quota, everything from here on out is a bonus."

"God reached you," Eustis said. "He reached you despite me fumbling around like a radiation-baked plumpkiss. What could he do with us as a team?"

"Not sure," Enzo said.

"Really," Eustis continued. "You've got some kind of photographic re-call or something."

"It's called indefinite eidetic memory," Enzo said. He eyed Eustis for a second. His expression of eager interest begged the kid for more. "Doctors call it IEM. Everyone has an eidetic memory to some extent, where an after-image remains in the mind for a few seconds. Mine just stays longer. Much longer. It's not that big a deal."

"Seriously? It's amazing! You've got an amazing mind. And that's not all. You know how to maneuver in a world that wants to eat you up." Eustis paused for dramatic effect. "You'd be a fantastic missionary."

Enzo rubbed his cheek with his palm as he looked anywhere but Eustis.

"I've got a lot more I'd need to learn," Enzo said. "There were a lot of parts of the Bible that I have questions about."

"I'll teach you everything I know."

"That shouldn't take long," Enzo said. They both laughed. "I've got some habits that—" Enzo brought his voice to a whisper. "Some of the things the Bible says not to do, I like doing them."

"I know," Eustis laughed. "Me too. But we can work on that. After all, we're part of the same spiritual team now."

"God's family," Enzo said.

"God's family," Eustis repeated.

"Me, a missionary," Enzo said with a smile. He sat on his bed and stared at the ceiling. "I guess If I'm going to be a criminal, it might as well be for a crime that is worth committing."

"True," Eustis said.

"Well, there's something we have to do."

"What's that?" Eustis asked.

"I need to get baptized, don't I?"

"Oh," Eustis said. "You're absolutely right. Great point. We should do that first thing tomorrow."

"But–" Enzo said. He scrunched his face. "I'm a little afraid to ask, but what is baptism? The Bible talks about it but doesn't give a definition." Enzo rubbed his hands against his knees. "Does it hurt? Do you have to cut any part of my body off?"

"No, not at all," Eustis said. "It's simple. I'd say a few words and dunk you under some water."

"You mean we've got to have enough water to go under?" Enzo asked.

"Sure, it's easy."

"Uh, not really."

"Why?" Eustis asked.

"Water is the most valuable commodity on Phobos. The water ration here is one and a half cups a day. It'd be cheaper to go swimming in molten gold."

"Oh, I see what you mean," Eustis said. "It's a challenge," Eustis agreed. "But we'll think of something."

CHAPTER THIRTY-FIVE

NAMED

The first night they spent in Maroon Housing was a frightening and sleepless affair. Unscrupulous voices, even screams, filled the bunk room all the hours of lights out. Sirens blared outside, and the ruckus of fist-fighting lent an eerie soundtrack to the horrid tumult in Eustis' mind.

He stared at the ceiling for hours, wondering why he was there, unable to drift off. At every insecure bewilderment, he reminded himself of Enzo's conversion, a small but worthy harvest. He hoped for more to come.

Laying on the dusty bed, Eustis gestured to bring up his cortex display. Checking the news feeds would pass the time. That's when he remembered there was no reception in Maroon Housing. He swiped the display away and stared at the ceiling in the dark. *I could talk to God,* he thought.

As he silently prayed the rest of the night away, he found some small comfort in his furry bedfellow, Tiny, Rudwick's giant cat. The enormous feline had taken up residence at Eustis' side, kneaded the blankets for hours, and now slept warmly. Despite the massive cat's frightening appearance, it was the kindest of the four. Eustis buried his fingers in the thick fur of his feline friend.

The single light at the corner of the bunkhouse clicked and buzzed to life without warning. Since Maroon Housing was buried so deep below Bezos City, this was the only indicator of the time of day. When Eustis sat up, he saw Marianna's empty bed. He stood and was about to start searching for her, but her voice came through the door before her body.

"Rise and whine," she said. Her hair was wet, and she had a towel around her shoulders.

"Are the showers warm?" Eustis asked.

"Shower doesn't work," she said. "Washed my hair in the sink. Freezing. There was a weird guy that watched me the whole time. Told him I'd punch him in the throat if he didn't go away. And I got bit by some kind of spider."

"Oh, no," Eustis said. "Want me to take a look at it?"

"Nope."

"Well, at least the sink has enough water to—"

"It doesn't," she said as she rubbed her head with her towel. "Tap doesn't work. I had to use my water bottle. Filled it up in the ship before I decompressed and shut her down. We're stuck with just what the water dispensary will give us. Water ration is only 1.2 liters. It's a desert down here."

"Oh," Eustis said. He had hoped there might be water adequate to baptize Enzo, but as the kid had said, they would have to get creative. Eustis watched Marianna for a few moments trying to gauge her mood. He got nothing, so he proceeded into uncharted skies. "Hey, I wanted to say I'm sorry."

"For?" Marianna said as she reached down and whacked a sleeping Rudwick. "Get up." She then stepped across the way and shook Enzo as well. "Time to rise."

"I've been thinking about what you said." Eustis wrung his hands as he talked to Marianna's back. "You were right. It was inconsiderate of me to get you and the others into such a tight spot without consulting you."

"Agreed," Marianna said. She was digging in her bag now.

"What time is it?" Enzo asked as he sat up but remained on his bed.

"A little after six," Eustis said. He stepped around to the side of Marianna's cot, trying to catch her eye line. "I still plan to share the gospel, but I will try to be smarter about it. I've been talking to Enzo about how we could come up with a strategy—"

"We?" Marianna said, catching the inclusive pronoun. Her eyes were wide for a second. She turned toward the kid. His hair was still in the shape his pillow had left it. "What? Are you a religionist now?"

"What's going on?" Enzo asked through a wide yawn. He rubbed his eyes. "I don't answer questions until nine." Rudwick winced at the mention of his least favorite number.

"Whatever," she said. She stepped over Striker, who had been sleeping on the foot of Enzo's mattress but now was stretching in the pathway. After slapping Rudwick once more, Marianna threw her backpack over her shoulder.

"What be the nature of such unwelcome intrusion into me slumber?" Rudwick said. He shoved his cat, Beverly Gertrude Lewis, to the side as he sat on his mattress. His feet hung off the end. The feline rolled to the center of the bed on account of the deep depression Rudwick's weight made in its contour.

"Listen up," Marianna said. "We can't just sit around for four months. We'll starve. Each of you needs to go find a job in town today." She turned to Rudwick and pointed her finger. "Nothing illegal. We can't afford the attention."

"What kind of jobs are there?" Eustis asked.

"Nothing fun," Enzo said. "Could probably get some bills for scrubbing the scuz tank on a scum trawler."

"What's that?"

"Don't ask," Marianna cut in before the kid could give his explanation. "It's just temporary. And remember, fake names only. Don't give your personal info to anyone."

"We be in need of code names," Rudwick said.

"No," Marianna said.

"Henceforth, I be addressed as first mate Bluffkin Blusterbang III, but me mates call me Hammer Hand."

"No, we're not going to do that," Marianna tried but Enzo was already gaining a head of steam.

"You're not the first mate," Enzo said as he pointed at Beverly Gertrude Lewis, who was licking her paw. "That fur ball is in charge of more than you are."

"It be a fictitious namenculture, lad."

"It's *nomenclature*, you dolt," Enzo said. "I'd be happy to call you Rusty Finger."

"I'll show you a rusty finger," Rudwick said as he raised his mechanical arm and posed it in an offensive gesture. Eustis couldn't help but laugh.

"What are you laughing at, Last Mate, Broad Bones," Enzo said in his direction. Eustis laughed once more as Rudwick joined the jest.

"Yes, but what shall we name our dear Marianna?" Rudwick asked. All three faces turned toward Marianna. Eustis didn't dare speak up, but he didn't have to. Enzo opened his mouth but didn't get the chance to name her.

"I don't think so," Marianna said. "Shut up. Get up. Get jobs!" She said as she turned and walked toward the door. It swung wide as a plume of dust settled back down to the floor.

Once she was gone, Enzo spoke up, "Oh, I've got a good one. She could be called–"

"Now, hold up," Eustis cut him off gently. "Let's give Mari some respect. She doesn't deserve to have us sitting around calling her names behind her back." Enzo looked as if he might explode, but he held his peace.

"She called you a scuz-licking mud gut while you were in jail," Enzo said.

"Nonetheless," Eustis said. "Let's be better than that."

"Be that a part of the Cripes code?" Rudwick asked.

"More or less," Eustis said. "Jesus *Christ* said, 'love one another.'"

"There be more fun in punching another," Rudwick said. "But I'll try me best to abide." They sat for a few moments with Rudwick looking as if he were a pressure vessel with a strike valve reaching its break-over point. After waiting as long as he was able, he erupted. "Nope. There be no shine in holding me peace. She's a ripe snarling Neptune tart, that Mari is. She be festooned with more flagrant faults than pass through a Titan toilet seat. As gripesome as a garden-gobbling Ganymede goat." he said. Neither Eustis nor Enzo laughed this time, though it took a powerful will to restrain for both.

"So, how did that feel?" Eustis said.

"Aww, it be no fun to bark alone. You've gone and made this old cut-throat feel a tinge of guilt. What you done such a dark act for?"

"Don't look at me," Enzo said.

"It's the amazing thing about Jesus' words. Once you hear them they get into your mind, and they won't leave you alone," Eustis said. "It's proof you have a conscience."

"The Cripes be of the dark mind maneuvers, you say? He be a hyper-terrestrial mind mingler?"

"No. It's not that at all. Quite the opposite, actually. The human mind is the dark place. Jesus is a light shining in the darkness."

"It be a pretty melody you sing, lad, but me mind be too dark a street to light with mere word lamps."

"We'll see." Eustis smiled. "I guess we better go find jobs," he said with an enthusiasm that didn't fit the arduous task.

They each rose and prepared themselves for the day. After getting ready, Rudwick pointed to Beverly Gertrude Lewis. She didn't look up as he spoke. "You be in charge. Eat all the mice you wish for. Daddy'll be back after yon voyage." With that, they walked toward the door and began to climb their way out of the tunnels that led up from Maroon Housing into the sprawling domes of Bezos City above.

Chapter Thirty-Six

PERFORMER

"What'd you find?" Marianna asked the crew as she plopped down across her bunk. They had each returned from a day of job hunting in Bezos City. The domed metropolis had been a bustling maze of activity, and Eustis felt as if his ears would never stop ringing, nor his eyes stop glowing from the incessant electricity of the tumultuous chaos above. He was happy to be back down in Maroon Housing. Far from safe, it was, but he was pleased to be away from the noise and busyness of the city above. There was something comforting in the quiet he found in the tunnels beneath it all.

"I tried to get a gig in one of those communication equipment shops in Horizon Dome," Eustis said. "No one would give me a chance since I'm not officially 'certified' in comms." He used his fingers to indicate air quotes. "Then I tried the ice mining operation in Water Dome, but they said I was too muscular. On earth, that would be a compliment, but I gathered that it's not a good thing out here."

"Nope," Enzo said. "Most born in low-G discriminate the thickness of earthers."

"So," Eustis said. "I wound up talking to the grease reclamation superintendent, and he gave me a job clearing the sieves on the grease filters," Eustis said.

"No," Rudwick said. "Eutychus be a greaser!"

"Aww, that's the worst," Enzo said. "Would have been better to get a job shucking fungal ingrown toenails at the tourist salon."

"Really?" Eustis said.

"Yeah, it's a pretty rotten job," Marianna agreed. Eustis thought he could see a slight smile stretch across her face.

"Should I quit," Eustis asked. "I could find another—"

"No!" All three said in unison. Biscuit arched his back and hissed at the sudden and loud outburst. Rudwick petted him as he explained their reaction.

"No matter how bad be the job," Rudwick said with one finger in the air. "It be deadly dumb to quit until you have got a new one."

"Actually," Enzo said. "Don't quit until you've got a new job *and* you've been paid for the last one."

"Let's make it simple," Marianna said. "Just don't quit. Word gets out you're not reliable, then even the greasers won't work you." She turned to Enzo. "What about you?"

"Scuz tank scrubber," Enzo said.

"Oh, that be too bad, lad," Rudwick said.

"They liked me because I'm small. They employ a bunch of kids from Maroon Housing. They said they'd have me crawl up in the drain lines and polish them by hand."

"Aww, sorry, kid," Marianna said. "It's—"

"I know," Enzo cut in. "It's temporary."

"At least it's something."

"What's a scuz tank?" Eustis said.

"Don't ask," Enzo said. "So, what about you, Cap?"

"I'll be working down pipe from you," Marianna said. "Sewage treatment plant."

"Oh, no!" Enzo said. "I'd hate to be you."

"That be a raw shake, lass."

"Well, that won't be fun," Eustis said, trying to get in on the round of remorse. He was beginning to see how this commiseration session was supposed to go. After a moment, all eyes turned toward Rudwick. The old swarthy cutthroat cast his eyes to the floor. "Did you find a job, Rudwick?"

"Oh, it be too ghastly to utter," Rudwick said. "Not because it be bad work, but because it be a grand opportunity for display of me skills, and I be afeared you each be envious of me good fortune."

"Well, now you really have to tell us," Enzo said, waving his hand at Rudwick's reluctance. "Out with it."

"I be abashed to say. I wish not to make you each a' greyed with jealousness."

"Come on, Rudwick," Marianna said as she sat up on her bunk. "What is it?"

"Brace yourselves." He came down to a whisper. "I be a guardian for life itself." He flourished his hand as he said it.

"Guarding life?" Enzo said. "What does that mean?"

"I be posted century near the most costly of commodities known to Phobosian man, water and wee people."

"What?" Eustis said.

"Wee people," Marianna said. "You mean genetically modified shorties?"

"No, they be the other kind." Rudwick pointed at Enzo. "Like the lad, but with more wee."

"You mean kids?" Marianna said. "Who would let you work with children? They'd have to be out of their mind."

Enzo started to laugh. They all looked at him. Through his guffawing, he said, "You mean you're a lifeguard."

"Yes, it be as I had already said, a guardian of wee lives."

"You're a lifeguard," Marianna said. "Where?"

"A body of water in the Recreation Dome," Rudwick said.

"You're a pool nanny?" Marianna said. "I'm going to be digging out solid waste from the sewage strainer while you sit by the pool!"

"You can't swim, can you?" Enzo asked. "I mean that anvil of an arm you have would sink like an anchor."

"The pool be only waist deep, lad" he said. "Old, Rudwick'll manage."

"What kind of pool is only waist-deep?" Eustis asked.

"It be very exclusive. A seven-and-under establishment," Rudwick said. "They only select from the most skilled to be the guardian of the most precious, the wee children."

"You're a lifeguard at the kidie pool," Enzo laughed as he leaned back on his bed. "How'd you land that gig?"

Rudwick picked up Striker, his genetically modified miniature cat, and pet him gently. "Took Striker along to ride upon me shoulder. Wore me best digs. Told 'em I been adrift for ages, assail upon the vast deep of blackened sky, and now me and me crew be marooned rock-side. I be scouting the domes for some industry to lay me hand upon. The kind lady took stock of me skills at a glance. Said I be a performer indeed. She had work for such a one as me."

"A performer?" Enzo said.

"It means I be perfect for *performing* the work of guardian to precious life itself, that be of the young, of course," Rudwick said.

"No," Enzo responded. "It means she thought you were putting on a show. She thought the cat and your accent were a performance you could put on for the kids. She thought you were an actor."

"It ain't so," Rudwick bellowed. "Proof I have." He reached down and opened the mouth of his duffel bag. He pulled out a wad of cloth and held it up. "To prove me industry, take privy of what treasure in weight of wardrobe she bestowed upon me. It be a fine uniform for performing the labor." He held up a pirate outfit. Enzo grabbed his stomach and laughed so hard he nearly fell off the bed. Marianna leaned forward and gestured for Rudwick to hand her the outfit. She held it up in the dim green light and smiled, trying to keep from laughing herself.

"Where exactly are you going to be working?" Marianna asked.

"It be none other than the Seven Seas Water Park," he said, but the tone of confidence in his voice was waning. "For me extensive experience and skills, I be tasked with the laborious job of guarding—"

"You're a party clown at a pirate-themed kiddie pool for the children of insanely rich tourists," Enzo howled with laughter. Rudwick looked at the costume for a moment, scratched his head, and plopped down on his bed. He stared at the floor.

"Oh, Rudwick be a crestfallen man," Rudwick said.

"And now Rudwick gonna be a costumed *man*," Enzo laughed. Rudwick buried his face in his hands.

"Sounds like a wonderful job to me," Eustis said, rising to his feet. "I'd trade you for your job anytime."

"Me too," Marianna said as she tossed the costume at Rudwick's bag. Enzo stopped laughing for a moment.

"So would I," Enzo said. "Except I don't think I'd fit into the parrot costume." He started with another round of laughter.

"Hey," Eustis said as he snapped his fingers. "Enzo, he works at a pool." He stared at Enzo, who let his laughter trail off.

"Now, even Euticus be rubbing in the sea salt to me wound," Rudwick said.

"No, I'm not," Eustis said. "This is great news. Enzo, you want to be baptized, right?"

"Well, yes, but...."

"Now we have our place," Eustis said. "Waist-deep water is all we need."

"Come on," Enzo said. "They don't let people like us into Recreation Dome."

"Unless you're dressed up like a pirate," Eustis said.

"Not a good idea," Marianna said. "Remember that jail cell?"

"How it be," Rudwick said to himself as he hung his head. "That Old Rudwick's fierce countenance could mutiny so frightful he be mistaken as a party favor for splash happy fatlings?" He took no note that the conversation was moving on without him.

"Think about it," Eustis said to Marianna. "We need a pool. He's got one." He patted Rudwick on the shoulder. "What's a little cloak and dagger to you guys? You're the best in the biz, aren't you?"

"Nope," Enzo said. "Pretty much the worst there is. In fact, I can't remember our last successful haul. Oh, let's see. When was it? Was it that bee job? Oh yeah. That's right, captain catastrophe over here really–"

"Don't start in on that again," Marianna jabbed. They began bickering as Rudwick mumbled to himself.

"How do an old pirate like mighty Rudwick regain his stature," Rudwick said. "There be something missing in me life. Where be the swash-buckling adventure and intrigue? Where be the plundering and pillaging and booty?"

"Well," Eustis said, rubbing his chin. He was pacing now. Marianna and Enzo were in a full-out argument about how many Gs a bee colony could survive, and Rudwick was muttering to himself about robbery and mur-der. "Rudwick," Eustis cut in. "What if instead of a pirate-costumed party clown, you were actually a spy in disguise, bidding your time, watching for a chance to let your crew mate come get baptized in the most exclusive section of Bezos City, the kiddie pool at Seven Seas Water Park?" Eustis was smiling wide as he made the offer. Rudwick looked up at Eustis and framed his eyes with a furrowed brow.

"It do have a ring of genuine piracy to it," Rudwick said. Enzo and Mar-ianna stopped their debate about the structural integrity of invertebrates and tuned back into the conversation. "This bat sighting you speak of, do it involve murder?"

"Well, *baptism*," Eustis said, overemphasizing the correct pronuncia-tion. "Is a symbol of dying to your old self and rising again in Christ."

"Ahhh," Rudwick shouted. All four of his cats looked up at him. "The Cripes be into murder and the making of zombies?"

"It's not exactly like you're thinking," Eustis said.

"Nonetheless, I be in the mood for a good drowning."

"Drowning while being baptized is extremely rare," Eustis said.

"But a possibility?"

"I think the danger is more related to what happens if we get caught," Eustis said.

"Do tell the grimness of it."

"If we're caught we could probably be—" Eustis looked to Enzo and put his hands up. "What?"

"Um, I don't know. What do you think?" Enzo said, looking toward Marianna.

"They'll murder you," Marianna said. "They'll send your bodies to reclamation, and turn you into plant food."

"It be perfect," Rudwick said. "How do we do it?"

"This is a really bad idea," Marianna said. Eustis ignored her.

"We plan, we pray," he said. "And when the time is right, we act."

Rudwick puffed out his chest and looked off into the middle distance with a gleam in his eyes. "So we shall prey upon the unwitting naves with a bat sighting, water murder, zombie thingy!"

CHAPTER THIRTY-SEVEN

GROWING

The weeks that followed were filled with hard disgusting day labor. They each returned in the respective filth of their occupation, all but Rudwick that is. After work, when the artificial evening was setting in the domes above, they would collect their water ration from the dispensary and head down through the eerie tunnels below the city. Once they were at the subterranean bunk house, they would divide up whatever they had left from their food stock and share a pitiful meal.

Since there was no data reception in the Maroon cave, they couldn't do what the uppers did: stare at their visual overlay for hours while avoiding human interaction. Instead, they talked late into each melancholy night until their eyes were too heavy to remain open. The conversation would eventually turn toward Enzo's questions about the Bible.

"But if He's God, why would he have to die?" Enzo asked during one of their late-night conversations. "Couldn't he just rewrite the rules and give everyone eternal life?" The sound of kids playing outside drifted in through the cracked door.

On the adjacent bunk, Rudwick was pretending to straighten the things in his bag. Since he had folded and refolded his socks five times, Eustis suspected he wanted to listen but was too proud to be caught paying attention.

"Rudwick, why don't you join us," Eustis said.

"Oh, I be too busy with..." Rudwick trailed off. "Outrageous busyness tasks, indeed." He went about a sixth sock folding. He stole glances at Enzo and Eustis throughout the remainder of their conversation.

Two stray children ran through the bunkhouse and slammed into the door, swinging it into a wide arc that impacted the wall. Eustis watched the kids disappear into a dust cloud outside before he turned his attention back to those before him.

"Marianna," Eustis said. She was lying on her bed, facing the other direction. She grunted in response. Eustis took that as a good sign. "Do you want to join us?"

"Yeah," Marianna said. "About as much as I want to clear another jammed sewage strainer." She didn't turn over. Eustis gave his attention back to Enzo.

"As for your question, Enzo. I'm not sure what Jesus *can* and *can't* do," Eustis said. "But He's called 'the lamb that was slain before the foundation of the world.' That seems to imply that even before mankind rebelled, He knew that it would happen, and he had planned on dying for our sins."

"Ok, but—" Enzo started to say, but the sound of the bunkhouse door cut him off. A young girl walked shyly into the room and paused about five steps away from where they sat.

"Hey, Enzo," the girl said. "Want to come play?" She was a scrawny girl, dust-covered, though her eyes were bright and shined a luminous blue that cut through the eerie light of the bunk room. Through the half-open door behind her, a half dozen other kids were kicking a rock around the central yard of Maroon Housing. In the low gravity, it flew higher with each pass.

"Enzo," Eustis said. "Who's your friend?"

"This is Liddy," Enzo said. "She works the same scuz tanks as me."

"Hey, Liddy," Eustis said, giving a simple wave. The girl studied the man with skeptical eyes.

"We're playing asteroids and aliens," Liddy said, offering the comment as if it presented a prodigious incentive for participation.

"Uhh," Enzo said to Liddy as he glanced back toward Eustis. "We're kind of in the middle of something."

"It's fine if you want to go play," Eustis said.

"There be plenty of time to play later," Rudwick said. "Now, be time for Cripes lessons."

"I thought you were too busy to pay attention," Enzo said. Rudwick huffed as he dragged the contents of his bag back onto his bed to start all over.

"Thanks, but I don't think I want to play right now," Enzo said to the waiting girl. She spun and moved toward the door. Once she was past the passageway, Eustis spoke up.

"Why don't you want to play with them?"

"They're kicking a rock. It's kid stuff."

"They don't always kick a rock, but you always turn them down," Eustis said. "You know, eventually, they're going to stop asking you to play."

"Well, better that than the other way around," Enzo said.

"What do you mean?"

"It's nothing."

"What?"

"I don't like to talk about it," Enzo said.

"I'm going to keep asking until you do, so save yourself the annoyance and spill it." Enzo took a long reluctant breath before he began to speak.

"Before my family—" Enzo seemed to choke on the word. "Before everything changed, I went to this prep school on Mercury. It was all the kids of Dad's colleagues. Politicians, GovCorp executives, famous research scientists, jerks, basically. Because of who Dad was, they expected me to be, well, you know, like them.

"I made friends with a kid named Tim. Son of a GovCorp account manager. Before I knew it, he was telling everyone I had a photographic memory, which isn't what it's called. Suddenly I became the school science experiment. Kids would flash pages of text in front of my face and say, 'what did it say?'

"At first, I played along because it was kind of nice to get some attention. But after a while, I noticed that being friends with Tim changed too. Suddenly it was like he was my talent agent for a talent I didn't really want on display. He just wanted to show me off. To him and everyone else, I was just a gimmick. Kids are the worst. Grown-ups aren't much better, but at least adults have something to lose, so you can usually figure out how to get them to go away. Kids are relentless once they know your secret."

When Enzo was quiet for a long moment, Eustis said, "Thanks for sharing that with me."

"Yeah, it was a real gift, I'm sure."

"Is Tim one of those kids out there?" Eustis asked after letting the moment of sarcasm pass.

"Well, no."

"Are any of your classmates out there?"

"I wish. This place would be a perfect punishment for those stuck-up jerks."

"When Rudwick was a wee one," Rudwick said. "He was mighty popular for his good looks and powerful physicalness."

"Thanks, that makes me feel great," Enzo said.

"Me as well," Rudwick agreed.

"I know what we need to do," Eustis said. He rose from his bunk and walked toward the door.

"What are you doing?" Enzo asked, sounding nervous.

"What was her name?" Eustis asked.

"Liddy," Enzo offered. "What are you about to do?"

Eustis stepped through the bunkroom door and disappeared outside. They could hear the sound of Eustis calling Liddy's name. Then the noise of the kid's play died down. The hush brought Enzo to his feet.

"What is he doing?" Enzo asked. A muffled conversation was taking place outside the door.

"Something idiotic, I'm sure," Marianna said from where she was pretending to sleep.

CHAPTER THIRTY-EIGHT
STORY

Enzo and Rudwick watched the door, listening to the voices outside. Eustis had stepped out, mid-conversation. The mystery of his exit was quickly unraveled by Rudwick.

"He be wrangling the wees."

"Oh, no!" Enzo said. He sat back down on his bed and then stood up once more. He yanked his shirt to straighten it. Eustis burst through the door with seven of the dirtiest children following in his wake. Their clothes were torn. Their hair was long and unkempt. There were few shoes among the group.

Eustis returned to his bunk, and the parade of children surrounded the place. Some sat on beds. Others took up places on the floor. Rudwick's cats mingled among the children, opportunistically seeking a scratch. The kids were supplied with giggles to match. Rudwick rudely closed his things in his duffle and cinched it tight.

"Get off my bed," Marianna said in an acidic voice to the child who had made her mattress his couch.

"What are we doing?" Enzo whispered with wide eyes.

"I told them we could do a storytime," Eustis said. They cheered at the words. "Now, let's see how my memory is. This is Liddy Carpenter." Eustis pointed to the girl and then went down the line. "Ava Sikes, Brad, Billy, and Bobby Gaines. Brothers, of course." The kids snickered. "This is Eddy and Samantha Crabbe. You guys aren't related, are you?" The look-alike siblings laughed as did the rest of the kids.

"What about me?" A little voice asked from behind Eustis. She was hidden in the shadow of his bunk.

"Oh, I'm sorry, sweetie," Eustis said. He put his hands to his head and pretended to squeeze. "Your name is Jewels—uh. Well, I'm sorry, Jewels, I've forgotten your last name."

"I doesn't have a last name," Jewels said.

"Her parents left here when she was three," Eddy Crabbe said. "She don't know her lastie. We just call her Jewels, cause she's the best pickpock-et."

"Jewelry my favorite," Jewels smiled.

"How do you remember all our names?" Ava Sikes asked.

"It's just a little trick I use to remember names. Maybe I'll teach you sometime. But you know who has a really great memory?" Eustis asked. Enzo's eyes went to the floor. Clearly appalled that Eustis was going to use him as a gimmick.

"Who?" the kids begged.

"A man named Jesus," Eustis said. At the words, Enzo looked up immediately and smiled. "Jesus has known all of your names from the time you were born."

"Who's Jesus?" Liddy asked.

"That's who we are going to hear a story about—" Eustis said, but one of the kids cut him off.

"What's your name?" Brad Gaines asked.

"I'm sorry, did I forget to introduce myself? I'm Eustis Grimes. This is Enzo Gatti. The big guy is Rudwick Nuske, and that sleeping lady there is Marianna Byrne." Eustis put his hand to his mouth and whispered loud enough to be heard. "But I'm not sure she's really sleeping." At the words, Marianna got up from her bed and headed toward the door wordlessly. The kids didn't notice, but Eustis's eyes followed her.

"What happened to your arm?" Bobby Gaines asked. Rudwick puffed his chest out and spoke in a fairy tale tone.

"Me and me crew mate were in a firefight with the Neptunian Scourge when a plasma cannon from a space squid tore a hole in the hull of me ship and severed me arm at the shoulder. All the air were being sucked into the darkness outside. We would be sucked into the black void of space, except for one thing," Rudwick leaned down and whispered. "Do you know what saved Old Rudwick?"

"What?" they all cried in unison.

"As everything not bolted down were sucked out, me blood spurting stump flew across the cabin, jammed the hole in me ship, and clogged the leaking air. When I tried to pull me arm free from the hole, it had already become part of the ship and tried to choke me." Rudwick pantomimed the rogue hand around his neck, making a sickly choking sound. The kids howled with delight. "When I got free, I shook the ship's new hand, which used to be mine, and started the search for a fresh one of me own." He clenched his robotic arm into a fist as the kids clapped, screeching with joy and disbelief, and begged for more. A half dozen questions were fired at Rudwick. He turned and pretended to be busy with his duffle bag once more, but Eustis could see a smile stretching across his face.

"Well, that was quite a story," Eustis said. "Would you guys like to hear another?"

"Yes!" They shouted.

"This one isn't a tall tale like Rudwick's. This actually happened."

"Do it have a cut-off arm," Jewels asked. "Cut off arms is my favorite." Though his back was turned, Eustis noticed Rudwick bouncing with laughter.

"No, this one is about someone named Jesus,"

"What did he do?" Liddy asked. Eustis turned to Enzo.

"Enzo, why don't you tell them your favorite Jesus story?"

"There's more than one story?" Bobby Gaines said.

"Uh–yes," Enzo said. "There are lots." Every eye turned toward Enzo. He shot a quick glance at Eustis, who nodded reassuringly. "My favorite story about Jesus? Ok. So. Once upon a time on earth..."

Enzo told three stories from the gospels. He recounted the time Jesus fed five thousand, walked on water, and healed a blind man. He quoted scriptural lines word for word while adding colorful commentary of his own between the biblical content. The children were spellbound. When Enzo had finished his Jesus stories, the kids had dozens of questions. Some of them Enzo answered, while most Eustis handled.

At a point that seemed far too soon, the light of the bunk room shut off. The red running lights, at least the few that still worked, clicked on along the decking of the floor.

"Ok, everyone," Eustis said. "That's bedtime." After a hardy cry of disappointment, the kids shuffled toward the door in the crimson shadowed darkness.

"Story time again tomorrow night," Eustis said. A round of cheers was the reply.

"Bring a friend next time," Enzo added as the kids shoved through the exit. Eustis and Enzo turned toward each other, both faces beaming. "That was awesome."

"Way to go, brother," Eustis said. "You did great!" He patted Enzo on the shoulder. When the last of the children was out the door, Marianna entered the bunk room once more. Without saying anything, she found her place on her bed.

"Aren't you going to tell us how bad of an idea our storytime was?" Enzo said.

"No," Marianna said.

"Boys, I be sad to be the barrier of bad tidings, but yon Jevus tale you spun for the wees, it certainly be tampered with," Rudwick said. "It bears all the marks of a story far exaggerated. I can say because Old Rudwick knows a thing about stretching a yarn."

"So, you were listening?" Eustis said.

"Well, between the bits where I were outrageous busy with the folding of me stockings."

"Why do you think the stories were exaggerated?" Eustis asked.

"This Jevus Cripes can't be," Rudwick said. "If a man were able to do such works, he'd be above the star gods in power. It'd mean he be magic."

"The stories Enzo told were verified by many eyewitnesses," Eustis said.

"How'd they be sure it t'weren't a hologram, or a trick of a cortex implant?"

"Jesus came before any of that existed," Eustis said. "Plus, the witnesses who saw him perform those miracles never changed their story, even when they were pressured to renege under pain of death. Most gave up their lives to prove the Jesus stories are true."

"It do fill me with mighty contractions," Rudwick said.

"Contradictions," Enzo corrected. Rudwick didn't hear him.

"Up until him," Eustis continued. "Power was almost always defined as the one with the biggest weapon, but he changed all that. Jesus had true power. Jesus was so powerful he could love those who didn't deserve it. Now that's real power."

"To feed five thousand be a mean feat," Rudwick said. "It be a power old Rudwick would fancy. No more roasted crickets."

"Who knows what Jesus can do through you," Eustis said.

"Old Rudwick don't want anything run *through* him, by your Jevus Cripes" he said. Eustis laughed, not quite sure if Rudwick was joking.

CHAPTER THIRTY-NINE

THAW

Over the next weeks, they continued to do their rotten day jobs, but Enzo, Rudwick, and Eustis looked forward to the evenings. Their story time was growing in popularity among the poor Bezos-stranded souls in Maroon Housing. The most frightening and dejected people, both children and adults, shuffled in and listened.

Sometimes Eustis had to break up fistfights or ask addicts to refrain from snorting powder while they attended. Sometimes he had to protect children from the violence that would erupt spontaneously among the adults, or break up hair-pulling matches between orphaned kids.

The attendance fluctuated, but there was a handful of regulars whom Eustis and the others got to know well. A regular group of about twenty never missed story time, and as many as a dozen new faces would amble in a night, having heard about the strangeness of the storytelling kid, the explainer, their mountainous space pirate, his gangly cats, and an aloof woman who never said anything but watched from the shadows.

Eustis always invited Enzo to tell a few stories from Jesus' life. His perfect biblical recall and comedic sensibilities made for an entertaining draw that no child could resist listening to, and hardly any grown-up either. One night someone from the crowd gave Enzo the name "The Three Story Kid," and the title stuck. A few nights later, they nicknamed Eustis "Talk Boss." This was mostly owing to the fact that Enzo told vivid picturesque stories, most often three in a row, from the gospels, and Eustis gave a *description* of the theological meaning when Enzo was done.

As of yet, no one but Enzo had become a believer, but the kinds of questions that some were asking led Eustis to believe at least a few were close.

Rudwick still didn't believe the content of the stories and insisted on calling the main character Jevus Cripes, but he never missed a story time and no longer pretended to be disinterested. Most adults avoided his scrappy cats, but the kids loved them. They couldn't get enough of Rudwick's odd mannerisms and feline friends. It wasn't long before they were calling him "Captain Rude Beard." He constantly had children begging to hang from his mechanical arm or surrounding him to get another of his non-biblical and often off-color stories. Most of his tales were contradictory fabrications about how he lost his arm. The more outlandish, the more the kids soaked them up.

Marianna watched it all from afar. Her angry demeanor had been replaced with isolation and silence. She kept her distance and rarely spoke more than a few words to Eustis or the others. She was often present for their story time but never truly attended. She listened from the edges of the strange growing community of interested story lovers. A few times, Eustis caught her looking in his direction, seeming almost to be studying him. When an entire week passed without a single cross word between them, Eustis decided he would seek out a time to talk with her.

"Can I walk you to work?" Eustis asked one morning. He had intentionally arisen an hour early so as not to miss her quiet exodus. She had a habit of slipping out before anyone had woken.

"I'm in Ross Dome," Marianna said. "It'd be way out of your way."

"That's not quite a 'no,'" Eustis said.

"Fine." She threw her bag over her shoulder and started toward the door. It would be up to him to keep up if he wanted a morning chat. He gathered his scattered things and made for the exit, charging after her. She was out of the bunk room and nearly to the tunnel entrance before he could close the gap.

"You're making me work for it," Eustis said when he caught up, already breathing hard. They were surrounded by the cave walls lit by inadequate points of low-wattage light. The cavern of rock offered an eerie backdrop for a sunrise stroll, though they hadn't seen the sun in over a month. "I said I wanted to walk with you, not chase you."

"What is there to talk about?" Marianna asked.

"A lot, actually."

"Better get started," she said. "My stop is one point three kilometers."

"I'll get right to it. I want to know how to be your friend."

"Why?" Marianna said.

"Everyone needs a hobby." he said. "I just don't know what else to do. I've tried apologizing, and you didn't like that. I've tried to talk about the situation, and you didn't seem open to it." He paused. "I've been trying to give you space."

"That *was* going well," she said.

"So, is that what you want; for me to leave you alone?" Eustis asked the question and then forced himself to stop talking, a difficult prospect when he was nervous. She didn't respond right away. She followed the curve of the tunnel into the light of Rogers Dome. As they emerged into the open space of the geodesic structure, Eustis' cortex display pinged, and news feed notifications appeared. It was tempting to look now that he had data reception, but he resisted the urge. He blinked, rubbed his eyes, and sped his pace to keep up. The daytime vendors were already hawking their wares along the dome's rim. Shouts of sales and bargains echoed in the shabby sphere.

"Do you know what I did before I had the *Scuttle*?" Marianna asked. "I mean before I had the *Resurrection*."

"Not a clue."

"You want to hear?" she said. "I can't tell 'em like the Three Story Kid."

"Of course, I want to hear."

"I was born on Titan. My parents were mineral prospectors and struck it rich before the rush filled the colony with the worst kind of people. Anyway, they had the money, so they gave me a trust fund to do whatever I wanted. When I was eighteen, I had stars in my eyes. I wanted to use my talents to change the solar system. I wanted to help people."

"That's awesome," Eustis said.

"It was dumb. I was a stupid kid."

"How?" Eustis asked.

"I joined FFSE. The Foundation For Solar Equality. You familiar with it?"

"No," Eustis said.

"It's a GovCorp volunteer program that claims to fight for social equality among the colonies of Titan, Europa, and Ganymede. I did anything they asked me to do and thought I was doing great work. After a couple of years, as I climbed up in the organization, I started to see behind the gleam. I realized the whole thing was basically a money-making scheme that lined the pockets of its officers, but none of that money, and I mean none of it, made it to the people who needed it. I jumped ship.

"Then I joined IFA, the Inner Relief Association, a non-profit that brings financial and housing relief to some of the poor colonies on the inner three. Or at least that's what its commercials claimed. I finally got certified to fly because they needed pilots. My job description was to relocate refugees who couldn't afford interplanetary travel. It was a total scam. In all of my time with them, you know how many refugees I moved?"

"I'm guessing not many."

"I was only assigned one transport of actual refugees, and that was after we received some bad press. The ship had as many reporters as refugees. Made me sick."

"You only flew once?"

"No, I flew passengers all the time, just not refugees. The organization was receiving kickbacks to transport wealthy elites who needed off-the-books trips. Hyper researchers, GovCorp officers, anyone who could pay and didn't want their trip recorded in all its corrupt and filthy detail. So, anyway, I quit when I realized what it was.

"I decided to find a smaller operation. I thought maybe the problem was the size. Maybe compassion work didn't work if the organization was too big. I joined a string of small relief groups. UNIF, BRE, TRLA, every acronym you've ever heard of. One by one, they all proved to be self-serving. I was so tired of always being the tool of the crooked. So I got stars in my eyes again.

"I decided to start my own relief organization. Solar Aid Distribution. Even the acronym was terrible."

"S A D," Eustis said.

"Pretty much says it all. I was going to do what those other organizations couldn't. I was going to do true compassion work. I cashed in that trust fund and bought my own ship. This was before the *Scuttle*," She said. "It was a beautiful new Ford Emperion Seven. Cherry red with black trim. It could transport a load of twenty-nine with a crew of six."

"Sounds nice," Eustis said.

"I did a couple of refugee runs before I realized the problem. It all comes down to funding. Refugees have a surprising inability to pay for services. So, I started taking side jobs to pay for the compassion runs. I had to. Otherwise, I couldn't keep gas in the tank. Before long, even legitimate jobs didn't catch enough profit for refugee work. I just wanted to help people, but I couldn't. The economy is stacked against honest work."

"Wow," Eustis said.

"So, there was this guy on Titan. Had a face that looked like he was in love with a crab. He saw my ship at the docks. Tracked me down and offered me my first shadow job."

"Shadow job?" Eustis asked.

"A black market run. Weapons. Ironic, right? Without the weapons flying around, we probably wouldn't need to move refugees. Anyway, I nearly passed out when he told me the payout. I did it, and it was a clean run. I got an insane payday, and I told myself I'd only do the one, and then it was refugees from then on. Then expenses changed, and I found myself back with Crabface. If I was smart, I would have seen I was already stuck, but like I said, I was stupid. I did more. The stupid stacked up." Marianna paused and looked up at the entrance to the water treatment facility. "This is my stop."

"No!" Eustis said. "You can't leave me hanging. What happened?" Marianna took a deep breath and bit her lip.

"I got caught. My ship was flagged for smuggling and impounded with no release option."

"What a punch in the gut," Eustis said.

"I lost everything. But I learned a lesson that was worth it all."

"What's that?"

"There is no true compassion in this messed-up Sol system. Everyone is just smiling while they pick your pocket."

"I totally disagree," Eustis said.

"I know you do."

"God's compassion is true, and it's here," Eustis said.

"I know you believe that." Marianna rubbed her palm across her forehead. "See, that's what makes me crazy about this whole thing. I see my old self in you, or I guess I mean my younger self. You've got stars in your eyes. You think you can help people. You can't. You won't. But you're so insanely stubborn you're not going to believe anything I say. You'll have to learn for yourself."

"And by *learn,* you mean...." Eustis said.

"Look, your storytime seems innocent now. It's nice. It brings some joy to those sad people. But I know how this thing ends. Word's going to get out, and they're going to come down on you like an anti-matter bomb. They're going to kill you, and I don't want to be here when they do."

"You're free to leave if that's what you need to do," Eustis said. "I mean, I don't want you to, but no one will hold it against you."

"No, that's not what I mean," Marianna said.

"Then what do you mean?"

"I'm not trying to escape. I'm trying not to care." She braved a second of eye contact, held it, and whispered, "But you're making it hard."

"But—"

"I'm going to be late if I don't go," Marianna said. Without another word, she turned toward the treatment plant and walked inside. Eustis closed his eyes and took a deep breath before beginning his walk toward the grease reclamation operation at the other end of Bezos City. He was certainly going to be late, but he didn't care. He had plenty to think about.

CHAPTER FORTY

IGNORED

"Bring the boys online, and have them assemble for inspection," Admiral Strafe growled. He had intended to make his way to Musk City and continue his search there, but with HEXA's report of the incompetence of Chancellor Montobond of Bezos City, he couldn't rule out the likeliness that Eustis Grimes was hiding like a cockroach on that crumbling rock. It would be easier to stop at Phobos before descending into the Martian environ, so that is what they would do.

"Yes, Sir," HEXA said. "How many do you—"

"All of them," he said.

"Even the scorch unit," HEXA asked. Strafe just stared at the hologram as if clarifying his instructions would detract from its strength.

"Of course," HEXA said to himself. "Stupid question. Bringing them online now."

"And set a course for Bezos City,"

"Yes, Sir," HEXA repeated.

"We have a religionist in Bezos, and that petrified dome-nanny won't ferret him out. So, I'm going to get the job done and destroy him."

"Sir," HEXA said. "Technically, we're not allowed to perform a tactical extraction from Bezos without authorization from—" He stopped talking mid-sentence. "You already know that," he said. "You have a plan."

Instead of answering the implied question, Strafe said, "Notify Madam Styx I will be arriving for a *personal* visit."

"Sir?" HEXA said. "Do you mean Madam Electra Styx, Chief Alien Liaison of Bezos City?"

"Yes!" Strafe turned and looked out the viewing hatch of his ship. *The Scorpion III* was only a few days out from an insertion burn for Mars Orbit. The change in course wouldn't add much time. Strafe muttered idly to himself. "I'm going to boil him in his own fluids."

"Your personal guard is online and ready for inspection. I'm signing them over to your voice command now."

"Right," Strafe said. He stepped toward the bridge exit and followed the corridor to the barracks compartment. A red glow issued from the bank of running lights at the head of the compartment. The room was filled with two dozen robotic soldiers cast in terrifying crimson shadows. "Attention!" Strafe shouted.

The cacophony of metallic footsteps clanged against the deck. The floor shook with the reverberation of the unified footfall. HEXA's hologram came up behind and took his post at the hatch opening.

"You rolled back their firmware as I instructed?" Strafe said.

"Yes, Sir," HEXA responded. "Their AI has been reverted. They will do whatever you ask without the updated restrictions."

"At ease!" Strafe shouted. The line of algorithmically intelligent soldiers relaxed into a broad position, and the room fell silent. At first glance, one could almost mistake the humanoid drones for men, though they would be enormous. However, these war machines were no more men than a rocket bomber was a sparrow. They were as conscious as a machine was legally allowed to be, but with the recent software rollback, they had nothing so ridiculous as a programmed conscience. *Machines with hearts, how stupid could you be?* Strafe thought.

"Soldier," Strafe said to the nearest unit. "State your O.S. version."

"GovCorp Security Drone Protocol Version 21.3.7, Sir." The robot's voice could have been mistaken for a man's, but behind the numbers burned the digital makeup of a cold unthinking killer. Just like the good old days. Strafe walked through the rank of robots and looked at each in turn. When he was satisfied, he returned to the hatch of the barracks compartment and addressed his force.

"Alright, boys," Strafe commanded. "To your hangars. We'll be dropping in before you know it." The man-shaped drones lifted themselves into their storage harnesses. The last to strap in was the flame-throwing soldier unit, characterized by a bulky backpack and fuel lines that led to throttled fire nozzles. He couldn't wait to unleash his super-mech soldiers on Bezos City.

"I'm going to pulverize that religionist cockroach," he muttered through what passed for a smile.

CHAPTER FORTY-ONE

PAYDAY

The first payday came after four weeks of grueling and disgusting work. It couldn't have come a minute too soon since their food stock had completely run out two and a half days earlier. On his walk back to Maroon Housing, Eustis felt like he could have floated up to touch the top of Bezos Dome. Apparently, it was payday for Marianna, Rudwick, and Enzo as well because he could hear their laughter as he approached the bunkhouse.

Enzo was singing the phrase "Payday" repeatedly as he spun in place. Rudwick was lying on the gross floor rubbing faces with his cats. Marianna caught him with a smile as he walked to his bed. He paused and stared back, confirming what he saw. *Yep,* sure as the moon was round, she had smiled at him.

"So, lads, and lass, what be our entertainment for this outrageous achievement?" Rudwick asked. "I be in need of a drink from Gruff's Fluids."

"You've never had just *one* drink," Enzo laughed.

"That be true, lad," Rudwick agreed as he rose from the floor covered in filth. Marianna dusted him off. "Be in need of *five.*"

"A steak dinner sounds good," Marianna said. "I don't care if it's synthetic."

"If we pooled our money, would we have enough to turn the air, water, and lights back on, and move back to the ship?" Enzo asked. He gestured toward Eustis. "How much did you make?"

"I don't have reception down here," Eustis said.

"It's black-linked," Enzo said as if it should have been obvious. "It should have downloaded before you came into the tunnel. Check it."

Eustis gestured for his display, and sure enough, his heads-up display had a financial notification waiting for his attention. "Alright. I made a little over fourteen hundred," Eustis said.

"Twelve hundred," Marianna said.

"Nine hundred fifty," Enzo said. They all looked at Rudwick. His lips were pursed. "Come on, big guy. How much did you make?"

"Don't be embarrassed, every bit counts," Marianna said.

"That's right, Rudwick. You've worked hard, just like the rest of us," Eustis said.

"Ok," Rudwick said. "Me take was the dreaded twisty six. Bad luck, to be sure."

"Nine hundred," Enzo said. "That's ok. That's ok. It's about what I made."

"How many digits be nine hundred?" Rudwick said.

"It's a nine then two zeros behind it," Marianna said. "It's ok. That helps. You did your part."

"Ashamed I say it. I be worth less than the nine hundred," Rudwick said.

"Ninety?" Enzo said. "Now that's a rip-off! What are they trying to pull?"

"Rudwick, what were the exact numbers on your pay stub?" Eustis asked. He made a gesture and was apparently looking at the stub because his eyes were scanning through mid-air.

"Ahh, here it be," He said. "They've given me almost nothing. Only a nine, and the rest be zeros."

"How many?" Enzo said. "Read it out."

"It be a nine, then a zero, then another zero, then another cursed zero."

"How many zeros are before the decimal?"

"I see no decilitral," Rudwick said. He made a sharing gesture and the image came up on Enzo's personal display. "Read it for yourself. I be a failure!"

"Rudwick, you invaluable monstrosity!" Enzo said. "You made nine thousand bills. What do they have you doing at that kiddie pool?"

"No way!" Marianna said. Enzo gestured to share it with the rest. Rudwick was the last to understand.

"What be the jest?" Rudwick asked.

"Buddy, you made ten times as much as any of us. You have the best job in Bezos City."

"Hear that, kitties? Daddy done good!" Rudwick celebrated. Enzo danced in a circle, as Rudwick rubbed faces with his cat. Eustis took a chance and spread his arms wide for a hug.

Marianna rolled her eyes but then said, "fine." She gave him a quick hug but then shoved him off playfully with a laugh. He hugged the others in turn.

"We have plenty of money to move back to the ship," Marianna said. The celebration died down slowly as the words sunk in. Eustis looked around at the bunk room considering what it would feel like to walk out of this place. It would feel good, very good. But.

A second later the door of the bunk room burst open with a dozen children. Some went straight for the purring cats who would soak up as much attention as the kids would give them. Others came in shouting, "Captain Rude Beard, tell us how you lost your arm." This was their daily greeting to the big man.

The three Gaines brothers surrounded Eustis and began peppering him with questions about last night's Jesus story. Enzo was captured by Liddy and Ava who had a story request. Jewels came up to Marianna and tugged on her hand. Marianna looked down at the little smudge-covered face. "When you going to tell a story, quiet lady?" Jewels said. For the next few minutes, they were each bombarded with kids vying for their attention and affection.

When the chaos reached critical mass, Rudwick came over to Eustis and caught him by the arm a little too hard. He tilted his head toward the door. Eustis followed. When they were out of the eye of the storm, Rudwick said, "It be a mighty temptation to move back to the ship. Would be a swell thing indeed. A hot shower. A not-dusty bed be tremendous." Eustis opened his mouth as if he would interrupt, but Rudwick put his hand up, and Eustis paused. "We could do it to be true, but Old Rudwick be thinking mighty thoughts with a new compass bearing."

After the big man had laid out his secret plan and Eustis approved with gusto, they called Marianna and Enzo over. Kids swirled around like a storm trying to hear what the grown-ups were talking about. They shared a rushed conversation above the vying faces.

"It's not a good idea," Marianna said. "You'd be better off spending your nine thousand at Gruff's Fluids."

"I like it," Enzo agreed.

"I think it's a great idea," Eustis said. "I'm in."

"Of course, you're in," Marianna argued. "You've never said no to a lead-headed idea."

"It be a better endeavor if we be united, lass," Rudwick said.

"You know, you used to call me Captain," she said. "If we do this we won't have the cash to move back to the ship. We'll have to wait another month in this rotting hole."

"Rudwick be happy in yon hole," he said. The three watched Marianna as she considered. Her body language communicated her disapproval.

"We are going to attract attention and we need to keep it small and quiet," Marianna said.

"Alright!" Eustis said.

"She's in." Enzo pumped his fist.

"Ahh, lass, you make warm this old hungbuzzled heart." He wrapped his arms around Marianna and lifted her off the ground, spinning her around.

"That's enough," she said as she wriggled free of the old pirate's grip. When he had set her down, the others caught the faintest trace of a smile despite her best attempt to mask it. When the conference was concluded, Eustis stepped out from the huddle and put his hands in the air. The kids hushed in eager silence.

"Everyone," he said. "The leadership council of storytime," he glanced back at his crew with a wink. "Has decided to make tonight a special storytime. Here's what we want you to do."

He then explained the plans for the evening, which the children could hardly believe. Before he was done, the kids were bouncing around the room like hydrogen ions. He instructed them to return in three hours with as many people as they could find among the bunk rooms of Maroon Housing. He dismissed all but ten of them, telling them he had a task for them. The rest ran out shouting the word about the special story time planned for three hours hence.

"So much for keeping it quiet," Marianna said.

Once they had run from the room, Eustis said, "Mari, you're the one with relief experience. How do we pull this off?" It looked as if she would resist, but her mean exterior broke.

"Fine," she said. "If we're going down, we might as well enjoy the descent." She quickly made a verbal list of provisions they would need. Rudwick divided up the children to go along to help carry what they would soon be bringing back. They made their way to the upper domes to buy everything needed for the occasion.

In two hours, they returned with their ten volunteer children carrying bulging bags of steaming items. They entered the bunkhouse. Eustis organized the volunteers to help with preparations. They overturned beds in an attempt to create the surfaces they would need. Mari and Enzo emptied the bags and laid out the items. Marianna took on a satisfied demeanor as she organized the entire affair. The vision of a joyful Marianna captured Eustis for a moment until she brought him out of his trance.

"Hey, Talk Boss," she said, clapping her hands toward him. "It's ready."

"Oh, right," Eustis said. "I'll go let them in."

CHAPTER FORTY-TWO

FEAST

When a little after three hours had passed, Eustis stepped out onto the front landing of the bunkhouse and addressed the large crowd that had gathered. He recognized some of the people from their nightly story time, but most were strangers. The crowd of faces demonstrated an array of varied expressions. Many wore rags that would have done little to keep them warm in the chilly caves beneath Phobos' surface. Knobby bones, sunken cheeks, pale sallow skin, and darkened eyes were prominent among the hungry hoard.

"Thank you for coming," Eustis said to the crowd. He had to raise his voice to its maximum to be heard. "I wish we could afford to do this more often, but we haven't had the means. However, what we do have, we would like to share with you. Tonight we feast!" The crowd cheered. When the sound died down, he said, "Before we do, I will return thanks."

"Return?" someone shouted. "We just got here!"

"No. What I mean is, we need to pray for the food," Eustis said.

"We need to pay for the food?" another grumbled.

"No you don't," he said. "I'll thank the Lord for what he has given us." Eustis bowed his head and said a prayer.

"What's he doing?" a woman said. Others echoed the question. Eustis kept the prayer short and hoped it was intelligible to at least some.

After Eustis said, "Amen," he looked at the door behind him. Enzo was standing halfway out watching Eustis' invocation.

"Here they come," Enzo said over his shoulder and then disappeared into the bunk room where Marianna was ready for the crowd.

Eustis stepped up and opened the door. Before him, a buffet of food was laid out on the upturned beds. The starving people could hardly afford the smell, not to mention the astoundingly expensive feast.

There had never been such fine dining in Maroon Housing, never so much joy shared beneath the domes of the city. Unless one was willing to spend a fortune, synthetic meat was all that was available in Bezos. However, Rudwick's massive paycheck had borne most of the burden of the feast's incredible price tag.

Real imported beef from Earth was included in the Europa-style pierogi and beef rouladen from a vendor in Little Titan. Enzo had found an authentic Bourguignon in the Callisto quarter. Eustis had gone for something with chicken, which was in short supply, but for a frivolous price, tube-grown poultry from Enceladus was the finest substitute on the market.

He discovered a Ganymedian chef in Dresden Dome who offered chicken pot roast, arroz con pollo, and a large pan of chicken souvlaki with spices from Mars. They had pies, connolis, and strudels. There was cream of mushroom, Mercury bean, and corn chowder imported from Earth. Where a simple slice of bread was a meal, the extravagant and eclectic offerings were a gorgeous feast, the likes of which overawed the gaunt feasters.

The ravenous crowd poured into the room, which was already claustrophobic, bordering on stifling. Seeing the congestion, Marianna told Rudwick to direct the traffic. He ushered the attendees through the food line and had them move toward the exit. At least a hundred and fifty people swept through the buffet, gathering heaping plates of food usually only available in a tourist dome or the GovCorp dignitary inns of Bezos Dome.

Since the room could not hold the feasting hoard, Rudwick directed them to find places to sit in the courtyard at the exterior of the bunkhouse. The noise dwindled to a light chatter as most of the mouths were full of the exquisite meal beyond any they had likely ever had. Eustis and the crew were the last to fill a plate. They emerged from the bunk room doors and found a spot in the packed courtyard. Eustis imagined the low-slung cave ceiling as if it were Earth's sky dotted with a million twinkling stars in autumn. When Rudwick found a place, a scurry of children relocated so they could sit next to the big man.

"Can we have a story from Three Story Kid?" Jewels shouted. She had not joined the circle, which had taken up spots around Captain Rude Beard. Instead, she had taken a seat next to the mysterious and aloof Marianna, where no other children dared go.

Eustis swallowed and said, "Great idea." Enzo stood, handed his plate to Eustis, and climbed up on the front steps of the bunkhouse. A smattering of light applause issued from the crowd, but most did not clap. When the few who recognized him let their clapping die down, he began. His voice felt warm and full as he reached out and touched everyone with his words.

"There once was a man who lived long ago on Earth, but he was not just any ordinary man." Enzo continued with the story, deftly maneuvering into the time Jesus cleared the Temple. Eustis let his attention drift across the spellbound audience. Eyes were wide with amazement. Bellies were being filled with the best food that maroon dwellers had ever tasted. Minds were being filled with God's word, which Eustis knew to be a greater feast still.

Enzo then effortlessly transitioned into the story of Jesus healing the man born blind. It was as if Eustis, too, had new eyes with which he was seeing for the first time. How had he found such a capable and talented kid? What other child of so few years could do what Enzo was doing? There was probably not another like him in the Sol system.

His perfect recall of Scripture and his effortless comedic timing made him solely unique. It was too much to be a coincidence. The beauty of Enzo's stories was in the details. He commanded emotion with the little flourishes he placed alongside the known material, always careful to stay within narrative boundaries. Although Eustis knew the stories by heart, he was always translated into another realm with Enzo's visual style and story craft. The crowd laughed together as Enzo sang out a humorous note from the melodic story. Eustis silently thanked the Lord for the Three Story Kid, his partner in this criminal endeavor, and his dear friend.

Rudwick's laugh could be heard above all else. Eustis' stare turned toward the old swashbuckler, who was absolutely festooned with adoring children. How had the old death dealer become such a life-giver? There were many among the crowd that looked as if they might have soon starved, but this feast–conceived and paid for by Rudwick–would be the very thing that would prolong their lives.

Rudwick's eyes were as big as Mars as he listened to Enzo's story. He had even stopped stroking his lap cat Striker. The children around him stole fleeting glances up at the bearded space pirate, taking cues from his rapt attention. They followed his listening lead and stayed closely tuned to Enzo. Eustis silently prayed that tonight might be the night Rudwick would finally believe the ancient truth being unlocked by Enzo's majestic words.

Eustis' eyes moved cautiously toward Marianna as if even a glance at her might unsettle the tremulous balance they had recently struck. She was sitting at the edge of the crowd but not alone. Jewels, the tiny parentless pickpocket, had found a place next to Marianna and now was sidling up to her, leaning sleepy-eyed into Marianna's personal space. The smudge-covered child burrowed beneath Mari's arm and found a warm place to close her eyes, a matronly lap like the one she had lost to the treachery of space so long ago.

Marianna looked down, pausing for a moment's hesitation—arm hang-ing in the air—before she laid her hand on the poor orphan's head and caressed her hair. This was probably the first time Jewels had drifted off to sleep in the arms of a grown-up in her entire living memory. Enzo began the story of Jesus feeding the crowd of thousands as Marianna squeezed Jewels a little tighter and Eustis secretly watched on.

The intrepid missionary took a deep breath feeling that familiar tickle in his nose and around his eyes. He blinked at the trickle that swelled about his lids. He wiped his cheek as he whispered a prayer, asking that God would continue to soften Mari's heart and bring her to believe in His only Son.

Eustis turned his attention to the crowd at large. Dirty children and adults alike, love-starved from birth, each now basking in an unknown warmth that came from a world away. God loved each, he knew, but it was Eustis who was here to explain that love. He prayed another silent prayer asking that the God of the Cosmos would direct his words.

"Thank you," Enzo said after concluding the story. His words brought Eustis out of his contemplative reverie. He set his plate aside, stood, and walked up the steps. The people who knew him clapped as Eustis–Talk Boss by title–scanned the crowd considering what he would say.

He knew as the words issued from his mouth that this was a moment of no return. Until this point, they had been cautious, even strategic, in how they shared the gospel. They spoke in whispers among small groups of mostly children. As he quoted the applicable Scripture, Eustis felt the gravity of the moment, a pull much more than Mars could ever draw down.

There would be consequences for these weighty words. He knew it in his soul. The consequences he hoped for—of people believing in the Lord Jesus—could not be disembodied from the constricting danger that a public sermon would bring. Nobody cared what a small group of children did in Maroon Housing, but this was no small group, and these unfamiliar adult faces were equipped with the most dangerous thing of all, mouths of their own. People would talk. Word would spread. Consequences would come. This might be the last sermon he ever gave. It was as if he were watching it all happen from outside his body.

He had talked for about ten minutes when he came to the conclusion. "Those of you who believe in Jesus for His free gift of everlasting life, have it. You have that everlasting, irrevocable life the very moment you believe." He was about to close their time in prayer when at the edge of his peripheral vision, he spotted movement. He turned.

Rudwick stood to his feet, letting Striker fall from his lap. His brow was furrowed, eyes closed, and face pointed at the cave ceiling above. A goof-ridden grin shaped his beard into a wide grey fan. He stood in the midst of a sea of people as he put both his arms out as if he would hug the entirety of Phobos. His robotic prosthetic moaned with a mechanical whine at the wide posture. The children around his feet stared up at the man's strange interruption. The Gaines boys were clearly trying to contain their laughter, probably not sure if this was one of his odd jokes.

"I believe!" he shouted. "I believe in Jesus Christ!"

Eustis was about to say something, though he wasn't sure what when Eddy Crabbe stood next to Rudwick and said the same, not as loud, but plenty as sincere. Ava and Liddy were next. Then all three of the Gaines brothers stood and said they believed. Then Samantha joined and did the same. The sound of footsteps through the crowd turned their attention. Jewels had woken, left Marianna's side, and was now rushing to join the other kids around Rudwick. She agreed that she believed as well. Eustis had hoped that some of the adults who had come to previous story times would stand as well, but none did. A silence fell.

"This is fantastic," Eustis said. "Each of you who have believed, you now have everlasting life. Welcome to God's family!" The children cheered, as did Rudwick. The surrounding audience did not, however. The hundreds of sets of eyes were heavy upon Eustis as he bowed his head and prayed for the sheep that had just been ushered into the fold. How many of those other eyes roving over this sacred scene belonged to wolves, he did not know.

"Amen," he said after praying. As he dismissed the crowd, the mood was ambivalent. Many wandered away without a word. Some lingered and talked with one another, but Eustis' focus was on the eight new believers. As they circled up to talk together, Marianna watched from the edge of the courtyard, once again alone.

"Mates," Rudwick said. "It be high time we make way to the water."

"What?" Eustis said.

"To the Seven Seas for a bat sighting water zombie ceremony."

CHAPTER FORTY-THREE

BAPTISM

"We be needing to avoid Bezos Dome," Rudwick explained as they crept the long way around the outer rim of the adjacent dome. "It be where wary eyes roam." The Seven Seas water park was in Recreation Dome, which was on the opposite side of Bezos City. Since they had to avoid the main central dome, they had a very long walk ahead of them. The transit system ran all hours, but it too was monitored with security AI, so they avoided it.

Rudwick routed them through Rogers, Horizon, Dresden, and then Ross domes. When they finally arrived at the Recreation Dome, it was nearing the middle of lights out. Light from above the surface line shone in at the peak of the dome, but the lights on the lower levels where they were had taken on their nighttime eerie green tint.

On the walk, which had taken more than an hour on account of the seven children they had in toe, Eustis explained baptism to Rudwick and the children. All but Jewels and Bobby Gaines, the youngest of the three brothers, were determined to be baptized as well. They wanted to see the others get baptized before they decided if they would go through with it.

"Here we be," Rudwick said pausing outside a powered gate terminal. He let Bobby down from his back, where he'd been giving the little boy a ride. "Beyond these bars be the sea we seek." The kids giggled at Rudwick's words. Jewels dropped Marianna's hand and ran to the entrance. The

Seven Seas Water Park was dark and deserted, humming greenly in the dim glow.

"Don't look at me passcode," Rudwick said to the kids. "It be a secret mighty protected." He made a big show of trying to block his hand as he made the gestures to unlock the gate. As he did he sounded them out aloud pretending as if he didn't know he was doing so. "Eight, four, seven, zero." The kids laughed. "Took me weeks to remember me number. It have an eight and a roundy zero in the line up. Them be two numbers Old Rude Beard have a rivalrous feud against."

"Access Denied," the panel beeped with an unfriendly voice.

"Kid," Rudwick said. "There be mysterious words." Enzo stepped up from the back of the pack.

"Not that mysterious," Enzo said as he waved his fingers at the panel. The display changed. "You don't have access between five and nine."

"There be another number me vengeance burns bright for." He gritted his teeth and spat the word. "Twisty Six."

"You big oaf," Enzo said. "You can't get in during lights-out hours."

"Lights out?" Rudwick asked.

"Are you kidding?" Enzo asked. "When the lights are green, stay off the scene." He pointed to a nearby illumination unit.

"There be no lock stern enough to keep Captain Rude Beard from the sea," Rudwick said. He reached up and tightened his mechanical arm. With the robotic prosthetic, he extended and took hold of the metal gate.

"Not a good idea," Marianna said from the gathered shadows behind. "There's got to be an alarm."

"I tend to agree with Mari on this one," Eustis said. However, before they could stop him, the gate gave way with a loud crack and clang of metal. Something metallic clattered to the ground, and Rudwick pushed the bars open. The kids cheered for a brief second, but Enzo was quick to hush them.

"Show us the way," Eustis said. Before they started to move, Marianna grabbed Eustis' arm.

"I'm going to hang back," she said.

"Are you sure?" he asked. "You might like to see what we're going to do."

"You need a lookout," Marianna said.

"Oh, good idea," Eustis said. "Thanks."

Eustis walked quickly to catch up with the others. They moved like tourists through the water park as Rudwick gave a noisy guided tour of his workplace. He didn't diminish the volume of his boorish voice but led the parade through the dim green as if there was nothing out of the usual going on.

"There be concessions, where the brats get sugared to the teeth," Rudwick pointed. "The wave pool," he gestured. "Josh, me boss, says after a year I be ready to guard life upon its treacherous waters." He turned and waved his hands with such pomp that the tiny kiddie pool might as well have been the Atlantic Ocean of Earth. "Here be me grand station." The little pool, hardly bigger than a bathtub, was surrounded by pirate-themed decorations. Rudwick crossed his arms and posed for everyone to see.

"Let's get to it," Eustis said. "Quicker we get out of here, the better. Enzo, you want to go first?" Eustis waded into the water, followed by Enzo. "Enzo, have you believed in Jesus for everlasting life?"

"I absolutely have," Enzo said with a smile.

"Then I'm baptizing you in the name of the Father, the Son, and Holy Spirit." Eustis helped Enzo down into the water and back out again. Eustis noticed how strangely the water moved compared to what he expected from his time on Earth. The kid's soft applause brought him out of his daze. Just as they'd been prepped to do, they cheered nothing louder than a whisper. They clapped ever so softly as Rudwick went into the water. The big man barely fit into the kiddie pool, but Eustis got him immersed after two tries. Then one by one, the children came in to do the same. When

Bobby and Jewels saw how simple it was, they too, decided that it was a perfect time to be baptized. When they were done, Eustis prayed.

"Can we swim?" Brad Gaines asked. The other kids rushed together, surrounded Rudwick, and begged him profusely.

"If you're done with your water ritual, we really should get out of here," Marianna said as she stepped out of a shadow. She'd come from her post as lookout without a sound.

"She's right," Eustis said.

"I agree," Enzo echoed.

"Nay," Rudwick said. "The poor bitties be in need of a water romp. Be you seeing the mighty distance we come?"

"It's not a good idea"

"This be me final word," Rudwick said. "The bitties get to swim." The kids cheered.

"Fine," Marianna said. "I'll be at the gate." She started back toward her post. "But keep them quiet, Rudwick. Seriously. We're exposed out here."

Enzo joined the kids splashing in the pool. Rudwick stood guard like a proud lion over a pride of cubs. Eustis watched the children play for a few minutes but felt drawn to the front gate.

"Hey, I'm going to go stand watch," Eustis said to Rudwick. He ran his fingers over his hair and put his hand to his mouth to smell his breath as he made his way toward the front gate where Marianna was waiting. He turned the corner and made his way around the wave pool when he saw Mari running full speed toward him.

"Nightguard!" Marianna whisper-screamed as she caught up with Eustis. "We've got to get the kids out of here!" Eustis spun around and began to run. In the low gravity, he leaped five meters at a time as he zinged toward the kiddie pool.

"Everyone out," Eustis said.

"Security guard is coming," Marianna added as she skidded to a bouncing stop behind Eustis. The kids scrambled out of the pool as quickly as they could. Before they were on the move, the night guard rounded the corner.

He was a rotund man in an illuminated uniform. The bright blue stripes that ran the length of his jumpsuit cast creepy shadows across his otherwise shadow-covered face.

"Hey, what's going on here?" the guard called.

Before he knew what he was doing, words were coming out of Eustis' mouth. "We were doing a—" He stopped when Marianna knocked him in the ribs with her elbow, as she probably realized his first instinct would be, to tell the truth.

"Let me do the talking," she whispered. She walked forward to meet the guard. Eustis noticed the extra va-va-voom she added to her step as she glided forward to meet the glowing night officer. She spoke to the big lunk in an overly sensuous voice. "Hey, there."

"Overdoing it a bit," Enzo whispered. The kids were lined up behind them now. Once they were out of the pool, Rudwick counted them. Luckily there were only seven.

"Ma'am, I'm the night guard. You need to—"

"Night guard!" Rudwick roared. He shoved Enzo, Eustis, and even Marianna out of the way. He squared off with the guard, who was not as tall but had more muscular girth than the aging cutthroat. "I be the guardian of life itself!" Rudwick was practically shouting.

"Take it easy, big fella," the guard said. "This is a restricted area. Tourists can't be in here after hours. Let me just scan your chips, and I'll get you back to your hotel." Rudwick didn't offer his wrist.

"I be no tourist," Rudwick said. "I be surprised. Surprised you don't know me. I be the scourge of the seven seas. I be—"

"Time to go," Marianna whispered to Eustis and the rest as Rudwick stood toe to toe with the guard. Their exit didn't escape his attention, however.

"Hey, stop," the guard shouted, trying to step past Rudwick. He was quicker than the old scallawag and maneuvered to where he could just reach Jewels. She screamed as the guard grasped and wrenched her wrist. When Rudwick finally caught up, the guard got more than he had planned on. Rudwick swept Jewels up in his human arm and used his robotic to shove the guard backward. As the guard tumbled, Rudwick set Jewels down and pointed after Eustis.

"Run, me hearty. Captain Rude Beard will mop the deck with this scurvy blighter."

With a roaring growl, Rudwick spun around and stood squarely in the path of the security guard. He thumped his chest with his fist as he bellowed. "I walked barefooted upon the surface of the sun in its mighty fury. I been three days bare chest in the void of space and lived to tell the tale. I stared death down a hundred times or be it a thousand. I know not. I be Captain Rude Beard, and nobody lays a hand on me beloved bitties." Rudwick was breathing hard, ready for action, poised for a fight. His speech was long enough to let the kids escape but not long enough that they could have gotten far. For a split second, the guard regarded him without emotion, then made a quick gesture that opened his comm app as he spoke.

"I've got a crazy man in Seven Seas," the guard said. "I need backup."

"Got to go," Rudwick said, and as quick as his old bones would allow, he turned and started toward the front gate.

"Oh, no you don't," the guard said. He reached behind his back and pulled a set of glowing power cuffs. Raising them over his head, the guard reached for Rudwick and caught him by his prosthetic. Rudwick tried to pull free, but before he could, the guard brought the cuffs down on his mechanical wrist. The power cuffs, which would have incapacitated him had they been on his human arm, sparked and zapped with a crackle of smoke. His metallic arm was suddenly lifeless. The limp appendage was like a metal leash connecting him to the guard who was now reeling him in.

"Hate to say goodbye," Rudwick said as he slapped the shoulder where his robotic was connected. The latch that held it in place went slack and released. With the sudden release of tension, the guard tumbled backward, holding his end of the power cuffs, which were still attached to Rudwick's mechanical arm. With one less arm attached to his body, Rudwick ran for his life, laughing like a madman, screaming, "I be Captain Rude Beard, Scourge Of the Seven Seas."

Chapter Forty-Four

VISIT

"Girls," Madam Electra Styx shouted as the deafening music reduced to an inaudible thrum. Delphi looked up from her dais, where she was performing her hyper-communication science rites. She put down the ostricular trange, extinguishing it in the shallow layer of cosmic water. "Gather!" Madam Electra shouted. Delphi stepped back from her commune kiosk, pulled the goggles from her eyes, and connected the buttons of her lab coat.

A bustle of activity swirled around the gothic mistress, who was standing at the center of the orbicular chamber. The hyper-terrestrial commune seemed to rush centerward as the flow of junior alien liaisons huddled around. The scent of electrified incense coalesced with the ozone created by a hundred open arc flashes at the available kiosks. The flashing colored lights continued as more than fifty girls, from nine to nineteen, encircled the mistress. The liaison guard, a motley array of black-clad boys and men, stood their posts at the chambers fringes.

Madam Electra clicked her lengthy black fingernails together, letting everyone know she was not happy with the sluggish response to her command. When the circle was quiet, she spoke in an eerie whisper. The sound of her saliva provided an irritating click that rivaled the volume of her hushed words.

"We have a distinguished guest arriving in about twenty minutes. Chief Executive Admiral Kynig Strafe, head of the Office of Dissident Management. I will be his primary service provider. However, if he speaks to any of you, do whatever he tells you. Now for inspection." She pointed to Delphi, the oldest remaining liaison understudy, and said. "You look like you're off duty." The mistress roughly jerked at the lapel of Delphi's lab coat, straightening it. Delphi closed her eyes and willed herself not to rebel. "Do you have something to say?" Electra whispered.

"No, Madam Electra," Delphi said. The mistress moved down the line.

To Clio Aura, she said, "A bit more makeup. You're looking starchy." She used the space-black nail of her index to lift Daphne Iris's chin. "Stand up straight. We don't want our patrons to know you've got a noodle for a spine." She continued down the row, barking orders that were to be obeyed as the highest priority. At the end of the line was Chloe Nyx, a nine-year-old girl with fear hiding behind her eyes. Her hands quivered, and her bottom lip stuck out. She was the newest recruit, initiated only three weeks earlier. The imposing mistress leaned down and spoke softly. "Junior Liaison Chloe, remember your lessons." When the girl didn't respond immediately, Madam Electra placed her long fingers around the delicate line of Chloe's jaw and squeezed.

"Yes, Madam Styx," Chloe said as if it had been rehearsed so often, it no longer held any meaning.

"And that goes for all of you," Madam Electra said as she stepped back. "We serve the hyper-terrestrials when we serve our patrons. How you perform today will determine your station in your upcoming ascension. Our cosmic role is to—"

"Appease the hyper-terrestrials in all we do," they all said in unison. Madam Electra walked around the interior of the circle, making eye contact with each.

"And this is—" Electra shouted.

"The most important science there is," the girls shouted in unison.

"Some of you are nearing your ascension," she said. Delphi tried to keep her cringe imperceptible. She steadied her stare forward, not daring to make eye contact with the mistress. Madam Electra paused for a fraction of a second, "and on that day, I will miss some of you." Electra stepped next to her, reached out, and ran one long, black fingernail down Delphi's face. "Then again, some of you, I won't." The mistress dropped her hand and stepped back. Delphi sighed quietly.

"That is all," Madam Electra shouted. The circle of girls dispersed in all directions. Many scurried off to their apartments to obey their mistress's orders. Delphi glanced around before surreptitiously reaching down and refastening the top button of her lab coat.

The hyper-terrestrial commune returned to normal operational standards for the next fifteen minutes. The music thumped, the lights flashed, and the girls returned to their kiosks, awaiting patrons. Delphi went through the motions, but there was a dark foreboding hanging over her as she turned and dipped the still steaming trange in the cosmic water.

"Admiral Strafe," Madam Electra's voice resounded above the music. "It is so wonderful to have your patronage." Delphi set down the trange once more, turned, and watched from her dais as Madam Electra greeted the Admiral in the middle of the domed chamber. Delphi tried not to let her face register the alarm she felt as an army of robotic soldiers filed in behind the Admiral.

"My, don't you travel with some handsome fellows," Electra said, gesturing to the killing machines that were taking flanking positions around Strafe. The human guards who had been occupying their previously held positions at the anterior of the main chamber shifted uncomfortably.

"Yes," Strafe said in an odd kind of intonation that was not exactly an answer. He was broad-shouldered with short-cropped hair. His physique was thick, as if he were planet-born, and boasted of the large man's formidable strength. His face was marked with deep dark lines running down from high carved cheekbones.

"Are you here for business or pleasure?" Electra asked.

"I make no distinction," Strafe said. Madam Electra strode close. Strafe made no indication of interest in her approach. She stood in front of him for a few seconds, but his eyes were not on her. She glanced back over her shoulder.

"Move," Strafe said. Madam Electra nodded in deference as she stepped back. With her out of the way, Admiral strafe turned his eyes slowly upward toward the central dais. On its pedestal stood the ever-arc, an always-lit beam of contained lightning in a shaft of cylindrical quartz crystal. It crackled and smoked and was never to be extinguished, as it was their way of channeling and communicating with the hyper-terrestrials. This being the chief Hyper-Terrestrial Research Commune in Bezos City, and therefore on all of Phobos, it was the primary channeling arc for Athima, one of the major and most powerful of the hyper-terrestrial beings.

"Bring me a trange," Strafe said in a loud commanding voice. His words echoed through the chamber. One of the nearest girls retrieved her ostricular trange from the closest dais and handed it off to Madam Electra. She, in turn, gave it to Strafe.

"Do you need some cosmic water and an arcing fork?" Electra asked.

"I follow the old science," Strafe said. Electra looked both admiring and shocked. So too, was Delphi, watching from the relative safety of her dais. In all her years as a researcher, Delphi had never seen a man enter the commune, skip the frivolities, opting instead for immediate communing with the hyper terrestrials. Most did the science rituals reluctantly. However, this Admiral Strafe was clearly no ordinary man.

He took the trange in his hand and placed the tip to his forehead. He lit off the spark and let the arcing electric current touch the skin near his hairline. He took in a deep gasp at the sensation and dropped the trange to the ground. As it clattered to the stone, he stepped forward, knelt to his knees before the main science shrine, and bowed low to the floor.

"Athima of Phobos Commune," Strafe said. At hearing him address their patron hyper directly, Delphi shuttered. *Who is this guy?* Chills ran up her back and neck. Her stomach twisted into a knot. She could feel the electric presence pulsing from the ever-arc. The smoke around the channeling arc swirled in a new direction, taking shape. Strafe continued his dark communion, "I have come to your City to hunt a traitor. If you give me victory, I will dedicate his blood to your pleasure and boil those who follow him in the harshest of vacuums. I will disintegrate his presence in honor of your power. I will cut him off from the living in your sight. I will devour his memory for the sake of Athima."

The channeling arc exploded with a loud crack. A dozen voices in the room let out a frightened scream. The smoke blackened for a moment, and the air filled with ozone. In another fraction of a second, a shape, tall and terrible, materialized out of the smoke. Delphi's stomach twisted into a knot. She stepped back and found the cold wall at her back. The channeling arc at the center of the room was blinding, spitting sparks of plasma, but she dared not look away. Made of the thundering crackle of the arc, a vile voice took shape. The sound of electricity formed into words so sharp they felt able to split stone. "You will capture your prey in Phobos." the horrendous voice was so loud Delphi thought her ears would be ruined, but she did not cover them. Suddenly the sound ceased, and the shape of the smoke dissipated. Admiral Strafe returned to his feet, nodded, and turned to look at the room of eyes that were all trained on him.

Delphi had never seen anything like it. A few times, she had witnessed a dedicated devotee interacting directly with the channeling arc, but none had ever gotten a response. Only a few times in all of her years had there been an arc event or a gathering of the smoke, and never together. In those cases, they were channeled by senior researchers, much more skilled than Delphi, and only after hours of fervent prerequisite science rituals.

This Admiral Strafe, however, communed with Athima without the cosmic water, the standard arc tools, and without the preceding dais rites.

With only a touch from an ostricular trange he had brought Athima from the arc smoke. Had she seen it a year ago, it would have filled her with awe and devoted delight, but not now. Witnessing this, after what she had seen and heard in the last months, especially her troubling dreams. It filled her with a deadly, black dread. She had to get out. She couldn't stand it anymore.

"Wow," Madam Electra said. "We rarely receive such dignified guests. Especially ones who know the ways of the ancient sciences." She gestured to an underling. The girl brought a tray of drinks. She snapped her talon-studded fingers, and another girl rushed around with a chair. Strafe, however, did not sit nor did he take a drink. Madam Electra took up a position behind the Admiral and attempted to rub his shoulders. When she laid her hands on Strafe's back, the admiral's robotic soldiers leaped into action. The nearest mechanical killer had the woman's throat in his grasp in a fraction of a second.

"Kill order, requested," the mech-guard said. The other robots immediately took defensive positions and had their weapons pointed at those who stood around. The black-clad men and boys who made up the alien liaison guard were now on alert with their spark batons drawn and crackling. The room was ready to turn into a battle zone.

"At ease, soldiers," Strafe said. The mech-guards dropped Electra and stepped back to the line of the others. "Weapons down." The sound of crying could be heard among the liaisons. Strafe turned to Madam Electra and looked down at her. She rubbed her throat where the guard had gripped her. She rose slowly. Strafe did not help her to her feet.

"I am not here to receive frills," Strafe said. "You will get me a meeting with Chancellor Montobond. The old stone won't take my calls, and storming his compartment would have unnecessary collateral damage."

"Ahh, yes," Madam Electra said. "Chancellor Montobond has become difficult to see—even more difficult to control."

"It's because he's old," Strafe said. "The old have nothing to lose. Makes them rigid." Strafe looked Electra up and down without a shred of shame. "If you perform this duty successfully, I might be inclined to use your services in the future."

"Maybe it's time for a new chancellor," Electra said.

"First," Strafe said, "I require a base of operations."

"Right this way," Electra said. He followed the woman up a spiraling flight of stairs into a gallery of residential compartments.

The robotic soldiers began to march in unison behind him. At the sound of their footfalls, Strafe turned and commanded, "Form a perimeter. Defensive protocol phalanx." The drones fanned out in a mechanical pattern and took up positions around the chamber entrance and the back exit.

Delphi turned and continued her science rites, trying to ignore the scary, non-human killing machines that had taken up offensive positions less than ten paces away. She let her mind wander, considering how she would escape.

CHAPTER FORTY-FIVE

DISCOURAGED

The trip back to Maroon Housing, post-baptism, was a brooding affair. Rudwick mourned his missing arm. Marianna sulked, giving them nothing but silence, and Enzo spent most of the walk trying to keep Jewels from crying. When they arrived back at the bunkhouse, the night was spent, and it was nearly time for work. They were quiet as they each left for their day's labor. The previous night's victory was swallowed up by the scare of nearly being caught by the night guard of Recreation Dome.

In the weeks that followed, they resumed their nightly story time, but their big event had changed the nature of the group. There was a trickle of people who added themselves to their number. Adria Churn and Gordon Festus were teenagers living on their own in Bunkhouse E nearby. They'd been abandoned in Bezos City years earlier. They were introduced to the faith at the feast and joined the devotees thereafter, both becoming believers in the days that followed.

In addition to the teens, Rymone and Geona Shaldon were a young couple in their mid-twenties. They were stranded on Phobos more than two years prior when a trip from Titan went sideways. They were still waiting for rescue but had given up hope of any help coming. Rymone and Geona, too, became believers through Rudwick, who had invited them to one of the nightly gatherings. He had to get Enzo's help explaining the faith, but they gladly believed not long after.

The tiny group was approaching twenty-strong, not counting Marianna, who still didn't believe. All of the kids and the teens moved into the bunkhouse where Eustis, Enzo, Rudwick, and Marianna stayed. Marianna wasn't happy about it, but she had taken a fondness for Jewels and endured the claustrophobic arrangement if only to be close to the little orphan. The community shared was unlike anything any of them had ever experienced. They played the roles of parents, teachers, mentors, and friends.

They didn't do another large-scale feast. They couldn't afford it since it wasn't safe for Rudwick to return to his former job, and they couldn't count on his massive pay, but they made sure the people who were now under their care were fed each night. It wasn't long before they didn't call their meetings story time anymore since they had morphed into something entirely different. They shared their water, meals, and time with one another. The burgeoning group of believers had the makings of a small church. *The Underground* was the name they eventually settled on.

"How do you think it went tonight?" Enzo asked after the children were bedded down for lights out. The crew had made a habit of sitting outside the bunkhouse to talk after the children were in bed. The four of them took their usual places on the steps. Rudwick's favored cat, Beverly Gertrude Lewis, rubbed Eustis' leg once he got still, and Tiny curled up next to Rudwick.

"It was ok, I guess," Eustis said.

"What be the disappointment?" Rudwick asked as he rubbed the place where his robotic arm used to be attached.

"Oh, it's just that—" Before he could say anything else, Enzo interrupted.

"Who's that?" He pointed to the tunnel opening about a hundred paces away. The shadowed shape of a person, possibly a man by the look of him, lurked. His posture and pose suggested he was looking in their direction. "Hey," Enzo shouted. "What do you want? We don't have any powder."

"Enzo," Mari said. She hushed the boy as they all looked at the stranger. The man stiffened, spun, and started walking away through the tunnel.

"Weirdo," Enzo said. "Anyway, Eustis, what were you saying?"

"I was just going to say that—" This time, he was interrupted from the other direction. Rymone Shaldon stepped out through the bunk door, followed by his wife.

"Need us to do anything else?" Rymone asked.

"Nope," Eustis said, smiling at the interruption as if nothing was wrong. "Thanks for putting the kids to bed tonight."

"Happy to," Geona said.

"If there's nothing else, we're heading to bed," Rymone said. They all said goodnight as Geona and Rymone walked toward a nearby bunkhouse, hand in hand. Eustis watched them for a moment, letting his jealous eyes soak in the vision of two so in love. He glanced toward Marianna and found her looking back. They both dropped their stare to the ground.

"You were about to tell us what's got you down," Enzo said.

"Oh, yeah. Well, it's—"

"Mari," a small shimmering voice called. Marianna spun toward the bunkroom door. Jewels was standing there, looking sheepish, clutching a tattered blanket. "I not sleep."

"Here," Marianna reached for her. "Come sit with me a while." Jewels brightened and sped toward Marianna. She nuzzled into her lap and laid her head against Mari's shoulder.

"Mari," Jewels said. "Why you not use your lastie?"

"My last name?" Marianna said. "I do sometimes." She glanced up at the others with a bewildered look. When she looked down at Jewels, the little girl was only centimeters from her face. "It's just that we don't use last names when we're with friends."

"If you not use your lastie," Jewels said. "Maybe I use yours." At the tiny innocent words, Mari gave her a smile that left the residue of remorse around her eyes. She wrapped her arms around the little girl and squeezed.

Jewels virtually purred at the affection. Instead of letting go of the hug, she rested her head on Mari's shoulder and closed her eyes. Apparently, she had found the perfect place to fall asleep.

"What be making you glum, mate?" Rudwick said. Eustis had hoped the distractions had excused him from the line of questions. He ran his fingers along the jagged stone of the bunkhouse steps.

"It's just that—"

"I'm thirsty." They all turned to find Adria Churn, one of the new teenagers who had joined the group, standing with the bunk door half open.

"Me too," Gordon Festus, the other teen, said from behind her, still shrouded in the shadow of the bunkroom.

"Did you get your water ration today?" Eustis asked.

"That yellow-toothed guy from block C stole it," Adria said.

"I got mine," Gordon said. "I drank it. I'm still thirsty."

"Ok," Eustis said. "You can have mine. It's by my bed. Gordon, just a sip. Let Adria have the rest." Adria and Gordon disappeared back into the shadows as the door swung closed.

"You're going to be dehydrated tomorrow," Enzo said. "You want some of mine?"

"That's ok," Eustis said. Enzo regarded him for a moment, tilting his head.

"Seriously," Enzo said. "What's wrong with you? You look like a suffo-cated addict."

Eustis looked up at the ceiling of the cave and let his eyes roam toward the tunnel that led away from Maroon Housing. He put the back of his hand on his forehead and rubbed the skin. It was dry and chapped. He pushed his fingers through his dusty hair. It made him sneeze. The distant sound of some motorized rover echoed through the tunnel.

"Things are great," Eustis said. "There are more believers on Phobos than anywhere else in the Sol system."

"Really?" Enzo asked.

"I think so." Eustis leaned back against the building's wall, folded his hands together, and put them behind his head. "Things are great, but I just feel..." he let his words turn to silence.

"Why be there such a hairball in your throat?" Rudwick asked. Eustis didn't sit up.

"What?" Enzo asked.

"It be a horrendous hacking to bring up what needs be said," he said. "Old Rudwick says what needs be saying, and that be that."

"Yes," Enzo leaned forward. "But, your prolific verbal excretions are a bit runny."

"Listen, you twerp–" Rudwick began in a booming voice.

"Rudwick," Marianna whisper-screamed. She gestured down toward Jewels, who was sleeping in her arms. She made a violent hushing sound in Rudwick's direction. Enzo turned toward Eustis.

"I'm just going to keep asking, so save yourself the annoyance and spill it," Enzo said, parroting Eustis' own saying back to him. Eustis sat forward and rubbed his chin.

"I was thinking about my parents tonight," Eustis said.

"What be they like?" Rudwick said.

"Dead."

"Ahh," Rudwick said. "Old Rudwick loves a tale of woe."

"Rudwick," Enzo said. "Have some respect." Eustis sat silently for a long few moments as his mind meandered through the shadows of his past.

"I can still see their faces the day they told me they were going to—" Eustis blinked twice. "The day they were going to do the procedure." He paused. He kept his eyes closed as he continued. "My parents were against suffering. Completely avoided anything difficult. They would get any procedure, take any medicine, or do anything to avoid pain. I was brought up mostly by a nanny–bot, cause, you know, raising kids hurts.

"So, at some point, I started asking the nanny-bot the big questions. Why are we alive? What's the point of all this? You know, standard kid stuff. The bot said I should discuss these matters with my parents. Yeah right. But whatever. I tried. Most of the time, they wouldn't answer. 'Course, they were atheists, so if they ever did give an answer, it amounted to cosmic meaninglessness.

"It was around that time my mom told me that when I was born—tube-birth of course—the A.I. asked her what my name should be. She didn't want to give me a name. Didn't care, I guess. When it asked again, she said I was just a, 'useless wad of grime.' The A.I. picked up the first three words and matched them to the closest names it had in its database. Eustis Wade Grimes. Her last name was Grace. I begged her for years to let me change it. She wouldn't let me.

"So fast forward to my eighteenth birthday. Mom and Dad call me on live chat. They're all smiles. Calling from some doctor's office. I'm like, what's this? I haven't seen you guys smile in years. Dad says they were excited because they were going to be voluntarily euthanized. I couldn't breathe."

"Euthanized?" Rudwick asked.

"Medically assisted suicide," Eustis said. "They were going to have the procedure done that day. I was like, 'What? No! Why?' So Mom says, 'It's illegal to be euthanized while you have children who are minors.' Now that I was a legal adult, they could take the lethal injection.

"I was like, 'no.' I asked, 'why not keep on living?' They went into how awful the world was. Aging is terrible. Everything is painful. Stuff like that. The whole time they were smiling. Smiling. It's been seventeen years, and I still see it like it just happened this morning. The smiles. The smiles that told me, 'You don't mean anything to us.'

"I begged them not to—to keep on living for my sake. Mom said they'd been planning to do this since before I was born. There was a government population growth program that would pay lifetime medical bills if you had and raised a kid. Turns out it would cover end-of-life assistance. They couldn't have afforded the euthanization otherwise. So they'd had me in the first place so they could get the procedure for free. My sole purpose for existing was so my parents could kill themselves. I wasn't useless after all. But being useless would be way better than all that.

"I asked them to at least wait so I could say goodbye. Dad said, 'Our appointment is in five minutes, and we don't want to keep the doctor waiting.' I hung up on them. That was the last we ever talked.

"They left me some money. Enough to live on for a while. So I sat around for a few years and felt the full weight of my name. My real name. The one Mom gave me. Useless. I was totally useless. I got an appointment with the doctor. The same doctor that did them. I was going to go through with it too. It was the day of the appointment. My death day. Then things happened, and I didn't go through with it."

"That's when you met Deb and Riley Wynters?" Enzo said.

"Yeah," Eustis said. He looked down at the step before him. "Most days are good. I can go for a long time without thinking about it now. But then, sometimes, it just smashes into me. I feel like I did on that day. I doubt myself and everything I'm doing."

"But look at where you are!" Enzo said. "Look at what you're doing. How could you be doing anything more important?"

"Still," Eustis said. "It's just how I feel." A thick silence wrapped around them.

"Eustis," Marianna said in a whisper. He looked up to find her eyes, direct, intense, real eye contact for maybe the first time. She looked into his eyes. She shifted Jewels' sleeping weight in her lap so that she had a hand free. She gestured for Eustis to come sit next to her.

He wagged his head and took a deep breath as he rose to his feet, moved across the steps, and plopped down next to her. She simply laid her head on his shoulder. He closed his eyes and leaned his head against hers. They existed in that moment for a thousand years. He felt Enzo's weight on his other side lean in against him. He was squeezed warmly between them for a few seconds before Rudwick rose, cats meowing around him, and came over.

"I be no good at hugs now that I be a one-armed man," Rudwick said. "That don't keep me from trying." He knelt in front of the three and laid his big arm across all of them, and leaned his massive head against theirs. His beard tickled their faces, but no one budged. Jewels let out a satisfying sleeping sigh from Mari's lap.

"You did this," Marianna said in the smallest whisper. Eustis could almost believe he imagined it. "This isn't useless."

CHAPTER FORTY-SIX

RECKONING

"Kick it here," Jewels shouted. She was the smallest of a chaotic group of kids who were kicking a piece of rock around outside the Maroon Housing bunkrooms. The scratch of feet and the ensuing cloud of Phobos' dust made it hard to breathe, but the kids played on. Jewels' giggle of delight pierced the noise of enjoyment with ease.

"Food's on," Eustis shouted to the playing children. The two teens, Gordon and Adria had the bread, and were ready to break it for the kids who were now rushing toward them. "Wait," Eustis said. The children paused in front of them. "Did everyone drink their water ration?" They nodded. "Okay, let's pray." He turned toward Rymone Shaldon. "Would you mind praying for us, brother Rymone?"

The hungry kids fidgeted while Rymone gave thanks for their meager meal. They had stretched their pay as far as it could reach, but their feast earlier in the month had left them little to work with. When Rymone said, "Amen," Eustis nodded to Adria and Gordon. They broke the bread, which sounded crusty.

"This is stale," Bobby Gaines said with his mouth full.

"I'll take it," his brother Brad said.

"Why can't we have another feast?" Ava Sikes asked.

The chatter continued as it skirted along the thin line between observing and complaining. Eustis patted Ava on the shoulder and smiled as Geona Shaldon, who had taken on a matronly role.

"What that sound," a tiny voice said. Eustis looked over in Jewel's direction. She was hugging Marianna's leg with one arm and had apparently had her thumb in her mouth, as it was still wet. Eustis cocked his head at the little girl and then looked up at Marianna, who shrugged. "Someone coming."

"Sometimes she thinks someone's coming to get her," Eddy Crabbe said.

"She used to do it all the time," Samantha Crabbe said. "Hasn't in a while, though." The Crabbe's went back to socializing with the other kids.

"Someone coming," Jewels said as she let go of Marianna's leg and placed her hands over her ears.

Marianna reached for the girl and lifted her up. "It's ok, Sweetie. I've got you." She held the tiny girl, smaller than her age should warrant, on her hip and hugged her tight. "I won't let anything happen. No one is going to take you away."

"What's that?" Bobby Gaines said. The group grew immediately silent and looked in the direction he pointed. Blue lights bounced off the walls of the tunnel to upper Bezos. Now that they were quiet, they could hear the sound of boots, lots of boots.

"Someone coming! Someone coming!" Jewels was crying now.

"I'm sure it's fine," Eustis said. He stepped toward the tunnel opening, placing himself in front of the crowd of kids. Only Jewels' sobs were heard over the growing sound of footfalls.

"Oh, no," Rymone said as twenty Bezos City custody troops in illuminated uniforms spilled out from the tunnel. They were in full riot gear. They had their firearms at the ready and looked eager to do damage.

"What seems to be the problem, officers?" Eustis said as he walked calmly in their direction. He made sure to keep his hands in sight as he moved slowly toward them. A man at the center, some kind of chief by the look of him, stepped forward and made a gesture. An image appeared hovering in mid-air between them.

"I'm Custody Officer Charles Yick of the Bezos City accounts delinquency force. Have you seen either of these two suspects?" Officer Yick said. His voice was husky and abrupt. He was underweight even for a Phobosian, and his brown teeth looked like he'd been chewing on a live grenade when it'd gone off. He swiped through a slideshow of hovering pictures as he explained. "They broke into a restricted area, accosted a security guard, and escaped custody. Luckily they were captured on body camera." Eustis let his eyes flit to the image as the officer continued. The picture was a dark but recognizable image of Rudwick holding Jewels next to the pool at the Seven Seas Water Park. "A little girl and a large man missing his right arm. If you have any information about their whereabouts, you're obligated to share."

"This is not—" Eustis tried, but another voice cut in.

"I know the big lefty," said a filthy man coming out of the shadows of a nearby bunkhouse. He gave a grey smile and pushed back a lock of wire-stiff hair. "Do I get a reward if I tell you where—?"

"Step back, you filthy fribble," the officer said as he drew and lifted his sidearm. "Your reward will be that I don't shoot you right here for interfering with an official investigation. Tell me where he is immediately,"

"Shew-wee, trigger-happy ninnyhammers," the man said. "The one-armed guy is right over there. The girl hangs around with him and the others too."

"Now, wait a minute," Eustis said. He tried to step in front of the officer but received a violent shove for his trouble. He felt a sharp pain in his lower back as he tumbled to the rock floor. The low gravity made it hard to keep from tumbling end over end. He shoved off and did his best to get his legs underneath him. By the time he was back on his feet, the squad of troops had descended upon the young congregation.

Most of the kids scattered instantly, knowing enough to realize there was danger. The soldiers spotted Rudwick and swarmed him. Even with a single arm, it took eight of the illuminated troops to subdue the old swashbuckler. Out of the bunkhouse ran four fierce cats, ready for battle. Tiny, the giant genetically modified tabby, reached the mob of assailants first. He leaped through the air and landed on the nearest soldier with a bone-crunching thud.

Tiny sunk his teeth into the arm of one of the officers. A scream of pain echoed through the cavern as the huge cat tore the flesh from his arm. The other cats entered the fray, and the cave filled with other-worldly screeches and cries. Eustis ran toward the action, hoping to help Rudwick escape.

Another detachment of officials was now surrounding Marianna, who was still holding Jewels. Despite her tender age, the little girl was on Bezos City's most wanted list, and the officers had spotted and targeted her. Only Marianna stood in the way of them gaining their prize. Holding Jewels away from the villains, Marianna swung wildly with her free arm and kicked at the resolute officers as they tightened their circle. Jewels clung to Mari's neck as she screamed for her life. Eustis glanced back toward Rudwick for a split second but changed directions and started toward the execution squad that encircled Marianna and the little girl.

A large officer grabbed Jewels and began a sickening tug of war. She shrieked as she looked to be torn limb from limb. Mari spun and gave him a well-placed kick to the gut. As he hit the ground, two more officers took his place and grabbed Jewels before Mari could react. She punched one and kicked the other, but a soldier grabbed her hair from behind and pulled so hard she stumbled backward with a shout of pain. Eustis was vaulting toward them when Jewels was severed from Mari's grasp.

"No!" Eustis screamed. "Take me! I'm the one you want! I instigated the break-in! Leave them alone!" He shouldn't have said anything. At the sound of his screams and the sight of his charging approach, three officers peeled off from the circle and faced him. They formed a barrier, keeping him from gaining access to Marianna or Jewels. He slammed into them as if they were solid stone. "Stop! Leave them. Take me. It's me you want." He swung his arms madly, grabbed at whatever he could reach, and yelled as he tried to shove his way through.

Two of the big men flanked him and wrapped their iron grip around his upper arms. They held him fast and forced him to watch as two officers held Marianna down. Another scooped up Jewels and tucked her under his arm as if she were nothing more than a bag of groceries. The little girl had more fight in her, though. She squirmed and kicked like a wild animal. She wriggled free from the man's grasp, hit the ground, and began to run.

The man lifted his firearm, at which point the color of his uniform flashed a deadly red, and a warning siren cut through the noise. Without hesitation, the soldier pulled the trigger. A blast of fiery white exploded from his gun. Ten paces away, Jewels fell forward, face down on the stone. A pool of red swelled around her head like a crimson halo. Eustis stared unbelieving, unbreathing. He blinked, willing her to get up. As the resistance drained out of him, the soldiers who held his arms let their grip go slack. A single scream pierced the thick numbness that was already setting in.

"No!" Mari screeched. The fight left her, and she went limp. Eustis stiffened. He stared at the spot where the little girl lay. He couldn't breathe. He couldn't think. He heard words, and at first, he didn't realize they were coming from him.

"Let me go to her," he said. "Let go of me. Let me go to her." His nose was running, and so too his eyes. He tasted bile at the back of his mouth, and his stomach was threatening to vomit.

"Fine," one officer said as he nodded to the others to step aside. He continued to mutter something, but Eustis didn't notice. He rushed to her side and stared down at the lifeless little body.

"Oh, Jewels," was all he could say. He took her diminutive hand. He tried to keep his eyes away from the gory hole in the back of her head. It was another few seconds before the soldiers let Marianna free as well. She was next to Eustis in an instant.

She said nothing. Enzo skidded up next. The three of them looked at Jewels' body for another few seconds before Marianna stood slowly. Eustis tried to grab her hand, but she jerked away. She looked down at Eustis for a second before she turned and walked with a singular resolution toward the bunkhouse. Halfway there, she stopped for a second and then burst into a run. She slammed into the front door and disappeared inside.

They heard the sound of Rudwick still struggling with his assailants. "Go calm him down," Eustis said with the deepest note of defeat his voice had ever carried. "He's going to get himself killed." Enzo was up in a flash. The enormous cat, Tiny, lay in a bloody heap. The others were nowhere to be seen.

"Rudwick," Enzo said. "Please! Stop fighting!" The sound died down. The tightness in Eustis' chest was so intense his breath came in shallow stabs, each more painful than the last. He reached down and laid a trembling hand on Jewels' back, wet with blood.

"God, help us," he said.

"Stop it," Enzo shouted. "He's not fighting anymore. Stop it. You're hurting him." Rudwick curled into a fetal position as the goons continued to rain blows down on him. They had gone from subduing to punishing.

Enzo screamed, "I said stop it!" He leaped toward a soldier's back, but the low gravity sent him high and slow. Officer Yick caught Enzo around the waist in mid-air before the kid could reach his target and slammed him to the ground hard. Eustis stood and was about to run to Enzo's aid, but in the periphery of his vision, Eustis saw motion.

"No!" Eustis shouted when he spotted her. "Don't!"

Marianna had exited the bunkhouse and was moving toward the line of soldiers with a pistol in her hand. *How had she smuggled it into the city?* He didn't know, nor did he care. She dashed toward her enemy, eyes ablaze with fury. She was on them before they realized what was happening, lifted her gun, and aimed for the murderer's chest. Eustis leaped toward her and put himself between her barrel and the murderous soldier's back.

"No," Eustis said. "Please." Marianna tried to step around him, but he pivoted.

She gritted her teeth. "I'll shoot through you if I have to." Eustis reached out slowly, placing his blood-covered hands on hers. They trembled together as he held on. "I'll shoot—" she faltered. "I'll—"

"No," Eustis said. "Please. There's been enough bloodshed." By now, the officers had realized what was happening and had their guns at the ready. All of their uniforms were flashing red. Their blood-thirsty eagerness was palpable. They fanned out around Eustis' back and prepped to take Marianna down in a hail of fire.

Mari let out a blood-boiling scream. She dropped the gun. It fell slowly and clattered to the stone. She collapsed on the ground and wept. The soldiers laughed. One said, "Aww, I was hoping to have an excuse to drop her like a pebble."

"Arrest her," Officer Yick said, walking toward the scene now that he had dealt with Rudwick and restrained Enzo. "Possession of a firearm, and aggravated assault of a custody officer." She put up no more fight, and they had her in power cuffs in seconds.

Eustis stood stunned as the officers moved around him. His breath was shallow, and his heart pounded like rolling thunder. His legs felt weak, and his stomach was spinning in place. He put his hand on his head as he watched the officers stand a cuffed Rudwick, Enzo, and Marianna to their feet. The goons chatted casually as they ushered Eustis' loved ones toward the tunnel. Eustis didn't know what to do.

"We need a reclamation team," one of the soldiers said into his shoulder communicator. "Two bodies in Maroon Housing. A human juvenile and a big cat."

"Should we call down an evidence bot to get a 3D scan?" Another officer asked.

"No need," Officer Yick said. "It's just Maroonies down here. We could grind through a dozen at a time, and it wouldn't matter." The other officers standing around laughed at the joke. Eustis tried to speak, to say something, anything, but his cold, empty breaths were all he could offer. Eustis bent over and vomited.

CHAPTER FORTY-SEVEN

AFTER

Rudwick, cuffed, bleeding, and incapacitated though he was, sobbed bitterly. When he learned of the death of his beloved cat, Tiny, his gusto was gone. Enzo's eyes were rimmed with tears, and his hands were secured behind his back. Marianna was sullen as if her face was set in stone. She had stopped struggling against her restraints and seemed resigned to whatever fate lay ahead.

The security rover soon appeared, barely fitting down the tunnel to Maroon Housing. Harsh spasms of blue and red danced off the walls of rock. Eustis tried to talk the officers into letting them go to no avail. Enzo, Rudwick, and Marianna were loaded into the rover drone and ushered away.

The silence that followed was black and hollow. Eustis stayed with Jewels' body until a reclamation team, three GovCorp employees in brown jumpsuits with an autonomous cart, came to collect the bodies. They loaded Jewels' remains before they moved on to load Tiny, Rudwick's genetically modified tabby.

"What are you doing with them?" Eustis asked as the three unscrupulous body scavengers began to move toward the tunnel. Their six-wheeled cart continued as one of the three paused to look at Eustis. He made a gesture with his hand which sent data to Eustis' personal node. He blinked twice to open it.

It read, *"Organic Reclamation Office, Reclamation Dome, Bezos City."* Underneath the heading, it said, *"We are sorry for your loss. All non-living organic matter present in Bezos City is the property of the Organic Reclamation Department and will be reintegrated into the macro-system via the Cyclical Biome Project at no cost to the bereaved. To make assisted euthanization arrangements or to donate found material, visit the offices of the Organic Reclamation Department between the hours of—"*

Eustis stopped reading and waved the hovering display away. The reclamation team was disappearing around the bend of the tunnel. Eustis knelt, intending to pray, but no words came. He leaned forward pressing his forehead against the stony ground. No prayer came. He curled his arms around his knees and stayed still for a long time.

It wasn't until after the reclamation team had gone that anyone ventured out of the shadows of Maroon Housing. The older children were the first to drift toward Eustis' cowering body. After enduring a few silent minutes in impossible emptiness, the sound of little feet came near. Eustis kept his eyes closed.

"Is he dead?" Bobby Gaines asked.

"No," Billy said. "If he dead, them goons would have loaded him."

"Poke him with something," Eddy Crabbe said. A foot or a hand, Eustis wasn't sure which, nudged his ribs gently. When he stirred the group of children gasped.

"Talk Boss," Liddy Carpenter said. Eustis sat up slowly and opened his eyes. "Where they take Jewels?" she asked. He couldn't answer. Brad Gaines cut in.

"What they do with Tiny?"

"Are they going to kill Captain Rude Beard?" Samantha Crabbe asked.

"Cut off his other arm at least," Billy Gaines speculated.

"Where's the Three Story Kid?" said another. The questions continued but Eustis couldn't hear what they were saying. He put his hands to his temples and closed his eyes once more. There was a tightness in his chest that wasn't there a moment ago. A burning enveloped the place where his heart had been beating. His face felt cold, and his hands were sweating. Vaguely he registered the sound of more feet coming toward him, running.

"What happened?" Rymone Shaldon said. The only adult present pressed through the throng of children. They were all talking at once, making it impossible to understand. Rymone knelt down in front of Eustis.

"Pastor Eustis, are you ok?" Rymone asked. The words sounded like a distant echo. Eustis laid a hand on his own chest and did his best to take a breath. He wondered if Maroon Housing had been depressurized because there was clearly no air to take in.

"Are you having trouble breathing?" Rymone asked. At this, the kids began in again.

"There were soldiers," Ava Sikes said.

"They had guns," Samantha added.

"They shot Jewels," Bobby Gaines said. One of the others disagreed, and an argument followed, but Rymone ignored it.

"Ava, go get Mrs. Geona," Rymone said and then turned to the others. Ava sped off as he spoke. "Brad, he needs water. Go see if you can find some." He tapped Bobby Gaines, the oldest of the children, on the shoulder. "Let's help Pastor Eustis into the bunk room."

Eustis hardly knew what was happening as hands wrapped around his arms. He was being pulled and then being made to stand. Geona Shaldon and the two teenagers, Adria Churn and Gordon Festus emerged from a bunkhouse at the end of the row of buildings. More questions that Eustis couldn't answer followed. More hands wrapped around him, virtually carrying him into the darkened interior of the building. A parade of children followed them into the room but were soon hushed to silence by Adria and Gordon.

The following hours he spent in a state of partial consciousness, reliving the horrific scene as if played on loop. His heart eventually slowed, and his breathing became manageable soon after. The tightness in his chest softened. His mind cleared enough to open his eyes. Dark shadows sat around him, unstirring in the green dim.

"He's awake," Geona said. Rymone came from across the room along with the teens and children. They pressed close, surrounding Eustis' bed. They were hungry for answers. He sat up slowly, rubbing his temples as he did.

"How long was I down?" Eustis asked.

"About an hour," Rymone said. "How do you feel?"

"I'm—" Eustis rubbed his hand across his chest. "I don't know. Feel a bit numb."

Something gently touched Eustis on the arm. A violent jolt shuttered through his body. Before he knew what was happening, he was recoiling backward across the mattress as if he were about to be struck. His post-traumatic response made him involuntarily ball his hands in fists. His eyes were wild, and his heart was pounding.

"It's ok," Geona said. "It's just the cat." Eustis looked down to see Biscuit. He let out a grinding sigh but watched warily as the cat stepped across the bed. Was it true? Had it only been Biscuit? He closed his eyes as the scene began to loop all over.

"We don't mean to pressure you," Rymone said. His tone was cautious, his voice soft. "It's just that the kids are scared. Well, we all are."

"You should be," Eustis said. *Don't be like that*, he thought. *They need you.*

"What should we do?" Geona asked. Eustis looked at the ground. Strange green shadows surrounded him, hinting at the darkness within this God-forsaken hole. He couldn't bring the impossible weight of his eyes up from the floor.

"I think maybe we should pray," Rymone said. "Come on, kids." The children knelt down, folded their hands, and prepared for prayer. "Bow and close your eyes. We're going to pray that God will—"

The bed creaked as Eustis stood. His abrupt movement stilled the room. Rymone's eyes followed him, as did everyone's, as Eustis fled headlong from the bunkhouse.

CHAPTER FORTY-EIGHT

EXODUS

Eustis walked without having a conscious destination. After climbing out of the tunnel that led to Maroon Housing, he wound his way through the streets of Horizon Dome. They were busy with the bustle of a quarter of a million souls going about their day. Shopkeepers spilled out onto the streets, selling second-hand goods loudly. Workers hurried by, trying not to be devoured by the voracious vendors.

At every corner, there were security officers. Eustis glared, attempting to see the face of Jewels' murderer in each. He considered what he might do. He could see it unfolding right there in the street. He could leap upon any of the stationed soldiers, and if he attacked with enough urgency, the officer would be forced to respond. His gun would come out. His suit would flash red, and his pistol would go off, and it would be over. Beautiful oblivion. *This useless wad of grime finally gets what he deserves.*

"What you looking at, slag?" an officer shouted. Eustis started. The soldier's hand had gone to his holster. "Move! you're holding up traffic." He was standing in the middle of the busy street, completely immobile and staring listlessly at the closest security force officer.

"You going to shoot me?" Eustis said.

"I just might," the officer said. He stepped forward, away from his post. Eustis bristled, feeling his heart rate rise. The big officer's hand was glued to his holster now, but he hadn't drawn it yet. In another few seconds, he was mere centimeters from Eustis' face. "How are you going to shoot me if you don't pull your gun?"

"Good point," the guard said. He tugged on his sidearm, which released it slightly from its holster. It was enough for the soldier's jumpsuit to flash red. "I swear to the hypers. I'll leave you bleeding in the street if you don't keep moving."

"A beautiful oblivion," Eustis whispered. The officer didn't respond. They shared a long, intense stare, but Eustis blinked, took a breath, and stepped back.

"That's right, you air-wasting gasser." The officer watched him for a few seconds before he spun and returned to his post as if nothing had happened. Eustis made his way down the street. His heart was still racing, and his breathing elevated.

A shop owner covered in grease yelled, "Parts for outdated models. Looking for anything off-market, this is where you'll find it." He ignored the offer and kept moving.

A woman at a mobile vending cart waved at him, saying, "Honey! Real honey! You've never tasted anything like this." He walked on.

A big toothless man with an empty tavern at his back shouted in Eustis's direction, "Gruff's got the best drinks in the dome." He surveyed the man, having heard of Gruff's Fluids from Marianna and Rudwick more than often. He was truly tempted by the offer. "I can see you want to, son. Bar's empty. You'd have the place to yourself. Come on in. I got what you need."

No, you don't, Eustis thought as he ambled by without talking to Gruff. *What I need is to get off this rock.* The whole thing had been stupid. To think he could do this work. It was idiotic to imagine that he would be able to make any kind of difference out here in this utterly filthy place. Why had he tried? After two months of toil, he had only convinced a few homeless children and a handful of aimless saps to believe. He had accomplished nothing and gotten someone killed in the process. *It should have been me.*

Images of Jewels' body flashed through his mind. He took a jagged breath and stopped the thought there.

"The hypers are calling you," a clear voice rang out from Eustis's right. "Commune with Hellion to receive statistical privileges, or with Dragbask to disadvantage your enemies. Consult with Athima, the powerful, and learn your destiny. The hypers are waiting." He glanced over. An ornate building set into the dome wall was the largest establishment on the busy street. The sign read *Hyper-Terrestrial Research Commune*. Beneath the sprawling archway were gathered a group of oddly-clad hyper-researchers. Of course, they were offering *communion* with hyper-terrestrials, supposedly beings from another world who made contact through alien liaisons, but Eustis knew the dark secret behind the lie. "Have you made your science contributions this week?" A young girl among them shouted at him.

When he looked, he noticed a face he recognized and one who apparently recognized him. Among the dozen hyper-researchers was Delphi, the young woman who had gotten him arrested a few months prior. Their eyes met. The other researchers were beckoning him, trying to bring him near with their words, but not her. To other patrons, no doubt, she would be doing the same. However, she watched Eustis quietly, studying him. She didn't look away. He raised one eyebrow at her and nodded. She cocked her head to the side at the surprising gesture and regarded him with curiosity.

He continued his walk through Roger's Dome, weaving cautiously among the narrow causeways of the Europa district. When the path dumped him onto the concourse between Roger's and Strong's dome, his pace quickened. Strong's hummed with Bezos City's main power equipment. The smell of fuel and grease filled his nose. He hadn't known where he was going until he was almost there. It hit him like a punch in the stomach when he realized what he was considering.

The southern end of Strong's held the massive conjunction course way leading out to the port. As he approached, he could hear the grumbling roar of rocket engines firing in the distance. The city transit sped by on its maglev railing twenty meters above his head. He passed under and stood in the tunnel that led to the exit. Not just the exit of Bezos proper, but if anyone was trying to make an exodus from Phobos, that tunnel was the way out.

He stared. He could do it. He could escape. He could find a freighter or private transport. He could return to Earth or maybe cast his fortunes farther afield and make his way to the asteroid belt. He could even try one of the moons of Jupiter. He stepped slowly toward a kiosk and made a gesture toward his own face. A display jumped to life before his eyes. He scanned the flight traffic schedule.

There was a mini-charter headed for earth. It didn't leave for another week, and the price was out of reach. *Three hundred thousand for a one-week trip!* He kept looking. A GovCorp shuttle was leaving on a round trip to Titan the next day. He motioned for the display to change. The price was, well, not great. He made a pinching gesture in the air, which brought up his bank statement. *It'd be tight.* He considered it for a moment. He wasn't sure what info they would scan for a GovCorp ship. Plus, there would be officers aboard. An entire month on a ship with them. What if *he*—the one who shot Jewels—was onboard? He winced. *No.* He waved it away and went back to the schedule.

"Perfect," he said when he spotted ID492R. Its flight plan included an immediate departure and stops all through the belt. It was a private fuel hauler with one seat available. Meals not included, *no big deal.* He could pick something up before the trip. It was leaving in two hours. He swiped through the air. *Wow. It's cheap.* Anything that cheap must be a dump, but it didn't matter. He was leaving one way or another, and the method was no concern.

He lifted his hand. He reached for the *purchase* button hovering before his face. When his finger was about to strike the gesture, a voice caught him off guard.

"Going somewhere?" a young woman said. Eustis swiped the display downward, making it disappear. As if he were looking at shameful images or illegal documents. He spun in place and found himself face to face with Delphi, the young hyper-terrestrial researcher. She had her floor-length lab coat buttoned up tight all the way to her neck.

"What?" Eustis said.

"Going somewhere?" she repeated. He squinted and cocked his head.

"What do you want?" he asked.

"I want to talk to you," she said. Her words were gentle, almost kind.

"Why are you here, though?"

"I followed you," she said. "If you're leaving Bezos City, I'd really like to talk to you before you go." She looked toward the port tunnel. "Are you leaving Phobos?"

"I uh—" he made a fist gesture to close the cortex display.

"We could go to my place."

"Listen, I'm not interested in your *religion*," he said, hoping the word would sting. Apparently, it didn't. There wasn't even a hint of disgust. What had changed, he didn't know.

"No, it's not that," she said. "I'm off the clock."

"Whatever," he jabbed. "Last time I saw you, I spent three days in jail."

"Yeah," she said. This time she blushed. "I'm sorry about that."

He puffed out his chest. "You might understand how I could be a little apprehensive about coming to your place."

"Please," she said. "I really need to talk to someone."

"I can't," he said. "My friends were just arrested. I've got to help them–" his words broke off short.

"How are you going to help them if you leave Bezos City?" she asked.

He lowered his eyebrows and glowered. "It's complicated. You wouldn't understand. I have to—"

"Do you know what they do to us?" Delphi asked. Eustis tilted backward slightly, not wanting to follow her line of thought.

"I have a pretty good idea what you get up to in that rotten place."

"No," her voice descended into a whisper. "I mean, do you know what the chief alien liaison does to us after we age out of the commune?" She glanced around as if someone might be listening. "When we get too old to work at the research commune, I mean. Do you know what they do?"

"No," Eustis said. "I haven't thought about it." He made a move as if he would walk on, but she had him hooked now.

She made a hand gesture that Eustis recognized. A notification popped up on his cortex display, but he didn't move to receive it. He considered trashing it. "Is this something that's going to scar me for all my days? I don't want to see—"

She reached out and laid her soft little hand across his arm. Her palm was cold, her skin pale. He could smell the sweet scent of some strong perfume. He looked at her hand before returning his eyes to her face. She took on an expression of pleading. "Please," she said.

"Just tell me what you came to tell me, and let's be done with it," he said.

"We can't talk here," she said. "The domes have ears."

"It's not a good idea," he said, parroting one of Marianna's favorite sayings. The memory stung.

"I'm begging you," she said. "Just look at the picture."

Reluctantly, he made the gesture to open the picture, and what he saw sent his heart rate into hyper-drive. He tried to swallow, but there was already a lump in his throat the size of an apple. His rapid breathing was accompanied by the sweat on his forehead. There was so much blood. *How could anyone do something like this?*

"I—" he stammered. "Is this—" He choked on his words. Her eyes were full of tears now. He saw her anew. Behind the brazen surface, fear danced in her eyes. "Okay," he said in a whisper. "Where's your place?"

CHAPTER FORTY-NINE

OUT

Eustis followed Delphi through the winding streets of Strongs, Rogers, and Horizon dome. A man with a large facial scar slept on the street under an old tattered GovCorp flag where they made their turn. A distant echo of laughter cackled down the hard surfaces of the passage. The lights pulsed a dim purple in this quarter. Somewhere nearby, the sound of rumbling music vibrated the ground. They turned down a walkway, too narrow for cruisers or rovers. A collection of old cluttered buildings lined the narrow alley, which curved in against a wall of Phobos' rock and so was hidden from the main street.

"It'd be better if no one saw you come in," Delphi whispered as she paused momentarily to ensure the way was clear. The alley reeked of smoke, and Eustis could taste the rust in the air. The young woman's hollow eyes continued to scan the shadows as she led him up a narrow flight of rickety stairs. The warped sheet metal of the thin door creaked as it swung open, and Delphi let Eustis inside.

The little place was carved into the rock. Its sparse decor hinted at the forced minimalism that accompanied her line of work. Thumping bass thrummed through the walls in a sepesprial cascade of thunder. A single door, not the one they had entered, was cut into the wall where the sound was most prominent.

"Does your place share a wall with a bar?" Eustis asked as he rotated to look at the tiny apartment. The rusty odor outside had been replaced with a sickly sweet incense, but it wasn't strong enough to mask the smoky aura.

"No," Delphi said. "That's the research commune." She pointed to the door, which was in the wall where the bass rumbled most profoundly. "They keep us close. Would you like anything to drink?" Delphi said.

"Nah. Thanks," Eustis replied. She looked down as she poured herself a glass of water. Eustis eyed the cup of clear liquid. Delphi approached and sat at one of two chairs that lined a little kitchen table. She moved with cool confidence. A single light bulb poured down a cataract of illumination.

He cleared his throat. "You know, I might actually take some water if that's ok. You're not on half rations, are you?" She nodded toward the little kitchenette, and he started toward the tap.

"Nope. That's one of the perks of being a researcher." She smiled, but the amusement didn't reach her eyes. "Free room, board, and water."

"It's not exactly free, is it?" Eustis said as he reached for a glass. "Seems to me like it's cost you quite a bit." His mouth felt like a desert as the clear liquid poured into his glass. He downed the contents and refilled.

"Yes, I guess it has." Her voice was a whisper. With a cup so full he had to walk slowly, he approached and took the other seat. She ran her finger around the rim of her glass in endless little circles. "About to cost me everything."

"And has it been worth it?" Eustis asked.

"Look," she bristled. "You have no idea what it's like." Her face hardened, and she was about to say more, but Eustis reached across the table, laid his hand across Delphi's, and spoke before she was able.

"I'm so sorry they've done this to you. No one should be forced to do what you're doing. It's terrible." Her angry look dissolved and was replaced by curiosity.

"Why?" she asked. "Why should no one have to do this?" She cocked her head to the side and furrowed her brow. "Someone has to do it, right?

Otherwise, we wouldn't know what the hypers want us to do. The hyper's will is supreme. If they want me to do this, then it's what I have to do."

"And you believe that?" he said before taking a sip of water. "The stuff about the hyper-terrestrials?"

"Do you always avoid questions by asking more questions?" she said. "I want to know why you think no one should have to do what I'm doing." Eustis smiled at her spark. He took a long breath and spoke over the drumming bass.

"Well, it's just wrong." he tried. The lines around her eyes deepened. "It's against God's laws." She leaned back in her chair and crossed her arms. "Okay, you know about GovCorp interplanetary law, right?" She nodded. "Did you know there are other laws, written into the fabric of the universe, that are even more important? No matter how much we might want to pretend they don't exist or erase them, they are still there. They're inescapable. A lot of them have to do with how we treat each other." She leaned forward, uncrossed her arms, and opened her eyes wide. Eustis said, "You're designed with a conscience. You can sense what's right, even if you don't always follow it."

"Sense?"

"Yeah," Eustis said. "The whole hyper-terrestrial system is designed to mask those deeper laws. It does nothing but distract, distort, and damage your conscience. Its ultimate aim is death." She was about to respond, but he put his hand in the air. "I answered one of yours. Now you answer one of mine," he said. She smiled and nodded. "That picture you showed me at the docks. Who was she? What happened to her?"

Delphi turned her glass upside down and slid it around on the table. "Hera," she said in a wispy voice. "She was one of us. She was a junior alien liaison like me but a year older. She turned twenty and aged out. So the chief liaison had her—" She paused and spun her glass on the table. "They sent her to reclamation."

"No," Eustis said.

"What?" She looked up with a bitter stare letting the glass wobble to a stop.

"No," Eustis said. "They didn't *reclaimate* her. They *murdered* her."

"Murder?" she said as if the word was unfamiliar. "But the hypers command it. They command that only a group of junior liaisons with a number equal to the smallest odd prime, that's three, be preserved for further service in the research commune. For the rest of the girls, their essence is released from their bodies so they can join the hypers on their home world of Elysium. They say it's the most blissful experience anyone can ever have."

"The Alysian Fields," Eustis said to himself darkly.

"What?" she asked.

"There's nothing new under the sun," he said.

"What do you mean?"

"This whole thing. The hypers. Their commands. It's an ancient hoax. It was all over Earth for generations."

"Are you saying the hypers aren't real?" Delphi said in a blast of rushed words. "Because I've seen things that I can't—" she took a gulping breath. "I've seen things happen. I've seen them do things. Recently I saw Athima in the smoke of the channeling arc. I heard her speak through the sparks. It was my ostricular trange that called her forward."

"No, I'm not saying they aren't real," Eustis said. "I'm saying they aren't who you think they are."

She closed her eyes and rubbed her face with her hands as if she both wanted and didn't want to go on. "I've felt weird ever since I met you on the street that day. Especially when it's my turn to do service in the commune. I feel—" Her voice broke, and tears began to well up at the corners of her eyes. She fixed her blue iridescent stare on him.

"You can say it," he whispered.

"I'm scared," she said, now the tears were streaming. "The hypers are dark. They're shadows. They love blood. And now there is this new guy that does the old science, and he's so scary. The whole thing is so—" she paused as if she didn't have the word. Eustis offered one.

"It's called *evil*," he said. "It's *evil*." She turned and looked at the little door in the wall that still rattled with thunderous music. He could imagine them bursting through at any moment.

"That day, they arrested you? You were about to say something right when they hit you." She was whispering now. "You said 'we worship–'"

"Demons," he said in a cool, even tone.

"Demons," she said, trying the word on. "What are they?"

"It's a long story," Eustis said. "And at the moment, there are people who need me. My friends were just arrested, and I've got to figure out how to get them out. I don't even know how. That picture you showed me isn't the first murder I've seen today. One of our kids was just shot, and—" He closed his eyes and breathed deep through his nose, trying to push the horrid vision from his mind. "The kids I take care of are going to be wondering where I am and—" He glanced at the exit and put his hands on the table, about to rise. "They need me." She put her hand on his.

"I'm so sorry to hear that, but I need you," she said. Eustis pulled back, wondering if he'd misjudged the nature of her invitation. "Not like that. I just need to tell you—" She wiped her eyes with the back of her hand. "I haven't told you everything. Ever since they dragged you away in that police rover, I've been having dreams. They're happening almost every night now."

"Okay," Eustis eased.

"In my dream—" before Delphi could finish her words, a loud thud, more present than the thrumming bass, filled the apartment. The door in the wall shared by the commune bent on its hinges.

"Oh, no!" Delphi said. She looked to the little door and rose from her chair with deep-set fear in her eyes. "They— They—" She couldn't get a breath, and her face was bright red. A shattering sound drowned the room in noise. Colored lights cascaded in through the broken passageway. In the door stood a handful of dark silhouettes.

CHAPTER FIFTY

MADAM

The door to the commune complex swung open and slammed against the wall. The thumping bass that had assaulted the apartment was now filled with loud, chaotic treble, and a wash of noise, Eustis stood his ground.

"Grab him!" a low female voice said when the men in dark robes started for him. Eustis backed up, opened the door, and was nearly out on the landing before three sets of rough hands dragged him back into the apartment. The sheet metal door smashed closed. The thugs smelled of sweat and cologne. "Hold 'em fast!"

"Yes, Madam," one of the men said. They were not dressed in traditional officers' uniforms but wore black robes, black undershirts, and black pants. Black everything. Even their eyes were black, which had to be an expensive genetic modification. They tightened their grip on his arms.

Eustis caught sight of the owner of the female voice. A tall woman in a floor-length lab coat stood in the doorway. She had to be at least fifty-five, but her age didn't stop her from wearing the otherwise revealing apparel of the researchers. Her face was sallow and pale. She towered over the men by at least a half meter. He realized that the imposing woman was talking.

"Aren't you going to introduce me, Jr. Liaison Delphi?" the woman said.

"My apologies Madam Styx. He's just a hyper enthusiast. I forgot to register his visit," Delphi said.

"I said, introduce us."

"Yes, Madam Styx," Delphi said. "Eustis, this is Chief Alien Liaison and head hyper-terrestrial researcher first-class, Madam Electra Isis Styx."

"Eustis," Electra said as she glided into the room and walked a tight circle around him. She touched his face with a handful of long black nails. She smelled like the burning incense of the commune and moved like its smoke. She squeezed his jaw between her finger and thumb, letting her dark nail jab into his cheek. "Is what my servant says true, little Eustis?" He was about to speak, but Delphi interrupted.

"Madam, it's just an innocent mistake. I should have—" Delphi's words were shattered. In one whirling motion, Madam Electra twirled and caught Delphi's face with the back of her hand. The concussion knocked her to the floor. Eustis lurched forward to help, but the men at his side gripped him tighter as they laughed.

Clearly a trained response, Delphi rose from the floor quickly and said, "Thank you, Madam Liaison. May the hypers allow you long life and blissful days." The woman then turned her attention back to Eustis, who was still squirming against the three goons' grasp.

"Tell me, little Eustis, what were you two doing in here?"

"That's none of your business, Nails," Eustis said. "I know you're some kind of chief witch of that smelly, noisy circus downstairs, but I don't care. You can turn the music down. Cut those ridiculous nails, and put on some proper clothes. As for the girl, let her go, and then we can talk. Cause that girl there, and all the others aren't yours."

Madam Electra Styx let a broad smile creep across her face. It spread into a toothy grin before it spilled over into full-throated laughter. The men at Eustis' side joined in, jolting him wildly as they cackled. Delphi looked at the floor, and Eustis remained stoic.

"I love it!" Madam Electra said. "No one has talked to me like that since," she paused to think, looked at the ceiling, and said, "well, never."

She turned to Delphi. "Where did you find this minikin? He's delicious." She didn't answer but kept her eyes on the ground.

"And another thing," Eustis said. "I know what you do with the girls who age out. This may be a rotten, no-good place, but there are still consequences for *murder*." Electra and her thugs laughed. Eustis had more he could say, but he bottled it up.

"When I was a young researcher," Electra said, "a smidge younger than little Delphi, I had a repeat visitor to my dais. Each time he arrived, he insisted that we converse before I did the science rituals for him. By *converse*, I mean he wanted me to ask him questions so he could talk about himself. If I asked him the right kinds of questions, he would be happy, and he'd be on his way before long. But if I asked a question he didn't like, he would fly into a rage and beat me. Since he was one of the commune's most generous contributors, the head Madam did nothing to stop him." She stepped close to Eustis.

"You want to know what I learned?" Her voice was eerie in its ironic sweetness. She reached out and petted her hand down his shoulder and arm. He tried to jerk away. "I learned never to ask a question that I didn't already know the answer to." She pulled her hand away and made a gesture in the air. A video clip appeared in the open space between them. Eustis recognized his own voice and image immediately.

"The whole hyper-terrestrial system is designed to mask those deeper laws. It does nothing but distract, distort, and damage your conscience. Its ultimate aim is death," Eustis said in the clip. He glanced around the room, looking for the hidden camera. It was well hidden, but based on the angle, it had to be near the ceiling above the door that led to the commune. He watched the video that had been taken only moments ago play out.

"Oh, this is my favorite part," Madam Electra said. She swung her hand to move the video forward. The video version of Delphi was speaking.

"You said 'we worship–"

"Demons."

Madam Electra made a pinching gesture to pause the video and then swiped it away.

"Did you know about this?" Eustis said in Delphi's direction. The girl didn't respond but kept her eyes on the floor. "Was this a setup?"

"You were wrong, little man," Electra said. "That little girl is mine. These little men are mine." She pointed to the black-clad thugs who held Eustis on all sides. "And now, you're mine." She spun around and began to march away. She pointed a condescending finger at Delphi and said, "Bad dog. Stay." She waved at the men who would be Eustis' escort. "Take him for a ride."

Rather than take the back exit, they pulled him, kicking and sometimes screaming through the research commune. Spastic lights flashed. Mind-numbing music rumbled in a bone-crushing drone. The smell of burning incense and ozone was strong in the colorful chamber. Girls stood at at least a dozen daises in lab coats taking part in strange pseudo-scientific rituals of various kinds. Standing around the perimeter of the domed main room were robotic soldiers. The death-dealing machines watched him with their roving lifeless eyes, yet they made no other moves. Eustis had been right to avoid the creepy place. He closed his eyes, let the men drag him, and prayed every step of the way.

When they hauled Eustis into the open space of the outer dome, he felt like he could finally breathe again. They shoved him into a black rover that was waiting outside the commune, and it sped down the street. Despite his attempts to talk to the sweaty, sullen, black-robed men, they were as quiet as space. In ten minutes, the rover came to a stop in front of a column that ran up toward the center peak of Bezos Dome. They dragged him toward the doors. Above them flashed a blue illuminated sign that read Bezos Municipal Compartments.

The atrium had a broad arching opening that looked down upon a complex of spiraling levels. It was familiar to Eustis, but he felt no fondness for the place. Somewhere inside were his friends. He'd give anything to see them again. He let his eyes follow the towering column that rose overhead toward the apex of Bezos Dome. A set of glass elevators sped up and down through a central shaft stopping at the twenty levels above to let passengers off.

"Listen, Ralph," one of the thugs said when they arrived at the front desk. "This guy is here to see Montobond." A portly man in a blue jumpsuit manned the counter. His name tag read *Ralph Sproket* with a little flashing notice underneath that said *on duty*.

Ralph's eyes did not come up from whatever he was looking at on his personal cortex display as he said, "This ain't a hair salon. Montobond don't take appointments. Get lost."

"Madam Electra Styx sent him," a thug barked. At the name Ralph glanced up from his seat and spotted the black-clad thugs. He rose and straightened his uniform. The thug continued. "She said he was to stand traditional trial before Chancellor Montobond immediately."

Ralph stepped back as if he had been punched in the chest. He smoothed his hair and nodded cautiously. He said, "Well, you'll have to see Montobond's assistant. I can't make appointments for him. I'm just the—"

"Ok, Ralph," one thug said. "Here's what you're going to do. Get a few of your blue suits out here to take this guy into custody. Put him in lockup until the chancellor can see him. We're not doing your job for you."

"That's not exactly my job," Ralph said, but he crumbled and made a gesture into the open air.

"I need a custody officer in the main atrium right away," Ralph said.

"Better make it two," the thug said. Ralph eyed him for a second. The thug patted Eustis' earth-born muscular shoulders. "He's a thick fella."

"Correction, make that two custody officers."

Within a few minutes, Eustis had been turned over to the officers in the blue jumpsuits. He was glad to be rid of the black-robed thugs but nervous about what was to come.

Chapter Fifty-One

DISCOVERY

"My apologies, Admiral, I had to deal with a—" Madam Electra paused long enough to find the word, "a situation." She gestured for the two girls to leave the room. As they hurried out, Madam Electra noticed that Chloe's right cheek and eye were red and already shifting toward blue. She could tell by the state of the apartment that Admiral Strafe had not liked the substitutes she had left in her place. She smiled in spite of the palpable tension in the room. "Where were we?"

"Nowhere but here," Admiral Strafe said, standing over a makeshift table where he had his weapon disassembled for cleaning. "By myself in this pitiful little room, where you left me in." He gave her a stare that could have pierced tempered titanium.

"I assure you it was an urgent matter," she said, hoping the excuse would be sufficient.

"No more interruptions." He spat the words as if he were talking to a dog. She imagined a half dozen snarky things she could say in response but bit her lip to keep them from spilling out.

"Yes," she agreed as she moved back to the center of the room and stood ready for his next command. "Of course." She could tell that her deference was inadequate, as the storm brewing about his brows indicated.

"And this urgent interruption," Strafe said, "it was more urgent than an Admiral's commands." He pursed his lips. "That *is* urgent."

Her practiced eyes noted the anger tightening his face, a warning sign not to be ignored. *Get low,* she thought. She knelt next to the table, careful to make sure her eye line was far below his. "It was a non-science visitor to one of my girls," she explained. Strafe bristled. She was immediately aware the words were too weak.

"You left me alone for a full eighteen minutes and forty-seven seconds on account of a non-paying customer?" Strafe said. His hands were in fists. He towered over her kneeling posture in a frightening pile of muscle and hate.

"Admiral, you are the most important person we have ever hosted at our humble establishment." She was keen enough to know she was fighting for her life even though the battle had hardly begun.

"Most important person?" Strafe repeated. "More important than Chancellor Montobond!"

She said the first thing that came to her mind, and as the words were escaping her lips, she realized a second too late that they were a mistake. "Montobond doesn't patronize this establishment," Electra said. A large hand swung free and caught her across the mouth. The force knocked her against the wall. Strafe leaped, lifted her, and pinned her against the stone surface by her throat. With his huge hand wrapped around her neck, he put his other hand over her mouth and pinched her nose at the same time.

"You didn't answer my question," Strafe said. She tried to speak against his palm, but no noise came out. He continued. "Eighteen minutes and forty-seven seconds. There are limits to my patience, and eighteen minutes and forty-seven seconds is certainly outside any limit I have. I pacified myself by thinking that five minutes might be given to a visitor as urgent as a chancellor, such as Montobond. That was the only person in all of Bezos City that could warrant leaving me alone in this room with my unmet expectations." He leaned so close to her face that his hot breath swirled around her cheeks. "Now, you're going to tell me what you were doing, and how in the name of Athima it was more important than *me* and my urgent mission to root out a religionist traitor from your crumbling city." He let go of her face. She gasped for air as the dry atmosphere rushed into her burning lungs.

"It was a—" she breathed, "a matter of life and death." Apparently, he wasn't satisfied. He tightened his grip on her neck and balled his free hand into a fist. It perched in the air, ready to strike.

"Try again," he said, letting his fist hover.

"A man was trying to sow abhorrent philosophy into the mind of my girls. The man himself is a peasant, a dog, a worm. But the urgency is in what he was saying... Very dangerous, poisonous ideas. He visited before and poisoned the mind of my most faithful liaison. She hasn't been the same since. She admits nothing, but from the moment that meddling slug spoke to her, she's been useless as a researcher, a terrible alien liaison, and avoids her supporters. I had to act. This man's words are venom and he's aiming to bring down this house on my head. It's embedded in our order, by the hyper-terrestrials themselves. No negative word may be spoken of the hypers within these premises or the entire establishment might fall to ruin. I had to go. I was compelled. If I didn't meet the challenge, there might be no commune for you to visit the next time you honor us with your presence. It's one of our most ancient dictums, that we defend the honor of our alien contacts with our lives." She was going to go on, fighting for altitude with her words, but she stopped. Strafe's fist had converted into a single finger poised before her face.

"Who is he?" Strafe said, squinting his eyes.

"He told one of my girls that going to reclamation is murder, and all this only a month before her ascension," Electra said. "Can you imagine? Not just that. He speaks ill of all the work we do here. He complains against everything we've achieved in hyper-terrestrial communication. He opposes the hypers themselves. He's a rebel that needs to be put down."

"Eustis Grimes," Strafe growled.

"You know of him?" Electra said.

"He is the one I am here to burn," Strafe said. He lifted his free hand and slapped Electra across the face. He then returned his hand, finger pointed, and poked her in the nose. "And you let him get away. You should have told me what you were doing. Don't forget I'm in charge."

"Yes, Admiral," Madam Electra said. "But I didn't let him get away."

"You have him here?"

"No, Admiral," she said. "I've sent him to Chancellor—"

"Montobond," Strafe rumbled. "That filthy curmudgeon!"

Strafe tossed her aside as if she were a piece of garbage and made his way toward the door. In three steps he had gestured to open a comm line with his robotic squad of soldiers. "HEXA, assemble my guard to my location. Take formation." He stepped through the door and into the corridor, shouting over his shoulder, "Woman, come!"

CHAPTER FIFTY-TWO

TOGETHER

Eustis watched the parade of jeering faces blur by as the custody officers dragged him through the Bezos municipality compartments. The narrowing corridors became claustrophobic as the familiar scent of the crystalline particulate in the air met his nose. When the big blue-suited man breached the semi-pressure lock hatch that led into the jail facility, a rush of cold dusty air blasted past them. Eustis was shoved harshly through the opening and squeezed into one of the miniature jail cells carved into the rock. His lungs were already protesting the thin air, and his eyes the familiar sight of a prison that three days' acquaintance had produced no fondness for. The custody officer said nothing as he exited the narrow passageway and disappeared through the hatch. A loud beep and a painful silence followed in its wake.

"Hey, newbie, what ya in for?"

"Enzo?" Eustis gasped. His own voice sounded flimsy. He pressed his head against the bars but wasn't able to see down the corridor. Both Enzo and Eustis started talking at the same time, then they both stopped, and an awkward silence followed.

"You first," Enzo said.

"Is everyone in here?"

"I be present, mate," Rudwick said. His voice was distant, and his tone tearful.

"Marianna?" Eustis asked, hopefully. When she didn't respond. Enzo's voice filled the separation between them.

"She's here, but she isn't speaking. Hasn't said anything since..." Enzo paused. His breath was long and slow. "Since the incident." At the word, Rudwick burst into blubbering sobs.

"Oh me sweet Jewels!" He wailed. "And me kitty!"

"He's been crying since we got in here," Enzo said.

"Marianna," Eustis said. "Tell me you're ok." He waited for a few seconds, but there was no response. He spoke cautiously. "After what they did to Jewels, I worried that you might have..." He choked on his words. "Thank God, you're alive. I just couldn't imagine if—" He flopped on the floor as waves of relief washed over him. He couldn't believe he had considered leaving Bezos City. This was where he was supposed to be.

"Why are you here?" Enzo said.

"It's a long story," Eustis said.

"We've got nothing but time," Enzo said. "Plus, I think a story might be good for the big guy. All this crying fits him like a sundress on a coal miner."

"I got tricked by Delphi," Eustis said. "Again."

"The researcher who put you in here the first time?" Enzo asked. "She called the fuzz on you again?"

"She acted like she had some urgent reason she had to talk. But it was a setup. Her head lady came in, and things got ugly."

"You talked to the chief liaison?" Enzo said as if it were impressive. "Wow. You must have caused some serious trouble."

"Why?" Eustis asked.

"She doesn't deal with the locals. Receives GovCorp uppers when they come to town. She's basically a commune diplomat. "

"She *basically* creeps me out," Eustis said. "I mean you should have seen the nails on that broad. Looked like vulture talons."

"A year ago we were doing a job that took us to Calisto," Enzo said. "The chief liaison there, Madam Artemis Rhea got her hands on me. Thought I was just some random street-creeping kid. Wanted to make me one of her research assistants. Nearly got her way, too, except Mari and Rudwick busted me out. They nearly got burned for it. She had her teeth filed to sharpened points. Looked like she'd been seeing a shark dentist. Creepiest lady I ever saw."

Eustis smiled at the kid's resilience. "You holding up ok?" he asked as he polished one of the cell bars with his thumb. The words required more exertion than they should have. He rubbed his temple where the headache was already setting in.

"Well, I'm hungry, but I'm not going to die of starvation," Enzo said.

"That's the spirit. God is watching out for—"

"I mean," Enzo interrupted. "We'll die of thirst long before we starve."

"Oh—"

"That's if the low air pressure doesn't kill us first," Enzo added.

"I spent three days in here," Eustis said. "Awful headaches and dizziness, but survivable." He gasped. "Do you think they'd turn the air up if we asked real nice?"

"Low air pressure is on purpose," Enzo said. "All the prisons do it. Keeps inmates docile. Hard to start a prison riot when even a trip to the pot leaves you wheezing."

"Right."

They sat there quietly, listening to Rudwick's weeping. The distant rumble of rocket fire shook the stone around them. A greenish light strip buzzed a lonely one-note melody from above. Eustis palmed his eyes, and white fireworks exploded across the black. An unexpected beep blared, and the hall outside the jail bars flashed from green to red.

"Prisoner, Eustis Grimes," said a voice over the loudspeaker. "Proceed from lockup to the chamber door and await a custody officer to escort you to your appointment." A metallic click followed the voice, and the jail cell swung wide. Instead of proceeding to the airlock door Eustis stepped into the hall and made his way directly to the barred face of Enzo's cell. Enzo's eyes were bright despite being rimmed with black and blue. He reached his hand through the bars as Enzo reached back.

"I love you, Brother," Eustis said. Enzo echoed the same words.

"Prisoner, Eustis Grimes," the loudspeaker's voice boomed. "Proceed immediately to the exit. Do not fraternize with the other prisoners." Instead of obeying, Eustis slid one cell down and found Rudwick in the compartment. He filled nearly the entire space with his massive frame. Eustis stuck his arm through the bars and spoke quickly.

"I love you, Brother," Eustis said. "We'll mourn our loss together soon." Rudwick burst into tears as he reached his thick arm through a slit, took the back of Eustis' neck in his massive hand, and pulled him against the bars. It was as close to a hug as they could manage.

"Prisoner, Eustis Grimes," the loudspeaker crackled. "This is your last warning. Move immediately to the exit, or you will be forcibly removed from the facility." The speaker clicked off for a second before the voice came back on. "You don't want that, trust me." Instead of complying, Eustis slid one cell down and stood before Marianna's chamber. She was already standing at the bars expectant. Her face was ashen white, and her hands were already reaching through the bars for him.

"I'm so sorry," Eustis said. "Maybe if I would have—" Eustis tried, but his voice broke off. "Maybe I could have—" Marianna reached up to his mouth and placed one finger against his lips.

"Make me a promise," she whispered.

"Name it."

"Keep your mouth shut," she said. He cocked his head at the strange request. "Promise me you won't say anything to them."

"What?" Eustis said. "Why?"

"I admire that you're willing to die, but I was just starting to like having you alive." She gave him a stare with so much gravity. He felt like he was falling down into those eyes. In his blissful trance, it took his greatest stubbornness to fight off the impulse to agree.

"I can't—" he started, but she interrupted.

"Tell me you'll try."

"Ok, I'll try to keep my mouth shut," he said.

She put her hands through the upper slits and twisted them into his hair. She pulled his face close to hers to the point where their foreheads touched. He could feel her warm breath on his face, and they lingered there for the briefest moment. He closed his eyes as her lips met his. With the cold bar pressed into the side of his face, he returned her delicate kiss. On contact, he felt a hot blast of electricity jolt through his body. His heart sped, and his stomach dropped. A loud beep sounded, and the red lights began flashing. The voice came back over the speaker, clearly more irritated now.

"Prisoner, remain still with your hands over your head. Any sudden motion and your custody officer is authorized to shoot."

Eustis put his hands in the air without breaking contact with Marianna's lips. It was her that ended the embrace. She shoved him back away from the bars. He studied her face. She put one finger to her lips and mouthed, *keep your mouth shut.*

He watched her as strong hands wrapped around his arms. There was a flurry of jostling and agitation, but he held her eye contact until a fist caught him across the jaw like a hammer. Another was buried into his stomach, buckling him over with the impact.

Once he was subdued, the three custody officers dragged him roughly down the corridor and through the partial airlock. Once they were outside, he drew deeply upon the thicker air as the custody officers attached a pair of power cuffs to one of his arms and locked the other side to a custody drone. The six-legged robot had a crane jutting up from its mechanical spine. It looked something like a giant police spider. The power cuffs clicked in place. One of the custody officers spoke to the drone as if it were a child.

"Take prisoner, Eustis Grimes, to Chancellor Phineas Montobond's compartment."

The robot walked, dragging Eustis. He didn't know what was waiting for him at the other end of this march. He intended to say a silent prayer as he walked, but his mind kept wandering back to Marianna.

CHAPTER FIFTY-THREE

APPOINTMENT

By the time Eustis was in the elevator, his arm ached from being pulled along by the custody drone. The three men who followed jabbered with a litany of gory exploits perpetrated on Bezos citizens. Eustis wondered idly if Delphi had been involved in any of their adventures in that dark, disgusting place. He did his best to ignore the inappropriate banter as the elevator climbed the dome's central shaft. The bustling movement that scurried about in Bezos Dome swirled and shrank below. Phineas Montobond's quarters were at the uppermost level of the column that reached into the only portion of the dome that wasn't buried in Phobos' rock.

The elevator ascended past the surface line as amber sunbeams coursed through the dusty glass above. He squinted into the radiant rays that seemed to dance about the compartment, little happy wisps of pure warmth. He closed his eyes and basked for a few seconds before the elevator dinged with a jagged bleep. The doors slid open, and he was, once again, being tugged roughly forward.

Instead of a waiting area, as he expected, the entire compartment was rimmed in the glass of the dome. He craned to look at the panorama that spread in all directions. Around the exterior of the dome was rock rising up on all sides. Its massive size almost allowed him to forget they were in a cave. Above the central peak of Bezos Dome hung that massive reflecting orb glowing orange a few hundred meters overhead. He stared at it, looking like a half-ripe orange effortlessly suspended in the yawning cavern space. An invisible cataract of sunlight poured in from the cavern mouth, only lightly touching the rim of the giant cave, the blinding beam painted the exhaust of every ship that ventured near enough. The illuminated plume trails looked like blinding streaks of fire in the half-lit cavern. Ships skittered about the cavern opening like moths drawn to the remaining embers of a once-great flame.

"Beautiful, isn't it?" said a voice as thin as atmosphere. Eustis shifted his attention to the room before him. The plush compartment that surrounded him was decorated with an array of expensive and rare items. Sitting in a high-back chair, fingers of both hands meeting in little archways, sat a man of considerable age. His white beard reached to the middle of his chest, and the whispy strands of grey hair hung across his pockmarked face. This had to be Chancellor Montobond. Eustis didn't respond, remembering Marianna's pleading. *Keep your mouth shut.* He would do his best.

"Do you intend to stand at the mouth of the elevator like a bucked tooth baboon, or are you going to come in?" he said. He didn't rise, but Eustis' six-legged custody bot glided forward as the human guards matched pace. "And who is this?" One of the guards next to him waved a hand at his own display node and began to speak.

"This is prisoner Eustis Grimes, undeclared crew of *Resurr*—"

"Blah blah blah," Montobond said. "Let's get to any pertinent information you have, shall we?" The guard bristled and made another gesture, this time more aggressive.

"Madam Electra ordered—" another guard began, but Montobond cut across his words.

"Ordered?" Montobond grumbled. "I'm sorry, I'm an old man, and my hearing isn't what it used to be. Did you say that Madam Eye Shadow ordered me to do something? I do not take orders from that featherless crow. What about you, Jaw Muscles?" he said, gesturing to the other guard who had not spoken yet. "Why don't you tell me what's going on?"

"Sir," the remaining guard said. "Madam Electra Styx *requests* that you send this criminal to reclamation."

"Reclamation?" Montobond said, raising one eyebrow. "Would she like me to hear his side of the story, or would she prefer I simply send him to the meat grinder without investigation?" Even the thick-necked guards were intelligent enough to recognize a rhetorical question. They didn't respond. Montobond took a breath, opened his mouth, but then paused. His eyes shot to one side. He waved his hand at an invisible alert.

"I'm in a meeting. What is it?" he said to the comm app as he turned his chair so that his profile was silhouetted against the glowing domed city below. "Prisoner Eustis Grimes, three muscle heads, and a custody tank. Why?" Montobond said to the person on the comm. "That's right. He's here with me right now. Why?" Eustis saw the Chancellor steal a glance in his direction. "What?" Montobond rose with more speed than a man of his age ought to possess. "What is that roid-riddled rhino doing in my city? Have security escort him to the—" Montobond paused. "That is ridiculous," he paused. "Ok. Make him wait." Montobond gave the standard gesture to end the communication and stepped toward Eustis.

"Things just got more interesting," Montobond said. He squinted his eyes and cocked his head to the side. As he studied Eustis, he stroked his beard and clucked his tongue. "It seems that Madam Smoky Eyes isn't the only one that wants you dead. You've been causing trouble in my city, and you've made some powerful enemies from the other side of Sol, too." Montobond spun around, scratched his head, and walked toward the dome wall.

"You know, I took this job almost forty years ago," Montobond said. "I took the job because I cared about the city. Really cared." Montobond paced in the space between the dome glass and Eustis. "You know how long that lasted?" He looked back at Eustis. "I cared for almost a year, then the numbness set in. Do you know about the numbness?"

Eustis watched the old man but resisted his near-insatiable urge to respond. Montobond gestured to the guards standing next to him. "These guys know about the numbness, right, boys?" They didn't respond either. "The constant grind of it all. What made you sick yesterday only makes you queasy today. On and on." He stepped closer to Eustis. "I can tell from your build that you're an Earther. You've been off-world, what, less than a year? Set out to the black skies with a big dream, probably. How long before that dream became a nightmare? How long before the numbness took the wind out of you?"

Eustis bit his lip and tried to look anywhere but Montobond's face. The old man whispered as he approached. "You've got to be feeling it by now. The dark. The cold. The oppressive pressure to conform to the whittling bitterness of it all." He reached a bony hand and pointed at the power cuffs that attached him to the custody drone. "Forty years ago, I would have cared about you. About all this. I would have had to get to the bottom of it. I would have had to put that old gothic bird, Madam Electra Styx, in her cage. I would have had to stand my ground against Admiral Kynig Meat Head Strafe. But this is what the grind does. It makes you so mind-numb that you just can't care anymore. There comes the point where all you have left is anger. The great justifier. I wish I could care, but I just don't anymore. In fact, I'm incapable of caring any longer. It's been burned out of me." He paused and squared up with Eustis. "Don't you have anything to say for yourself?"

When Eustis didn't respond, Montobond took a deep breath and spun. "I just got a call that Admiral Strafe is on his way, and he wants you. He's an absolute murdering butcher. But what's worse, he has bad manners. Technically, he's got no jurisdiction here, and I'd love to slam the door on his fingers."

"Madam Electra insists—" one of the guards spoke up.

"Shut up," Montobond said. "Bribes are still illegal, you know. I don't care what Madam Crow Claws is paying. She's not in charge here." The man quieted immediately. Montobond closed his eyes and rubbed his head until his hair looked like he'd been standing in front of a drive plume. With his eyes still closed, he scratched one eyebrow with a pinky.

"Whatever," Montobond said. "I don't have the energy to fight these goons anymore. I'm going to give you to Strafe. He's going to kill you. I'd say sorry about that, but lying to a dying man isn't any more efficient than telling the truth." Darkness squeezed around the edges of Eustis' vision like a black boa constrictor. His heart thumped so hard he was sure everyone in the room could hear it. A chilled sweat shoved its way through the pores on his forehead. He clenched his hands into fists and closed his eyes. *Lord let me stay faithful,* he prayed, *even until death.* He felt a tug on his power cuffs as the custody bot started to pull him toward the elevator. He heard the shuffle of footsteps as the custody guards followed the drone.

He took a deep breath. *Sorry, Marianna,* he thought. *I have to.*

"You're wrong!" he said in a grave voice.

"Yeah, yeah, yeah," The guard at his left said. "Life isn't fair."

"No," Eustis said as the elevator doors slid open. "You're wrong about the numbness. You can care again."

"Wait!" Montobond called. The guards spread out as Montobond stepped into Eustis' personal space. "Say something else."

"You don't have to give in to the numbness," Eustis said. "There's another way." At Eustis' words, Montobond's eyes grew wide. He laid a hand over his mouth and stood completely motionless.

"It's impossible," Montobond said through his fingers. "It's just impossible." He looked suddenly intense. "Custody drone, release the prisoner, Eustis Grimes." The three guards protested.

"Get out, or I will have this custody bot remove you!" Montobond shouted. A long staring contest followed, but the men started to move toward the elevator.

"Madam Electra will be—" one of the guards said, but Montobond sliced into his words.

"Get out of here, you slags-crusted grumbletonians!" They filed into the lift, and one of them stabbed the button with a knife-like finger. When the elevator doors finally closed between them and the guards, Eustis was left alone with Montobond. The old man walked circles around Eustis, looking him up and down. Clearly, something had changed.

"Say something else," Montobond said. "I want to hear you."

"I—I'm Eustis from Earth, and I'm talking. I'm talking."

"Now say, 'loved the world so much that he gave his only son.'"

"Wait a minute," Eustis said as the breath left his lungs involuntarily. "Where did you hear that?"

"You're taller than I imagined you," he chortled. Montobond was about to say more, but a chirping beep blared through the compartment, and a voice Eustis didn't recognize spoke through a public address speaker. "Sir, Admiral Strafe is coming up. We tried to stop him, but we couldn't. He's in the elevator. On his way up now."

"That fool," Montobond said, only allowing the news to half douse his effervescent demeanor. "Come on. We have to get you out of here." He followed Montobond across the plush apartment to a small hatch that had been hidden from Eustis' view by the elevator. "Sorry, kid. You've got to take the fire exit." Montobond spun the manual hatch wheel and was stuffing Eustis in before he had time to realize what was happening.

"Where did you hear John 3:16?," Eustis said, trying to buy a moment.

"No time for that now," Montobond said as he shoved his legs into the cramped compartment. It was a little pod, not much bigger than a jump seat. "Strap in," Montobond commanded wildly. "Find a place to hide out. Strafe is a nasty goon." Montobond shoved on the hatch door. Before he got it closed, Eustis stuck his hand in the opening.

"Sir, my friends are in jail, would it be possible to have them re—" Montobond shoved his hand in, slammed the door, and spun the latch.

The sound of the blaring siren died away. Through a small hatch window, Eustis saw Montobond working at a little panel next to the escape pod. A metal window shade slid down like a guillotine over the window, and the pod interior was dark. He could hear the sound of his own breathing and the muffled noise of Montobond working outside the capsule. A second later, an interior light clicked on, and a rumbling sound erupted from underneath his seat.

Suddenly he was moving. Being on Phobos for months had given him a feel for the standard microgravity. This was not standard. It was propelled motion. He was pressed into the metal seat as his weight increased five, maybe six times its normal. He tightened his abdomen muscles as Enzo had taught him to do under a heavy burn. As quickly as the crushing thrust had enveloped him, it was gone. He went from weighing more than he had for months to weighing nothing at all. His stomach twisted into a knot.

He reached for the metal window shade and slid it out of the way. A blinding orange orb filled his entire field of vision. He panicked as the pod fell back toward Bezos City.

CHAPTER FIFTY-FOUR

REMOVED

"What is the meaning of this?" Chancellor Montobond shouted as the locked elevator door which led to his office fell to the ground in an explosion of bent metal. "Desist at once!" Despite his strong words, Admiral Strafe was preceded through the hatchway by three robotic soldiers. The murderous drones took up positions and trained their weapons on Montobond. Once Strafe was in the door, he squared off with the Chancellor and smirked. Behind him, Madam Electra Styx and two of her black-clad goons breached the hatch and followed Strafe in.

"Montobond," Strafe said. Behind Strafe, Madam Electra was smiling.

"You can wipe that stupid grin off your face, Electra," Montobond said. "I'm surprised you can smile with as much xenoplastic as you've had pumped into your poor face flesh, speaking of which, who gave you that beautiful bruise? It's quite an improvement to your horrible face." The gothic woman stopped smiling at once.

"Give him to me, Montobond," Strafe growled. He gestured, and two of his killer drones stepped forward and took custody of the old man. They gripped his upper arm with their vice-like fingers.

"You can stay, Strafe," Montobond said. "But your pet crow will have to wait outside."

"A joke," Strafe said.

"A genius," Montobond said. He leaned around Strafe to see Madam Electra. "Electra want a cracker?"

Before Montobond could say anything else, Strafe stepped forward and rammed his fist into the chancellor's stomach. He stood over a wheezing Montobond with a grin.

"Give me the religionist criminal Eustis Wade Grimes. Now," Strafe thundered.

"Let me check my criminal collection," Montobond said. "If I don't have him, would you take a substitute?" Strafe punched him again. He would have doubled over, but the mechanized soldiers held his weight.

"We know he came to you only moments ago," Electra said.

"Oh," Montobond said. "The guy you sent over this morning? I sent him to reclamation. He's been ground and downed by now. Sorry, you just drank him."

As Strafe drove another fist into Chancellor Montobond's stomach, one of Electra's thugs stepped forward and delivered a whispered message.

"An escape pod was just spotted," Electra chimed in. Strafe straightened. He didn't turn in her direction, but he was clearly waiting for more. She continued. "Report says it will touch down portside in just a minute."

"Very well," Strafe said. He stroked his shaved chin for a few seconds as he looked at Montobond, who was still trying to catch his breath. "By stricture code five one six, section nine point two, I hereby relieve you of your duties as Chancellor of Bezos City."

"Five-one-six doesn't apply in this situation," Montobond said. "You'd have to be a sitting member of the council to—" Strafe punched him again as he continued to speak.

"Let the record show that Chancellor Phineas Montobond is unfit for duty."

"Ha!" Montobond said between gasps. "I've been unfit for duty for three decades. That hasn't stopped me from doing my job."

"Electra," Strafe said. "Come here." She stepped forward. "I'm appointing you acting chancellor of Bezos City until such a time as Phineas Montobond can sit a hearing in Musk City. Effective immediately."

"This is ridiculous, Kynig," Montobond said. Strafe spun on his heels, apparently not liking being called by his first name. "There's no way that order sticks. You can't—" This time, Strafe's fist found Montobond's temple, and the scene went dark.

CHAPTER FIFTY-FIVE
REUNION

When the escape pod descended to around thirty meters above the tops of the domes of Bezos City, it fired a tooth-crushing blast of thrust that brought its downward motion to nill. When the descent vector was zeroed out the tiny craft cut thrust to nearly nothing allowing the module to drift lightly down. Eustis leaned forward to get a piece of the minimal view. The hatch window allowed him only a few degrees field of vision but he spotted the location immediately. He was coming down into an open bay door at the far end of Bezos City. He watched ships zoom by on their way to the docking port. He must have been a speck in a sea of metal and movement.

The little capsule dropped into the nearest bay and set down automatically at one end of the port gangway. The bay doors overhead closed. He heard the hull of his little escape pod creak as the airlock equalized the external pressure. When it got quiet the hatch popped open and the internal light clicked off. He had taken his first solo flight in a private spacecraft, but he had no time to appreciate the experience. He needed to disappear, as Montobond had instructed, but how? He glanced around as if he were even able to identify the difference between friend and foe on Phobos. A few seconds later the airlock between the main port and his bay clicked open. He began the long walk down the passageway that led to Strong's Dome.

"Last call for Flight ID492R," a booming voice repeated in three languages over the loudspeaker. It was the flight he had marked down for his quick exit. Eustis paused in the pathway and looked for the terminal as passersbys bumped and jostled him. Three decks away, there was a sign with the flight ID blinking with a countdown. It would burn off this rock in three minutes. He could get on the ship. He could leave the Mars' little moon. He could do it. He *could be* gone. It gave him an idea.

He made his way through the thickening crowd toward the dock port. He could only see the loading zone of the ship, but it was rusty and beaten. He raised his hand and shouted at the docking agent. In another second, he was talking to the loading manager. He made sure to repeat his own name multiple times aloud. When the arrangements had been made, he transferred the bills, signed his name, and walked onto the cargo ship bearing the name *Hugo*. The cargo hold smelled like raw fish. Next came the tricky part. This would be easier on a flight packed with passengers, but he'd have to find a way.

He stood by the cargo door and watched the loading agent finalizing the cargo. When she spun the other way, Eustis leaped out of the corner of the cargo bay and hid next to the landing gear. A minute later, the loading agent boarded the ship, the cargo bay closed, and the engine reactor started to hum. Now that he was sure the coast was clear, he sprinted for safety, knowing the loading bay would depressurize soon. He made it to the airlock just before the hangar started to close and pump out the atmosphere.

He wasn't sure how much time that would buy him, but he hoped it would be enough. He wove through the crowd being sure to slouch and hide his face from any possible cameras mounted around the Bezos port walkway. When he made it to Strong's Dome, he took a right and worked his way through the down-level slums. The odor of rotting food and sewage never left the hovels in Rogers and Horizon. He put his hand over the bottom half of his face as he maneuvered through the narrow makeshift shanties.

It took much longer to get to the entrance tunnel which led to Maroon Housing than it should have. However, he wanted to make sure he wasn't followed, so he took the most circuitous route possible. He waited at the entrance of the tunnel for fifteen minutes before he dared start down the shaft. Although it had been less than twenty-four hours that he'd been away, the dusty smell and green-tinged lighting reminded him he was coming home.

Maroon Housing was a squalid haunt cast in eerie green shadow. He paused as he came to the place where Jewels had been murdered. A ragged breath tore from his lungs as he stared down at the splatter of dark crimson on the rock. *Keep moving.* He walked toward the bunkhouse watching for signs of movement. *Where is everyone?* There were no kids playing in the courtyard. There were no adults loitering around the edges. It was Ava Sikes whose voice split the spooky calm.

"He's back!" Ava cried from the porch of the bunkhouse. Her little feet carried her Eustisward as quickly as possible. Brad's face peeked out from around the bunkhouse.

"Hey, Talk Boss's back," Brad said as he came out with the Gaines brothers in tow. The wash of familiar faces blurred toward him now. Liddy and the Crabbe siblings were next. Adria Churn was holding Striker and Gordon Festus had Beverly Gertrude Lewis in his arms. Geona and Rymone were last out. The crowd was warmth. The group was comfort. This miniature congregation was home. The questions came in five at a time.

"Where's Captain Rude Beard?" Eddy said.

"Is Enzo coming back?" Samantha asked.

"What did they do to Mari?" said Ava. The questions felt like repeated knife wounds to the chest, but the one that left the deepest scar came from Adria Churn. She let Striker down from her hold as she questioned him.

"Why did you leave us?" The other questions stopped. This was the black hole that sucked all the others in. "We needed you. We were scared." Eustis could have laid on the ground and cried at the way the question made him feel. It wasn't the asking that was hard, but the answer that swelled in his throat like an apple. He gulped as they waited for his answer. He was tempted to lie; to make up some excuse.

"I'm so sorry," he said. "I'm sorry to all of you. It was selfish of me to leave you at such a terrible time after what they did. What they did to Jewels—" He choked on the name. "I'm ashamed that I left you alone."

"Are you going to leave us again?" Liddy Carpenter asked.

"I won't run away again," Eustis said. His words were concrete and steel. They were more solid than the rock they stood upon. He could see the collective relief in the kids first. When they all relaxed Eustis said. "There are so many things we need to talk about. Everyone gather around."

He had them sit on the steps of the bunkhouse and told them of meeting Delphi, Madam Electra, being jailed with the others, Montobond, and Strafe. The children were enthralled by the tale and had so many questions. After he had caught them up on the story, he turned to the delicate matter of Jewels' death. He thought it would be a difficult and sensitive conversation, but the kids were able to talk about it more readily than Eustis. Probably owing to the fact that they had all seen death so many times, they had scores of questions about what happened after life's end. He did his best to keep up with their rapid-fire inquiries. When he explained the tradition on earth of doing a memorial service they all agreed that they should do one for Jewels and Tiny when Enzo, Mari, and Rudwick returned. The subject then shifted to these three loved ones who were still incarcerated.

"Any idea if they'll be released sometime soon?" Rymone asked.

"I have no idea," Eustis admitted. "If we had money we could pay off the judicial recompense fee and get them out, but—" Before he finished his sentence, Billy Gaines was on his feet. He disappeared into the bunkhouse at a run. A moment later he returned with something in his hand. He held it out to Eustis.

"Would this be enough?" Billy asked. In his hand was a valve stem that had been polished. "We could get half a bill for it if we sold it to the scrap hauler."

"That's very generous, Billy, but I don't think—" This time all of the children rose at once and made their way into the bunkhouse. The doorway was clogged as they all rushed in. Another moment and they each displayed their various trophies. Nothing of any real value was present, but Eustis smiled back at the little philanthropists.

"Wow," he said. "You guys would be willing to give up your most prized possessions?"

"We've fifty-seven bills on our account," Geona said. "We'd happily give it to free them."

"I've got twelve," Adria offered.

"I have nineteen," Gordon added.

"How wonderful it is to be part of such a generous group," Eustis said. "We'll give what we can and pray for the rest." He led them all to bow their heads and close their eyes. Each in turn sent up the most sincere prayers he had ever heard. If it didn't bend the ear of God, then what could? After *amen*, he said, "I'd like to tell you all the story of the widow's mite." A stab of pain reminded him that the Three Story Kid was still gone.

Eustis was about to start the story when Eddy Crabbe interrupted. "Hey, who's that?"

Eustis looked up and said, "Oh no." He was on his feet before he realized it. "Kids. Quick. Hide. Don't come out until I tell you it's safe." The children scattered in every direction as Eustis stepped down from the landing to meet the group of strangers that was coming.

CHAPTER FIFTY-SIX

DREAMS

"No, no, no!" Eustis shouted. A group of eight girls was emerging from the entrance tunnel at the mouth of Maroon Housing. Two of them were mere children, the others were teens. Eustis put his hands out as the pack of girls, wearing floor-length lab coats and far too much makeup approached. "Don't even think about it."

"Please," Delphi said as she ducked her head and looked at him under her eyebrows. "Just listen."

"No!" Eustis growled. "I should have learned my lesson the first time you got me thrown into jail. I certainly won't ignore the second."

"I didn't know—" Delphi tried. The girls around her cowered at the unsavory tone of the conversation. The littlest girl, not much older than Jewels had been, rubbed her eyes as if tears might spill over at any moment.

"What?" Eustis interrupted. "You didn't know getting me thrown in jail could be so much fun? You're practically making a sport out of it." Eustis gestured to the broken-down bunkhouses behind him. "I have people that rely on me. I can't take any more risks."

"What's that?" One of the young girls at Delphi's side asked. She was pointing to the spot where Jewels had fallen. The blood that had soaked into the rock was dark brown under the dim lights. Delphi looked as if she were going to ignore the girl, but Eustis spoke to the child.

"That's evidence that I can't even protect those that are still here," Eustis said. The words were like acid in his mouth, and speaking to a child with such bitter contempt felt black and cold. He watched the girl's face as her eyes were cast to the ground. "I'm sorry," he said softer this time. "We've had a terrible few days. We can't risk any outsiders."

"Are you going to tell him your dream?" one of the teenage girls asked in Delphi's direction.

"Please don't," Eustis said. "I've had enough of your mind games, and I've already heard everything you have to say."

"No, you haven't," Delphi said. "In my dream, I'm trapped in a dark room with this terrible smoke, and there are dark shadows all around me telling me to kill myself," she whispered as if the words were sharp against her tongue. "Suddenly, there's a man standing in a bright doorway. The shadowy monsters hide from him. I rush toward the light of the opening, but he closes the door before I can get there. From the other side of the door, he says, 'What is the door's name?' I tell him I don't know. Then he says, 'The door's true name is useless. Wade into the grime to find the underground.'"

She continued to speak as a shiver spiked up Eustis' back and made the hairs on his neck stand on end. He studied the young woman's face as she recounted the dream.

"So I kneel down and start scratching at the ground below me. It's not a normal floor, but instead, it's like this grimy muck, like you'd find on earth, I guess, but there's nothing there. Then the voice says, 'The grime is among the underground, and the underground is among the grime.'"

"How long have you been having this dream?"

"It started about two years ago. It only happened occasionally back then. But since the day I met you, I've had it every night. The things you were saying about God were so strange, but it was like—" She paused and pushed a curtain of hair out of her face. "It's like I was numb before that moment, but as soon as I heard the things you were saying, they kind of grew bigger in my mind until I couldn't stop thinking about it. I mean, I didn't understand, but I wanted to. I told Madam Electra about the dreams. She said the hyper-terrestrials were trying to communicate with me."

"No," Eustis said. "The dream isn't from the hypers."

"I know," Delphi said. "I'm not sure how, but as soon as Madam said that, I knew she was wrong." She reached over and put her hand on one of the younger girl's shoulders. "Then I started to kind of talk," she squinted. "I don't know what you call it. In the commune, it's called correspondence when we open the comm link to the hyper-terrestrials, but I'm not sure what you call it when you're talking to—"

"It's called prayer," Eustis said.

"Ok," she accepted. "So I started to prayer—ing" she paused on the new word and looked at Eustis to see if she had used it right. He gave an understanding nod. "I just started to say, if someone or something is out there, please give me a way out. Once I started prayering, I couldn't stop. I wasn't sure if it was doing any good, but I just kept talking. From then on, it made me sick to keep up my duties at the commune, but I was scared to leave. They've sent more girls to reclamation than I can count."

"Murdered," Eustis corrected. "We call ugly things by their ugly names."

"Yeah," she looked at her hands. "So then I started telling some of the girls about my dreams. I showed them how I was prayering. So some of them started doing it too."

"So, why didn't you come to me earlier?" Eustis asked. His cutting and bitter tone had been replaced with a soothing calm.

"I looked for you," she said. "I came to the jail after the first time you were arrested, but you had been let out. I figured you had left Bezos City, or that they had reclaimated—I mean, murdered you. I didn't know how else to find you. Then when I saw you the other day, I followed you. And the rest—"

"But why didn't you tell me all this then?" Eustis asked

"I was going to, but we got interrupted."

"That's an understatement," Eustis said. "You're living in a different world than me if you call a kidnapping an *interruption.*"

"Sorry," she said. "I'm not used to calling ugly things by their ugly names."

"Right," Eustis said. "How did you know I was in Maroon Housing?"

"I didn't," Delphi said. "After they *kidnapped* you," she gave special emphasis to the ugly word. "Things went bad. There's this GovCorp guy Madam Electra is working with. He's an Admiral from dissidence management. He travels with about fifty robotic killers. And he's always muttering about how he's going to crush, pulverize, or maim someone. He practices the old sciences. I think he might be under alien possession. He talks directly to Athima."

"Admiral Strafe?" Eustis asked.

"Yeah, that's the one," She pointed at Eustis. "He was there at the commune, and when he heard that they had taken you to the Chancellor, he just about knocked the walls down, getting out of the building. Said you were a dangerous criminal."

"Yeah," Eustis gulped. "He doesn't like me much."

"Well, on his way out, he ordered that everyone associated with the Criminal Eustis Grimes was now contaminated with religionism and needed to be sent to reclamation," Delphi said. "Since I'm scheduled for reclamation before the end of the year, anyway, my time had come. I had to get out or—" Her words broke off as a single tear ran down her cheek. "All the girls I had taught to prayerize would be—"

"We were in danger, too," the youngest of the girls said. Eustis knelt down and perched at eye level with the little one. Her blue eyes shined despite the dim light, and her golden hair beamed through the darkness.

"And what's your name, my lady?" Eustis said, reaching out his hand.

The little girl giggled as she replied. "I'm Jr. Liaison Chloe Nyx, under-research sister to Jr. Liaison Delphi Persephone," the girl said. Eustis smiled, but inwardly his stomach twisted into a knot at hearing the child's words. He went down the line and shook each of their hands. Daphne Iris, along with Cloe, couldn't have been any older than seven. Phoebe Selene, Clio Aura, and Thalia Xanthe were all teenage girls. He could see in their wary eyes and cautious stance that they had suffered too much at the hands of Madam Electra and the research commune system. At each of his movements, the girls shifted nervously. The oldest two, who must have been near Delphi's tender age of nineteen, were Asteria Calypso and Delia Echo. The motley squad of alien liaisons was much more than Eustis knew what to do with. He stepped back from the little crowd.

"I'm a bit concerned that you found me so easily," Eustis said. "How did you know I was in Maroon Housing?"

"We didn't," Delphi said. "Asteria thought we should go to the port and find a ship off-world. I was worried it'd be too hard to sneak eight girls across town."

"I thought we should go see the Chancellor," Delia Echo said cautiously. "I knew a research sister who visited him. He didn't lay a hand on her. She said he asked her all kinds of questions about how Madam Electra was treating her."

"It was a good idea," Delphi said in Delia's direction, "except that Strafe and Electra were going straight to Chancellor Montobond's office so we couldn't go there."

"So, we went *underground*," Clio Aura said.

"Because of Sister Delphi's dreams," Daphne said.

"It's the only thing we knew to do," Delphi said. "I didn't know what was down here. I've never been below dome level. I don't know why I didn't think of it earlier. The dreams said to find the underground. I didn't know it was so simple."

"The underground isn't what you think," Eustis said. "I mean, yes we are literally underground, but that's not what the dream meant." At Eustis' words, Delphi gasped, stepped back, and a handful of the other girls gazed at him with wide eyes. He tilted his head forward and pressed his lips into a thin line.

"Did you send me the dream?" Delphi asked. "Do you do mind science? Do you use an ostricular trange?"

"No," Eustis laughed. "Sometimes God gives people dreams to set them in the right direction." At the revelation, the girls all stood a little taller and leaned toward him for anything else he had to offer.

"So, where is the underground?" Delphi asked.

"You're not looking for a place," Eustis said.

"What is it then?" Delphi asked.

"I never told you my full name," Eustis said. "I'm Eustis Wade Grimes, but the truth is, my given name, technically, was Useless Wad of Grime. It's a long story." Delphi put her hand over her mouth.

"It's like your dream," Clio Aura said, tugging on Delphi's lab coat.

"So, what is the underground?" Delphi asked. Eustis spun in place and raised his voice.

"You can come out," Eustis said. "It's safe." He turned back toward the newcomers. "Girls, meet The Underground." From a dozen shadows, the believers of Maroon Housing emerged into the green light. The kids were the least cautious in their approach, rushing out to meet new potential friends. He gestured broadly as they began introducing themselves.

"Geona," Eustis said. The woman looked up from her mingling chat with one of the newcomers. "The girls are going to need a place to stay. Could you find them some beds? Maybe bunkhouse B?" Geona nodded dutifully and began to lead the parade toward the bunkhouse. The entire mass moved as a single organism across the courtyard and into the structure.

"Are we sure about taking them in?" Rymone asked when the group was inside.

"Nope," Eustis said.

"How are we going to feed the extra mouths?" Rymone asked.

"Don't know," Eustis said.

"Any idea how we're going to get Rudwick, Enzo, and Mari out of jail?" he added.

"Nope," Eustis said.

"So, what are we going to do?" Rymone's face was stretched tight with concern. He was awaiting something, anything. Eustis smiled, slapped him on the shoulder, and spoke with as much confidence as he could.

"What do we do?" Eustis repeated. "We do what we can, and pray for the rest."

CHAPTER FIFTY-SEVEN

MITE

With the addition of Delphi's girls, the bunkhouses felt cramped. While everyone else was sleeping, Eustis and Delphi spent the lights-out hours talking about Jesus, the Bible, and faith. Eustis read passages from his priceless copy of Scripture, and she marveled at its wisdom and insight. She had a constant flow of questions, each leading to the next verse Eustis shared. He repeatedly brought the conversation back to her need for eternal life, and Christ's offer.

It was difficult for her to imagine that such an awe-inspiring gift, eternal life, could be received by nothing more than faith. However, Eustis relentlessly worked his persuasive powers. He paused the conversation often so that they could pray for wisdom. Little by little, and with the help of the Holy Spirit, he was sure, he broke down her reticence. Somewhere around three A.M., her questions slowed, and her skepticism dissolved. After explaining multiple times, Eustis once again returned to the saving message, and she happily believed. She was eager to share what she'd learned with her sleeping companions, but Eustis suggested they get a few hours of sleep before everyone rose.

In the final hours of the waning morning, Eustis laid in his bunk wondering if troops were going to storm in and murder the underground. He repeatedly reminded himself of the harvest he had just experienced—and a hyper-terrestrial researcher at that. Certainly, God had not abandoned them. When the little green light in the corner of the bunkroom clicked on, and no blue-clad officers had come, he was sufficiently satisfied to rise and face the day with a measured hope.

Delphi was already up chatting with Geona in hushed tones on the front steps of their bunkhouse. A few of the younger children under their care were already up and mingling in the courtyard. The Gaines boys showed some of the new arrivals how to derive the most sport out of a kicked rock. Eustis moved toward the women.

"Morning," Eustis said. "Did you get any sleep?"

"A little," Delphi said.

"And did you have any..." Eustis trailed off, not wanting to tread on a sensitive subject. Striker meandered up and rubbed Eustis' leg.

"No dreams," Delphi said. "Well, none of the recurring type."

"She was just telling me she wants to help out," Geona said. "I told her about our nightly meetings, assuming they're still—" Geona let her words break off, but her eyebrows stretched upward in a questioning posture.

"Yes," Eustis met her inquiry. "We're still doing them. We'll resume tonight." He paused and lowered his voice. "But listen. I think, all things considered, we better not invite any new people for the time being. I don't think we want to attract any more attention. Let's just quietly spread the word among the regulars."

"Good point," Geona said. "I'll get the word out, but I'll do it discreetly." She suddenly spun her head toward the sound of children playing. "Billy, no!" She protested as Billy led a game of *dodge the rock* with the newcomers as the primary target. "Someone is going to get hurt. You can't just—" she continued spouting instructions as she hurdled into the courtyard. Geona redirected their youthful ambition as Eustis and Delphi returned their focus to the present conversation.

"What do we do now?" Delphi asked. "Is there anything I can do to help? I want to do my share. That is if me and my girls *are* part of your group now."

"Absolutely," Eustis said.

"So," Delphi said. "What do you need me to do?"

"Well," he ran his hands over his chin. "Honestly, we're in a tough spot. Most days, everyone sets out mid-morning to find whatever work they can. We scrape by with the meager water rations and by pooling whatever money we have to make sure no one starves. But yesterday, a few of our founders got arrested. We're scrambling to figure out what to do."

"They get dumped in reclamation?" Delphi asked.

"No," Eustis said. "They are still alive, thank the Lord."

"Thank the Lord?" Delphi repeated the odd phrase.

"Oh, it's an expression of gratitude toward God," said Eustis. "So, we don't have enough to pay the judicial fee to get our friends out of jail, but it's tearing me up to think of them in there. It's terrible in there. You can hardly breathe. There's no water. It smells like death." He looked down at the steps and took a long drag on the thin subterranean air. He could hear Geona in the courtyard lecturing the children about the golden rule. Eustis added, "I have a contact at the Bezos City Municipal Authority, but he told me to hide out for a while and—" Eustis paused. "I really just don't know what to do."

"How much do you need?" Delphi asked.

"How much what?"

"How much money to get your friends out."

"Oh, sheesh." Eustis blinked his eyes at the dry air. "I think it cost fifty thousand to get me out, so times three."

Without an instant of hesitation, Delphi raised her hands into the air and began gesturing. Her eyes focused on her own internal display, which was invisible to Eustis. He was about to ask her what she was doing when she said, "What's your middle name?"

"Wade," he said. "Why?"

"Oh yeah, that's right," she said. Then as if talking to someone else in a formal tone, she said, "Eustis Wade Grimes."

"What are you doing?"

"Ok," she said. "It's done." She smiled. He was about to repeat his question when a notification pinged. He gestured to bring it up in his personal display. His eyes grew wide as his arms dropped to his sides. He stared past the superimposed image, at the girl who had just blown the door of opportunity wide open.

"Are you serious?" he asked. "I mean—"

"It's my gift to you," Delphi said. "If you need more, please don't hesitate to ask."

"How did you come by that kind of money?" Eustis said.

"In my *former* line of work, money was the least of our worries." They stared at each other for a long few moments. How could he have doubted the loyalties of this incredible young woman? No, that wasn't the half of it. How could he have doubted that God would provide?

He waved away the translucent display and put his arms out. He reached for Delphi and gave her a hug. He held her shoulders and looked her in the eyes as he said, "Thank you. You've reminded me to never lose hope."

"So," Geona said, returning from her impromptu lesson with the kids. "What'd I miss?"

Eustis let go of Delphi's shoulders and said, "We're going to pay their fine and get Mari, Rudwick, and Enzo out of jail!"

CHAPTER FIFTY-EIGHT

RESCUE

"Why can't we just call the jail from here?" Delphi asked.

"There's no signal down here below the city," said Geona. The few adults, and those who were close enough in age to be considered so, were huddled up making a plan.

"I transferred the money while I was down here," Delphi questioned.

"It's brick-linked—" Eustis started to say.

"Black linked," Rymone corrected. "It doesn't need service. It will update as soon as either of your embedded terminals re-link."

"Let's hope so, anyway," Adria Churn said. "What if they catch him?" The waver in her voice wasn't lost on the rest.

"It's okay, you guys," Eustis said. "I've got to go." They all protested the idea. Now that the money was sitting in his account, Eustis was eager to get his friends out of that rotten place. A shudder rippled up his back as he remembered the cold cell he had spent three days in. His breath came jagged as he recalled that deep well of remorse that churned in Marianna's eyes the last time he'd seen her.

"I don't think it should be Eustis. He's being hunted by that Admiral guy," Gordon Festus said. "If he shows his face domeside, he's going to get tagged."

"And Madam Electra," Chloe Nyx added.

"Plus," Delphi said. "The Chancellor said to stay hidden."

"Listen," said Eustis. "I appreciate everyone's concern, but it's got to be me. If something goes sideways..." he paused. "It's just got to be me." They tried to protest, but he set his face in stone and didn't budge. He listened gently as their fuel was expended on persuasion attempts. The protest died down. Eustis reached out and laid a hand on Adria's shoulder. "It'll be okay."

"At least, wear this," Rymone said as he handed Eustis a mask. The emergency rebreather, standard apparel in most docking ports, was a threadbare piece of kit. He would have been surprised if it worked. Although it was less common in the domes, it wasn't completely out of place to spot a few stray individuals who were suited for vacuum even in the relative safety of the city. "I removed the tracking chip, so it won't ping the ID receivers. It'll make it harder to spot you with your face masked."

"Thanks, Rymone," Eustis said. He let his eyes move across the group that surrounded him. "All of you. Thanks."

They hugged him each in turn and stood watching as he dawned the worn-out, old mask and headed for the tunnel. The walk toward the upper dome was labored with the mask on his face. He dutifully kept it in place, but its grimy face plate smeared the green lights of the corridor. Its smell reminded him of a rat he'd pulled out of a scuz-tank jam-line a few weeks earlier. Through the haze and stench, he offered up a short but fervent prayer. "Lord, please let this work."

When he exited the tunnel his cortex terminal reception returned with a ping. Notifications about his newly acquired fortune sounded as he maneuvered resolutely through the milling crowd. The remainder of his walk was uneventful, but that didn't mean it was free of stress. There was no way to get to the municipal compartments of Bezos Dome without passing by the research commune. He skirted the opposite side of the street as he passed without incident.

The walk in the broken breathing mask left him feeling like he might pass out. His lungs burned and his muscles felt like they would cramp at any moment. He wedged a finger under the edge of the mask to let in some fresh air. The air that rushed in was anything but fresh. He turned the corner and faced the municipal column of compartments that rose up in a central spiral of Bezos Dome. He wondered what had happened in Chancellor Montobond's compartment after he had been whisked away. He shoved the thought aside and pushed the front door open.

"I need to pay the judicial fine for three prisoners you have in—" Eustis wasn't allowed to finish. The blue-suited officer with the nameplate reading *Snuff* didn't look up from his post as he cut across Eustis' words.

"Not all prisoners can be released," Officer Snuff said. "Depends on the sentencing. If they are up for judicial recompense, you can pay the fee and get them out. Fee is forty-nine-five for each. Paid in full before the release request can be filed."

"How do I know if they are up for release?" Eustis asked.

"You don't," Snuff said. "Pay first. We'll check if they're up for release. All trials and sentencing are done by A.I. when they are booked in. If they are sentenced to judicial recompense, then fine."

"But what if they're not?"

"It's a non-refundable judicial recompense fee," Snuff said.

"So, I pay you a hundred and fifty thousand bills," Eustis said. "And if they're not allowed to be released, I just lose that money? Sounds more like a bribe than a fine. Couldn't you just check first and—" Snuff leaned back and stuck out his chest. His hand lightly landed on the pistol in his belt-mounted holster. The paunch around the rotund man's cheeks stretched as his eyebrows rose. The officer cocked his head to the side, clearly studying. Eustis looked down immediately. Even his grimy face mask couldn't obscure his identity at such close proximity.

"I'm sorry," Eustis said now staring down at the counter. "That's fine. I'll pay the fee."

"Really?" Snuff asked. "And you understand it's non-refundable?" Apparently, most didn't fall for the ridiculous shakedown. Eustis nodded but didn't look up.

The officer made the applicable hand gesture, shoving his own translucent display across the counter to the available display node. A ping verified that it had been sent and received. Eustis ventured a glance through the smudged faceplate. Officer Snuff was at work, a smile stretching across his face.

"Prisoner's names?" Snuff said.

"Marianna Byrne, Enzo Gatti, and Rudwick Nuske."

"Ok," Snuff said, leaning forward in his chair. "Weird."

"What's weird?"

"They're gone," Snuff said. Eustis' hands balled into fists. Every muscle in his body tightened. Adrenaline hit his system like an avalanche. He could feel his heart thumping in his ears. The echoed sound of his breathing increased. He envisioned leaping over the counter and—but he took that thought hostage and sent it away.

"Can you tell when they will be marked for release allowance?" Eustis said, trying to keep the acidic edge out of his voice.

"No," Snuff said. "You didn't hear me. A.I. sentenced them to reclamation. And we don't have them in lockup anymore. Reclamation team must have come early today."

"I—" Eustis stammered. "Do you mean—" He felt lava rise in his throat. His legs threatened to give way below him. He reached for the counter. He was sucking air now, but his lungs overrode his need for anonymity. He felt his hands moving without giving them a command. His mask was being pulled from his face, and his mouth was wide with the inhalation.

Snuff was on his feet looking over the counter at a choking sputtering maniac. Eustis looked up at him with a fire burning behind the skin of his face.

"It's not reclamation. It's called murder!" Eustis screamed. Snuff reached for his sidearm, as his suit blinked a varied shade of red. "We call ugly things by their ugly names!" His vocal cords felt as if they would tear.

"You alright, buddy?" Snuff said.

"No!" he bellowed. "I'm not alright!" He rose abruptly from his knees feeling like the world was spinning. He choked on the dry, cold, dusty air. The room, no the dome itself was falling in on him. His legs didn't have their normal stability. He shuffled like a wounded bird toward the exit and spilled onto the street.

"Hey, buddy, you left your mask," Snuff said but Eustis didn't hear him.

CHAPTER FIFTY-NINE

BACK

Eustis stumbled into the street as if he'd just spent the night at Gruff's Fluids. He clutched his chest. His vision was blurry, no longer because of the mask. Black elbowed its way toward the center of his vision. His consciousness was trying to exit his body. *They couldn't be dead!* He staggered to an alleyway next to the municipal compartment tower. He had to get out of the rush. The flow of people and vehicles was too much. He reached for the wall and leaned his forehead into the stone so hard it was sure to leave a bruise.

He stumbled deeper into the alley and found a place among the shadows. He flopped down and leaned his back against the rigid surface, closed his eyes, and did nothing other than breathe for five minutes. When his heart was nearer a controlled state, and his breathing was adequately low he opened his eyes. Without thinking much of what he was doing he gestured for his display to come online. He began thumbing through the few pictures he had of Rudwick, Enzo, and Mari.

He smiled at one he had of Mari in the cockpit of the *Resurrection*. She had not liked that he had taken it. She had questioned him about it, but suddenly it was one of his most prized possessions. His eyes welled with wetness as he choked on the memory. If only she had believed—he cut the memory off midstream. *Maybe she had. Maybe she hadn't told him yet. But what if she hadn't?* An involuntary rush of air hit his lungs.

Inevitably he would come back to the photo again, but he couldn't stand to remain in the horrid visions that were bombarding him at the moment. He thumbed it aside and found the picture of Enzo, shirtless, and smiling from the engine room of the *Resurrection*. He was covered in grease and looked happy. Eustis swiped to the next, Rudwick posing proudly with his cats. However, as the image of Enzo slid by and out of view, a small dot of red caught his eye. *What was that?*

He swiped back to the photo of Enzo. He gestured toward the red dot in the corner. Words popped into the display. *Enzo's Current Location.* He and Enzo had set up location sharing when they had arrived on Phobos. Eustis had completely forgotten. *A lot of good that did.* It was supposed to keep them both safe. *What a joke.* Certainly, it only had old data. By now the location of Enzo's body was already dispersed in the biomass recycler. There was comfort in knowing that his Spirit was with the Lord. Eustis was about to swipe away the location data, but something, a small stab of curiosity in the back of his mind moved his hand in the other direction.

A map filled his cortex display. A red dot with Enzo's name blinked somewhere north of his location. *Wait, what?* He moved his hands to bring the location closer. The dot was moving. It was in Ross Dome. *Why?* Reclamation wasn't in Ross Dome. Eustis's mind was already racing.

Eustis was on his feet without realizing it. He gave the map a half twist which shrunk it to a quarter of the size and made it transparent. He started to move. He was out of the alley in a few seconds. Another minute and he was through the gauntlet of Bezos Dome's city center. He worked his way through the layers of the slums around the lower levels of the massive main dome of the city. All the time he watched the dot. When Eustis was nearing the concourse junction between Bezos and Ross Dome, the red dot stopped moving. He zoomed in and sure enough, the dot was still. It blinked relentlessly.

Eustis doubled his speed, nearly flying through the residential compartments of Ross. He had rarely had reason to come to this part of town.

The living spaces that were laid out in this neighbordome were palatial compared to anywhere else in Bezos City. In fact, these would be immaculate even on Earth where space and resources were comparatively plentiful. Eustis followed the dot, begging it not to blink out. He passed entire levels devoted to massive single-residency apartments. One compartment even had a fountain; a real gushing, splashing fountain. Of course, it was locked behind a wall of impregnable glass. Another semi-dome had a garden as green as any on Earth. The gate was barred with heavy stainless steel, but he could sense the familiar scent of vegetation, moisture, and life. He wished he could stop and stare but he kept moving, willing the red light to keep flashing.

A police rover took the corner up ahead and meandered slowly down the street. Casually, Eustis side-stepped and found a narrow alcove in the wall to obscure him. From the speed of the vehicle, Eustis was trying hard to convince himself it was just a routine route and not a man-hunt unit. When it got close, he could see there were no duty officers aboard, and it was just a patrol drone. *Of course,* Eustis thought. *Keep the riffraff out of the rich neighborhood.* When it had passed, he came out from the shadow and continued toward the blinking dot.

Behind this wall, Eustis thought when he had gone as far as the open street would allow. Before him, a massive residence spread in both directions. It was the only one on the block that rose high enough up the dome wall to receive reflected sunlight from above the surface line. This had to be the biggest house in Bezos City. The word *castle* would be fitting, despite its old-world overtones. Eustis walked the lateral alley that lined the wall around the estate. It was a few minutes before he arrived at its termination point, in the rock. He turned around and went the other way, looking for an entrance. Another three hundred paces past where he had started, he found a second alleyway that drifted down lazily from an upper level. Set in the wall was a gate. On either side of the gate was a turret drone with plasma cannons embedded in the stone edifice. *Someone doesn't want visitors.*

The ominous pit that the sentries put in his stomach was enough to turn him around and send him in the other direction. He stood stone still for a moment. "Lord, I'm not sure what to do." He took a deep breath and started toward the weaponized guard station. Without another word, he knew. His path led through that gate, it had to, and he would try or die.

When he was within ten paces, the plasma turrets came online and bounced to life. Their barrels slewed like active thrust drives to his location and tracked him as he moved. The titanium of the guns began to glow red, then orange, and were approaching white-hot. A sharp crackling like a welding torch came from the plasma barrels as they readied to spit fire. Eustis stopped in the middle of the alley.

"Who's there?" A disembodied voice came from a speaker. Eustis didn't know where to look, but clearly, he was being watched.

"I need to talk with—" *who?* He wasn't sure. "The owner of the house."

"He's in a meeting," the voice bade. "Go away."

Ok, the owner is a man, Eustis thought. "He has guests?" Eustis ventured.

"What's that to you?" The voice said.

Yes! Eustis could have jumped up and down, but he couldn't be sure the plasma cannon-toting A.I. wouldn't take that as a sign of aggression. Eustis took a chance. "I'm so sorry, I'm late. I'm with the *other* guests. We came separately." Technically it wasn't a lie.

"Hold please," the voice said, now drained of its emotion. A few interminable seconds passed. Without another word, the plasma barrels stopped crackling, dropped to a resting position, and began to cool. The wall behind the cannons, which had previously given no signs of being a gate, split and swung on loud metal hinges. The path was clear, and Eustis walked through.

Chapter Sixty

LEAD

As Eustis walked into the courtyard of the massive estate the first thing he noticed was the smell. It was like being on Earth in a forest. He paused, closed his eyes, and took a deep breath of the moisture-laden air. It smelled green, rich, and alive. He opened his eyes and could have been dreaming for the presence of the impossible sight.

Most of Bezos City's plants were being grown in the food sectors of each of the ten domes, and its water was in the filtration and recycling plants. It felt strange to be in a place, not only with plant life but a pond teeming with fish. A coy danced against the surface of the reflecting pool. The body of water surrounded a single island, like a mote of pure serenity. The island was growing a tree from its center. Eustis squinted. *Is that possible? A real live tree on Phobos!*

Artificial misters washed the entire scene with a layer of mystic fog. Through the mist, a narrow bridge crossed the water and connected the tiny island to the path he was on. The sidewalk cut through a canvas of green grass. The entire scene was bathed in warm amber light. He looked up and saw a mirror array pouring down recaptured thrice-reflected sunlight.

"Hello?" Eustis called out. A boy, probably no more than twelve, stood from behind one end of the bridge. He had a trowel in one hand and a potted plant in the other. He didn't say anything but watched Eustis approach. "I don't know where I'm supposed to go." The boy pointed with the little shovel. Eustis nodded, turned, and made his way down the path toward the grand structure which was its inevitable destination.

The giant building was made of glass and titanium, and in the specular glare of the wall of windows, he could see the reflection of the city behind him. He walked slowly as the boy went back to work. Through the mist, the materializing structure glowed with the purples and oranges of Bezos City lights, but it might as well have been a black monstrosity for all Eustis knew about it. He could see himself looking dumbly lost in the mirrored surface. There was no handle on the wall of glass. He spun around in place, trying to decide what to do. Only a moment passed before his curiosity was answered as the doors slid open noiselessly. He stepped inside.

The entry alone was as large as any of the bunkhouses in the Maroon Quarter. Although, the decor in this single room was worth more solar collateral than Eustis had ever seen. On the high walls hung works of art, many of which Eustis recognized and others he didn't. He didn't know their names or the painters who did them, but they must have cost more than ten fortunes. He could hear footsteps approaching.

"Eustis Grimes, my boy," came a familiar voice. "I'm so glad to see you in one piece." The white-bearded, grey-haired man that approached was a welcome, albeit confusing sight. He stepped into the light, revealing the face that was so pockmarked with age. "I was just trying to work out how to find you."

"I —Uh—" Eustis stammered. "I followed a location beacon here." He was feeling the weight of anticipation beating in his chest.

"There is rarely sense to be had when you don't have all the information," Chancellor Montobond said.

"You were trying to find me?" Eustis asked.

"Yes, after our abrupt interruption yesterday," Montobond said. "I was hard-pressed to make out your location. And that's saying something, considering I have—or at least had— access to everything." As the old man talked Eustis felt like his insides might burst.

"Please tell me you have my friends here? I was sure they were murdered, but then I saw this location beacon."

"I'm sorry, my boy," Montobond said. Eustis could hardly hear what came next for the concussion the words offered. "I would have told you, but I didn't know how to contact you." Eustis' eyes welled with tears.

"They're dead?" Eustis gasped. The words were like broken glass in his mouth.

"No," Montobond said. "They were my plan for finding you." Eustis watched Montobond expectantly. He continued, "I'm an old man, but before we were interrupted, you said you had friends in jail. I wanted to find you. After no residence information came up on the database, I realized I could just ask your friends where you're staying. I had to do a bit of a jailbreak. I released them this morning before the guards got the memo that militarized ape had canned me." Montobond paused. "But they are stubborn as a stuck kidney stone. They wouldn't tell me a thing."

"Are you torturing them?" Eustis said balling his hands into fists. "Let them go. Take me!"

"My chef isn't the best in Bezos City, but I wouldn't call it torture," Montobond laughed. "They were nearly starved when they came out. They're in my dining room upstairs." Eustis didn't say anything else. He rushed past Montobond feeling that if his feet failed him he would sprout wings. "Other way," Montobond shouted after him. Eustis's feet screeched across the shiny black marble as he changed directions. He took the stairs three at a time and emerged into a grand, glass ballroom. A long slender table was stacked as high as his head with food of all kinds. Sitting along one side were Mari, Enzo, and Rudwick eating as if they hadn't had a meal in a decade.

Before he knew what he was doing he had rushed to Marianna's back and wrapped his arms around her. He meant it as a hug, but he immediately realized he should have warned her of his approach. With one swift move, she kicked the chair backward, flipped Eustis over her shoulder, and slammed him down on the table. Food went flying everywhere. It knocked the wind out of him, but he lay still unable to breathe staring grinningly up at her. In another instant, she was pulling him off the table and wiping the food from his clothes. A flurry of activity surrounded him as Enzo and Rudwick helped him to his feet. He smiled through his winded state at each of them in turn. He hugged them all at least three times.

"I thought you guys were dead," Eustis said. "I tried to pay your judicial recompense fee but—" he choked on his words.

"Coming here was a bad idea," Marianna said. "There's an old creep trying to find you."

"We would have come straight home, but he would have followed us to get at you."

"If I had me arm," Rudwick said rubbing the place where his prosthetic used to reside. "I'd be breaking me crew from this dreaded place, but—"

"Guys," Eustis said. "It's okay. He's a friend." Eustis regaled the entire adventure to them in a breathless eagerness. They grilled him on every detail from the time he left the jail to the moment he entered the dining hall. Rudwick wanted to know about his remaining cats. Marianna asked about the children in Maroon Housing. Enzo seemed particularly interested in more details about Delphi and her new arrivals. By the time he had them up to speed, Montobond had topped the stairs and was listening at the edge of the room.

"You have loyal friends," Montobond said. "I've been trying to get information about your whereabouts for almost an hour, and they were determined to protect you until the end."

"Oh yeah," Enzo said. "Creepy guy with a big dark house wants to know where my friend lives. Can't imagine why we'd keep secrets."

"Yes, well," Montobond began but Enzo wasn't done.

"I mean, you basically kidnapped us."

"From *jail*," Montobond grumbled. "It's called being *rescued.*"

"It be goons of your own possession that slapped me and me mates in irons in the first," Rudwick said.

"Now wait a minute," Montobond said. "It's a big city. I can't approve every grab and tackle of the custody force. They've been known to take too many liberties."

"Might be time to take a little more active role, Chancellor," Marianna said.

"Me best kitty were killed by your blue boys," Rudwick growled. His eyes were red around the edges. "There be no retribution paid for the crime."

"We also had a young girl," Marianna said with a detached distance. "Jewels was only five years old. She was gunned down by your custody thug squad. When is there going to be justice for *that* crime?" They stared hard at the flustered man.

"Yes, well," he said, putting his hands in the air. "I wish I could do something about it. I wish I could go back and fix a great many things. But I can't. I was removed from my position by that rotten scag Admiral Strafe. Madam Electra now occupies the chancellor's seat. Sorry folks, I've been deposed."

"Disgusting," Rudwick bellowed.

"Means, he's not the Chancellor anymore," Enzo explained.

"Ahh," Rudwick said. "These be treacherous times."

"Oh, I have something for you, big guy," Montobond said. He moved to a large case that hugged one of the walls. He pulled out a bottle and a few glasses. "We'll need these in a moment, but first..." He heaved as if lifting a weighty object. From the case, he produced something wrapped in a cloth. Eustis thought he recognized the metallic clatter. He pulled the cloth away to reveal Rudwick's mechanical arm. In Montobond's hands, the disembodied appendage looked like it must have belonged to a giant.

"Blasted buster bang!" Rudwick erupted. "Me dignity be restored."
He lunged at the arm that Montobond was offering. As Rudwick began
strapping it to his shoulder, Montobond explained.

"It was among your possessions at the jail. Thought you would want it."

Rudwick strapped the metal to his shoulder. It hung limp and showed
no signs of movement. "I be deep debited to you. You still be the canceler
to me, indeed." Rudwick wrapped his human arm around Montobond in
a broad bear hug. When Rudwick released him, Montobond looked at the
four of them for a long moment before a smile stretched across his face.
He walked to the table, grabbed a glass, and poured some wine. He took a
long swig and lifted the glass.

"You were quite right, young lady," he said nodding to Marianna. "I
should have taken a more active role in running the city. In the course of
events incumbent upon a Chancellor, there is the tremendous weight of
duty, thus enumerating—" He was clearly going into speech mode, but
Eustis cut him off. He blurted the question he had been wanting to ask for
the last twenty-four hours.

"Where did you hear John 3:16?" Eustis said.

"Ah, yes," Montobond said lighting up like a Saturn sunrise. He pulled
a chair and gestured for the others to do the same. They didn't, but at least
Eustis sat. "Where to begin."

CHAPTER SIXTY-ONE

ANSWERS

"About three and a half months ago," Montobond said. "I received a report of a signal transmitting contraverbs that was being broadcast on an old band radio wave. We figured it was most likely an unregistered ship broadcasting illegal messaging somewhere between here and earth orbit." He took a long drink of his wine and reached for a slice of real bread. The others eased their posture and returned to their plates as Montobond talked. Eustis remained spellbound. "I assumed it was rebel activity or organized crime. Maybe even GovCorp corruption. All of those would have been normal. I ordered the team jam the signal band and spread the news of the hack to the other colonies.

"It all went as these things do. I stamped the case closed without paying much attention and assumed the problem was taken care of. Then a few weeks later another incident took place. This time a similar message was being broadcast through a distress beacon channel. Same order of business. Jam the frequency and put the case to bed.

"Then, again, another anomaly popped up. This time it was a Rider signal, buried under a transponder carrier wave."

"Busted," Enzo said.

"That be me slippery mate, Eustis Grimy at his dark work," Rudwick said.

"Ahh, so you all knew," Montobond said.

"Nope," Marianna said. "He did all that on his own. Nearly got spaced for it too."

"Yes, well. For some reason, I don't really know why exactly, after I had closed all three case files I decided to reopen them and take another look. Something about how it was reported was odd. I was shocked. The message was certainly illegal, but it wasn't rebellion, insurrection, or criminal in nature. It was religionism.

"You've got to understand. This job is mind-numbing. It was curiosity as much as anything else. I opened the only sample message the case file included. It was a young man's voice, talking about something he called Jesus Christ. I only had about a two-minute sample, but I listened to it over and over. I kept a copy. I've listened many more times since then. Your voice is branded into my mind, Eustis Grimes.

"The broadcast was incomplete. It started midway through, and I've been dying to know the rest of the story for months." Montobond reached for a bowl of grapes and plucked them one by one. His chewing didn't slow his story. "So, when you showed up in my office, and your voice identified you unmistakably as the mysterious pirate broadcaster, I had to know more. Except that, we got interrupted by Strafe. He's made it his personal mission to see Eustis carved up and sent all over the Sol system."

"He be a scurvy dog of ill and darkness," Rudwick bellowed.

"What happened after I left your office?" Eustis asked.

"Strafe arrived with that disgusting woman, Madam Electra, and his army of robotic triggermen. He demanded I turn you over to him, but I told the truth. You had already left. He put Electra in my chair, my favorite chair, mind you, and I was pretty sure he was about to have me shot when he got a report that you had left Phobos on a cargo ship hauling synthetic fish." At this revelation, all heads turned to Eustis.

"Oh, yeah," he said. "I bought a ticket on a cargo hauler. Made sure they had my full name spelled right."

"You were going to leave?" Enzo asked.

"No," Eustis said. "Well, not that time. Anyway, I scanned in, boarded, and then jumped off the ship when the attendant wasn't looking. I figured it'd buy us some time."

"It did," Montobond said. "He loaded up his goons, and he's burning as fast as he can to catch that hauler. Of course, he'll realize he was duped before long. It'll take him a couple of weeks to get back to Bezos City, and he'll be aiming to remove your head from your body when he gets back, but it was a clever move, my boy."

"Eustis is a sneaky wrinkler," Enzo said smirking. The rest ignored him.

"Now," Montobond said, setting his cup down and leaning in toward Eustis. "I have questions about your Jesus."

"And I'm eager to answer them," Eustis said.

"But?" Montobond anticipated.

"But, I have a lot of people relying on me," Eustis explained. "They're waiting for me to return with these three. If I don't come back soon, they'll be worried and I just can't do that to them."

"And where are they?" Montobond said. Eustis cocked his head and squinted his eyes.

"I'm not comfortable sharing that with you, Sir," Eustis said. "You've been very hospitable, but—"

"Don't do it," Enzo said. "Don't go speeching." Eustis ignored him.

"You've been very hospitable, Sir, but we've experienced a lot of trouble at the hands of your administration. Less than fourty-eight hours ago your soldiers arrived at the secret place we've been living, shot one of our young girls, and arrested my friends. I hope you'll forgive us if we're not quite ready to trust a former GovCorp chancellor. I've got my people's safety to think about."

"Of course," Montobond said. He made a broad hand gesture and fixed his attention on an invisible point that hovered over the table. He made a few adjustments as he poked at the transparent display.

"You gave him too much," Enzo said.

"What?" Eustis said. "No, I didn't!"

"That little speech had plenty of info in there for him to look up the incident report."

"Ahh," Montobond said, returning to the conversation. "Makes sense. Where better to hide an *underground* movement but under Bezos City in Maroon Housing?"

"See?" Enzo said.

"Well, great!" Eustis said. "That was a total bait and swap."

"Bait and switch," Enzo said.

"Whatever," Eustis grumbled.

"How about this," Montobond said. "Bring them here. There's plenty of room, and there's no safer place in Bezos. Nothing gets past Beetlejuice and Canopus." Eustis was about to ask about the odd names.

"It's what he calls his plasma cannons," Enzo said. "He brags about them constantly." Eustis turned his attention back to Montobond's offer.

"We're a big group," Eustis argued. "I don't think it's a good idea."

"How many?"

"Don't," Enzo said.

"He be too deep," Rudwick said. "He be ready to reveal all the coin."

"Twenty-four," Eustis said.

"My household staff alone is over thirty people. We have plenty of room for a few more." Montobond leaned closer. "Please, I want your people safe too. There is no safer place in the city than my home. I will feed them and give them a warm place to sleep. All I ask in return is that you answer my questions."

"Sounds like a mass kidnapping," Marianna said.

"Please," Montobond said. "Satisfy an old man's curiosity, and let me show some kindness to your people."

"He's decided," Enzo said, studying Eustis' face. "Now I'm going to have to give up my favorite bunk in the maroon caveworks."

Chapter Sixty-Two

MEMORIAL

A group calling themselves The Underground secretly migrated toward a new location in the green-lit dim of night sometime after Phobos' lights out. The congregation of clandestine nomads divided into groups consisting of no more than five each. Twenty-four humans and three cats quietly traversed the eerie nighttime cityscape, each cautiously moving with thumping hearts and ragged breaths. The final group to pass through Phineas Montobond's compound gate consisted of Gordon Festus, Bobby Gaines, and a very puffed and noisy Striker.

Hugs, celebration, and happiness saturated the scene inside Montobond's estate. Most of the Underground had not seen Enzo, Rudwick, or Marianna since the catastrophe in Maroon Housing. Waves of jubilation were matched by undulations of mourning for their losses suffered on that fated day. Only now could the congregation finally mourn as a collective, and so the group recounted their sadness and victory with a unified voice that echoed about the walls of the vegetated courtyard. After the commiseration had gone on quite some time, Montobond, who had been lurking about the edges of the gathering, found his way through the crowd and acquired the attention of Eustis.

"Now that your people are in this safe haven," Montobond said, gesturing to his estate. "You owe an old man some long-awaited answers."

The noise of the others was ringing so loudly that Eustis had to lean near Montobond's ear to be heard.

"There is something we have to do first," Eustis said. He spun in place and spoke to Rudwick, who had Striker perched upon the shoulder where his mechanical arm was strapped. The arm, which Rudwick had been working on, spasmed awkwardly but was otherwise lifeless. On his other arm hung three giggling children. At Eustis' words, Rudwick let the cat and the children to the ground gently and took a deep breath.

"Everyone, quiet!" Rudwick bellowed. The crowd of excited migrants hushed and awaited whatever word would come. Eustis stepped to the center of mass.

"Let us thank the Lord for his kind provision," Eustis said. Those familiar with the phrase among the undergroundlings bowed their heads.

"Oh, that's not necessary," Phineas Montobond said with mock shyness. "I'm quite happy to provide." Only a few nearby heard him, but Eustis continued with his intentions.

"Dear Lord," Eustis began. The prayer that followed was one of the most sincere expressions of gratitude Eustis had ever offered. None of Delphi's girls prayed, but the rest of the underground spoke a varied array of supplications. Although the new additions to the group were still cultivating their understanding of prayer, it was Chancellor Montobond who appeared most intrigued by the odd practice. "Amen," Eustis said after more than ten minutes of genuine prayer had concluded.

"Fascinating," Montobond erupted when the prayer was over. "I take it that was some type of cosmic communication?"

"We will get to your questions soon," Eustis said where everyone could hear. "But we have something we must do first." Some had chosen to sit on the ground during their prayer, but Eustis gestured for everyone else to sit. Montobond smiled as he excitedly mirrored the posture of the undergroundlings. Some of his household staff stood at a distance studying their master's new group of uncanny friends.

"We agreed that once we were united, we would hold a memorial for Jewels," Eustis said. "As some of you know, a few days ago, our beloved sister in Christ was taken from us. Her murder was a tragic loss, but we know that the loss is temporary. We will see her again."

The alien liaisons who had come in with Delphi showed signs of surprise, and Montobond gasped. Eustis continued, recounting the moment Jewels believed and what tremendous events awaited her at the moment her spirit was separated from her body. Eustis called on Enzo to quote certain passages from the New Testament on the topic. Enzo recited with pinpoint accuracy as Eustis gave the explanation. Even those who had been with the underground the longest were spellbound by the words that spilled from Eustis' mouth like warm silken comfort. Eustis then shifted.

"Maybe a few of you would like to share your favorite memories about Jewels," Eustis said. He then sat, and a silence filled the space, only penetrated by the distant sounds of Bezos City's nightlife, and the water gently lapping around the small tree island in the courtyard. Brad Gaines stood. He rubbed his open palms against his upper thighs as he talked.

"She was the best pickpocket I ever knew," Brad said. "One time, she stole my sock while I was wearing it." The crowd laughed and murmured enthusiastic agreement. Brad sat down as Eddy Crabbe rose.

"Member that time, before Talk Boss came, we were alone?" Eddy said. The others of the maroon kids nodded. "Member that time Jewels stoled that apple from some earther in Dresden Dome?" The other maroon kids giggled and agreed, clearly excited to relive the story. "It was mostly ate up already. Liddy told her she ought'n eat it cause she'd get earther cooties. Member how she buried it behind the bunkhouse and kept getting it out every little bit to look at it. It was so brown and covered in Phobo-dirt."

"Then Samantha told her there's no such thing as cooties," Bobby Gaines said, laughing, unable to contain himself. Samantha spoke up.

"Yeah, and she ate it straight away, dirt, brown and all," Samantha said. "Looked like some kind of gobble monster." The kids laughed so hard it was impossible not to be drawn into the levity.

"She had Spit-mud all round her mouth," Ava sikes erupted.

"She said she didn't know why them earthers liked apples so much," Liddy Carpenter said. "I told her, I don't know nothing bout no earther, but she had eaten more of Phobos than apple." The laughter that followed came in warm cascades of glowing hope. As the laughter died, others stood and shared memories of the kind, industrious, and affectionate girl. Some were funny. Others were somber. Some expressed anger at the soldiers, and others cried. When it seemed that every memory had been shared, Eustis was about to stand and conclude the memorial service, but a movement caught his attention.

Marianna stood. She was wringing her hands and staring at the ground that had only enough gravity to hold her lightly. Eustis settled in place and marveled at the vision, cast like an angelic statue in a cathedral of rock. The hard layers of her gritty persona were peeling away in the light that reflected from the companions close at hand. Eustis could hardly blink as he took in the gentle transformation he saw. This battle-hardened space-faring smuggler, now surrounded by loved children, spoke in a whisper so delicate it could have been a dream.

"I know I don't usually—" Marianna paused and put her hand over her mouth. She closed her eyes and took a breath. "I know I don't normally say much," she fidgeted. "You all know I don't believe the—or I mean—what Eustis said about dying—it's very nice." She ran her fingers through her hair and shook her head. "I don't know what I believe, but I know at least this. If Eustis' god is real, and he really does accept the spirits of people into his—uh—place or whatever. I want that to be true for Jewels. I—" Marianna gasped for air with a sudden burst of emotion. "She was so special. I—" she gasped again. "I loved her so much."

Marianna sat back down and buried her face in her hands. The children around her piled in, surrounding her with tiny arms of warmth and comfort. Rudwick, Eustis, and Enzo, along with the other adults and teens, joined in. For a long few moments, the group was entwined in a collective hug of mourning. When he sensed it was time to let go, Eustis rose and addressed the group once more. He offered up another prayer and concluded the memorial service with a few final words.

"Now," Eustis said. "Chancellor Montobond has prepared a meal for us. You'll find his household very generous and welcoming. You can follow Jeera through those doors there." He gestured to Montobond's assistant as she quickly led the processional toward the doors. Eustis lingered at the end of the parade of hungry bodies, and as he expected, Montobond caught him by the arm.

"Please," Montobond said. "I have so many questions."

CHAPTER SIXTY-THREE

QUESTIONS

The relative comfort and safety of Montobond's estate filled the entire congregation with an overawed sense of peace and security. The children who grew up in Maroon Housing were astounded by the facility and abundance. The alien liaisons who had arrived as Delphi's faction were amazed by the warmth of the community. The weeks that followed their arrival were ones of immeasurable satisfaction for those tucked away in the protected enclave behind the walls of the idyllic compound.

Enzo and Eustis led story time and Bible study each night in the walled garden of Montobond's estate. Delphi and most of her girls had expressed belief in Christ in the days that followed. Montobond listened intently every day and was full of questions at the end of session.

With their permission, Montobond had filed each of the new guests as household staff so they could come and go at will without being detained or questioned by the Bezos City custody force. They had been given aliases and clean union IDs. Everyone had accepted certain tasks and chores around the manor with pleasure. The natural grouping among the undergroundlings melted into one seamless cohesion as time went on. They prayed together each morning and ate together each night. The sounds of laughter and joy were common in the halls of Montobond's fortress on Phobos.

After one particularly moving story time, Montobond caught Eustis by the arm as everyone was dispersing for their evening routines. Montobond's eyes were wide, and he had his characteristic volley of questions.

"The girl who died," Montobond said.

"Jewels," Eustis offered.

"Yes. So, you really believe you will see her again?"

"Yes," Eustis said.

"How do you know?" Montobond said.

"Jesus rose from the dead," Eustis said. "His resurrection, along with his other miracles, verified that he has the power to fulfill his promise."

"Which is?" Montobond asked.

"Resurrection and eternal life," Eustis explained. "It's a free gift to those who believe in Him."

"But—but—" Montobond's eyes were darting around, an outward demonstration that his mind was racing. "If you're right, then that changes everything."

"So, I guess you better figure out if you think I'm right," Eustis said.

"What you're saying is that it's not all meaningless?" Montobound looked at the dome above their heads. "Do you realize how different this is? It wouldn't all end at reclamation."

"I'm not just saying it," Eustis said. "I'm living evidence that you don't have to live a useless life."

"The numbness," Montobond practically sang. "What could we accomplish if we weren't choking in the horrid pressure of numb-minded worthlessness?"

"Phineas," Eustis said, making eye contact. "You were designed by a loving Creator. You were placed at this time and place for a specific, important purpose. You have talents that the creator wants to use to accomplish his grand plan in the Sol System. It's not just that you have some vague meaning. You are here for an incredible reason. You can make your life count for something huge, and powerful, and eternal."

"I'm astonished," Montobond said. "I'm amazed. I'm—I'm—" He stuttered, looking for more synonyms. "I have so many questions, and I'm sure we'll get to them, but more than that, I have a strange feeling. I think it might be—if I might be so bold—it might be a feeling of hope." Eustis smiled and laid his hand over Montobond's, which was gripping his own arm tightly.

"It's contagious, isn't it?" Eustis said.

"I feel so alive!" Montobond nearly shouted. "Do you feel this way all the time?" Eustis just smiled at the man. Montobond stroked his beard. "We have to find a way. Bezos City needs to hear what you have to say."

"Are you saying you believe?" Eustis asked.

"Believe?" Montobond said, running his fingers through his wild hair. "I'm swimming in belief!" Eustis reached out and hugged the man.

"Welcome to the family, Brother," Eustis said. "Speaking of swimming, here follow me." Eustis turned toward the place in the courtyard where they had previously held their story time. Those who had attended were mostly still mingling. Eustis raised his voice above the crowd. "Attention, please," he said. The noise quieted. "Our gracious host has just believed in Jesus!"

Montobond bowed his head slightly as the group cheered for him. The smile across his face was enormous. "Do you be intending to baptize him, or be it I who shall do the dunking?" Rudwick said. The crowd laughed as Eustis turned toward Montobond.

"I'm afraid of the electric shock putting your arm underwater might give me, Rudwick," Montobond said. "We better let Pastor Eustis do it." Eustis nodded as they both moved toward the tiny island garden. They stepped down in the cool water, and in another few seconds, Montobond had been baptized. He came up from the water to the uproarious applause of those standing around, and almost as soon as he was up, he was talking at full speed.

"Others need to hear what you've said," Montobond thundered. "The City! We need to tell the city about Christ?" Eustis stepped up out of the water and reached down to help Montobond out as well.

"It's illegal," Eustis said, ringing out the front of his shirt. Montobond let go of Eustis' arm and put his hands on his grey head, smoothing down the dripping wet hair.

"Yes," Montobond said. "Illegal. Illegal. Illegal." He was muttering to himself as much to Eustis. "Yes, well. Certain risks are worth the danger."

"I agree," Eustis said, raising his eyebrows and cocking his head slightly. "What do you have in mind?"

"I don't know," Montobond said, "but it will be something big."

CHAPTER SIXTY-FOUR

PLAN

After they had been in Montobond's compound for almost two weeks, Montobond called a meeting of the leaders of the movement. They were sitting in his study, waiting for a tardy Enzo as they chatted.

"Rumors gotten out about us," Geona said.

"What are they saying?" Delphi asked.

"Some say we be a new hyper-terrestrial guild," Rudwick said and then spat on the floor. He pointed to Eustis and added, "They say we be led by a Commander who communes with the dark forces without aid of ark or trange." He spat again.

"Feeds say we're led by an Earther rebel," Rymone said.

"I just brought it up because I'm concerned," Geona said. "The more people that know about us, and especially know about Eustis, the more danger we are in." There was a long silence. No one disagreed with her, but it wasn't a subject anyone seemed eager to tackle.

"I heard a lady in Dresden talking about you guys," Marianna said. "She was convinced that Eustis is a genetic clone of the first Emperor of Musk City sent to spy on Phobos."

"I will neither confirm nor deny," Eustis said. The group laughed.

"What's funny?" Enzo said as he entered Montobond's study.

"Eustis is a tube-grown mutant with royal blood," Marianna said.

"Oh, Okay," Enzo said as if it weren't news at all. He shifted the subject as he took the remaining open seat. "Just heard from the shipwright. The magnetic containment bottle should be here in a few more weeks."

"Magnetic bottle?" Eustis asked as Enzo slid into his seat. The pre-meeting chatter died down.

"Yeah. The part we need to fix the ship," said Enzo.

"You're not leaving, are you?" Montobond said in Eustis' direction. Geona and Rymone sat up straighter, craning their necks to hear the answer. Delphi furrowed her brow. Eustis and Mari shot each other a furtive glance. Rudwick didn't notice the tension latent in the room, being occupied by Beverly Gertrude Lewis, who was kneading his lap into submission.

"Well, we—we were thinking—" Eustis started. Enzo cut across his words.

"Yeah, just as soon as you loan us half a million bills to get the tub gassed up, aired, watered, and repaired," Enzo said. He was idly thumbing through some display to which he hadn't offered the others access. "We strained the magnetic bottle casing when we—"

"You are planning to leave us?" Geona said as if she were pulling a knife from her abdomen. "You said you wouldn't run away again."

"Leave and run away are two different things, Honey," Rymone, her steady-handed husband, said gently. She looked as if she were going to say something else, but Marianna cut in.

"Why'd you call us here, Chancellor?" Mari said with an abruptness that was sure to leave emotional casualties. Geona and Delphi were reluctant to turn their attention away from Eustis, but they spun slowly toward Montobond. Eustis gave a nearly imperceptible nod of thanks to Marianna. She raised one eyebrow ironically.

"Yes, well. Something has to be done." Chancellor Phineas Montobond said.

"He's kicking us out?" Enzo said as he flicked to a new screen.

"Be it not so," Rudwick thundered. He was on his feet in an instant. Beverly Gertrude Lewis rocketed across the room and out the door at Rudwick's sudden aggression.

"No," Montobond said, looking up at the big one-armed man. "You are all free to stay as long as you like. You're family." Rudwick moved back toward his chair, looking pleased with his accomplishment. Montobond continued. "It's quite the opposite, actually."

"What's the opposite of leaving?" Delphi asked as she subtly cast a sideways glance at Eustis.

"We simply must get the word out to Bezos City," Montobond said. He took a breath to continue, but it caught in his throat when Delphi cut across him.

"The word?" she asked.

"The word about the Supreme Lord Jesus Christ," Montobond said in an airy tone. "There are a quarter of a million people on the other side of that garden wall that need what we have in here."

"That's not a good idea," Marianna said.

"Says the unbeliever," Delphi fired back. Mari pursed her lips. She took a breath before she spoke.

"No," Mari hissed. "*Says* the only one with some semblance of objectivity. Look, I see the beauty in what you guys believe, but it's possible to be blinded by the beauty and forget how ugly this place is. They'll kill you. Even you, Chancellor. GovCorp doesn't care about your former position or your wealth. The bigger the group, the more danger you're in." By the end of Marianna's speech, Delphi was practically bouncing in her seat. She was about to retort, but Eustis raised a hand in her direction. She furrowed her brow a second time.

"Thank you, Mari," Eustis said. "Jesus said to count the cost. Mari has helped us to see the stakes. Anyone want to add to that?"

"I agree with her," Enzo said. "It's super dangerous." He swiped his hand downward, dismissing his invisible display. He leaned forward and injected his attention into the room for the first time since he'd been there. "All the more reason to do it! I'm in it for the eternal reward." At Enzo's words, Delphi's tension dissolved. Enzo gave her a smile and an over-confident nod for his tender age. She smiled back.

"I mean," Geona Shaldon said. Her voice trembled slightly. "Whatever we do, I want to ensure we do it together. I want to make sure we're not going to be abandoned if things go wrong." Her words were rising in pitch. Rymone put a steadying hand on her arm. She looked at it, then at him, and turned back to the room looking slightly abashed as if she had just discovered she was wearing shorts to a formal dinner.

"Unity is the greatest defense against danger," Montobond said sagely.

"I'd prefer a plasma cannon," Mari said.

"I have those too," Montobond bragged.

"I think what my wife is trying to say," Rymone said. "We're scared."

"Me too," Eustis said. He was about to expound, but Rudwick thumped the table with his human arm and rose to his feet. None of the others felt the need to be standing while talking, but the man's massive stature had an imposing effect on his audience. He spoke slow, low, and severe.

"Be it far from me mind to be afraid of what the Lord Good and Loving hath woven me old bones into," Rudwick said as he looked at each face one by one. "Me think it not a surprise the High Lord hath called upon savy pirates to do pirate's work. No mamby slop trotter be adequate to do tasks of such grave difficulty and import. If what needs be done be easy, He'd a called upon the soft palmed lilly-livered souls, but instead, he called forth a leather necked swatchbuckle, a stowaway more stubborn than ever I seen, a boy more brilliant and mean than there be in all the colonies of the sun. Even though she be unbeliever still, mark me words in inky black. The Good God of sky and void hath a play for the indomitable Marianna Byrne too. And be it true of each around this here fateful table. You each bear marks and scars given You from this dark foreboding place, and yet you be here. You be ready. You be bold."

There were tears welling in his eyes, and he was roaring with a fiery inspiration. "Be it not far from our poor, inadequate minds to be honored. We need not discuss whether or not. We be compelled by Maker and kin to take up the mantle, whether to life or to death, such as the Good Lord hath beckoned for our mere time around His otherwise tiny and insignificant star. We faint not at the heralding morn, come it with blood or broken bone. We be fast in stance, ready for all we be called to do."

A long heavy silence filled the room as Rudwick closed his eyes, looked at the ceiling, and slapped his closed fist against his chest.

"Oh, so we're giving speeches?" Enzo said. "I didn't get the memo. I don't have a speech. Was I supposed to have a speech ready? Did anyone else know this?" Delphi laughed a little too eagerly, while the rest sniggered. It was a long moment before anyone responded.

"He's right," Eustis said. "God makes unique teams for unique tasks."

"There's probably never been a more unique team," Rymone said, still eyeballing Rudwick.

"Yes, well," Montobond said. "This is all very well, but there is still the matter of how to get the word out. I was thinking a plenary meeting. We throw the doors wide and take our chances."

"Not a good idea," Mari said. Delphi bristled.

"Three months ago, I would have been all for it," Eustis said. "But I tend to agree with Mari on this one. We don't *just* want to get the word out. We want to continue to grow the group we already have as well. I think we need to have a layer of protection for those we already have in the fold." Montobond looked as if he were about to protest, but Eustis interjected.

"We could send everyone except me into hiding," he said. "I could hold a preaching meeting. If things go well then—" Before he could get the rest of his idea out, the group erupted.

"No," most of them said in unison.

"They'll kill you," Mari said. "Where would this group be with you dead?" Eustis tried to double his effort, but the others talked him down with surprising vigor. Eustis was trying to press his point, but everyone was talking at once. Some were standing. Others were leaning over the table, rumbling in raised voices. All the while, Enzo sat quietly in his chair. Once again, he was flicking through invisible display screens, but now he was not idle. His intense stare into the open space above the table was fixed on something, something important. He clenched his jaw and leaned back in his chair.

"Shut up!" Enzo shouted. They all quieted and looked at him. Their faces were red, and some were breathing hard. He closed his eyes.

"Eustis," Enzo said. "To hack the *Resurrection's* transponder, you would have had to build a posi-induction base unit that could transmute 56-bit encryption, right?"

"Yeah," Eustis said. "But it was just—"

"Shut up," Enzo repeated less aggressively. "What would you need to do that for a 256-bit encryption?"

"Well," Eustis considered the question. "I don't know why I'd need to. There's no use for an encrypted comm matrix."

"Let's just say you needed to. What would it take?"

"Okay," Eustis rubbed his chin. "I could probably do it with a quad-latis interface and a pair of adjoined scopes." He paused. "But that would be impossible to get here. There's no way—"

"There's a dual-latis interface in a galaxy four transponder," Enzo smiled. "And we have one on the *Resurrection*." He smiled bigger. Delphi's eyes were wide as she studied the boy at the end of the table.

"Now, wait a minute," Marianna said. "You're not talking about gutting the transponder on the *Resurrection*! It's in GovCorp docking. They'll never let it out of impound without a transponder. We'd be stuck here for good." Geona perked up at Marianna's comment. Enzo ignored the others as Eustis started to pace.

"It's semi-parallel reverse binary," Eustis said. "It would work. But why?"

Enzo made a simple flick of his wrist, and the display image he'd been viewing became visible to everyone in the room. No one but Eustis understood the implications. He said, "That's here?" Enzo simply nodded and smiled. "You brilliant little brat."

"Can you do it?" Enzo said. Eustis looked at him with a distant glint in his eye.

"I can," Eustis said, sounding as if he was surprised by his own usefulness.

"Although it's terribly exciting to watch you two incomparable nerds play gadget footsie under the table, would you mind letting the rest of us in on your incomprehensible chatter?" Montobond said.

"Yeah," Eustis said. "We have a plan."

CHAPTER SIXTY-FIVE

HACK

Marianna and Rudwick were tasked with repressurizing the ship, which required them to sneak into long-term docking, quietly attach the life support umbilical, and initiate the startup sequence. They burned most of the day, and the remaining O2, but they got it done. Eustis was going to need a pair of adjoined spectroscopes to make the plan work. To avoid the risk of getting any of the most-wanted members of the underground out in the city, Geona and Rymone volunteered to visit the shipwright to procure the needed equipment.

After days of studying schematics, Eustis and Enzo determined that the *Resurrection* was going to need to be hardwired to a terminal point. This was a complication since it was humming quietly in long-term docking a kilometer away from any terminal porting location. After looking at the options for another day, Montobond offered his own private hangar, which had an exterior dome-side ship hatch. Relocating the ship was risky, but Eustis and Enzo realized that the only viable plan was to get the ship to the hangar, so they suggested it to Marianna.

Once again, Marianna and Rudwick were chosen for the clandestine task. The ship wasn't safe for interplanetary travel, but they hoped it could make the trip across Bezos City without blowing a pressure seal. The trip required them to fly low and slow around the rim of the mouth of Phobos' cave so they could come at their destination undetected. They arrived short of breath as the *Resurrection* had completely run out of fresh O2. Despite the heavy breathing, Marianna parked the old rusted tub in the private hangar of Phineas Montobond and ripped open the hatch to let fresh air flow. They had succeeded in bringing the ship only a block from Montobond's estate, which was the underground's headquarters.

It took them another day to tie the ship's aged comm array into the city's interconnected emergency relay. Then the real work began. Eustis and Enzo toiled away in the *Resurrection*, speaking a language that no one else understood. Small groups of visitors from Montobond's estate would come a few times a day to bring meals. Delphi's visits were more frequent than any other's, owing to her fascination with the Three Story Kid. He seemed to enjoy the attention but would dutifully usher the beautiful young woman out when mealtime was over.

The main task, while clearly not impossible, proved more difficult than Eustis had originally supposed. Doubts came in waves as he and Enzo tried everything they could think of. On day three of the modifications, the bridge of the ship looked like a horrific scene of electrical surgery, and he was ready to give up. After a short prayer and a suggestion by Enzo that they unplug their makeshift patch and reattach everything one by one, Eustis had a stroke of inspiration. With a gleam in his eye, he maneuvered to the panel where they had been most intensely focused, dug for a wire hiding in the array of spaghetti, and pressed it into place. The whole cockpit came to life with dancing lights.

"What did it?" Enzo asked after an obligatory round of celebration.

"Forgot to connect the power modulator to the induction base plate."

"Of course," Enzo laughed. "Are we ready for a test run?" They trialed their hack with enthusiastic results. When the job was complete, they stared at one another for a long moment hardly able to believe what they had accomplished. "So when do we start?" Enzo asked.

"Tomorrow," Eustis said.

They cautiously walked the block back to Montobond's estate, careful not to be seen by any of the patrol drones that prowled the streets of the dome. When they passed through the gates after three days away, it was like a family reunion. The crowd surrounded them and showered them with affection.

"Did you do it?" Ava Sikes asked as the din died down.

"It's ready," Enzo said. The congregation erupted with jubilee. They ushered him and Eustis into Montobond's house. Their lack of sleep drove them toward the nearest beds, and they were out in no time.

The next day was an odd mix of excitement and nostalgia. Everyone spoke in hushed tones as if the sacredness of the coming task might be vanquished by rude joking or noises above a whisper. For the morning, Eustis paced in Montobond's study, rehearsing and polishing spoken lines quietly to himself. His open Bible lay across the desk, and he returned to it often, running his finger down the page to remind himself of particular phrases and words.

When he emerged from the study, Bible under his arm, Marianna was sitting in the hall with her head on her knees. Eustis glanced both ways, finding no one, he knelt before her.

"Mari?" Eustis said gently, having taken on the reverent whisper that so permeated the house's mood. She looked up, rubbed her eyes, and smiled. She reached out a hand that Eustis thought was meant to lend her aid in rising to her feet. He reached, but she pulled him to the spot next to him against the wall.

"What's going on?" Eustis asked, but she didn't speak. Instead, she laid her head against his shoulder. He leaned his head against hers. They remained there together for a long time, but when a stirring came, it came too soon. She tugged his hand away from his knee and held it in both of hers. She traced the lines of his palm with her finger as she looked down at it.

"You don't have to do this, you know," she said. "We could just run away."

"Not after what we did to your ride," Eustis whispered. He sensed an aimless smile on her face but didn't look up.

"Just for once, I wish you would do the selfish thing." Her stare turned slowly from his hand to his face. Her eyes were soft and wet. Her expression was pleading. Her gaze lingered. She leaned toward him. He closed his eyes, taken by the moment, caught in the flow. His heart thumped so hard he could feel it in his ears. He leaned over and let his nose graze the side of her face. Their lips met in an instant, and he was suddenly encircled by the warmth, the glowing passion, which rose so strong in his chest. He put his hand against her cheek as he kissed her.

"Talk Boss," a little voice called. Eustis could almost hear the sound of shattered glass dancing to the floor as the delicate moment was dashed to pieces. He pulled back and looked up to find Liddy Carpenter in the hall, giggling at the embarrassing moment. Her expression was quizzical. She smiled, "Chancellor is looking for you." She hovered there, waiting for him to come. Eustis turned back to Marianna, but the momentum was gone. She was rising to her feet and offering him a hand.

"But I was doing the selfish thing, remember," Eustis said, trying not to sound as if he were begging. Marianna laid a gentle hand on his chest and looked up at him.

"No, you weren't," she said. "You were sacrificing more of yourself to make a scared woman feel better." She patted him, rose to her tip-toes, and gave him a passionless kiss on the cheek.

"Eww," Liddy squealed with a fascinated disgust. It was much less than he wanted, and he would have waited for more, but more wasn't on its way.

"Come on, you, selfless black-void wanderer." She turned, started down the hallway, and reached out for Liddy as she passed the place where she was. The little girl took Marianna's hand and skipped joyously along. Mari turned and looked over her shoulder as Eustis tried to pull his feet from the wet concrete she had left him in. She smiled at him before she turned the corner and was gone.

"Ahh, my boy," Montobond said, rounding the corner looking as greyly disheveled as ever. "We have a new development." Montobond reached out a hand in Eustis' direction. "Your ploy bought us some time, but he's back."

"Who's back?" Eustis said.

"Admiral Kynig Strafe," Montobond said, putting his hand on Eustis' shoulder. "He's just landed in Bezos City. Your decoy bought us a couple of weeks, but he's back and hotter than ever. He's made you public enemy number one." Montobond made a gesture that sent the information to Eustis' visual terminal. A wanted poster sprang to life with Eustis' face plastered front and center.

"He wants me dead?" Eustis said.

"Hunting you as we speak," Montobond confirmed.

"He'll have to get in line. By tonight, the whole system will be after me. Maybe even the Chief Executive Emperor herself."

"So, you're still going to do it?" Montobond said with an airy effervescence that exuded awe.

"Of course," Eustis said. "This doesn't change anything." They both turned as the sound of fast-falling footsteps came rushing toward them.

"Master Montobond," Jeera, Montobond's chief staff member, said breathlessly. "It's that Liaison woman. She's at the gate swearing and screaming."

"Madam Electra?" Montobond asked.

"Yes," Jeera said. "She's got at least ten black-robed guys with her. Do you want me to authorize the plasma turrets to cut them down?"

"It would make things simple," Montobond said. He looked over at Eustis, his eyes asking for moral permission. Eustis shook his head.

"Of course not," Eustis interjected. "No murder."

"Yes, well," Montobond was about to argue, but Eustis put his hand in the air. "Very well. We will have to try diplomacy, which is a huge hassle with such a dark-eyed skinflint."

"She says you are illegally harboring eight of her girls, and she's going to break down the gate and take them back."

"Where are Delphi and her girls?" Eustis asked.

"We're moving them to the safe room," Jeera said.

"What's that?" Eustis asked.

"Bunker. They'll be safe there," Montobond said. "Madam Electra isn't fond of you either. It might be a good idea to get you down there."

"Not a chance," Eustis said. "If you're confident that Delphi and the others are safe—"

"There's no way that old bat will find them," Montobond said. He turned to Jeera. "I will deal with Madam Electra directly. Tell her I'm on my way. If she causes trouble, bring Beetlejuice and Canopus online. That will give her a chill." He turned back to Eustis as Jeera sped off in the direction she had arrived from. "Best take the back alley. God be with you, brother." Montobond put both his hands on the back of Eustis' neck and looked him in the eye for a moment before letting go and following Jeera's direction. When Montobond was gone, Eustis gestured to his embedded terminal. The communicator came to life. He opened Comm with Mari, Rudwick, and Enzo. A second later, they were all on the line.

CHAPTER SIXTY-SIX

FIRST

"Change of plans," Eustis said making his way toward the back exit of Montobond's house.

"What be the new heading, mate," Rudwick said.

"We've got some trouble at the gate," Eustis explained. He tapped the keypad next to the door hoping the sound couldn't be recognized through the comm. It beeped and he peered out into the passageway. He unzipped his jumpsuit just enough to hide the Bible and pulled the zipper back to its place at his neck. He hugged the hidden treasure to his chest as he moved through the relative darkness. The alley was empty so he stepped out and started making his way. "Enzo, you still in the courtyard?"

"I'm looking at it," Enzo responded. "And the trouble sure is ugly. Long black nails. Not nearly enough clothes. Neck wrinkles deep enough to suffocate an elephant. And she's got about a dozen black-gowned thugs at her heels?"

"Yep," Eustis said. To the others who likely didn't know what Enzo was talking about he said, "Madam Electra is at the gate of the estate looking to take Delphi and her girls."

"Nay," Rudwick bellowed.

"Over my void-boiled corpse, she is," Enzo added in a cold determined voice. It was strange to hear the kid speak with such venom.

"And you need us to stay behind," Mari said without any sense of agreement in her voice.

"That's right," Eustis said. He peeked around the alley corner and stepped into the shadowed lane that led to the hangar. "If things go sideways, I need to know the underground has you guys at hand."

"Rudwick and the Kid are enough," Mari said. "I'm coming with you. You'll need someone watching your six."

"Actually there's more," Eustis said as he leaned near the ID terminal at the hangar entrance. It chirped and the door unlatched. He was in one step later. He gestured for the lights. Sitting like a sleeping giant skinned in rust and negligence, the *Resurrection* hummed and hissed. "Admiral Strafe is back in town with his brigade of rumble bots and he wants my head."

"Oh, Eustis," Mari said. Enzo and Rudwick both swore. Mari's voice was pleading. "Postpone. There's no reason it has to be now. You can—"

"I don't know how long I have," Eustis said. "If he gets me—I mean—if I wait—this might be my only chance." The silence that followed was filled with a hollow emptiness.

"But," Mari said. "Why?" she gasped. Eustis remained quiet as he stepped aboard the ship. "Why can't I come and—" She gasped again with realization. "I'm the backup plan."

"Yes," Eustis said. "If I die, the underground still has you. A very capable captain, who can take them out of here and to safety." Eustis slapped the panel that closed the hatch on the *Resurrection* and flipped on the lights.

"Eustis," Mari said with iron in her voice. "I'm coming with you. Where are you?"

"I'm already there," Eustis said as he stepped into the cockpit and began flipping switches.

"You stubborn stowaway," Mari said.

"I know," Eustis said pulling the Bible from the hidden recesses of his jumpsuit. "I'm intolerable." He laid it next to the captain's seat and opened it. "But somehow you tolerate me." He sat down in the seat and took a deep breath.

"More than tolerate," Mari said. A long silence followed.

"Godspeed, mate," Rudwick said before dropping off the comm line.

"Good show, Talk Boss," Enzo said. He too left the call.

"Eustis," Mari said now that the call was private. "There are some things I need to say to you." A labored breath issued from Mari's comm. "I'm not good at saying what I think—what I feel." Eustis closed his eyes, wondering if this might be the last time he'd ever hear her voice. She continued in the thinnest and most delicate whisp. "I was planning to kill myself."

"What?" Eustis said. "When?"

"Before we came to earth," she said. "Before I met you. We'd had a string of terrible luck and I was so tired of always losing. I was drinking enough to kill me already, and so depressed. I couldn't see any point in going on. I'd decided to commit suicide. I was just trying to figure out how to do it without pain."

"Oh Mari, I'm so sorry," Eustis said. "What changed your mind?" Eustis asked.

"You did. I mean, I—I didn't understand it at first. That first day, when we talked. You were such an oddity. You made me mad. I wanted to punch the nose right off your stupid face. After we left you behind, I couldn't stop thinking it was a mistake. I wanted to go back and find you, but I was too proud. So I just drank the doubt away."

"Wow," Eustis said.

"Everything before meeting you was just shades of indifference. But there was something peculiar about you. I was feeling something. Especially when you showed up on the ship uninvited. I felt—pure rage. But it made me curious. How could I hate someone so much who I just met? Why did you make me so crazy?" Her words turned upward into a smile. "So, after you showed up on the ship, while I had Rudwick beat you to a bleeding mush, I decided right there, I wouldn't kill myself. Not yet, anyway. Since then, like a hundred times, I've been so mad at you. I've thought about killing you a few times. But—" she paused. "Imagining killing you always made me sadder. I used to really like thinking about killing people. You ruined that. Thanks a lot."

"Sorry," Eustis said.

"Anyway, I kept asking myself, why you made me so mad. While I was in jail I think I figured it out."

"Why?" He questioned.

"It's like this. Everyone else in this rotten Sol system has a manipulation point. Find what a person can't stand to lose and with enough pressure you can control them. It can be anything in the world. You've got them if you can convince them they stand to lose that thing. It works with everyone—except on you. It's because the thing you want the most isn't part of this world, it's outside the Sol system. I was furious, not because you're a stubborn slag—which you are—but because the thing you really care about isn't here. It isn't something I can touch, threaten, or take away. It gives you a kind of power that's unlike anything I've ever seen. You're unstoppable because of what you believe."

"I—uh—" Eustis tried to respond.

"And then you started turning my shipmates into the same thing you are. They're different than they used to be. They're like you. So that made me crazy because your weird brand of power was spreading to everyone around me. And now everyone I love has it. It took time to get okay with that, but I see it's better. Better for them. It's good. But there was still something bothering me."

"What?" Eustis asked.

"I knew that a man like you could never love *me* more than he loves his god. If I gave in to what I was feeling, I'd only ever have second place. I think that's what I resented more than anything else—that I couldn't force you to love me the most or need me more than you need your Jesus. I'd never have first place in your heart. I could sense that from the beginning, even though I didn't understand it. I hated you for it because I wanted you so much, and I knew I could never be loved the way I thought I needed to be loved."

"The way you needed to be loved?" Eustis asked.

"Yeah," she echoed. "That's what I thought love was. Being first. Being the only."

"But now?" he questioned.

"But now I'm not sure," she said. "I'm not ready to lose you. Before you, my life felt like a dead end. You saved me from that."

"It's God who saves," Eustis said. "I'm just trying to let Him use me."

"I don't know about any of that," Marianna said as her old bravado returned. Eustis could sense that the place where she kept her vulnerability had just been shut. "Anyway, I didn't want you to die without knowing—you know—whatever."

"Thanks, Mari," Eustis said. "That is very meaningful to me."

"Ok," she grumbled awkwardly. "I guess it's time. Give 'em hell."

"I'm trying to give 'em heaven, actually," Eustis said.

"Shut up and get to it."

"Will do Cap," Eustis said with a smile. He made the gesture to kill the comm link and lowered his hand. He was alone in the cockpit surrounded by wiring harnesses and blinking lights. His head was spinning from all that Marianna had just told him. He slowed his mind and pushed it all away. He keyed in the appropriate hand gestures and waited for the system to boot. He bowed his head and began to pray.

CHAPTER SIXTY-SEVEN

CAST

Phineas Montobond allowed Madam Electra but not her goons to search his estate. As he promised, Delphi and her girls were well hidden. When the Madam couldn't find them, she spewed vile epithets at the former chancellor and promised to report his insolence to the hyper-terrestrials. When he remained nonplused, she gave more colorful options, and among them, she would certainly have him executed. Her threats included a promised visit from Admiral Strafe and his automaton soldiers, but Montobond brushed her poison away with steely defiance and ushered her from his walled estate. She was gone for now, but the matter seemed far from concluded.

Delphi and her girls came out from the safe room and gathered with the rest of the undergroundlings in the courtyard next to the pond. They sat on the grass, waiting for what was about to happen. There was an electric buzz in the mood of all those gathered. Only hushed and subdued tones were used as they anticipated the next few moments.

"Your attention please," a voice, a very familiar voice, said. Marianna's stomach twisted into a knot. Around her, everyone cheered.

"You did the miraculous," Rudwick bellowed as he slapped Enzo on the shoulder and pointed upward. The celebration was quickly quelled as Marianna stood to watch and listen.

"Your attention, please," Eustis' voice repeated. It echoed off every hard surface in Bezos City and emanated from ten thousand emergency alert speakers positioned throughout the domed metropolis. A live video of Eustis hovered near the top of the dome, where anyone within could easily see. With the help of Enzo, he had high-jacked the emergency address system, and now Eustis was speaking directly to two hundred thousand people from the bridge of the *Resurrection*. The ship was hidden away in Montobond's private hangar a block from where Marianna stood staring up. She hoped his hiding place would stay a secret long enough for him to give his talk and escape. She wrung her hands unconsciously as Eustis began.

"Dear friends of Bezos City. My name is Eustis Grimes. I'm from Earth, and I've come here to share a very important message with you. It's a message that has cost me dearly to deliver and will no doubt cost me much more very soon. I would not have hacked into the city's emergency alert system if the circumstance wasn't dire.

"For generations, you have been lied to. An ancient truth that has the potential to set you free has been hidden from your eyes. I am here to reveal that truth.

"An all-powerful, all-knowing, and benevolent Being created the universe. In the beginning, the human race was engineered to live in peace and harmony with its Creator. People were designed to experience bliss-filled life forever with their Maker. However, a rebellion occurred while our people were still in their early history on Earth. The rebellion resulted in a severance of peace and harmony between the human race and our Creator. The rebellion is why the worlds are the way they are now. The revolt introduced evil, corruption, and even death itself. The relationship between humans and their God, which had been the chief purpose of the Maker's design, was nearly obliterated. However, being a kind and patient Creator, He promised to end the separation.

"One day, centuries later, a man was born miraculously. He lived a life without darkness, corruption, or evil. He claimed to be the Eternal Maker's own Son, wrapped in a human body. He proved his claim by demonstrating incredible power, even raising the dead. Only someone with the Maker's power could perform such amazing acts. His name was Jesus and he made an amazing offer. In an ancient collection of eyewitness accounts, which have been banned but not completely lost, we can discover his main claim and primary offer."

Eustis shifted in the video feed and lifted the thick Bible into the frame. He began to read. "'For God loved the world so much that He gave his only Son, that whoever believes in Him will not perish but have eternal life.' Even today, the Creator's offer still stands. Anyone who believes in Jesus for the free gift of eternal life will receive it. Little more than three years after Jesus spoke these words, he was captured by an evil governmental corporation and put to death. Even his death proved to be part of the Maker's plan in that it had been predicted with accuracy generations prior. The Maker's plan was more marvelous than anyone could have imagined. After being dead for three days, Jesus rose from the dead, finally proving that he had the ultimate authority and power to grant eternal life to those who believe in Him. It's for this reason that—"

The video feed flashed white for a split second before returning to normal color. Eustis spun in the captain's seat. Over his shoulder, a silhouetted figure stood at the cockpit door. Eustis returned his attention to the camera and spoke twice as fast as he had before. "Those who believe in Jesus will receive eternal life. If you want to know more, find The Underground—" Two metallic hands gripped Eustis around the neck and pulled him out of the frame. Marianna's hands were over her mouth as she watched helplessly.

"Mari," Enzo shouted. "Come on! He needs us." She looked in Enzo's direction to find that he was already in motion, running toward the estate gate. Montobond was following close on his heels. Marianna rushed after them.

"I'll stay here and guard the kids," Montobond said as he fiddled with the gate kiosk. "Activate gate defense protocol." Enzo and Mari squeezed past him and through the closing aperture. They ran full out, making their way down the street that led to the hangar. Above them, people hung from balconies, watching them run. Through the city's emergency speakers, they could hear the echo of what was happening to Eustis, and when they dared a glance skyward, they caught shaky glimpses of the circumstance.

"Finally, I meet the indomitable Eustis Grimes," said Admiral Strafe. He rounded on Eustis, who was being held in the titanium grip of one of the robotic guards. Strafe looked around at the wires and blinking lights strewn about the command cabin of the *Resurrection*. He turned to the mechanical soldier that was holding Eustis and said, "Bring him outside." He started to walk but then paused and spoke over his shoulder. "Bring the camera. I want Bezos City to see what happens to this rebel. And, bring that too." He pointed at the Bible lying on the deck next to the bulkhead. A soldier bot reached for the Bible and the camera and followed Eustis, who was being dragged through the interior of the *Resurrection*, then Montobond's private hangar. The robot tossed Eustis roughly into the street outside right as Marianna and Enzo were arriving. Marianna tried to rush to Eustis, but three of Strafe's soldiers blocked her. Another kept the camera rolling as the scene unfolded.

Chapter Sixty-Eight

BEAT

"Create a perimeter," Strafe said as he unfastened his flack jacket and began rolling up the sleeves of his jumpsuit. Eighteen of his mechanical soldiers spread out like an impenetrable phalanx of titanium and carbon fiber. "I don't want any Phobofilth getting near me while I'm flaying my prey." Strafe thrust his right hand into a holster at the waste of his jumpsuit and pulled it out clad in a glowing power glove. He flexed his gloved fingers and then tapped a button on the side. A high pitch whine issued from the illuminated mitt for a few seconds before it gave a ready beep.

"Burn that," Strafe said, pointing at the Bible. The soldier who held the ancient book dropped it on the ground. It landed rudely with the delicate pages splaying bent across the pavement. A soldier bot, whose shape was different than the others, stepped forward and pointed his flame thrower at the Bible. A superheated blast of fire shot out of the stem and enveloped the priceless book. The pages curled black and sooty as the orange swallowed the only copy of scripture Eustis had ever held, possibly the only physical copy left in the Sol system. From second-floor balconies, cracked doors, and nearby sidewalks, voices of bystanders booed and jeered.

"No!" Eustis screamed at seeing his precious Bible burned. He tried to wrestle free. "You can't!"

"Ahh, but I can, and I did." Strafe said. Eustis continued to struggle for another moment. Until Strafe threw the first punch. As the charged glove made contact with his face, it let out a white-hot arc projecting a ten-thousand-volt bolt of electricity into Eustis' cheek. The electric impact laid Eustis on his back. He saw nothing but bright sheets of white for what could have been hours, though no true time passed at all. When his eyes opened, he saw the thick form of Strafe standing over him, smiling. The screams of Marianna, Enzo, and others watching from balconies were distant and hollow. Eustis touched his face where the glove had landed. The raw flesh sent spikes of pain, tremoring through his body.

"Hurts, doesn't it? Eustis Grimes," Strafe said. Eustis blinked, trying to shove down the agony. "That's just the first. We have so many more." Momentarily, he couldn't remember what was going on. As his eyes struggled to gain their focus, the memory came back in sharp bursts. Eustis rolled and pushed himself up from the ground. Even the microgravity was almost too much to fight. Slowly he rose. He felt like his brain had been scrambled inside his skull.

"You won't be able to stop it," Eustis whispered.

"Speak up, Eustis Grimes," Strafe said. "We're streaming this video to the whole city." He gestured to the camera. "And you have a live audience too." He pointed to the balconies of people. Others were now lining the street to watch.

"You won't be able to stop it," Eustis repeated no louder than before.

"Stop what—your heart?" Strafe chuckled as he took a cigar from the front pocket of his jumpsuit, held it out letting the blaze bot light it with his burning pilot flame. With the glowing tip, he tapped Eustis' chest. Eustis winced. "It's easier than you'd think."

"You can kill me," Eustis said. "But it doesn't stop the underground. It won't stop the—" A fist rocketed into Eustis' temple, sending him to the ground with a flash of blinding white. This time it took twice as long to rise to his knees. His face was on fire, and his mind was shrouded in fog. Instead of talking to Strafe again, Eustis interlocked his fingers, knelt, and looked upward.

"Decided to beg?" Strafe said. Eustis closed his eyes.

"Dear Lord," Eustis said as he bowed his head. "Please forgive this man. He doesn't know what he's doing. I pray that he would be allowed to see your truth and experience your love. I pray you would give me the strength I need."

"What is this?" Strafe said. "Some kind of religionism, no doubt." Strafe raised his gloved fist and brought it down on Eustis' crown like a war hammer. He crumpled to the ground at Strafe's feet. "Any last words?" Strafe said with a sickening laugh. Slowly Eustis rose to all fours, unable to ascend any further. He drew a breath that was more labor than relief.

"Get him up." One of the electronic soldiers lifted Eustis by the collar of his jumpsuit and hoisted him into the air. His feet dangled a few centimeters above the ground. Strafe began raining blows anywhere he could reach. Enzo and Mari tried to push through the line of autonomous battle bots, but they couldn't make it past the wall of killer machines. A few angry bystanders shouted profanity at the Admiral, but it did no good. They watched helplessly as Eustis quivered with each blow until a strike to the temple rendered him limp.

"Aww, Eustis Grimes fell asleep," Strafe said. He raised his voice to the crowd. "See, Bezos City. This is what happens to those who oppose power." He raised his hands in the air like the victor at the Sol Games. "But I'm not done yet." He lowered his arms, reached out his gloved hand, and touched one finger to Eustis' chest. A cracking spark made Eustis's body lurch, and he half-opened his eyes. Bloodshot and distant, he looked around. "Do you know where you are? Do you know who I am?" Eustis blinked away the blood and tears that were pouring from his eyes. Red saliva dribbled from his open mouth. He struggled to keep the weight of his head up. His response was slow and slurred.

"You're a scared man," Eustis said in a gentle voice.

"And what am I scared of, Eustis Grimes?" Strafe asked.

"Violence is the tool of those who have no other options," Eustis said. "Your fist is a sign of your fear. You're scared because if this doesn't work, you're out of options."

"It will work," Strafe said. "It always works."

Eustis whispered. "It's only when you've stopped my heart you'll know that it didn't."

"That sounds like an interesting experiment. Let's find out if your hypothesis is true." Strafe reached for his sidearm, tapped the slide, and pointed the plasma barrel at Eustis's chest.

"No!" Marianna screamed, unable to break through the phalanx line. Eustis willed his head to turn, his eyes to scan, his vision to focus past the wall of robotic soldiers. Her eyes were drowning in tears. A crimson curtain of death blurred his eyes. Pleading. Hopeless. He gave a weak red smile. Even smiling was pure agony.

"It's ok," Eustis mouthed. His eyes tried to close, but he fought their tremendous weight. He wanted her to be the last image in his mind before he went to God.

As he watched Mari's face, a moving figure caught his attention two hundred meters down the street. Barreling through the causeway with guns spitting fiery balls of plasma was Rudwick. He was shouting like a madman. People hanging over balconies to watch ducked, and people standing in the streets dived out of the way.

"Monsters of the deep?" Rudwick bellowed. "Captain Rude Beard be not afeared, and come armed with hook and harpoon for the white whale's reckoning." Two battle bots exploded in flames from Rudwick's mad firing. Rudwick laughed with churlish delight as he poured fire bolts upon the robotic hoard.

"Rudwick, No!" Eustis tried to scream, but his voice was too weak. He flopped to the ground when the robot soldier who had been holding him marked the approaching threat. All eyes, even Strafe's, turned toward the charging mountain of a man. Another autonomous soldier dropped in a spray of sparks as Rudwick screamed his victorious epithet. Strafe fired before any of his bots got off a shot. A spire of plasma exploded against Rudwick's mechanical arm spinning him in place. The entire appendage, along with the gun it held, shattered and fell away. When he righted his balance, he continued his assault with his remaining arm, dropping two more battle drones.

Around the corner came Rymone Shaldon at a run. He rolled, picked up the fallen rifle, and started to fire. Another bot dropped. The one-way fire was now being answered with a fierce volley. From the bots exploded a cascade of plasma, pouring down the narrow street with meteoric chaos. Rudwick and Rymone spun and leaned into a nearby open doorway for cover. The autonomous soldiers began to march toward their hiding place.

Things began to fall from above. A hundred voices, both young and old, shouted as scavenged items rained from the second-story balconies. People threw whatever they could get their hands on. Chairs, light fixtures, and even the broken pieces of an antenna array spiraled down on the military drones. The robots' A.I. defense protocols were momentarily confused, and attention was divided as they assessed the balcony-born projectile.

They slewed upward and began firing on the invisible assailants, who had quickly disappeared into their second-floor homes. The short distraction was enough for Rudwick and Rymone to lean out and dispatch another three drones. They were quickly driven back into their hiding spot with the return fire. In the chaos, Marianna rushed to the place where Eustis lay, knelt, and lifted his head onto her lap while Enzo opened a comm with Rudwick.

"Rudwick," Enzo shouted, "lead them to the gate!"

"What be your meaning," Rudwick shouted through the crackling comm.

"Beetlejuice and Canopus," Enzo shouted over the din of battle.

"You have a gift, me boy!" Rudwick sounded with realization. A few seconds later, Rudwick and Rymone appeared further down the street, having entered an open door and come out at a safe distance. They fired aimlessly at the line of remaining deadly drones. "Be me followers, if you dare," he screamed as they fired over their shoulders and ran the length of the block toward Montobond's estate. The bots pursued and gained ground on the two human men. They rounded the corner and went out of sight.

"You stupid drones," Strafe called. "Return to my location at once!"

It was too late. The sound of the two plasma turrets mounted at Montobond's gate tore at their ears even from a block's distance. Beetlejuice and Canopus exploded with flashes of light and thunderous echoes through the streets. People in balconies with a better vantage point on the mechanical melee cheered uproariously. A moment of silence followed.

"It worked, me boy," Rudwick said. "Now they be nothing but smoking rubble."

"Stupid robots," Strafe shouted. He turned back toward the place where Marianna had Eustis' head cradled in her lap. Eustis was moving in and out of consciousness.

Without the aid of his mech guards, Strafe rounded on Eustis and Mari. He lifted his gun and was about to fire when Enzo came into view. He struck Strafe's arm with a piece of shattered antenna array. His gun clattered to the ground, and Strafe shouted. Enzo leaped on the pistol and had it in hand before Strafe could find his balance. Enzo stood and pointed the pistol at Admiral Strafe's barrel chest. When the admiral saw what was happening, he put his hands up and smiled.

"Now, boy," Strafe said. "Do it if you dare." He gave a sick grin.

"Shut up!" Enzo shouted. There was a wild rage in his eyes. The pistol trembled in his hands. His finger applied ever so little pressure on the trigger.

"Don't," came the weak voice of Eustis. Enzo darted his eyes between them.

"Listen to Eustis Grimes," Strafe said. "He's right, at least about this."

"I said, shut up!" Enzo said. "I could blow a hole in you so big—"

"Enzo," Eustis whispered as he put his weak hands against the hard-packed stone. It took all his strength to rise, even with Marianna's help. Three teetering steps and Eustis moved between Enzo's barrel and Admiral Strafe. Putting himself in the line of fire, he lifted his shaky hand covered in his own blood and placed it on the gun. "Live by the sword—"

"Die by the sword," Enzo finished.

"Don't become a murderer for me," Eustis whispered. The moment could have lasted a month for all that was shared in their stare. Enzo let his grip loosen and allowed Eustis to take the pistol. He gave it an underhand toss toward a second-floor balcony. The gun clanged against the wall and landed out of reach.

"Wrong move, Eustis Grimes," Strafe said as he reached one arm around Eustis' neck from behind and pulled a hidden knife from his belt. Marianna screamed and leaped on Strafe's back when she saw what was happening. Enzo's view was obscured, but Eustis's face told him all he needed to know.

Eustis felt a piercing pain to the right of his spine, and then something cold shoved its way through the flesh and organs of his abdomen. A sickening gasp issued from Eustis's mouth as his head drooped, and a blood-chocked gurgle drowned his breathing. Marianna, who was on Strafe's back, tightened into a chokehold. Enzo shouted and reached for Eustis. Strafe closed his gloved fist and swung blindly for Marianna. His powered glove found contact with Mari's forehead. The impact knocked her from his shoulders, and her limp frame flopped on the ground.

Enzo huddled over Eustis's body, screaming for help. Strafe backhanded him with the powered glove, knocking him to the ground five paces away. He didn't move. People that lined the street screamed for the brutality to end, but no one was brave enough to engage the wild-eyed Strafe. Many of the witnesses who surrounded the horrific scene made the hand gesture to record video of the events that were unfolding in the street.

"I'll want my knife back, Eustis Grimes," Strafe said as casually as if he were ordering supper. He reached down and pulled the dagger from Eustis's back, wiped it on his pants, and replaced it in its hidden scabbard. He charged his glove once more, knelt, flipped Eustis over, and straddled him. "I could just kill you now, but what would be the fun in that? Let's get to know one another, Eustis Grimes." Strafe tapped the unconscious Eustis on the forehead with one finger. "Wake up."

A silent moment issued from the street where the horrific scene was taking place. An eerie quiet lay like a blanket over the watching crowd. Then a breath broke the stillness. His eyes opened. His chest rose. His mouth moved. Through gurgling gasps, Eustis mouthed a weak melody.

"I'll lift my eyes to the hills,

From where does my help come."

"Singing?" Strafe said. "That's a first." He slapped the back of his power glove and waited for it to beep once more. Viewers from balconies above screamed for the admiral to stop. He ignored their pleas. Admiral Strafe pounded blow after electrified blow into Eustis's face, each time allowing his glove to recharge. Between strikes, Eustis sang on.

"My help will come from the Lord,

Who made the earth and sky."

"What a songbird you are, Eustis Grimes?" Strafe growled when he had to stop for a breath. The melody, weak at first, grew as Eustis gained his breath. He could feel the blood pooling in his lungs. He coughed crimson spatters. Through blurred vision, he could see Admiral Strafe reach with his free hand for the power glove. "Let's see how you like fifty-thousand volts." He made some momentary adjustments to his glove and reached high into the air, ready to strike once more. Eustis closed his eyes and sang louder now between every hammering strike of Strafe's electrified fist.

"He who His People He keeps,

Will not slumber nor sleep."

The pain of each punch was growing distant as Eustis continued the song in short labored breaths.

"Won't let them drag you away,

From evil, he will save."

Strafe was no longer waiting for his glove to charge. He was showering down blows with all his might in rapid fury. The screams of those watching from balconies were growing to a fever pitch. The crowd of strangers was tightening their circle, looking almost ready to take action. Strafe ignored them. Eustis continued.

"The Lord is your rest and shades,

Sun won't strike you by day."

"Praise Athima the powerful!" Strafe shouted as he slammed his bleeding fist into Eustis' face and body. Still, Eustis sang on.

"Nor the moon hit you by night,

The Lord is your rest—"

Finally, Eustis' body went lax, and the singing ceased. Strafe rocked back, watching the silenced missionary. He was breathing hard, and blood was splattered all over his face. "Ok, Eustis Grimes, I've had my fun. Now it's time to do my job," he said with a sickly satisfied grin. Once more, he pulled his knife from its hidden sheath and held it high in the air before driving it once more into Eustis' motionless body. The crowd's cries rose high and chaotic. He stared down at his gory work with a gleeful satisfaction in his eyes.

The sound of footsteps brought him from his focused gloating. Rudwick and Rymone, followed by a score of people, were charging in Strafe's direction. The crowd split with their advance as Strafe stood from the violence and readied his knife. He looked at the blade for a second and then at the coming hoard. He turned and ran through the parting crowd leaving the carnage behind.

CHAPTER SIXTY-NINE

BEGINNING

Blackness enveloped. For time unending that is all there was. A tiny pin-point of white light swelled to envelop. *I exist.* The dying darkness was accompanied by an unmanageable cold. So many thoughts, little pieces of dangling meaning, unanchored, floated in the inky void. An eerie tingling crept from the extremity inward toward the center of—what? *A body. I have a body. And it's cold. So cold.* The thoughts gathered into a spiraling gravity well, coalescing, mingling, and building. *I'm—what? I'm alive.*

His eyes sprang open. He wasn't ready to test the limits of his broken body, but he let his eyes scan the scene above him. He was on his back to be sure, but the view was not what he expected. Strafe was gone, and so too was the block of Bezos City, the dome, and the crowd. He blinked, the light was too powerful; too immense. The tingling in his arms and legs felt like a million little injections, drilling into his bone. Squinting, he ventured a second try. A room surrounded him. A high ceiling. Blinking colored lights at his left. Medical equipment. At once it came. Montobond's study. He was in Montobond's study.

A blurry figure rose into his field of vision. Apparently, the muscles of his face worked because he felt his cheeks tighten involuntarily into a smile, but there was something unfamiliar about the sensation. The woman that stood over him, reflecting his smile had tears at the edges of her penetrating eyes. The delicate lines of her features brought comfort and warmth though he couldn't quite bring the image into sharp focus. Something warm squeezed his hand. That was good, he still had his hand, an altogether pleasant realization. He wondered if all parts of his body were as fortunate.

"Eustis, can you hear me?" Mari said. Her voice was like an anchor tying him to the mortal world. He opened his mouth to speak and found that his voice possessed an unfamiliar quality.

"Did we win?" he croaked. The words came out in an airy rasp. Marianna's face twisted into a smile then shock and then she was wholly overcome with emotion. Her hand covered her mouth, and her eyes poured a cascade of warmth that splashed down on Eustis' fingers. She brought his tingling hand to her mouth and kissed it repeatedly.

"You're back," Mari said as she leaned over the bed and stroked his hair away from his forehead. It was longer than he remembered it being. "I just can't believe it. You're back. I thought—" Her grip throbbed with the sobs that followed.

"Did we at least tie for second place?" Eustis said. Mari let out a chuckle that cracked halfway into a new round of joy-filled sobs. Tears ran down her cheeks and she sniffled. She bounced with the weight of weeping on her overburdened shoulders. Eustis discovered that his other arm worked, as did his upper body. He sat up cautiously and reached for the crying woman. She encircled him with her arms and nested her face into his neck.

"I have to call Doc," Marianna said. She stepped out of the room for a moment and returned with a doctor who Eustis had never seen. After introducing Dr. Strauss, Eustis endured about a thousand medical questions. Tubes and wires were pulled from sore spots on his arms and he was forced to drink what felt like a gallon of nutrition-infused mush. It was the most delicious slop he had ever tasted.

"Something's wrong with my eyes," he said. He devoted his free hand to rubbing. "Everything's blurry."

"Yeah," Dr. Strauss said. "It's a potential side effect of repeated blunt force trauma to the ocular bone. Considering the nature of the assault, it's amazing there wasn't more damage."

"We nearly lost you, Eustis," Marianna added. Her tears were nearly dry now.

"Where is everyone?" Eustis asked. "Is everyone ok?"

"Yes," she said. "Everyone is great. They're all at the service. I stay with you during meetings."

"There were a couple of lacerations, but no one else suffered any long-term injury except you," Dr. Strauss said.

"They're at what service?" Eustis said. "What does that mean?"

"You'll see," Mari smiled. Eustis turned to Dr. Strauss.

"We're in Montobond's estate, right?" They nodded. "So are you a—" He paused not knowing how to ask the question.

"I'm so sorry," Strauss said. "I forget you are just coming up to speed. I feel like I know you since I've been seeing you every day for so long. The others have told me so much about you. Montobond hired me to be your primary care doctor."

"Would you mind if I told you about a man named Jesus?" Eustis ventured. "Many years ago on earth—"

"Eustis," Mari said with an affectionate giggle. "She knows all that."

"So you're a believer?" Eustis asked.

"Sure am. I joined The Underground shortly after your broadcast. It was an inspiration." This filled Eustis with so many questions he could hardly find an onramp to the highway of his mind.

"Well, at least we reached one," Eustis said leaning back in the bed. Through his blurred vision, he thought he noted Marianna and Dr. Strauss sharing a smiling glance.

"It's true. The Strafe incident was an inspiration, but it was so terrible," Marianna said looking like she was nearly at an exploding point. "I begged God not to let you die."

"You begged—who?" Eustis tilted his head. "Maybe my eyes are worse than I thought. Marianna, is that you?" He reached out and touched her face with his fingers. Her cheeks were still wet with tears, but he could feel her smile as she laid her own hand atop his and pressed it warmly against her own cheek. "Are you saying—"

"Yes," she said in a whisper. "I believe. I believed a little while after the Strafe incident. The Three Story Kid has been teaching me a lot. I've even learned a few things from Captain Rude Beard, though I always make sure to fact-check them with Enzo and Rymone." Eustis moved his hands from her cheeks to the back of her neck and pulled her close once more. He held her to his shoulder, letting his fingers entwine her hair. Dr. Strauss covered her mouth with one hand and dabbed at her eyes with the back of the other.

"And all I had to do was get stabbed and beat near death to get you to believe," Eustis whispered in her ear. He could feel her smile against his own cheek. "If I knew that's all it'd take, I would have done it a long time ago."

"It *was* a long time ago," she said. He loosened his grip so that he could look at her face. His eyes were dim, but he did his best to focus them on her piercing stare.

"What do you mean?" He said. "How long?" She glanced at Dr. Strauss.

"Eustis, you've been in this bed for months," Strauss said.

"We thought you might not ever wake up. Doc was worried you had brain damage. You've been in a coma." She reached out and caressed his arm. He stared back with a growing understanding of what she had been through. Past the glaze in his eyes, he could tell she looked tired and nearly spent, but she radiated a kind of peace he had never seen her wear.

He took a deep breath as he looked down at the body that had been confined to the bed. He used his hands to confirm what his blurred eyes couldn't. The muscles of his legs and arms were atrophied from long disuse. The previously healthy physique had been stolen away and swapped for a gaunt, emaciated stranger's. His knees were knobby, and his arms were rail-thin. "About a week ago, you started mumbling things."

"Nothing embarrassing, I hope," Eustis said.

"Enough to let us know you had access to your memories," Dr. Strauss said.

"What does that mean?" Eustis asked. "What did I say?" He was directing his question toward Marianna, but she blushed and looked at the ground. Strauss put her hand on Marianna's shoulder and whispered.

"You were calling for Mari."

"Well, that's not embarrassing at all," Eustis said. Mari squeezed Eustis's arm.

"Embarrassing or not," Strauss smirked, "it was nothing short of a miracle. Since then, you've been getting more restless. A couple of days ago, you started to move. Just a little at first, but then gradually, you seemed like you were coming back."

"Some of the others thought you'd never come out of it, but I kept praying. Yesterday your eyes opened for a few seconds. I tried to talk to you, but you went back under," Marianna smiled.

"I'm glad I was calling your name. I couldn't have woken to a more wonderful sight. And I couldn't be happier to be here with you." He leaned over past Marianna and said, "And you're a neat gal too, Doctor." They shared a laugh as Strauss busied herself rolling up the tubes and wires they would no longer need. As she did, Eustis moved his hands to his face. The skin was warped and distorted, weirdly smooth in places but contorted in strange patterns.

"What happen to my face?" he said. "Did you guys leave me out in a meteor shower?"

"When Strafe—you know—" Marianna tried.

"It's a result of a high voltage electrical shot," Strauss said as a matter of fact.

"His power glove," Eustis said with a note of realization. "I guess a million watts to the face meat makes for quite a cheek barbeque." He used both hands to survey the damage, which had long since healed over. Up the left cheek and stretching past his hairline well into his scalp, gnarled scar tissue was all that remained. "He must have favored his right hook 'cause I'm missing half a head of hair here. I was hoping for a more traditional pattern of male baldness." While he was surveying, he stuck his finger into his mouth, feeling along the space where he used to have a row of molars. "Well, good news. He did some free dental work too."

"How can you be so—" Marianna said. "I mean—I would be—"

"I bear on my body the marks of Jesus," Eustis said without a beat missed.

"What's that?" Marianna said. Strauss had stopped to listen as well.

"It's a quote from the Bible," Eustis gasped. "My Bible! That troglodyte burned my Bible! What kind of bibliophobe burns a Bible? Seriously!"

"It's amazing," Mari said, leaning back on her heels and studying the man. "He ruined your eyesight. No problem. Melted half your face. Forget about it. Stabbed you through the lung and left you for dead. Who cares? But he torches the Good Book, and you blow chunks."

"Priorities, my dear," Eustis said, feeling around his chest. "He stabbed me through the lung? Really?"

"Yep," Marianna said. "Collapsed it. Doc had to remove two-thirds of your right one." Eustis took a deep breath, testing it.

"Good," Eustis said. "I needed to make some room." He patted his chest. "I have Jesus in my heart, but I've always thought he must feel a little crowded in there."

"Brilliant," Mari said, rolling her eyes. "You were slightly funnier when you were dead." She gave his cheek a playful pat.

"Well, Strafe gave me all the best punch lines."

"Ok," Mari said. "Puns are a sign of brain damage. Doctor, we're going to need some sedative."

Strauss laughed. "You know, a stroll might be a good idea. He hasn't been out of this room in months."

"Seriously?" Marianna said. "You'd be ok with that?"

Strauss nodded but added, "Nothing strenuous. But yeah, a change of scenery might do him good."

She turned to Eustis. "There's something you need to see."

Eustis looked down at his legs. "There's no way I'm brave enough to venture out on these twigs, even in microgravity."

"We've got wheels, silly," Mari said, pointing to the corner of the room. A motorized wheelchair was parked, waiting for an occupant.

"Thirty minutes, tops," Strauss said. "Then back here for some rest."

"Will do. Thanks." Mari said.

CHAPTER SEVENTY

FAMILY

Marianna walked next to Eustis's wheelchair as they rolled toward the front entrance of Montobond's estate. The house was empty but the motion-detecting lights clicked on as they moved through the space. The glass doors auto-swung wide as Eustis rolled out into the courtyard and gasped at the blurry sight. A group of what had to be five hundred people was sitting in the grass listening to someone speaking.

Eustis blinked his eyes, trying to make them focus. A fuzzy figure with a voice resembling Enzo's, but deeper, stood at the front of the spellbound crowd telling the story of Jesus's resurrection in a powerful commanding tone. Eustis and Mari lingered near the doors at the back edge of the crowd. He looked up at her, begging to borrow her eyes.

"Is that—" Eustis asked. She knelt and spoke softly in his ear.

"Yep, that's The Three Story Kid," Mari said. "Not so much a *kid* anymore, though." Eustis rubbed his eyes wishing he could see him clearly. When that didn't work he resigned his attention to his ears. Enzo's voice had dropped half an octave since Eustis had last heard him speak. His delivery was enchanting and his rhetorical skill was something of a marvel. He was confident. He was decisive. He was fantastic.

"What is this?" Eustis whispered in Mari's direction. "Is this a dream? Are you sure I'm not still lying on that bed?"

"This is our church service," she said. "After the Strafe incident, people from all over the city came to pay respects to the brave man who stood up to oppression. They wanted to give their support to a mysterious man named Eustis Grimes. Enzo was brilliant. He didn't let a single well-wisher pass without telling them about Jesus. The underground exploded. A hundred. Then two. Now we have meetings like this every day. It's thousands, Eustis."

"The underground," Eustis whispered. "Name doesn't fit anymore, does it?"

"Nope," Marianna said. "It's called Bezos City Church now." She laid her hand on the arm of his wheelchair. "There are other groups too. Adria and Gordon hold regular meetings in Maroon Housing. Delphi and her girls do one in Horizon. Montobond teaches daily at the municipal compartments. It seems like every few days a new group is popping up somewhere in Bezos City."

Eustis wiped his eyes and ducked his face into his hands. Gratitude washed over him in overpowering waves. Marianna patted the back of his neck. When his emotion subsided, she continued. "It's spreading too. A couple of months ago we got a message from some people in Armstrong City. They said they wanted someone to come and tell them more about the religionism of Eustis Grimes. Apparently, the video of the Strafe incident was leaked. So, Rymone and Geona are planning to move to Armstrong to start a group there. Oh, and they adopted the maroon kids, by the way."

"Which ones?" Eustis asked.

"All of them," Mari smiled. "Ava, Liddy, the Gaines boys, and the Crabbes. They also just had their first baby. They named her—" Mari's words were cut off by a sharp breath.

"Jewels," Eustis guessed.

Mari nodded as she wiped her eyes. "I never used to be like this. I was tough once, you know." She laughed at herself. "Anyway, they're moving to Armstrong to start a new work there."

"Armstrong?" Eustis said. "Admiral Strafe won't be happy about that."

"Oh," Mari whispered. "You're not up on the latest news. Strafe was arrested and taken to Musk City after the incident. He's awaiting trial."

"Really?"

"Yep," Mari said. "He didn't have the authority to remove Montobond from Bezos Chancellorship. Only the chief executive emperor can do that. Who knew GovCorp had any limits of power in place?"

"Wow," Eustis said. "Now there's an idea."

"What?"

"Break some laws, get a free ride to Musk City, Mars," Eustis smiled and tapped the tips of his fingers together as if he were hatching a devious plan.

"Don't even think about it," Mari said.

"What about Madam Electra?" Eustis asked. "Is she still acting chancellor of Bezos?"

"Nope," Mari said. "She split. We heard she fled to Titan after the Strafe incident. Haven't seen her since."

Two unexpected hands reached over the back of Eustis's wheelchair and squeezed his shoulders. Montobond leaned down and whispered in his ear.

"I'm so glad to see you up, my boy," Montobond said. "We've been praying for you constantly." Montobond wrapped a hand around Eustis's shoulders and gave him a hug from behind.

"I bet you'll be glad to get your study back," Eustis whispered.

"Nonsense," Montobond said. "I'll tell the others." Before he could respond, Montobond crept over to a large blurry silhouette sitting near the back of the crowd.

"What's he doing?" Eustis asked.

"Oh great," Mari said. "He's telling—" Before she could get the words out, a bellowing voice erupted from the direction Montobond had gone.

"It be the man Eustis back from the deep void," Rudwick's unmistakable voice shouted. Enzo's sermon stopped, and five hundred heads turned first to Rudwick and then in Eustis' direction. "It be Eustis Grimes the Brave." There was a rush of heavy footfalls, followed by the shape of a large one-armed man barreling toward him. "Me brother be returned from the hallows of shadow!" Eustis felt a single thick arm reach around him and lift him out of his chair.

"Rudwick," Marianna warned. "Be careful."

"There be no better medicine than a hug from old Rude Beard," Rudwick said as he spun Eustis around like a rag doll. Eustis's thin arms gripped Rudwick's neck as the merry-go-round spiraled.

"I'm so glad to see you too." By the time Rudwick was placing him back in his wheelchair, Enzo's voice was near, as were dozens of thronging people's murmurs. The crowd was now encircling him, making it impossible to tell which was Enzo. A blurry figure squeezed through the line of whispering onlookers and knelt before Eustis's chair. Even through the blur, Eustis could see that his shoulders had broadened, and his face had taken on the stronger lines of manhood.

"I was looking forward to hearing the rest of that sermon," Eustis said. Enzo rose and wrapped his arms around his chair-bound brother. He didn't lift him aloft, although he had grown so much that it felt like he could.

"Praise the Lord," Enzo said after leaning back and placing his hands on Eustis's shoulder. His voice sounded like a man's. Rymone, Geona, Delphi, and all of the children came close. He had more hugs than ever he'd experienced in his life. His heart was full to the bursting point.

When all of his loved ones had greeted him warmly, Enzo pushed back the line and gestured toward Eustis. He increased the volume of his voice to be heard by the entire crowd. "I'd like to introduce you all to my friend and mentor, the bravest and most stubborn man I've ever even heard of, the unkillable Eustis Grimes." With the words, the hundreds who had encircled them uplifted their voices and applauded. The clapping persisted longer than Eustis was comfortable with, but he resisted the urge to dampen the spirit. These people were looking at a miracle, and he didn't want to take that from them. When the clapping died down, Enzo said, "Eustis would you like to say a few words?"

"Sure," he said, clearing his throat. Enzo gestured for everyone to sit down so those in the back could see. From his wheelchair, Eustis began. "I'd stand up to address you, but my legs have gotten thinner than carbon fiber nanotubes." The crowd laughed generously. "Seeing you all here, I'm more shocked than I've ever been." He reached up to the burnt scar tissue of his face. "And that's saying something." The crowd laughed again. "My eyesight is almost completely gone, but I feel like I'm seeing more clearly than ever before."

"You've called me brave and many other kind things," Eustis laid his hand across his chest. "Those words warm my heart. But if I've done anything good, credit that to the Lord. I'm only a dim reflection of the Lord's great power that works and moves within the lives of those who believe and love him." He paused and smiled. "Now my doctor says if I am not back in my bed soon, she'll sedate me for another year. I love you all, and I look forward to getting to know you better very soon." Eustis and Mari moved slowly back through the doors of Montobond's estate to the standing ovation of hundreds.

CHAPTER SEVENTY-ONE

VISION

The months that followed were a time of sweet fellowship among the believers in Bezos City, but there were difficulties as well. Although Eustis was more concerned with the health of the budding church, Dr. Strauss insisted on a disciplined physical therapy schedule. The grueling regimen was not made easier by the microgravity, but Eustis worked daily to grow his physical strength. Little by little, he gained back his muscle mass and physical fitness. Strauss often encouraged him to get cosmetic surgery to remove the burn marks from his face and scalp, but Eustis refused. He wore them like badges of honor. Every time he passed a mirror, his blurry reflection reminded of the sacrifice he had made and hoped he would never stray from doing so once more if he were ever called to.

The missing part of his right lung made it hard to keep up in the oxygen-deprived environment in which he lived, but physical therapy was helping him overcome his deficiency. His eyes, however, were never the same. The world, which had been full of light and color, had grown increasingly dark and blurry in the months that followed Eustis' awakening. Each morning he woke to find his eyes less reliable than the day before until he perpetually lived in a shroud of near darkness. He was fortunate to have so many around him who were eager to help. He almost never went anywhere without someone gripping his arm to guide him along his path. Many times Dr. Strauss offered a medical solution to the problem, which Eustis would have accepted. However, ocular implants of the kind he needed were only available in certain colonies, and Bezos wasn't one of them. He could still interact with data through his cortex implant, but the real world around him was dark.

He spent countless hours teaching and mentoring those who were taking leadership in the burgeoning church of Bezos City. They saw growth month over month, and the church enjoyed a good reputation with those in the City. With Phineas Montobond reinstated as the chancellor of Bezos City, the church had a champion and protector. Most of the believers no longer lived in Montobond's estate since the city had become friendly to religionists. In the absence of Madam Electra Styx the believers had converted the hyper-terrestrial research commune into a church building for daily meetings. It was a place of learning and spiritual growth.

Most had returned to a better kind of life than they had left. The quality of life that Eustis and the others were experiencing was unrecognizable from what had come before. Life was good. Everything had turned out well, and yet Eustis found the edges of his mind pulled skyward.

Enzo was growing into a man who had the respect and affection of all those whom he taught. With his eidetic memory, Enzo had become the single source of Scripture, since the burning of Eustis' Bible. Although Enzo had the words of Scripture recorded in the stone of his mind, he still relied on Eustis' interpretation of much of what came out of his mouth. Memorizing Scripture and understanding it were two different things. Eustis had often encouraged Enzo to take the time to make a record of those ancient and invaluable words locked in his mind, but his teaching and administrative schedule had so grown that there had been no effort to do so.

Rudwick's love for children and a constant supply of needy younglings kept the old pirate a cheerier chap than ever they had seen him. He visited Maroon Housing at least once a week, looking for newly abandoned children to unofficially adopt. When there were no human kids, he would regularly return with new furry friends of the feline persuasion. At any given time, he had no less than a dozen children and as many in his growing pride of stray cats following him around. The children giggled at his every joke, marveled at his wisdom, and basked in his effusive affection for them. He taught them to care for the strays, both cats and each other. The man constituted a kind of wandering orphanage and animal shelter, a band of needful but merry younglings charming the heart of old soft-hearted Rude Beard.

In the weeks that followed, Eustis often found himself being led by the arm by Marianna. As his duties with the church were increasingly managed by other responsible parties, he found himself with free time to take long walks through the City, and Mari was rarely absent for these regular strolls. Many had gradually changed in the months that followed their belief in Christ, but none had made such a surprising turnaround as Marianna Byrne, and Eustis was the chief benefactor of her newfound compassion and joy. He found her tender yet stern when the need arose. Like him, she had a streak of impossible stubbornness, but it had become an asset rather than a liability in her transformation toward Christ-like bravery. She spoke her mind with new freedom and listened relentlessly when he needed to search for a solution to a given problem through verbal meandering.

"I keep thinking about Musk City," Eustis said on one of their walks.

"Really?" Mari asked.

"Yes," Eustis said. "I know what we have here is great, but how long can it last before GovCorp takes action? I feel like we're sitting on a ticking time bomb. Strafe's overreach bought us some time, but—" He took a breath and imagined the gruesome scene. "This time it won't be one deranged maniac and his robot toys. It'll be a dozen GovCorp gunships. As long as the church is in only one City, we're exposed. We're in danger. We need to—to—" He couldn't bring himself to say it.

"Eustis," Mari interrupted. "I already know." Since he could no longer rely on his eyes, he reached up a nervous hand and touched her cheek.

"You're smiling," he said. "Why are you smiling?" He put his other hand against the smooth skin of her face. She covered his with hers. "What do you know?"

"I know you're the most stubborn man I've ever met," she said, still smiling. "But I know that stubbornness is just the kind of light this shadow-drowned crater needed. And it's what a hundred other craters throughout the Sol system are waiting for." She moved closer to him, shrinking the chasm between. He could feel her warm breath on his face. Her smile was wider still. "Me and the boys have been talking about it for weeks. You look like you're going to explode. They thought something was wrong, but not me. I know what you're feeling." She leaned forward and put her forehead against his.

"What?"

"God made you this way," she whispered. Shivers trickled down his neck. "To always be looking at the horizon."

"A horizon I can't see."

"And yet you're still staring off into the black, dreaming of doing it again, of starting over in a new place, of spreading the gospel, of changing minds, and lives one stubborn conversation at a time."

"But I can't. I can't even walk across town alone," Eustis said. "God took away my eyes."

"And gave you me," she said, letting the smile fade. Now her hands were on his face, warm and comforting.

"Do you mean that you would—" Eustis started.

"I said I know what you're feeling," Mari said. "Because I'm feeling it too. These black worlds need this. They need what we have. It's worth every beat of our hearts we can give it and every breath from our lungs we can offer. It's burning inside me. I have to let it out, whether by my life or by death."

"Is it an inappropriate time to—" Eustis started to say, but Mari had an uncanny ability to anticipate his words.

"Not in the least," she said.

Their lips met almost involuntarily. It was unlike the previous kisses they had shared. He had only ever dreamed unimaginatively of their kisses being made of physical affection. However, the moment was so much more, being suspended in the dewy mist of hopefulness, adventure, and Godly yearning. The embrace was the strong, tingling, and warm elixir of belabored longing drunk under the blissful arora of effervescent passion. When they drew back, sharing their precious breath, cascading warmly face to face, a smile between grew.

"So," Eustis said. "On to Mars?"

"On to Mars," Mari repeated.

He reached for her and leaned close once more, eager to revisit the newly discovered adventure that waited at the horizon of her delicate smile.

A NOTE FROM THE AUTHOR

I've been dreaming of the Sol System for years, and it was thrilling to get the ship off the ground.

In Missionary To Mars I merged two topics I love: Christian missions and sci-fi. I've been reading/writing sci-fi for years, but in the research for this book, I began exploring missionary biographies as well. I was amazed.

Good missionaries are idealistic, stubborn, and unstoppable. Because of their idiosyncrasies, they rarely fit into "normal" society. Sometimes their success hinges on some unexpected skill or characteristic that they had never seen as useful before. They are born for another world, and they can do nothing but draw the rest of us upward with them.

I have seen this in my life. What seemed like anti-social behavior, and a useless tech fascination when I was 15, has proved to be the driving force in how I share the gospel of Christ now. I consider myself a missionary to the indigenous people of the internet, and my purpose is to make media that points people to Jesus.

So, I hope this book has helped you to imagine what God can do with you and your uniqueness. He wants to advance His kingdom plan, and he's willing to employ you to do it. No matter your interests, enthusiasms, and characteristics, you can make your life count for eternity by spreading the news about our amazing Savior. If you take up that challenge, let me know. I'd love to hear your story.

If you would like to send me a message, learn about the ministry that made this book possible, or receive notifications on upcoming releases, visit us at www.freegrace.in and subscribe. If you'd like to see the other books I've written, you can find them all at lucaskitchen.com.

Please, if you enjoyed this book, will you leave a review. The simple act of reviewing this book on the platform where you got it, could be what convinces someone else to read the book, or listen to the audiobook, and think more deeply about our Lord and Savior Jesus Christ. Reviewing great Christ-honoring books, like this one, can be a ministry the has a lasting, even eternal effect.

Thanks for reading! Let's meet in space again soon.

— Lucas Kitchen

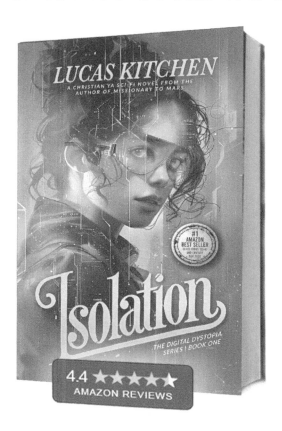

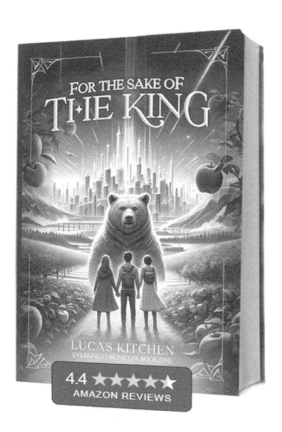

ABOUT THE AUTHOR

Lucas Kitchen is an American author of Christian fiction and nonfiction. He has written over twenty books. Readers have reported a glitch, that his novels can't be put down, but he has a technician looking into the issue. He writes blogs, releases podcasts, and publishes social media videos about Jesus, the faith, and AI robots. His social media content is occasionally viral, but no antivirus has yet been found. He lives in Texas with his wife, four kids, and his scratch-addicted cats.

Made in United States
Cleveland, OH
10 July 2025

18410314R10223